THE LAST EYE OF TIME

GUY W NETTLETON

Abeno Star Press

To my family

for always believing in me.

Contents

CHAPTER ONE
ESCAPE

A HAND REACHED THROUGH the thick morning fog as it rolled over the dock, hiding the port town from the sea. Blood-stained mail covered its owner, who bobbed his head and grasped for a short wooden post for support. Grog and vomit still stained his stubble from the night before. Gaelenn studied the figure from the water, wrenching his head a little to the side to get a better look.

Lucky, he thought, *that anybody'd be here at dawn. Strange, but lucky. There might still be a chance to warn them. A guard?*

He tried to shout to get the man's attention but his screams were drowned by the waves and the ropes between his teeth. All he could do was catch a few stray rays of sunlight in his shimmering, odd eye. But today the sun hid behind dark clouds. Gaelenn sighed and relaxed the muscles that buckled against his restraints. Tied to the bowsprit of the ship approaching the shore ahead, he cursed to himself.

How did I get myself into this?

The man on the dock craned his neck toward the sea, paused tentatively, and inched toward the warning bell hanging nearby.

He sees me! He sees my eye! Gaelenn blinked to draw more attention.

The guard stumbled sideways, rubbing his disbelieving eyes, and searched for the bell with his free hand. Before he found it, the boat carrying Gaelenn—and two dozen pirates—pierced the fog and eased onto the beach's soft sand in total silence.

The warning bell still a yard to his left, the man above gargled and coughed, frantic, attempting to warn the town. But just as he cleared his throat, an arrow from the boat pierced the middle of his neck and he fell to his knees, gasping. Another arrow hit his chest and the last thing his eyes fixed on before he dropped flat and drove the arrow the rest of the way through his back was the sparkling green in Gaelenn's eye.

The pirates, clad in sun-worn linen, jumped from the boat's deck to the sand and knelt around the hull, their hands tracing its knotted, rotting wood. Once it had been a modest ship, fast and nimble, made for a small crew to take it from point to point along the coast. Now, it was a husk of a boat, battered and beaten. Running out of life, much like these once-plentiful port towns that fell, one by one, day after day.

The captain looked behind and winked at his first mate, a half-toothed, leathery-skinned woman in sparse braids, and she grinned back at him with menace and hunger on her lips. His eyes glistened, eager—this town, at least, was not deserted. Maybe the last. He looked above at Gaelenn, the odd-eyed vagabond who tried to steal their dinghy during the night, as he hung topless from taut ropes. Salt and streaks of dried blood from lashings the night before painted white-and-crimson stripes across his down-turned body.

"Hm? Whassat? Nothin' to say?" the pirate captain whispered. His breath reeked of fish and decay. "Be a good lad and take care of the boat. Jus' be a few hours. We'll be back to collect you."

He put his weight into a slap on Gaelenn's gut and smiled toothlessly at his crew. The crusty skin on his face rippled with his soundless laugh into a hundred sun-worn creases.

Gaelenn winced and jerked, but the rope easily resisted his formidable strength. His voice, leaking out in a muffled, wheezy hiss, had no chance of alerting the townsfolk of the incoming raid.

Damnit. I can't move an inch. Can't even scream.

The day before he had tried to send warning and failed. Paying his way from port to port on whatever boat was sailing, as he had done for seven long years, he had counted his lucky stars to find this one.

How could I have known they were pirates? He thought, grinding his teeth into the ropes. *And how could I have known they'd be coming here, of all places?*

Hours after he bought his ticket with the last of his earthly possessions, he overheard the planning of the raid and the town's name: *Key Rock*. His heart had dropped to his stomach. Key Rock was his home until he came of age and left his mother and his old life behind on his fruitless quest. Now, years later, back again—though in a bitter twist of fate, a silent bystander in what was sure to be a bloody reunion. He cursed to himself again and his eyes bulged, their whites a hateful shade of red.

The captain nodded to his crew and leered at Gaelenn once more, looking into both his green eye and his gray, unsure of which to use. Desperation and fear hid in the depths of his gaze, his own way of life and the lives of his crew nearing their end. Gaelenn knew it and almost pitied him, and the pirate noticed, cleared his throat quietly, and puffed out his chest.

"No funny business or we'll gut the entire town, yeah? Including yer mum. But if I do see 'er I'll make sure to give 'er a kiss from ya." He puckered his cracked, filthy lips.

Gaelenn glared back, his pity forgotten. Perfect knot-work prevented his slightest movement, so he used his strange eyes and clenched jaw to express his welling desire to kick the pirate leader's rotting jaw with everything he could.

If you touch her I will kill you.

The pirate withered under Gaelenn's stare and muttered under his breath.

"Shoulda drowned this one when we caught 'im." His upper lip exposed the blackness of his mouth where teeth once were, and he shook his head, returning his focus to the beach.

He's right—I should have been killed in the night. Gaelenn replayed yesterday's events briefly in his mind, his brow twitching, looking for alternate paths and better choices. *No, I shouldn't have been caught at all. If only I'd rowed faster. Started earlier.*

Caught cutting away the small rowboat he intended to take ashore during the night while the corsairs waited for the fog of dawn, he bought his life with the promise of ransom: all the treasure he owned and a one-of-a-kind, priceless diamond in return for sparing his mother and himself. Unfortunately, his mother owned no treasure and would rather die than lose her husband's stone pendant, her last connection to the man Gaelenn had scoured the known world to find. But Gaelenn had no intention of going through with any trade; as soon as he could secure their lives, they would both disappear.

Hopelessness invaded his mind as he reviewed his plan. His burning, raw skin reminded him of his odds, and he sighed.

If I pull this off, it'll be a miracle.

On a silent signal from the captain, the pirates inched low over the sand toward the town. Gaelenn battled against the ropes to get a better view, his neck convulsing and bulging with the strain. He managed to turn his head slightly, but the grinding of his skull against the wooden bowsprit forced a low, painful grunt from his throat. The assailants, focused on the task ahead of them, paid no notice, and Gaelenn's eyes followed them up the beach to the town. All the air in his lungs left his body in one great heave.

The corsairs were too late; somebody had beaten them to the raid.

Crumbling walls, battered doors, rising smoke—nothing out of the ordinary from a pirate's eyes, maybe. Not Gaelenn's, who had spent his childhood running through its alleyways. He drew a deep breath through his nose, and sure enough, the air carried nothing of the bread in bakers' ovens or the aroma of fish soup—only the vague reek of blood, flame, and death.

Gaelenn's eyelids flashed open. *This could be my opportunity, if I can—wait. Mother.*

He turned toward the dock involuntarily, ignoring the pain in his head. The dock where he had last seen her seven years ago, weeping, begging him not to leave. That his father would come back someday. That he did not have to go find him.

Father...why did you leave us? Gaelenn allowed his mind to drift further. *Why?*

He ground his nails into the rope around his palms.

No...I don't care why anymore. It doesn't matter. There's no excuse. No forgiving how you abandoned us. And now, Mother might not survive this day.

Gaelenn's jaw muscles convulsed and a tiny thread of rope snapped between his teeth. *She might be dead already.*

"The beach!" came a shrill voice, breaking his thoughts. A dozen more shouts followed along with alarm bells, all calling attention to the pirates slithering across the sand toward the town.

Arrows burst through the air in sudden volleys, striking both sand and body with dull thuds. Voices and screams littered the air. Above, the pirates' returning darts chipped at the town's stone walls and buried themselves into wooden beams and chinks in armor, drawing more screams and more soldiers. A brief silence took hold of the beach for a frightening moment before giving way to the clashing of swords and cries of battle.

Gaelenn squirmed helplessly against the knots, desperate now, forcing his skull against the bowsprit with violence. Blood trickled from the back of his head, following the strands of his messy, dark brown hair and falling to the sand below. Everything was a blur of pain, both in his head and in his heart—until one particular dark blur under the dock caught his eye and stopped him cold.

The sewers!

His father's warning should danger ever threaten: "*If anything were to happen, not that it would, of course, you go down to the sewers and find the deepest place there. Hide.*"

He had droned it into Gaelenn's head, long ago, over and over—almost as if he had predicted this very moment. "*If I don't find you, your mother will. You'll be safe there. You can get home.*"

With a painful whistle, an errant arrow slammed into the hull of the ship just below Gaelenn, drawing a gasp from between the ropes in his mouth. A foot higher and it would have split his head in half. He peered down, mystified.

Not an arrow for boars. This is for piercing armor. Not something a guard of the town watch would be using in these parts. What is going on up there?

Neither his ears nor his eyes answered him. Chaos reigned. A trail of blood and bodies stretched from the beach and disappeared into the town.

There must have been an entire army here when we arrived. Is this the one that's been leveling all these towns...?

The few pirates who were still alive scattered into the streets between the houses above, still searching for loot, catching stray blows from chasing soldiers. They were finished. Gaelenn's brow knotted.

And so am I. And Key Rock. If I'd only stayed instead, I could have been here to stop this. To fight.

Instead he had roamed the known world and witnessed its ruin for seven years. Staying would not have changed his hometown's fate—or his own, he knew.

Maybe I was meant to die right here, right now, no matter what I did. Destined to die.

The smell of flint and oil hit his nostrils and shocked his eyes wide open. The air above the beach filled in a single instant with the sound and scent of powder and flame, and a gruff voice barked.

"They're going back to the boat—don't let them escape! Light it up!"

A rain of fiery arrows slammed into the ship and the pirates sprinting back to it. Gaelenn squeezed his shoulders together to make a smaller target but the wake from several darts kissed the open skin of his face and arms. Smoke dominated the air. A brief pause as the archers reloaded preceded a second torrent and another wave of fear. The air itself seemed to die for a second as he held his breath and forced his eyes shut, waiting for the next volley. Sure enough, missiles drummed into the wood, sending vibrations up and down his spine. He closed his eyes tight, knowing that the next arrow could be the last for him.

A quick thud just above his head knocked the beam and severed a cord, whipping it out into the smoky haze—and out of Gaelenn's mouth. He sputtered and gnawed at the freshly loosened rope, free now to move his head from side to side, until he conquered it and spit it to the ground. He gasped, glad of the taste of air, full of smoke as it was.

"Not much consolation to get my voice back *now*," Gaelenn mused to himself. He followed it with a cough, swallowing dryly between breaths. "Going down with the ship on land. I'd have made a terrible pirate."

His lips curled up into a black smile, and his head fell, crowned in smoke. But the smoke might be his salvation. Slowly, it gave birth to fire, and Gaelenn followed its path as it trailed over the deck and into the ship. Snake-like hisses escaped from between the loosening boards of the hull and Gaelenn took a deep breath and held it. The danger finally dawned on him.

BOOM

The hull exploded from the sides, rocketing wood and metal into the sand and water. Kegs of powder, stored for raids, caught fire and ruptured one-by-one while the tattered sails fell in ashes and the deck smoldered. The renewed heat lashed out at Gaelenn's boots, his ears ringing, but he still hung in one piece, just as trapped as before. The bowsprit held.

"No fighting the inevitable."

He spat, steeling his jaw and closing his eyes tight, preparing for death. The next explosion might be the one to end him. The fire's scent drew closer and closer. But instead of an explosion, a subtle crackle tickled his ears. A rope broke and flew away from his chest, cracking the air with a quick snap.

Gaelenn squirmed. "The bowsprit's on fire!"

Threads continued to burst and snap, and he jerked his limbs to force the ropes free where the fire was too slow to finish them off. Flames crawled down the sides of the horizontal wooden pole, their heat sizzling away his pouring sweat. With a single, great shout, Gaelenn broke the last of the bonds on his torso just as the fire wrapped around to the bottom of the bowsprit. He swung under it, caught by the ropes around his boots, his face thrust right into the fire bursting from the hull.

A scream slipped from his throat. He covered his face with his left hand, pulling desperately at the remaining rope at his feet with his right. The fire had trapped him. Although the thick leather of his boots protected his skin for the moment, in seconds they would burst into flames, too.

Just below him, the glint of the arrow that had nearly ended Gaelenn's life minutes earlier caught his eye. He swooped backwards, stretched his body as far as he could, and swung toward the arrow with all the momentum he could gather. His burning hands yanked it out and in a single, panicked stroke, he stabbed at the rope that trapped his feet.

A second later, he landed in the sand, dazed, his neck and back bearing the brunt of his fall. Fear left him, seeping away into the sand with his sweat and blood.

The grimace of pain faded from his face and the lines above his eyes hardened into determination.

Mother.

The sewers.

CHAPTER TWO
THE SEWERS OF KEY ROCK

THE TUNNELS WERE DEAD black except for light from the entrance behind. It caught the occasional ripple of brackish water and the glint of the long knife Gaelenn picked out of a dead pirate's hands—along with a shirt—on his way in. His legs moved slowly, tentative and searching. He knew the town above like a tattoo in his mind, but the sewers remained foreign. They were an ancient, puzzling maze, unused for hundreds or thousands of years; the air held the rotten breath of undisturbed centuries. Dirt, dust, fetid pools of what was once water—even without sight, it reeked of age beyond comprehension. Onward.

His fingers probed the brick walls, sometimes for support and sometimes for direction. Tracing his vestigial memories, he sensed where he was, but there was no straight path to where he was going: his old house. Resting on the outskirts and likely away from most of the fighting, Gaelenn and his mother would be safe there.

I hope, he thought.

Clamors above from the din of battle faded in and out, and clots of soot fell into Gaelenn's eyes. He had no need for sight here anyway so he closed them, hoping to enhance his other senses. He exhaled all his breath through flared nostrils and held it, in spite of the pain in his still-burning lungs. Now, aside from the screams and metallic crashes above, he could discern two sounds: the uncontrollable pounding of his heart and the barest, gentlest flow of air.

There was a way up from these tunnels, after all. He willed himself to hope. "Just hope I can find the exit in time to save her. Damnit—hold on, mother...!"

He doubled his pace and resumed breathing.

Halfway there, at least, he held another breath and paused. The liquid at his feet was deepening and the smell turning from bad to worse. He began to feel for potential doors or hatches, the walls closing in with every step he took. Panic that he might not find the way out took root.

"Tsk," he hissed, attempting to control it. Another corner, another long passageway, and guess after blind guess. It was a labyrinth—his prison. Perhaps his grave.

After a time the sounds above stopped, the battle either over or not yet this far from the beach. Gaelenn's hand unconsciously squeezed a brick that stuck out an inch more than the others. Its edges crumbled into his fingertips.

"I've got to get out. I must be close, or under."

He took care to speak under his breath. His foot crept forward a half-step and froze—there were voices above again. Harsh voices, arguing about something. But not fighting; only speaking. Hands still on the wall of the sewer, Gaelenn lurched forward without a sound. He should almost be under his old house by now, he felt, somehow. But knowing that someone was there robbed him of any comforting thought.

His mind went back to his father's words: "*The sewers. If anybody finds you in there, they're a friend.*"

Gaelenn rubbed his eyes, unsure if the memory was real or just a dream—his memories had faded over the years—but he could almost swear the next part of the sentence was, "*when they come looking for you and your mother.*"

No—it couldn't be. After all, he still remembered the village's strict rules *against* going into the sewers—the only reason he knew of this hidden entrance was because he found it while playing under the docks—also strictly forbidden—with his best friend Kell as a child.

A brief smile in the dark distracted him for a moment; it was one of a small handful of happy memories he clung to. But it was just as likely that Kell was already victim to whatever was happening in the town as his mother.

Gaelenn paused. The voices above suddenly became clear. A man—no, two men—and a woman. His eyes opened and shot up. The soft flow of air blew over his face, but there was no light. He angled his head back and twisted it awkwardly in circles to try to see if there might be a way up. Craning his neck all the way backward behind his body, he sensed the soft gradation of a shadow above and followed its trail until the top of his skull brushed the low part of the sewer's low arch behind him.

He raised his arms above his head, using the grimy stones to balance and maneuver his body in search of more precise vantage points. Second by second, he grew more desperate to rediscover the source of the faint light. The voices above were heated, and although he could not yet discern the topic or even a single word, panic was again beginning to boil in his stomach.

His mother could be right above him, for all he knew. Evil thoughts unsettled him and then broke away at once, his focus returning. The tiniest, softest beam of light caught a fleck of dust near his outstretched hands, and he explored the ceiling above with renewed hope. His fingers traced a perfect circle a yard or so in diameter, directly above him, cut—or perhaps built—into the brick. It led upwards.

His hands probed further up for a recess he could use to pull himself up. His lips curled up into a grimace as his shoulders began to burn, and all at once he found two slits on either side. A few inches above them he found identical holes—a ladder. *Two* ladders.

He lifted both hands and pulled himself up as he jumped, vaulting high, counting on finding two similar holes higher in the vertical tunnel. At first, panic set in. His fingers jammed against solid brick. But as he began falling at the crest of his leap, he doubled down, forcing his limbs against the walls and ignoring the pain sent down his spine by the nerves in his fingernails, tearing away from the skin of his fingers with each inch he fell.

A deep breath rushed out of his nose when he caught the next holes, three inches down. Most of his fingers were bleeding, but he ignored them. Bringing his legs up, split-fashion, he stuck his toes in the bottom holes and pushed himself upward with one hand over his head, searching for the ceiling. He breathed in slowly, conquering his pain, and then squinted into the air, struggling to ascertain how high it stretched. He could *feel* the ceiling more than he could see it—it was only a foot or two above his reach.

His dry throat ached as he swallowed. The voices grew louder. And Gaelenn climbed. Again his hands reached upward, his feet braced in the recessed rungs, and found the ceiling: an iron-hard, perfectly circular plate. It was cold and damp and on its surface was a kind of writing or shape that his fingers could not comprehend. Around the circle's circumference, a perfect divot; it was a door or a latch or a lid.

He tried to force it upward. No use. It was sealed or rusted shut. He again located the source of the weak light he had noticed from below. No brighter from up here. But his hands surmised that there were a series of holes in the iron-like plate above. With his index finger he scratched at some of the compacted dirt within them, focusing on the circular indentation from which the light had found its way, somehow, under the earth.

Shuddering above sent a clot of dirt into his mouth. He spat and cursed to himself and rubbed his eyes, though he could not be sure if he had gotten the dirt out or not. Either way, it was pitch black once more, and the voices had become muffled. They were moving around above him and becoming more heated. But even though they weren't clear, they were growing loud enough to make a few words out.

"...This...is it...key...the Lord's plan..."

The voices were a blend, impossible to tell who was speaking or whether it was a man or woman, except for the occasional grunting sounds that seemed to Gaelenn too deep to come from a human's mouth at all. Some of the guttural words did not even sound like the same language, but that could not be right—he knew, as everyone knew, that while there used to be countless local dialects from town to city-state, nobody on this continent had spoken different tongues for generations. There was neither word for nor concept of another language. Here, at least. It could not be.

Gaelenn waited for the voices to retreat, slid the knife out of his belt, and brought it to one of the holes with care. He chipped at the dirt with soundless twists, his sweat from the effort of holding himself dripping down his face and stubble, mixing with the dirt and tasting of salty ash. His legs shook.

The knife was a finger-width too wide to fit completely, but the first inch of the hard clay came slowly loose. He stowed the blade away when it lost traction and reverted to his fingers to scrape out a little more. With a wincing effort he pushed his bleeding middle finger through the years of earth in one of the holes all the way to his knuckles and twisted. At the last hair's breadth, the dirt gave way to air.

When he excised his finger, a gray column of light poured into the catacombs. Gaelenn's eyes adjusted slowly and the voices, completely clear now, came from several yards away. Venomous and spiteful, their heat made it evident that those above had not noticed his finger poking out of the ground. He put his aching arms down and pointed his ear at the opening, his heart beating hard against his chest.

"...Our Lord has commanded it," a feminine voice said in a threatening hiss. "Finally—finally! We have found it. In the very last place we've looked. And at what cost? You must bring it back immediately."

The tone shifted suddenly, now less demanding but somehow much sharper and more dangerous. "The Eye does not tolerate treason. Nor do I."

A low, feral grunt echoed in agreement, followed by a few sounds in the foreign language from before.

"Treason?" a male voice scoffed, smooth, almost slimy, and unworried. "Never. Of course. As we planned, I will be only three days, then I will meet you. I will simply test the key and…"

A pair of footsteps accompanied by two screaming voices interrupted, coming straight at where the three argued. The foreigner screamed deep, his cry reverberating into the hole and raising the hairs on Gaelenn's neck. A swoosh from the single swipe of a weapon—an axe or massive sword, perhaps—preceded two brief, simultaneous grunts, two small thuds, and then the obvious crumpling of bodies to the ground. The heavy feet of a massive being walked back to the others. More of the foreign tongue spewed forth, then a blood-curdling laugh.

"Don't be so selfish next time. We all deserve a little fun and glory," the woman spoke again, teasing and placating, as if training a dog, then paused briefly before continuing in her venomous voice. "You were saying—and…?"

The other man spoke again after a pause, "And nothing. I will return to you in three days and we can enter the city together with this gift. Our Lord has waited long enough for it. We'll have a parade in celebration."

The others responded with silence, and the man continued, lacing his voice with a politician's verve. "Listen—three more days means nothing to our Master. I simply want to test the key first. For authenticity. As you know, Master *also* hates having its time wasted."

Gaelenn frowned; he was wasting his own time—and maybe his mother's—right now. Bringing his feet up two rungs on each ladder, he dug his toes into their recesses, set the back of his neck and broad shoulders against the plate above, and pushed. His legs burned and the skin at the base of his neck bled, but he persisted. It began to give way.

The plate itself was heavy and solid, but it was the ages of compacted clay and rust that resisted the most. In a desperate final effort, Gaelenn conquered it and held fast, keeping the lid open just high enough to peer out at the scene. Mindful, he shut his green eye. Outside it must have been noon, still overcast but now fog-less. The fresh air wafting in restored him somewhat but his heart kept racing. A few broken houses lay several paces away.

Seaward, he thought. He knew the narrow trail before him. It led straight to his old house—right behind him. The three voices continued from that exact direction.

He swiveled the lid around, passing two corpses, beheaded, still emptying their vast supplies of blood into the brown earth. Several yards beyond them lay his home. Or, the remains of it.

The invasion had not been kind. It sat broken—the door had been busted off its hinges inward, its dozens of boards littering the floor inside, and the thick plaster-wood walls bore holes from top to bottom. Fire had eaten the roof and smoldered.

Gaelenn's jaw set and his hands trembled, barely able to hold up the heavy plate atop them. His heart pounded in his throat. Inside his old house, through a hole in the wall, he saw them: a man, a woman, and a giant the height of two normal men. They dressed in official-looking armor, intricate and exquisite, more decorative than functional, and all wore purple bands on their arms near their shoulders under green capes. He had seen the colors before in his travels, always preceding destruction, death following in their wake. The legions of Maynon Ohza, the ruthless, mysterious city-state that sprang from the ashes of the kingdom of Sithica, overthrown a decade ago. Rumors were all anybody knew about what had happened there, but now it was swallowing up the whole continent, painting it red in blood and black in ash.

The three stood silent, pitted against each other for the moment in stalemate. Something under them caught a ray of light. Gaelenn strained for balance as he bent to the edge of the sewer hole. His neck ached, a sharp pain pulsing down his spine, but he set his head all the way over to the side of the opening where he could get a better view of the floor of the wreckage.

Then, a deep quake rumbled in his chest—the most profound he had ever endured—and his legs and arms weakened. His feet slipped out of their rungs and he plummeted. Though the metal plate fell harmlessly and noiselessly back into its place, muffled by loosened dirt, Gaelenn himself crashed hard onto his side on the sewer floor below. But pain did not touch him; the single pillar of light hitting his face revealed only rage, eyes bulging and teeth grating.

On the floor of his old house he had seen what they were arguing over—a body out of sight except for the long, brown hair on its head and an arm holding a pendant. His mother's. He was too late.

CHAPTER THREE
The Hunt

WHEN THE FOG BEGAN to lift from Gaelenn's mind, he wondered how he had come so deep into the forest. The mesmerizing flow of greens and browns somehow sent him deeper into his trance, and only now did his brain find its way out of the haze. He concentrated, brow intense, keeping his eyes wide and on his target ahead, while a fraction of his consciousness diverted itself.

What just happened? He thought, silent as the windless leaves surrounding him.

At the bottom of the sewers, his first instinct was to act on his rage and jump out in a torrent, but with only a small knife against three heavily armored warriors it would have been a suicidal assault. Still, he might have done it if he had not seen the bodies of those two pirates...

So instead he had gone back up and listened and waited for his chance. It came quickly. The three above continued their spat, escalating moment by moment, calming down only when one of them mentioned, "the Lord," or "the Master."

But Gaelenn did not have the luxury of time to ponder the meaning of their words. He had to be ready for his chance. Something about the three figures struck him. Their movements were a little too quick, too powerful, their voices far too on-edge.

He recalled the smaller man, about the same size as himself—taller than most, lean, and sturdy—speaking as they broke their meeting. "Then it is settled. You will wait for me before beginning the parade. I will validate the authenticity of this key and meet you at the South Tower, as planned, and we will return with our quarry to the city in triumph. This was our last task. Our *master* will soon reward us, as promised."

His face bore a prideful grin, inviting the others to exult in their collective victory, but the woman answered him with an icy stare and the giant just grunted and leered. Gaelenn's mind lingered on the word.

"Master." *Master of what?*

"Well then," the man had continued, "I'll leave you two to organize this mess. I know you'll have your fun, at least, *Triumvir* Visha."

He flashed her a knowing, perverse, demented smile.

She rejected it with a laconic reply: "*I always do,* Triumvir Anwir. As does *Triumvir* Yajuu."

The giant lifted his great axe, at least the length of a man, onto his shoulder like a toy and forced out a rehearsed sentence in his own language. At length, he left the house and headed toward the center of the town.

"All-seeing Eye guide us," the woman replied while staring at Anwir. She teased a short whip holstered on her belt with her fingertips for a moment, then departed with the giant.

"All-seeing Eye guide us...," the last remaining Triumvir replied. When they left, he smiled again, this time at Gaelenn's dead mother. He reached down, pried the pendant free, admired it, then put it around his neck and under his armor.

Gaelenn had watched the scene, seething, barely able to restrain himself. He could not take all three at once, perhaps, but he could take this one. All of them in time, but *this one first.* His anger swelled until his vision went blurry, and he set the metallic plate down for a moment to gather the strength in his arms for an attack.

But when he opened the lid once more, the man was gone. Panicking, Gaelenn swiveled the lid around. Not a living soul in sight.

Damn!

He thrust up on the lid, slid it to the side, and pulled himself up. Keeping himself low, he closed on his old house and just before he reached the door, caught sight of Triumvir Anwir stalking at a torrid pace toward the thick forest bordering the town. Gaelenn was desperate not to lose him but he walked up to his mother's corpse and took her hand. Cold. At least an hour since she died, bled out at the neck. He could not bring himself to look into her haunted face.

"I'll be back. I'll bury you. I'm sorry," he had cried softly. A tear gathered in one eye and fell, and the next thing he could recall, the forest surrounded him. His memory whole again, he came back to the present and drew a great, careful, much-needed breath.

Several hundred yards ahead, Triumvir Anwir covered impossible distance despite the thickening underbrush and trees. Gaelenn kept up thanks only to the many large, oddly-shaped mounds of earth scattered around the forest. Whenever the man passed one, he stopped, scrutinized it with his hands, and moved on. It gave Gaelenn much-needed chances to rest, catch his breath, and drink from the plentiful streams that flowed rapidly through the trees.

As a child he had played here nearly every day, imagining the trees were towers and the mounds forts and castles. They resembled old houses, square sometimes, or rounded. He knew it was forbidden—he and Kell, who always cried and dragged Gaelenn back home. The old stories of the evil witch of the Windy Woods who snatched up young and old alike to eat kept them from being too adventurous.

A thin smile flashed on his lips. Even if it were true, it could not scare him now. Seven years of riding the wild seas and roaming the known world in the fruitless search for his father had, at the very least, taught him how to hunt and fight. Today, though—with a little patience—he intended to arrest and capture his prey before violence had an opportunity to strike.

Stay with him. Stay with him. Stay with him, he repeated to himself. The air eased out of his lungs in slow breaths; Gaelenn willed himself calm.

This is my element, my only chance at vengeance.

He continued at a safe distance and his prey plunged deeper and deeper into the forest, hour after hour, racing along with the same swift gait, never tiring, never slowing. Soon they had gone farther than Gaelenn had ever been in the forest, and not long after that they doubled the distance, and then tripled it. The forest would not end.

He occupied his mind with thought in an effort to forget the pain building in his legs. Beyond the woods lay the Ash Cliffs, according to folklore: a massive, sheer, near-vertical shelf that jutted up from the ground and cut a circle in the forest like a razor, running straight up into the air further than the eye could reach. Nobody he knew had ever gone far enough to see the cliffs except his father, but he would never say more.

Gaelenn had wondered in his youth if it ever stopped rising. Perhaps the witch was up there. The elders of Key Rock could not say, but the children told tales at night about strangers with see-through eyes and pure white hair.

"No time for stories."

Gaelenn surprised himself by speaking out loud, although in a low whisper. It was enough to knock himself out of his aimless daydream. He gritted his teeth; he needed the pain, if not to remind himself of the task at hand, then to stay awake.

But creeping doubt slowly built within him and weighed on his shoulders, bringing them ever so closer to the ground. For the last hour, no matter how swiftly he moved, he could not catch up with his prey. Yet when slowing down, he lost no ground. Something was dangerously amiss and he could taste it in the stale air.

He risked a short dash but again drew no closer. He took a shortcut but when he emerged back into view, he had not gained. Every step closer Gaelenn took, the figure ahead matched exactly. Again and again and again thereafter, hour after hour. Reality dawned on him far too late. He was just too exhausted to notice.

His heart started pumping hard again, drenching his whole body with the cold sweat of adrenaline. And fear—now, he was not so sure that *he* wasn't the prey.

Twilight fell. Colorless clouds gave way to clear but stark black skies, draping the inside of the forest in deep shadow, highlights of trees shooting out of the ground at random. Sight and movement grew labored and dangerous. But the pursuit went on. On and on he followed, fear creeping up on him little by little, minute by minute, step by step. Soon the second day came and went. No rest. Gaelenn's throat burned as the fresh streams dwindled and faded away, and his legs ached worse, begging for reprieve. He fought on.

The second night came, and following it, the next morning. Still no rest. Miles and miles and miles gone, possibly miles more to go. Gaelenn's listless body fell forward more than walked, and his hands bounced against his legs as his back lost its strength.

He strained against his agony for a moment, willing himself up straight. The Ash Cliffs must have been a myth after all, or they would have reached them by now. He pinched the skin of his wrist hard to wake himself up. Black rings framed his sunken eyes. He had reached his limit.

He sighed, no louder than the ruffle of a leaf on a bed of grass, and immediately panicked. The man ahead stopped. Gaelenn's eyes shot open, temporarily restored in strength and wits, and he fell to a crouch, half confused and half joyous of the break. His target stood as still as a rock, staring straight ahead.

Gaelenn crawled for cover behind a large tree, praying he had not been found, keeping his gaze ever forward, and slid his knife from his belt. The tree, a gangly collection of several smaller trees, wrapped around itself in strange patterns and made for odd cover. Gaelenn glanced down to set his feet for only a second and when his eyes flashed back up, the man was no longer there.

He was not there.

Panic again hit Gaelenn's empty stomach and twisted it in knots. He scanned the forest before him, desperate. Nothing. Nothing at all.

He swallowed hard. But his Adam's apple stopped short on its way back down in his throat, caught on something hard, cold, and steel. A sword.

CHAPTER FOUR
DANCE IN THE WOODS

"The suspense was killing me!" Triumvir Anwir's voice cried out with half amusement, half exasperation. "How long have we been dancing here, days? You did well not to fall asleep on your feet."

Gaelenn did not dare respond. He was not meant to. The sharp blade dug into his throat, triggering a small trickle of blood. The man could cut his head clean off with the flick of his wrist if he wanted.

"What in the world would an idiot pirate be doing following me into these woods? Isn't this a little far from your boat? I'm awfully sorry to say that I have no booty worth your effort."

His voice lingered in the air and he studied Gaelenn. He pulled the long knife from Gaelenn's grasp, and without looking hurled it at a nearby tree, burying it to the hilt. The sword at his neck relaxed slightly. Having firmly established their hierarchy, the man was finally ready to hear Gaelenn speak. But no words came. His mouth hung open, gulping in lungfuls of air. His eyelids fluttered with exhaustion, relief, and confusion.

Suddenly, the man squeezed the flesh of Gaelenn's shoulder in a super-human grip and forced him several feet to his side until he fell back onto a large fallen log. In front of the log's stump two yards away, he then began unloading a few of his burdens: a waist pack, a short rope, a water sack, and his sword, whose fabulously detailed hilt sparkled despite the lack of sunlight. Somehow, the man was almost jovial, his eyes alert, unbothered by lack of sleep or rest.

In fact, up close, Gaelenn noted no sweat upon his forehead nor a single heavy breath whatsoever. His immaculate attire was matched by a clean face, paler than most, with little stubble and nothing to mar its beauty other than deep lines between the eyes.

Anwir swept his green mantle around the stump and sat down, letting loose a dramatic sigh. He tapped an exquisite sack hanging from his belt, marked by a peculiar gold symbol—the outline of an eye crossed with a scythe—and bore his eyes further into Gaelenn's.

"Come now, it's obvious you're not just some common pirate. You have all your teeth." His voice lingered in the air, snake-like and vile.

"And you have some skill at that. I don't think I noticed you until yesterday."

He wore a taunting smile, resting his elbows on his knees so he could lean closer. His hands wrangled together into a knot and he stared again, penetrating his quarry, allowing dead silence to continue the interrogation for him.

The will to speak lurched into Gaelenn's throat, but hung there without leaping out as he studied his options. His hands and legs rested, unbound, and the sword lay well within a second's reach.

But he knew better. The man caught Gaelenn's trail of vision and raised an eyebrow. Both of them knew it was pointless to resist.

A cough forced itself from Gaelenn's throat, followed by his dry, crack-led voice, "What did you want in that town?"

"What town? That? Just a pile of rubble now!"

The man laughed as if he were making a joke. In his very next breath, his smile morphed into a threatening sneer. "How long were you following us?"

"Following? No. I saw nothing," Gaelenn said, and tried to force a change in subject. "What happened to that place? Why is it in ruins? Who are you?"

The man in green did not answer. Instead, he grew more curious; the questions themselves seemed to set his thoughts onto an altogether separate track. His eyebrows met at a point just at the top of his long, thin nose and his gaze was something between confusion and contempt.

But he was patient, despite his physical and aggressive manner.

"Answer my questions first, then I will entertain yours. Why did you try to follow me all this way?" he asked. His thoughts snowballed and other questions burst out, his patience suddenly lost: "What are you doing? Who are you? Speak up."

Gaelenn hesitated. There had to be some reason he was being kept alive—he should have been killed as soon as he stepped foot into the forest. He made it this far only because the man was toying with him for fun. He knew it as soon as he had seen those giddy, brown eyes, when the sword was at his throat. But it did not explain why his head was not cut off right then.

"I'm a pirate. I heard what happened and wanted to see if there were scraps left over. Hard times," Gaelenn lied. "That's all."

The swordsman frowned, unamused—he neither was used to nor liked being lied to.

"Hard enough indeed. You really don't know who I am?" he asked with some importance.

The two men sat opposite one another and glared. They were at a stalemate. Between them raged a natural, instinctive dislike, and they stared each other down with untraceable hatred. Finally, after a long gap of tense silence, the man stood up and grabbed his sword. He had reached his decision: execution.

Gaelenn bowed his head slightly, understanding, and steeled himself for his fate by forcing as blank an expression as he could muster. But the sword was heavier in the man's hand than before. Not that he was tired—the weight was in his head, and it dragged down his every movement. He crept toward Gaelenn, considering the death sentence with each small step. *Stalling.* Something was making him think twice about his decision, and Gaelenn could not decipher what it was.

The man's lips stretched, pensive, and his narrowed eyes deepened their search into Gaelenn's. Killing the wrong person could be a problem, apparently. The swordsman's instincts, again, were impeccably accurate.

"Ah, you've noticed my hesitation. Although I'm very happy to end your life here, I just find loose threads appalling."

He made a wry, unsettling grin and raised his sword until its edge rested under Gaelenn's chin once again. He moved it very slightly to the left and then to the right, using the reflection of the morning's light through the trees to examine his face more closely. Cheeks, nose, the green eye and the gray eye he studied; still he was unsatisfied.

"I feel generous—I will give you one last chance to save yourself," he said, resting his free hand on his hip. There was a struggle in his voice between humor and anger that could only be explained by insanity.

"I'm sure you've realized that I have no qualms about shoving this right into your throat. Tell me who you are and why you followed me, and maybe we can negotiate the losing your head part."

However jovial his offer appeared, there were achingly few answers that would help Gaelenn avoid death. He scoured his mind for some excuse, or lie, or plan that might give him a chance, but without time he was unable to conjure up a single sentence. He was a man of action, not a thinker. The truth seeped out.

"That was where I was born. You destroyed my home," Gaelenn said, relenting. At last he let loose the air in his chest that had been frozen there. His head drooped onto the sword, which, as if made of stone, refused to move. Blood dripped from its edge and fell to the ground, and Gaelenn closed his eyes in defeat.

No stroke came. When Gaelenn reopened his eyes, the green-clad man met them, brow raised in satisfaction.

"I didn't destroy your town personally, if it's any consolation," he said. "I can't say I'm not totally blameless, of course."

His humor seemed to come back to him. "But now I think we're set. I've got things to do."

Gaelenn looked up. "You're going to let me go?"

A bemused chuckle hit the swordsman's throat.

"Of course not," he said. "Lucky for you, though, I've decided against torture."

His sword arched up and readied for a quick, merciful strike at Gaelenn's neck. They looked each other full in the eye. A crazed flash swept over the face of the executioner and his muscles tensed for the stroke.

"At least tell me what you need with my mother's amulet," Gaelenn said. He had not planned on speaking; the words just slipped out. They were the exact right ones.

The swordsman turned to stone, sword above his head, legs still bracing for the strike. Every part of him froze except for his eyes, whose whites flashed into perfect circles around the tiny dots of his irises. He was in utter shock and, for the first time, *fearful*.

Gaelenn looked again. Fear—or elation? There was no way to tell whether he was grinning or grimacing.

For a moment, all was silent. Nothing could be heard by even the keenest ears—not a bird chirping nor leaves blowing. A minute later, the man's breath poured out in heaves, the cogs in his head churning behind his glazed eyes. Slowly and carefully, he moved backward, his blade pointed at Gaelenn's face. His feet sought stronger footing among the fallen branches of the forest floor—a purely *defensive* stance.

Gaelenn hid his bubbling confusion as best he could. The man acted as if he had cornered a kitten that had somehow turned into a lion, and moved back toward the tree stump. He was absorbed—entranced—and without breaking his stare, he reached down and wrapped his fingers around the rope set against the old dead tree. Rope for binding.

The green eye on Gaelenn's face caught the glint of a tiny ray of sunlight, and the swordsman took one last moment to look back and forth between it and the gray one. He was working things out in his mind. He *knew* something.

But his focus was too consuming to notice the slight rustling of leaves in the distance just over Gaelenn's shoulder. A whistling projectile broke his trance, but not before it lodged itself with such force into the dead tree behind him that only half of it remained visible. Pinned to the stump was a bloody mess of finger, rope, and palm.

The man howled in excruciating pain, dropping his sword to bring his right hand to rescue his left, now a mangled mess of blood and bone; the metal arrow had taken a finger and part of his thumb.

The spell of fear shattered. Gaelenn dashed forward as fast as he could, just in time to nab the sword on the ground and avoid a wild, desperate kick. The Triumvir was, for the moment, anchored to the tree. And livid.

"This way!" a voice rang from where the arrow originated. "Quickly! Run!"

For Gaelenn, the time to think, as excruciating as it had felt, was over. It was time to act, just as he liked it. He sprinted toward the voice hidden in the trees, leapt over the sitting log, and hit the ground running on the other side. He did not need to look back to feel the foaming, screaming, crazed grimace of the swordsman—the flowing stream of obscenities in his and several other languages sufficed.

"Faster! Come on," his rescuer's voice prodded. Gaelenn couldn't make out its owner between the flashes of deep green, but he knew that this wasn't the time to pick and choose an ally. He followed the figure through the trees and soon they were step for step, separated only by shadows. Gaelenn could not remember running this fast in his life—but then again, he had never been this scared before, either.

The screaming, now a safe distance behind them, reached a terrible fever pitch and suddenly—dreadfully—ceased. The shadow running next to him looked over and Gaelenn saw the whites of its eyes widen with panic.

Go! Move! They begged. Gaelenn obliged as fast as his feet could take him.

"Ha!"

A maniacal laugh echoed between the trees behind them. "Hah!"

He looked left and right, but that didn't help—it was coming from everywhere. And it was gaining. Fast. The forest came alive behind them in a flurry of senseless expletives.

Light broke through the trees ahead.

"We made it!" Gaelenn said, his heart pounding harder and harder the closer he and his newfound friend came to the end of the forest. "Almost!"

They broke free of the shadows and burst out into the light. Beneath them laid nothing but stark, blackened, rocky rubble; Gaelenn traced it up from his feet, stumbling now instead of running, until he saw the wall in front of him: solid black rock. To the left, black rock. Right, black rock. Up, all the way up—forever, it seemed—black rock. The Ash Cliffs. He could see his companion now slightly ahead of him, and still running nimbly over the stony ground, directly at the walls.

Raising his hand, Gaelenn called out to warn his new friend: "You're going to run into—"

But he was already in the air.

"Grab on!" the man, still only a shadow, shouted.

Gaelenn shrugged his shoulders and put his hand over his eyes to block the sun until he saw it—a thin, gray line against the black background of the cliff. A rope.

"Better hurry!" the man said again as he drifted above and away.

Gaelenn found a large boulder and vaulted off of it, grabbing the flickering end with both hands. Softer than silk yet strong as steel, it felt more like it had latched onto him than he on it. They coasted upward together in a smooth line.

"Is this magic?"

Below, the screaming man broke out into the open and watched them ascend.

Gaelenn and his friend looked down to see the man in green's chest heave before uttering the most awful and inhuman bellow either had ever heard. It was pure hate.

Blood spurted from the disfigured hand laying at his side. But his other hand refused to give up. He pulled a short knife from his belt and arched it backward behind his head where it caught a glimmer of sunlight.

In that good hand he held certain death for either Gaelenn or his companion. They clenched their teeth and squeezed their ropes.

"Watch out!" Gaelenn yelled just as the projectile shot into the air.

It flew with a sharp song, cutting through the air so fast that neither target could keep track of it. A second later, it struck true in the dead center of the rope above them—and bounced off, lodging itself deep into the black rock. Gaelenn looked up in awe and disbelief.

His friend looked down with a smile.

"It would take a lot more than that to cut this rope," he laughed out of the corner of his mouth. "I was worried he was aiming for one of us! Lesson learned, I'd wager—don't be greedy."

Gaelenn's neck craned up and down over and over. The ground fell away until it was nothing but a green blob of forest.

Ahead of him in the air grinned his savior, and for the first time he was more than just a shadow. His smiling eyes had almost no pigment at all, just two specs of black in white sockets and no color in his eyelashes to frame his eyes. His hair was pitch black, though, and flowed to his shoulder over his dark, padded shirt. Somehow, despite the odd appearance he was instantly likeable. Gaelenn already trusted him. In fact, he thought he might have seen him before.

"Hold on, we're almost there," the man said.

"Almost where?"

He looked up one last time at the odd face just in time to catch the smile fly away in the wind.

CHAPTER FIVE
LAST RETREAT

THE DISTANCE UPWARD WAS impossible to fathom, but the pair crossed it faster than Gaelenn could run downhill. Yet it was still several minutes before they finally made out the sharp edge at the top where the cliff cut the sky.

The air was thinner at this soaring height, making breathing a conscious effort, and the land below seemed a distant, foreign canvas. But in the distance lay the sea he knew and northward he found Sapphire Mountain, the great volcano split in two by its translucent blue gem, shining majestically with blue fire.

He submitted to the serenity of the scene below for a moment and found his nerve again just as they cleared the cliff above.

Gaelenn and his companion let go of the rope that had been pulled up by a peculiar system of pulleys and tip-toed to the ground over the black lip of rock that he could now see was over a yard thick and perfectly straight. The ground, a half-yard below the edges, consisted of packed dirt and dotted with strange, long-bladed grass that lead to a lush, dense forest of twisted branches and trees that looked like towering clovers. He marveled at the intense darkness it radiated.

"Welcome to safety! Guess our welcome party's gone ahead and spoiled our arrival. But how lucky was that!"

The man laughed and smiled and slapped Gaelenn's shoulder with an open hand. "I think I know who you are but you don't know me yet—I'm Rin."

He reached his hand out to Gaelenn, who failed to understand the gesture. A look of utter confusion was all he had to say.

Another laugh. "Oh, just a silly thing we do as a greeting."

Gaelenn had been all around the known world and had never seen a greeting like this. But it was easy enough to guess that he should grasp the offered limb, so he did by the wrist.

"No, no—the hand, like this!" Rin used his left hand to guide Gaelenn's to a proper handshake. "A bit firmer...there."

He grinned, satisfied.

Gaelenn brightened for a few seconds before his brow furrowed and he threw up his guard. "How could you possibly know who I am?"

"Anybody up here would know who you are. There's no mistaking that eye of yours," Rin said, examining both, one at a time.

All Gaelenn could do was blush and look away.

"I'm not coming onto you!"

His strange savior's white eyelashes clamped together as he laughed again. His own eyes were hard to focus on since they were almost the same color as his skin, which was just a shade pinker.

Gaelenn gave a half-smile. "What do you mean, 'anybody up here?' There are people up here?"

Rin nodded and Gaelenn tried to hide his surprise in a chuckle.

"There's nothing special about my eye, anyway," he said to deflect attention. But his defense only lasted a few seconds before he shook his head, defeated. "But who cares. None of what you're saying makes any sense at all to me."

"Come with me. There's no way I'll be able to really explain it with words," Rin said. "We've got somebody else who'll be able to tell you. That...and a whole lot more."

His eyes lit up for a moment before he turned his face toward the towering forest a few yards away from the edge. "Now you can hold my wrist. It gets pretty dark in there."

"I've had enough of trees for a while," Gaelenn said. He grabbed Rin's outstretched arm and followed him into the black.

For ten minutes, silence dominated. Leaves made slight whooshes here and there, but the thin air muffled the footsteps the four feet should have made. Finally, Gaelenn spoke, though in an instinctive whisper.

"You can see?"

"We've been up here for a long time. We've gotten used to it," Rin spoke back in his normal voice, not bothering to keep quiet. He even laughed in apparent jest before continuing, "I mean, you saw my eyes, right?"

Gaelenn would never forget them.

"How long is that?" he asked, but before the answer came, the floodgates in his mind broke open, and a thousand more questions begged to be unleashed. One in particular stood out: "And how did you find me down there?"

"I didn't find you—you and your little friend walked right past the tree I was parked in. Like I said, we were lucky. And then unlucky in another way," Rin broke off, following some internal train of thought. "That guy was trouble. If you hadn't been so obviously following him and keeping him distracted, there's no way he wouldn't have noticed me. Where were you following him to?"

Gaelenn responded with hesitation. He forgot to use words and shook his head, paying no heed of the darkness.

"You don't know? This just keeps getting weirder," Rin said.

"Wait, so you *can* see me? It's pitch black!"

"Shhh! Quiet!" Rin started.

Gaelenn put up his guard again.

Rin slapped his shoulder and laughed. "Relax. It's just that this next part is a whole lot more dramatic when you're totally silent."

For a short time longer they walked on, weaving left here and right there, up and over and under the wild, wooded maze. Rounding a large tree that Gaelenn braced against, having almost struck head-on, a pale blue light reached out from several yards ahead and bade him open his eyes, which had closed instinctively.

He released Rin's wrist without a word and walked toward it, spellbound. He bent down to examine the source of the glow: an orb of light at his feet. A misty blue radiance emanated like clear water from its flawless, translucent surface, and in its center, a ball of pure white writhed in a dance of smooth chaos.

The two men and all the trees surrounding them were awash in a strange, otherworldly glow. Gaelenn's fingertips traced a tentative, absent shape on the globe, then, reassured, he pressed his entire palm against its cool surface. He could not remember how long he sat there on the back of his legs—it felt like days—but he paid no heed to the pins and needles building up around his knees until he stood up. He took a few steps beyond the tree ahead and found a hundred more of the head-sized globes, illuminating a large clearing and revealing a massive stone gate.

The woods swam in undulating blue light, as if submerged in the shallows of a white-sand lagoon. It was like a dream.

A familiar dream. Gaelenn felt around from globe to globe, as if one of them might tell him why he knew them—as if one would jog his memory. It was the strangest sight he had ever seen, yet somehow it was not the first time he had seen it. He clenched his teeth together and shook his head.

"What is this place?"

"Home," Rin said. He smiled at Gaelenn and nudged him with his elbow. "Apparently the entrance was a big hit when the others came here, too."

Gaelenn shot him a confused look. "Others?"

"You'll see." Rin allowed a few more seconds for his guest to absorb the grandeur before pushing on. "We'd better head in and let some people know what's happened. I'm sure *she'll* be excited."

They walked past the gates where guards flanked either side. They dressed in a hardened, matte material with cloaks so black that they seemed to suck in the fantastic blue light surrounding them.

They acknowledged Rin with deep nods, keeping their focus on Gaelenn's bright eye, which glowed more gold in the blue light than green.

The two men stepped through the giant, door-less gate into a courtyard more wondrous than even the mountains of blue orbs outside. Scores of people populated the open area and fabulous buildings rose up at the end of neat little stone pathways, some two or three stories high. Hundreds and hundreds more of the wondrous blue spheres overflowed with their blue light, making the air up to the canopy of trees overhead almost as bright as the outside sky.

"You all live here? How many people? How long?" Gaelenn asked. His mouth hung open, breathless.

"Thousands upon thousands, and thousands more," Rin replied wistfully, happy to add to the moment. His hand waved in front of Gaelenn's eyes. "We've been here for a very, very long time."

"That's impossible—I grew up a stone's throw away," said Gaelenn.

"Well, we are pretty good at staying out of sight," Rin said. "I don't want to spoil anything, but you'll probably find that you grew up closer to us than you think. After all, I know who you are already, right?"

A playful wink dotted his question.

Gaelenn nodded absently. He was still so absorbed that he failed to notice the equally awestruck crowd gathering around him, gawking and murmuring secrets among themselves. Rin grabbed Gaelenn by the wrist this time and used his other hand like a knife to cut a gap in the crowd.

"Please, let us pass, let us pass," he spoke gently, over and over.

They walked through the hidden city and its twisting streets and opulent courtyards until Gaelenn's feet began to drag on the stone path. Looking back, Rin noticed him stumbling and put his arm around his broad shoulders to prop him up.

"You haven't slept in quite a while, have you? You need to rest," Rin said with an encouraging pat. "We're almost there. Hang on."

But before they took another step, Gaelenn fell asleep on his feet.

CHAPTER SIX
THE PRIESTESS

YELLOW CANDLELIGHT FLICKERED IN Gaelenn's eyes for two full minutes before he realized he was awake. The feather pillow under his head was the softest thing he had felt in years. Maybe even since the last time he had slept in his own bed. It begged him for a few hours' more rest.

Just before his eyelids fused together again in blissful acquiescence, his brain clicked.

"What is that...?"

On the ceiling his gaze followed a trail of naked little babies dancing around clouds, holding hands, flying among the beautiful gold-painted spires and domes of the ceiling. A painting. He rubbed the sleep out of his eyes.

"I swear I've seen that before," he said. His voice was dry and low from countless hours of sleep.

He sat up and stretched his back and opened one eye wide to protect the other from the light. It was not a candle, he noticed. It was just another glowing ball—a warmer color than those outside the little house, sitting on a tall table stand at the other end of the room.

Rin's voice startled him. "Up already? Sure you don't need any more sleep?"

Gaelenn turned his head around to find his new friend standing against the wall.

"I'm...fine," he said. He stretched and rubbed his limbs under the soft linen sheets until his hands found his stomach. "Actually, I'm starving. I couldn't tell you when the last time I ate was."

Rin brightened up with a smile and a chuckle.

"Then let's go," he said and waved his hand. "It's time for you to meet the Priestess. I'm sure there'll be food. She's always eating."

He paused and looked Gaelenn in the eyes, the laugh disappearing from his face instantly.

"She's really been looking forward to this. Gave me a promotion for all the fuss, even."

"Looking forward to meeting me? Who? Priestess—what priestess? And what would she want to talk to me about?"

Rin's smile returned and Gaelenn caught the hint. "I guess you're going to let me see for myself this time, too? For effect?"

He swung his legs around and pushed himself off the bed with almost a jump. His pants, along with a fresh, unused tunic and leather jacket, lay cleaned and neatly arranged on a fine wooden shelf—the finest he had ever seen—near the globe lamp, and he walked across the room in a new, white undergarment. Somebody had seen him naked. He looked sideways at Rin.

"Wasn't me," his new friend laughed.

As Gaelenn unfolded his clothes to inspect them, the smell of flowers hit his nose and he smiled before he could think.

"Well, a big thanks to whoever washed these. I was traveling for...quite a while."

"I'm sure the Priestess'll be asking all about that," Rin said, his voice light, enjoying the pleasantly confused expressions on Gaelenn's newly shaven face. "And a whole lot more. If there's one thing she likes more than eating, it's talking."

"So who is she? Are you guys some kind of cult—" Gaelenn paused and rethought his question. "Uh, everybody here is of the same religion?"

He buckled the jacket over his new tunic and strapped on his arm guards, which had somehow also survived his journey. His weapon, the sword he stole from Triumvir Anwir, was just as it was before. He almost gasped in surprise that it was returned to him freely—he must not look as dangerous as he pictured himself.

Apparently at least not tough enough to be a threat up here. There was a carafe of water on another table and he drained it without asking.

There was no chamber pot, but Rin guided him to an elevated hole in a small, separate room to relieve himself, waiting politely before answering.

"Cult? No. Religion? Something like that. The Priestess is our 'spiritual leader,' you might say." He framed the phrase with open hands, like it was inside an invisible bubble. "She's something of a mystery even to us. You'll see."

Gaelenn nodded, refreshed but ravenous. "Ready anytime."

"Oh, and she's pretty old, too. But don't let her age—or her looks—fool you. You'll get more answers than you ever wanted to hear, I'm sure," Rin said before he led Gaelenn out of the house and back into the glowing maze of streets.

The crowds had dissipated and gone back to their daily lives, though pale white eyes cut through the air at Gaelenn wherever he walked. The people were washing clothes, preparing food, walking about here and there. A man swept the dust off a small pathway. Guards walked to and fro. It was like any other village except that it was a mile above the rest of the continent, and the light came from all around instead of from the sun above.

But something else was peculiar about this place. Gaelenn cocked his head.

"How do you know whether it's day or night?" he asked, looking up at the pitch-black ceiling.

Every one of the villagers had irises like Rin's—so pale that they were almost all white.

"It's always day here—well, it's always night, too. We're used to it. We just turn out the lights at home when we sleep."

Children played jumping games on the round stone paths and a crowd had gathered near a small well. The people there were taking turns dipping their heads into buckets of watery paint. Those who were waiting in line had roots of colorless hair, almost translucent, which they washed into pure black. Others, men and women both, plucked hairs from each other's eyebrows and chins and painted them back on in color.

"What are they doing?" Gaelenn asked.

Rin smiled again. "You really do have a lot of questions, don't you? It's a cultural thing, I guess. We'll talk about it all later. We need to hurry. She's already been waiting a while. You were sleeping for an entire day."

"A whole day...? I thought you said—"

"Exactly, what's the hurry? You'd think somebody as old as she is would be more patient, right?"

Several minutes later they came to an enormous covered courtyard with a central building decorated in strange, ornate script and figures carved in stone. Vines crawled around it like veins. Rin pointed teasingly at the increasingly puzzled wrinkles on Gaelenn's forehead.

"Our lights keep the plants healthy even in dark places. Have to keep them alive so that they can help keep us alive." He grinned when Gaelenn's expression failed to change. "I could tell you were going to ask me. Does that make me as prescient as the Priestess? Ha!"

"I don't understand a single thing you say."

Rin's head bobbed backwards and he giggled. "It'll all make sense in a few minutes. Maybe."

With no further words, they walked up toward the decorated wooden door at the end of the walkway to the house and Rin rapped his knuckles against it a few times. It echoed like a drum and two cloaked guards greeted them and raised their hands, palms up, to invite the visitors. Gaelenn walked in but Rin remained at the door.

"I'll see you in a little while. Lots of work to be done. Oh, and, like I said earlier," he said as he departed with one last smile. "Don't let her looks fool you. Good luck."

The doors closed behind the visitor and a third guard appeared from a side door.

"This way, please," she said politely.

He paused for half a step to make a mental note that it was a woman's voice that came from under the helmet; here, it seemed, the men and women wore their hair and their clothes the same way. Here, everybody seemed equal, and thinking about it, in the city, most jobs were done by just about anybody. But the thought disappeared as soon as it had come, slain by the sheen of lacquered wood and the glimmer of gold accents that lined the huge, luxurious room. Delicate paintings hung on every open wall. Massive sculptures of nude figures stood upon the perfectly-polished marble floor. And an ornate silver rail snaked around an ivory staircase leading to the second level where a hand-carved door hid what must have been piles of treasure.

"So, this...priestess? She's got quite some taste, doesn't she?" Gaelenn asked no one in particular.

The guard shook her head and motioned to a door next to the stairs. "The Priestess prefers more modest accommodations."

Gaelenn walked past her into a dimly-lit room. He neither thanked the guard for opening the door nor looked back to see it close behind him; he simply stood, frozen, and stared. He was not prepared. At the end of a polished obsidian table sat the Priestess. His heart skidded across his rib cage and slammed into his throat, muting him—she was not the old, haggard relic he had envisioned. This must be the precise effect Rin had been expecting.

"Hello, Gaelenn," she said.

The smile he had worn as he had daydreamed of the fabulous riches that must hide somewhere in this magnificent mansion vanished like a phantom. The face looking up at him could not have been more than twenty years old. Her innocent smile was even younger. A star-shaped diamond pendant lit up her neck and chin in a brilliant rainbow of color.

She continued, ignoring his reaction. "It's been a long time."

"A long what? I'm sorry, I—" Gaelenn stuttered, coming back to his senses. Something about her was familiar, but it was almost as if he had seen her in a dream.

She wore a flowing dress, purer white than anything he had ever seen, and her long platinum hair fell freely behind her shoulders; there was not a place in the entire world where she would not look completely out of place. She was too clean. Too different. Too perfect.

"I...," Gaelenn started and then jumped back. "Wait, how do you know my name?"

"I know a lot about you!" she said with an even warmer smile. Her eyes gleamed, different from the eyes of the people outside—different from any eyes he had ever seen: blue. "For example, I know that you must be hungry. I am, too."

Gaelenn broke into a smile, admiring her ability to set him at ease. Her voice was light and bright and happy. But it was older than her face—weaved into it somewhere was the weight of many years. "Yeah, actually."

"So—let's eat," she said. Her first finger tapped the monolithic stone table beneath her and, to Gaelenn's surprise, it lit up like a perfectly still pond reflecting the daytime sky. A vibrant painting of rolling, green hills, far too fine for an artist, glowed under her hands.

"Is this magic? Are you...?" he asked and lurched his head back toward the wall. This was not the usual sleight of hand employed by street magicians; he had seen plenty of that in his travels. But there was no other way to explain what he was seeing.

"No, no, no—not magic. I suppose they told you I'm the 'Priestess,'" she laughed, motioning toward the guards outside the door. "Actually, you can call me Livvy."

Her smile seemed to push the air around the room like a current. She tapped a blue circle on the image in the table and watched it turn white. "But it really must *look* like magic, right?"

Gaelenn did not reply. He just stared at the table.

"Oh, I'm sorry—I don't mean to make fun! I know it's a bit strange. But it's just a machine," Livvy said with a gentler, motherly smile. "I'll just order our food. It will be here shortly."

"Machine?" Gaelenn could not fathom how a machine—in his mind, a bulky, brutish device like a grain mill—could do something so sublime, so magical. He closed his eyes tight for a moment and swallowed.

"I'm sorry, I don't understand," he admitted.

Her head tilted to one side with narrowed eyes and she stared into him. "Your parents—didn't they ever tell you about us? About this place?"

"My parents? Tell me about you? How would they know this?" Gaelenn was aghast. "My dad was a merchant, not a priest or a magician!"

Livvy frowned. "I'm sorry. I didn't know. There is a lot to talk about. I think we need to start from the beginning."

"That sounds like a good idea." He crossed his arms. "What in blazes is going on? What is this place, who are you really, and how does everybody know who I am?"

Her kind eyes smiled at Gaelenn, sympathetic, and she spoke in the gentlest voice he had ever heard. "First, I will answer your questions. Then I'd like to ask you some. Is that okay?"

He nodded. "Okay. I'm not sure I have any answers for *you*, but okay."

"Good enough. Oh—the food will be here in just a moment." She made a few noiseless taps on the table and the painting on it vanished.

Gaelenn had not noticed his fingers grinding into the back of the chair in front of him. He pulled them away and looked at Livvy, waiting for her to speak again.

"So, the beginning," she said. "Okay, you do know, at least, that your eyes were not like that when you were born—right?"

She pointed at his face.

"What?" Gaelenn's knees buckled as if he had been physically shoved. His distinguishing birthmark was not a birthmark.

"No? Okay then, the *very* beginning." She traced a shape with her pointing finger as she searched for the right place to start before finding it with a quick *a-ha* poke in the air.

"I knew your father and mother. And your father's father. And his mother, and on and on and on, as far back as—well, as you could imagine. And the first time I saw you, you weren't even a week old." She smiled warmly.

"That's insane. I'm older than you are—obviously!" Gaelenn braced himself against the edge of the table.

The Priestess simply raised her eyebrows and shook her head gently. She was still smiling. Gaelenn got the feeling that she enjoyed spilling revelations like this. And that she was used to it.

"Alright then," he said. "Let's assume you are older than me. For the sake of our conversation. So, I've been here before?"

He had no real memory of this place. Only a sort of far-off familiarity. A feeling.

A few long strands of hair swung to the front of Livvy's shoulders as she leaned forward. "I'm quite old, Gaelenn, though I don't look it. I'm one of the last of my people, who were lost long, long ago. Yes, you've been here before. And I've watched over your line for eight hundred generations."

CHAPTER SEVEN
A History of Ruin

THE DOOR BEHIND GAELENN creaked open and two female guards placed large plates of cut red meat and pale vegetables in between him and the Priestess, who closed her eyes in lustful focus on the savory aroma.

Gaelenn did not even remember sitting down. He certainly had not spoken for several minutes.

"At my age, good food is about the only thing that can still really bring me back down to earth," Livvy said, breaking through the tension with an anticipating grin. "Let's talk while we eat!"

Gaelenn's hand reached for his stomach and rubbed it. Empty. He had forgotten that he was starving, and he let the smell penetrate his nostrils.

"I'm so hungry."

"So am I!" The Priestess beamed.

They devoured their meals—she slowly, savoring each bite, and he on the brink of abandoning his silverware to scoop the food into his mouth with his hands. Ten minutes later, Gaelenn sat, gorged, and watched Livvy's delicate and refined manners in a satisfied stupor. He had forgotten his questions for the time being.

"So much for talking while eating," she said and laughed, pointing at Gaelenn's plate.

He looked down at the fine dish, scraped almost completely clean of any trace of food, and laughed at himself. Blood rushed to his cheeks as embarrassment and nourishment crawled around his body. A guard came in the door, refilled his glass of wine, and left again.

"So, as I was saying," Livvy continued, "I am very old. But I'm not a priestess, or a witch, or whatever our mutual friend Rin told you. I'm more like this machine here."

She pointed happily at the table with her palm face-up. "Old, but new. You could say there are machines like this inside me."

Gaelenn's head tilted like a dog's upon hearing a whistle as she looked at the table with her own sense of wonderment.

"You know, actually...I think this machine is older than me. Though it's pretty close. But at least it's had a much more recent tune-up."

Gaelenn did not understand enough to return her laugh. "You...don't age? Doesn't that make you a goddess?"

"No, it does not."

"Well then, why do they call you 'Priestess?'" He stared at her sparkling necklace.

She grasped it at her neck and glanced upward toward the ceiling. "That's just a nickname. An old one. And a long story. How about this: I'll tell you the whole boring thing tomorrow over lunch. Okay? Today there are a few more pressing things to discuss. For today, let's just agree to trust each other. As is."

Gaelenn sighed and shook it off with a wave of his hand. "Fine, then. Something more urgent? My hometown was destroyed. Do you know about that?"

Livvy's eyes drifted downward. Her happy mood died.

"Rin said you know a lot," he continued. "Did you know that this is happening all over the world? All I've seen over the past seven years is destruction. Everything's in ruins."

She nodded. "I know about it."

"And do you know why the people who destroyed my house would go around looking for my mother's amulet?" He threw his hands up in exasperation, allowing his raw emotion to control them instead of his manners. "I know I'm shooting arrows in the dark, but—"

"...Yes," she responded, this time looking him straight in the eye.

Gaelenn jumped in his seat. He had not intended to actually get an answer.

"Let me show you how I know," she said and rose to her feet, wiping her parted lips with a soft towel and setting it down. "Follow me."

She was a full foot shorter than Gaelenn, and thin, and carried the suppleness of youth. There was a bounce in her step that Gaelenn would have expected of a young girl. But not from the ancient being she claimed to be.

She walked to her left through a small dark door and Gaelenn followed her. As they entered, pure white light flickered and came to life above. Gaelenn looked right at the nearest bulb reflexively and nearly went blind. He had been in the dark too long already.

"Oh, better not look right at the light!" Livvy said. "But you can open your eyes now."

After a few more seconds of wincing, he did.

Right in front of him, in the exact middle of the room, stood a strange table, almost like a bed. It was raised from the floor to around waist-level, covered in straps made from the same material as the rope that had brought him up the day before. Above it a large, metallic, sharp-looking object—another of the Priestess' machines, Gaelenn guessed, hung from the ceiling.

He walked around and examined it from each side.

Livvy waited for him to stop before speaking.

"When you came here, both of your eyes were still gray. That day...of all my long days, that is one I'll never forget. You were still a tiny baby. Just six days old. This is where your eyes changed—or at least one of them."

"What do you mean?"

"This machine made your eye that way. They don't turn that color naturally."

"Well, I kind of noticed nobody else had one this color except for my father. And he had two."

"...Yes—before it could complete your other eye, it stopped. The operation failed before it could finish. That's why only your left eye is different."

She ran her finger around the lower part of the steel hanging between her and Gaelenn. He watched her trace its sharp, cylindrical lines, paying equal attention to it and her delicate fingers. They were younger and purer than his, which were rough and calloused from years of use.

"After thousands of years, this machine broke. And this time, we couldn't fix it. We scoured the world—what's left of it, at least—for another working one like it. But they're all either gone or destroyed. Or the wrong kind. We're still working on it, but..." Her forehead wrinkled like a wrung sponge and her eyes cast downward onto the bed. "Now, the game has changed."

"Because of this? I can still see. Out of both eyes."

She looked at him, understanding, with a sad smile. "No, not that. This is where we kept alive the hope of humanity. This is how we were supposed to, one day far from now, show the people of the world the truth of their past. Of what was, of what could be. And what should never be."

Livvy walked closer to Gaelenn and looked up into his eyes.

"Your eyes hold the key to our history, which we have kept in rooms like this around the world. Or at least...your eyes were supposed to. When this machine broke, it was the end of our ability to protect our legacy."

"What legacy?"

"Our legacy. Everybody's. Your line has descended since the end of my age all the way down to now, keeping the key safe from one generation to the next."

He put his hands palms-out in front of his chest. "No, not that—what 'key?' My mother's amulet? That's why they were after it, wasn't it?"

"No. No—well, yes, in a way. Luckily for us, the amulet is just a diversion. A ruse we planned as a layer of defense. But I'm sure the ruse won't buy us much time. It has some function, of course, but it can't do what the real key can do."

She walked back to the bed-machine and caressed it as she walked, keeping her eyes locked on Gaelenn, and stopped beside him. "The key is inside you, woven into the very fabric of who you are. You were born with it, just as your father was, and his mother, and on and on, all the way up the line. This machine just makes your key usable; it was meant to take your key and open the way to our most important resource. And our only real weapon—our history."

Gaelenn felt the bed with his own hands. It was firm and smooth but gave a little. Just enough not to be uncomfortable. He closed his eyes and rested his mind for a moment, thinking about how ragged his own hands and clothes looked compared to the pristine cleanliness of the strange material.

And the woman across from him.

"I'm having a tough time understanding any of this," he sighed. "Please, just speak plainly. What am I?"

Again a hint of pity came to her face and she frowned.

"If only your father had done as he was supposed to," she said, exasperated. "What every one of his line had done all the way back to the beginning. But after what happened to you here I almost can't blame him for changing his mind. Inside of you—deep, deep inside—is a code that nobody can understand. This machine translates that code and imprints it directly onto your irises."

She pointed to his eyes and traced his green iris in a circle with her thin finger.

"Those eyes were to become the key which you were to keep safe, as your ancestors had done since I was born, waiting for the day we could finally share the treasure with all the people of the world. I...was supposed to protect you."

"Treasure," Gaelenn responded, "I have no need for."

"Not that kind of treasure." Livvy lifted her fists up to her chin. "You carry with you the key to all the history of the human race. Thousands and thousands of years of joy and peace and war and suffering. Every song, every event, every mistake, every success—and every secret."

Her usual intonation was absent at the last word; she was deadly serious.

"And I guess that some secrets are worth hiding," Gaelenn said. A picture formed in his mind, though it was still too blurry to decipher. "But keep them from who? And why?"

Without a word, Livvy walked back to the door and went through. Gaelenn followed her like a puppy. She stood above her black table and touched the surface, and again it came to life with a brilliant-colored tapestry. Seeing it much more clearly this time, he stood next to her and watched.

He barely noticed the smell of fresh flowers in her hair. But he did notice.

"This will come as a shock, perhaps. But when I was a young girl, this world was destroyed."

CHAPTER EIGHT
OUR ENEMY

GAELENN DID NOT LOOK up at Livvy as she summoned image after image of herself on the table, looking just as she was now, but in a different place—a different time. They were more than drawings or paintings, things he knew and had seen before. They were *her*, images of her life.

And people were with her, wearing the same style of strange clothing she was wearing. Some even stranger. They were smiling, making silly faces, obscene gestures, living strange and wonderful lives. Around them were structures beyond imagining, and perfectly formed glass windows in careful order, and vivid, lively landscapes of a tamed world. A world built by gods.

They must be gods, Gaelenn thought, though he had never entertained the thought of a deity himself. Some pictures even showed Livvy using machines just like the table in front of them, but so small that they fit on her lap and in the palms of her hands.

A deafening sigh floated from her open lips.

"This was my world," she said. "Too long ago."

Gaelenn could only mount a whisper in response. "What happened to it?"

She closed her eyes and waited for the emotion to pass. "You'd think I'd have gotten over it after all this time. Time beyond time. But whenever I reach myself back that far in my mind, it happens all over again."

Tears welled up in the corners of her eyes. Gaelenn resisted the attempt to console her with his arm—it was wrong. Not yet. Probably not ever.

"I gave up letting go after the first thousand years," she said.

"You don't have to talk about it...if it hurts you."

"No. No, I do need to talk about it—you need to know." Strength returned to her voice; she choked down her emotion and forced it back into the hidden compartments in her mind. "Something is about to happen, and *you* need to know more about this than anybody."

He lost himself in her eyes, which were still focused on the table, and felt how close they had drawn together, arms almost touching. Or maybe he had edged closer without thinking.

"What happened was...our fault. We built it. We made it—we gave birth to our own reaper," Livvy said. Each word fell as if gravity itself pulled it down. "Or maybe it was inevitable. We'll be lucky if there are people alive to debate it someday."

Gaelenn squinted to focus his imagination. "I still don't quite understand—"

"There was this war," she continued, anticipating the question, "among all the domains of the world. I was only a few years old at the time, really, but I still remember. And a lot of people died. And then for a while, there was peace, and we rebuilt."

She looked up from the table for just a moment to stress the word 'peace.'

"Everybody was so tired of fighting, and so sad. So we took all the energy we'd put into fighting each other and we pushed the human race further than it had ever been. Maybe ever will be. We made monuments to ourselves. Worked to make our mark on the world. Tried to make things that last forever. Like this mountain."

"This mountain? Your people *made* it?"

Taking a deep breath, Livvy finally seemed to notice their proximity. She looked up straight into Gaelenn's eyes, and the room, dark now except for the pale glowing table, illuminated their faces in blue light from below. He could barely breathe, and he did not know if it was her or the story she was telling him. They froze there for what felt like an age itself.

A moment like this must be less than the blink of an eye to her, he found himself thinking. *And I must be nothing but a child.*

Still, up close, he had never seen any human even close to as beautiful as her. He cleared his throat and walked around the table where he could compose himself. He had to force himself to resume breathing.

"I don't really quite get it. What kind of 'reaper?' Some sort of weapon?"

"No, not exactly. It was...a being. A person, you might say, though not human. Something that existed but not physically," Livvy tried to explain. "You might say it was like a spirit that could take form."

"So, you were gods—and you created a god."

"No, and yes," her voice grew somewhat frustrated while she searched for the right way to explain. "We created this 'life,' but we weren't gods. I'm not a god—I don't even believe in gods. We just reached a point where humanity was ready to create life on its own. At least, we thought we were ready. It just became inevitable. Our 'child' didn't think of us as its masters, it thought it was our successor."

Gaelenn stared at the table, as lost as ever. His head was swimming and he found it difficult to stand. "And it's still alive? Still fighting?"

"I fear it may never die."

"Then why doesn't it come up here and wipe you all out? Can't it?"

Livvy sighed.

"It may very well be able to. But we're lucky. We found old things like this," she said, stroking the edge of the table, "when we came up here. There are some other 'magic' things that let us hide. Or at least make it look to anybody else that the only thing up here is rock and sand."

"I still have no idea why something you created could end up being your enemy."

She nodded. "It was supposed to help us and to liberate us from toil, and fighting, and war. We were confident that when we succeeded in its creation that all our problems would go away. We somehow knew of the dangers, but we still had hope. In only a matter of years after we created it—it lived inside machines just like this—it turned on us, though we didn't know."

"I see...maybe," he said, although both were aware he did not really see.

"Oh, if only your father had done his duty, this would be so much easier. You'd already know it all!" Livvy almost laughed as she spoke, though Gaelenn easily sensed how painful it was for her to say.

"My father knew all this?"

"Of course. It's been taught to the firstborn in your family for almost as long as I've been alive! My father and a group of survivors set the precedent and I've been keeping it going ever since," she said, then walked back to her room, and plopped down in her chair, giving Gaelenn another moment to reflect before following her.

"Let's assume I understand all of this. Any of this. Whatever happened, it happened so long ago that I don't think it makes any difference, and if it made any difference at all, it doesn't anymore because this machine here broke."

He motioned toward the door to the room, where the white lights had gone black as soon as they left. "What matters to me is what happened to this country and what happened to my home and my friends and my family."

"That is *exactly why* it matters. The same enemy that destroyed my world also destroyed your home," she said. "And it's not going to stop there. This time, I think, it is out to end the conflict for good. You see, we've been fighting against this enemy ever since it destroyed my world. And every time it comes back, it takes a little more away from us. For every injury we inflict on it, it injures us tenfold. We've been teetering on the edge of destruction now for a long, long time."

Livvy put her hands lightly on her lap, wresting control of her emotions back from her memories. "This time, I honestly don't know if we can survive."

Gaelenn stood tall, finally understanding the connection. Destruction and violence were much easier concepts to grasp.

"How do we stop it?" he asked, as much a statement as it was a question.

"I'm afraid I don't know how. I don't think we can. Your father went off in search of its source some years ago, and we haven't heard from him since," she said, taking notice of the brief wince on Gaelenn's face and adjusting her tone accordingly. "Now, we only have your key. And the most important thing is that we keep you safe. If our enemy ever got a hold of you, it would have all it needs to wipe us out, once and for all."

She gave a dramatic sigh, this time with a smile. "You don't know how relieved I am that you returned to us. And at this exact time, of all times."

"I have no intention of staying, though," he replied without thinking. "I didn't come here knowing that I would find you, or any of this. I came to find who did this to my home. Now I know. I can't sit here and do nothing."

She stood up, walked around the table and held his arm, looking at him face to face. In her eyes the shadow of desperation tried unsuccessfully to hide.

"Please listen. There is nothing you can do, there is nothing that anybody can do right now except for to protect ourselves, protect you, and wait for our chance to fight back. It's what we've done for thousands of years. Our chance will come."

"Why don't you just tell the people about what's happening? I'm sure they'd band together. And then you could defeat this...enemy!"

Livvy shook her head. "We have tried everything. Until humanity reaches a certain level of...advancement and openness, they can never accept the truth. We've tried it before. We've tried just about everything over the past twenty thousand years. Our civilization has been destroyed time and time again, no matter what we do."

Gaelenn stared ahead without focusing on anything. He did not believe in magic and subscribed to none of the plentiful religions he had encountered during his travels. But he believed every word she said.

"I trust you. I believe what you're saying," he said. "But I can't stay here forever. Maybe for a couple days at most. I just can't stand by and do nothing. Not with what happened to my village. Not with what's happening all over the world. I've seen it! And now I know who's behind it. You said that if your enemy—"

"*Our* enemy," she interjected.

"If *our* enemy gets its hands on me, how would that change anything? You said your machine wasn't able to finish its job on me before it broke. This key, or whatever it is, is broken. *I'm* broken."

"You're not broken. You're whole, even if you have one half of a key."

Her desperation dissipated and her hands fell back to her sides and her thin lips curved back up into a kind smile. She spoke like she was addressing a small child. "I think we should go back to the beginning. Since you'll be staying, why don't we talk again tomorrow? I have some things to take care of and a lot of thinking to do. And I'm hungry again."

"Fine," Gaelenn started, but a rush of air hit him from the swinging door behind.

"Lady Priestess, the west guard rotation hasn't returned," a voice blared. It was Rin's. "All the other teams reported as usual."

"Rin," Livvy's controlled voice responded as she swiveled her whole body gracefully on her heels to receive his news. "How late?"

"One hour," he said, his usual playfulness completely absent.

"One hour? What's one hour?" Gaelenn asked. Punctuality was not a highly valued trait in most of the world these days.

Livvy stiffened to attention, ignoring him.

"Set up a recovery party and dispatch them immediately," she ordered. "This is not a coincidence."

"Our guards are never late coming back—never," Rin said. "We can track the precise time, down to the second, if we must."

The Priestess swiveled to Gaelenn. "Rin is now the Lieutenant Captain of our Guard. He explained to me every detail of your escape yesterday. But I need some more information from you."

Rin closed the door softly behind them.

"Unfortunately, he was unable to hear the conversion you were having with your captor, so I'd like you to fill in the blanks," she continued. "And quickly, please."

"There wasn't much conversation to speak of," Gaelenn said. "All I could tell is that there was something...inhuman about him."

Rin and Livvy exchanged brief glances.

"Yeah, we're pretty certain that the man you were talking with wasn't all human," Rin said.

"Not all human? What does that mean?"

"We used to call them 'EN,' sort of short for 'enhanced.' Or sometimes just 'the Legion.' We suspect he has been modified—he moved too fast for a normal human being from what Rin said. ENs are capable of dangerous things."

She paused and considered the best way to explain. It was not quite long enough for Gaelenn's thoughts to catch up.

"We thought they were destroyed after the last conflict. But now, it appears our hopes were misplaced. Somehow the enemy has found a way to resurrect them." Livvy's nose crumpled up in a sneer.

"And if they are around, things will be much more dangerous for you," she said, pointing at Gaelenn. "As long as they are around, the enemy has...hands. Hands that can strike. No one will be safe. We can only hope that he doesn't know who you are...but we can talk about that tomorrow."

Suddenly, she snapped upright. "First, tell me—what did he say to you?"

"Almost nothing, really. He wanted to know who I was and why I was following him. That's all. But I didn't tell him anything," Gaelenn said, scanning his memory for any other details.

"Good. That's good." Livvy exhaled with relief. "Rin, organize a search party to find the missing patrol. Small and mobile, and keep out of sight. He might still be around—"

"There was one strange thing," Gaelenn interrupted. "Well, the whole thing was strange to me. But one thing stood out. He was about to...execute me, I guess. But something changed his mind. Pretty suddenly, too."

"What did?"

"It was when I asked about the amulet he stole."

The priestess looked all around the floor, as if checking it for vermin, but the vermin were in her head. "What were your exact words, as best as you can remember?"

"Um... 'Why did you take my mother's amulet?' Or something like that."

"Oh, god."

"What? What's the difference?" Gaelenn asked.

"You didn't know. You didn't know, you couldn't have known—I don't blame you," Livvy said, almost wincing, trying to smooth her harsh tone.

"But we've gone to great length to keep that amulet the focus of the enemy, and not you, yourself. That the enemy even knows about the amulet bodes poorly for your father's fate...but as its owner's son, you most definitely piqued that man's interest. You painted a target on your own back."

She rubbed her forehead. "It will come for you again, that's for certain. Wherever you are."

Gaelenn's mind was still minutes behind. "Wait—so, do you know if my father's alive?"

The shockwave of the mere word father had hit his knees and he staggered. He had spent the past seven years searching the world for his father without even a whisper.

"No, I'm sorry—I don't think so. Not after this news. But there will be time to discuss that, since you'll be staying here. We'll keep you safe."

She tapped the table rapidly as she spoke.

"Rin, prepare a team to go immediately. Our most skilled, and you lead them."

The lines above her brow deepened, but Livvy showed absolute control.

"I'm going, too," Gaelenn blurted out. It was almost instinct for his words to precede his thoughts.

"Please, Gaelenn—we agreed that you would stay. Remember what's at stake. Remember all that we have yet to discuss," Livvy pleaded. "If you go, you could be found and captured. Who knows what would happen to you? What would happen to everybody!"

He clenched his teeth, torn between keeping his word and his own reckless nature. "I have to do something. I can't hide away."

"I'm sorry, Gaelenn. I can't allow that."

The door behind them opened again, bringing two cloaked guards. Livvy nodded at them and before Gaelenn could react, he found his hands in chains.

"What are you doing?"

"Please understand, Gaelenn. I have fought this war for too long to risk everything like this. You are our last hope. We had lost you. By some miracle you came back. You had no siblings and our means of salvation broke down. We have no backup plan."

Sensing his confusion again, she reassured him. "Our people will do what they can. They are skilled. And maybe after we've talked more about these things, you will understand why I need you to stay."

Her delivery was soft and gentle, but her face was hard as stone.

"Then tell me one thing before you lock me up," Gaelenn said. There was a dark side to her, after all. "What's really at stake? What's *our* enemy going to do?"

Pity came to her cheeks in a red flush. It wasn't easy for her to have him bound. "I'm afraid it intends to end the conflict for good. The faster they find you, the faster they'll come for the rest of us."

CHAPTER NINE
REUNION

BACK IN HIS ROOM, the ornate ceiling above Gaelenn's new bed was quickly becoming familiar—and old. Suddenly he was a prisoner instead of a guest—the entire cabin was locked down with guards at the door and each window. Sleep would not find him; the anger at being caught off guard by the Priestess had kept it at bay. Hours passed in silence as he sat near the window and waited for nothing in particular.

He looked at the backs of the guards' heads from the window and huffed. It would not be a challenge to overcome one or two of them. But he would not get far, and there was no way he would make it down to the ground below even if he did. He was a prisoner, and the thought drew his proud shoulders down to his chest.

The window—and the freedom beyond it—was the only thing that could occupy his mind. He watched a young man only a few years younger than himself apply jet-black dye to his hair, whose roots were so white he could see the pink of scalp from several yards away. A group of men and women gathered around in a small court, gossiping perhaps, and at a fountain in the shadow of a large building, and a few residents shaved their arms and legs with small razors.

Gaelenn shut the curtain. "This place is another world."

With it shut and the strange new world gone from his view, he resolved to force himself asleep. He launched himself onto his pillow and without shedding his clothes, closed his eyes. They were only closed for a minute.

Three voices came from the door, followed by a muffled thud, and he opened his eyes and sat up. The door opened and Rin appeared, dragging in the body of an unconscious guard. Gaelenn rushed to the door and eased it shut. He understood. The shadows of the guards outside the window on the other side of the house had not moved.

Rin put his finger to his lips. *Shhh.* They spoke in glances and nods, moving the still body to Gaelenn's bed and covering it with a blanket. Rin took two sets of short-chained hand irons from his belt and put one on the guard's wrists. Then he motioned toward Gaelenn's wrists. He winked and smiled as he bound Gaelenn's arms.

Gaelenn did not know whether to laugh or frown; he had just gotten out of the things a few hours earlier, and they were not exactly comfortable.

Rin chanced a brief whisper: "Don't answer. Don't speak. Whatever was in the forest is gone now. I'll help you out, so play along. Remember, not a word, and move quickly."

They walked toward the door and stepped out. One of the guards must have been sent away because the entrance way was clear. Rin once more put his finger to his lips to emphasize silence and grabbed Gaelenn's arm by the elbow to lead him on through the winding pathways. In the opposite direction of the Priestess' house, the visitor noted.

Every guard they encountered made Gaelenn's heart jump, but Rin looked perfectly at ease. Or maybe he was just a talented actor. He led Gaelenn through just about every back alley he could find, in a confusing, round-about pattern that would expose any tag-alongs. There was nobody following them, thankfully, only quiet attention from curious eyes.

The edge of the forest, black as night, crept closer and closer. Escape. Behind a hut and past a well and behind this and that, they made their awkward journey with ever more speed and urgency. They walked faster and faster until they were almost jogging toward the tree line. A lifetime seemed to pass before they finally arrived and walked through.

"Lieutenant Captain!" a harsh voice rang out from behind. They were found.

"What is it, Captain?" Rin rapped, spinning his half-lit body around to face the approaching figure. It was a woman, tall and strong and beautiful, hair dyed black as the others but dressed more decoratively and crowned with a golden helmet adorned by a large red plume.

Gaelenn had no time to turn around to see any more of her impressive entrance—Rin pushed him right through the first row of trees out of sight, flinging the handcuff key blindly past him, then continued his conversation with the captain. The dense, waxy leaves dampened their surprisingly soft words.

"Are you to go out again? Who will you take?" Concern weighed down her voice.

"I've got a crack team. Only three of us is enough. We already checked once—it's clear. We'll do one extra sweep to make sure. I'll be back soon."

"Take care. Don't be gone so long this time," she continued. "I almost went after you myself after the second hour."

"I'll miss you."

"Me, too."

A sly smile crossed Gaelenn's lips that disappeared in the blackness. Rin had a girlfriend—none other than his boss.

The key!

He fell to his knees and searched. It would have been a lot easier had he not been cuffed. He struggled for a moment to remember the tinkling sound of the key hitting the ground. He had not heard it. *Great*, he thought.

Struggling blindly against the dirt and vegetation, a strong hand grabbed his forearms silently above his restraints and used the key to remove them.

"Let's go," the hand's owner whispered, and with a brief whiff of coal and sweat, Gaelenn found himself led right out of the forest. With the luster of wonderment on his first trip through gone, this time was much faster. But just as dark. The light of day blinded Gaelenn when they broke the tree line thirty minutes later. He shielded his eyes with his arm.

"I thought they were lying to me! But here you are," a rough but happy, grunting voice declared. It was loud enough to surprise Gaelenn; he had grown used to the unnatural quiet of the forest and its hidden city, and it took a few seconds for his eyes to adjust.

"Kell!" Gaelenn exclaimed.

The two men embraced. His childhood friend—the only real friend he had ever had—stood in his grasp.

He had grown into a fine man over the past seven years. Not tall but tough and stout; his fingertips were, as always, caked with black dust, as any good smith's should be. The tips of his reddish beard hair were, as well, and his light brown eyes shone with the fire of a forge.

"How...? What...?"

"I'd ask you the same thing!"

"I'm so relieved to see you. I thought you were dead for sure. You've got to tell me what happened," Gaelenn said.

Kell's smile faded as he detailed his escape from the onslaught at their hometown.

"Not many of us made it out of Key Rock before they came. A couple weeks ago, now. Soldiers swept through the entire countryside, took out every cottage, village, and city between the mountains and the sea," he said, and stopped to catch his composure.

"They didn't just raid or invade either. They wiped out everything. Mowed down hundred-year-old buildings like they were grass. Never seen anything like it."

"I walked through, I saw it," Gaelenn said. "Your dad, your family?"

"...Didn't make it." Kell looked at the lip of the mountain on the ground. "I don't know anybody else who did, either, even though they said they were able to save a handful. Haven't seen many yet except for you. Gaelenn...your mother..."

The ripe shock had been compartmentalized over the past three days, but it leapt out at the word and skewered Gaelenn's heart. A jolt ran through his body when he recalled her cold body lying face-down in blood. He could only nod and look away. In the seven years since he left, he had already mostly come to terms with losing his family, he thought.

His back straightened. There would be another time for grief. There would need to be.

"The 'Faithful' up here came down and did what they could to rescue the survivors, as I've heard," Kell said. "Faithful—that's what they call themselves sometimes. Like that old witch we used to talk about, eh? Had no idea they existed before, but they took good care of me."

The hair above his mouth moved with his deep breaths, and his eyes drifted downward. "Think about that—less than a hundred people made it out."

The two friends found themselves both facing the edge of the mountain, over the carcass of their home country, pain in their voices and their faces and their hearts.

"What in hell for...?" Gaelenn asked, but not to Kell. He knew there was no answer. Not yet. They stared for a few minutes at nothing in particular, not needing to fill the silence with words. It was often that way with them, and they found their friendship had not diminished.

Two hands reached through the trees and grabbed onto their shoulders.

"Sorry about that, boys, had to take care of my lady," Rin's voice rang, clear now. "Not to worry, though. We're safe. Ready to go?"

Gaelenn spun around.

"Why did you help me?" he asked. "You're supposed to be serving Livvy."

"*Livvy?*" Rin replied with honest shock. "It didn't take you long to get familiar, did it? *The Priestess* is my boss, sure. She's led us for thousands of years. But..."

His eyes sharpened and he looked down toward the forest. "I can think for myself, right? And I don't think a man should be kept against his will. I'm talking about you, of course."

Gaelenn ignored the jest. "That's all? Just a noble sense of justice?"

Rin's eyes met Gaelenn's. "I don't necessarily agree with everything the Priestess says. That's it. I think that you staying here and reading books isn't going to help anything. Besides, you made your intentions perfectly clear. Who are we to hold you against your will, right? The way I see it, I'm doing her a favor by reminding her of everything she's ever taught us. Anyway—"

He pointed down at some fresh ruins in the distance, a thin pillar of smoke climbing into the sky. It was a clear day all across the landscape. "It's still safe to assume she's right about a lot of other things. Our enemy is coming after us—well, her—eventually. Which is exactly why I also agree with what *you* said to her. The time for magic eyes is long gone. We need everybody who's willing to fight back to actually fight back. Some of us here do."

Rin brushed off his uncharacteristically serious speech with a happy smile.

"So, there you go. You're free!" With a smack on Gaelenn's shoulder, he added, "Besides, your little magic eye key is broken, right? Couldn't help but overhearing that bit."

"Actually, it's—"

"Well, let's just say it is so I don't feel so much like a dead man walking when they catch me!" Rin laughed. "Anyway, you can fight, can't you? I can tell."

"Oh, you can fight now, can you?" Kell raised an eyebrow and a rough smirk blossomed between his mustache and beard. "We'll have to catch up on the way down, it seems."

"Yes, we will," Gaelenn smirked back.

"Sorry to break up the reunion, boys, but in case there's a fight waiting for us down there, we'd better not keep it waiting," Rin interrupted, and the three men descended.

CHAPTER TEN
THE WINDY WOODS

THE WINDY WOODS FELT a lot different now. Despite the two friends at his side, it was a more dangerous place for Gaelenn now that he was a little more aware of the nature of his enemy. For all he knew now, he could be the prey today. They all could.

The three men waded through the brush, communicating through gestures. Each man scanned his surroundings and scrutinized the movement of everything, even the bugs. It was a slow and painstaking process, made more arduous by fear. The clearing where Gaelenn had almost met his fate less than two days earlier was empty; a hand-shaped splatter and a thick line of mostly-dried blood painted the fallen log's bottom half, the arrow broken off at the end but still lodged in the wood. The strength required to snap its mysterious metal must have been immense. The party moved on, perturbed. Some hours later, Rin was the first to speak, and that in a hushed whisper.

"We're getting close to now to where the guards disappeared," he said. "Here's the post that went missing. We checked the whole forest earlier. Nobody's here, or wasn't when we checked."

He pointed up to a tree above with his eyes. Concealed in a clever bundle of leaves and sticks, Gaelenn and Kell could make out a harness in a split high in the trunk where a human might hide.

"And I mean we couldn't find our guards *or* your friend. Let's move on—quietly," Rin prodded. "Best be safe. Our sentries are never away from their posts. Never."

His eyes opened wide, ready for any surprise.

"These guards...their job is to make sure nobody gets close to the wall?" Kell asked with a quiet, muffled grunt.

"Kind of. We watched your town. And we guard a couple other landmarks, too. We're almost at one of them. The Priestess mentioned it might be worth a look after she heard the amulet story from Gaelenn. I dunno."

The trio moved on, more alert than before, reacting in unison to the slightest snapping branch and calling bird. There were a lot of birds today. Some of them were carrion—odd, this deep into the trees.

So much for catching up with Kell, Gaelenn thought to himself. At his side his old friend carried a short sword for protection, which looked odd and out-of-place, its blade much thinner than the robust forearm that bore it.

Rin planted his feet and flung his palm up. *Stop.* He nodded at a small, protruding hill among the trees a few hundred yards ahead. It was not tall, two or three yards at its apex, but was somehow conspicuous on the otherwise flat land. He put his index finger to his lips even though none of the men needed the reminder. They continued, ever more thoughtful of their steps, inching closer and closer.

They took almost a half hour to reach the mound. From afar, though awkwardly jutting out of the ground, it was easy to dismiss as a simple, grassy hill populated with rocks and moss and rubble around its base and a couple of thin trees on its dome. But up close, like so many of the other hills and mounds in the Windy Woods and around the continent, some unnatural message seemed to emanate from deep below its surface.

A shiver climbed up Gaelenn's spine and he shot a confused look at Rin and Kell. The hill was round—perfectly round, now that he studied it more closely. It looked like a bubble had raised up the earth just under the surface.

It looked *hollow*, though there was no entrance, at least from this side. Kell, a few yards to Gaelenn's side, checked from his angle, too.

Rin looked at them both and shook his head, his finger moving in an arching gesture. *The other side*. Hiding behind brush and timber, they curled around the mysterious mound. Halfway there, Gaelenn's chest swelled and his breath stopped cold. The smell of iron leapt up to his nose. Blood.

He glanced at Kell, sweating profusely despite the cool breeze weaving through the trees, and they moved on, the two friends tracing one side, and Rin the other. They arrived at its rear and caught a shadow within the shadow cast by the earth against the quickly setting sun.

It was a door, if a hole in the ground could be called such. A hacked-up, empty divot in the side of the earthen hill that was barely large enough for a man to pass through. It was at least an arm's length deep and the raw earth around it was packed hard, the marks of fingers and hands all around its circumference. In front of it lay a path made from the displaced earth. From it came neither light nor sound.

Rin's gaze fixated on the rough opening, his face wrinkled and contorted into a mix of disgust, anger, and sadness. He crawled forward, hunched over with one hand on the forest floor and the other securing his unsheathed long knife in a fierce grip. Gaelenn followed his lead, sword in hand, and Kell pulled a heavy iron hammer, a tool he made himself, no doubt, from his belt. He eased his thin, awkward long knife into the ground, discarding it blade first, and suddenly looked much more formidable.

After an eternal minute of trepidation, Rin lunged into the hole. The two men waiting outside braced themselves for some reaction—the sound of metal-on-metal, or perhaps a scream, or maybe even Rin running back out of the hole. But all that came out was more silence. Kell and Gaelenn met eyes and swallowed in unison.

"Come in," echoed Rin's voice from within. "It's safe."

Kell poked his head in and out, then pulled a black mask from a pack at his waist to fasten over his face. Gaelenn's brow wrinkled, confused.

"This is how I got through the dark up there on the clifftop. Lot of interesting toys they have. You didn't get one?" Kell said as he stretched the mask over his eyes and disappeared into the hole.

Gaelenn took a deep breath, sheathed his sword, and crawled into the darkness. A chamber inside opened up just past the entrance, allowing him to stand up. He squinted his eyes into paper-thin slits, but felt rather than saw that Rin had stepped past him back toward the entrance.

The Lieutenant Captain used his short sword to cut a smooth shape in the earth on the wall of the chamber above where the three had entered, then sunk his fingers into it and yanked it down, revealing a totally symmetric, proper doorway. A wide ray of dim light spilled in and illuminated the small room.

"Mercy for the dead!" Kell uttered the common saying of the continent, pulled the mask off his head, and rubbed his eyes with his dirty palms.

He and Rin had already surveyed the room, so they allowed Gaelenn a few moments to inspect the bodies lined neatly against the unearthly wall. They were cleanly eviscerated; no excess wounds to show signs of some valiant struggle. Their deaths were quick and precisely executed.

"I'd say they were killed one at a time, probably without even knowing what was coming," Gaelenn said. He had seen plenty of death in his short life. "Or maybe they tried an ambush...and failed."

Rin stared at his slain comrades, bottom lip between his teeth. "These guards were not green. They were some of our best."

"Women, your best guards?" Kell said, not totally disdainfully but with a hint of disbelief.

"You know the Captain," Rin retorted swiftly. "Each of these guards was worth 3 imperial soldiers. Half of our army is women. We don't judge who can fight by what they are. Only what they make of themselves. If someone wants to fight, we let them fight."

"As skilled as they must have been," Gaelenn stepped in, trying to ease the tension exacerbated by the emotion of the scene, "the person who did this to them was stronger."

He glanced at the sword loose in his hand and lifted it up. "And he didn't even have a proper weapon."

"I think it's safe to say he's an EN. Just like the Priestess thought," Rin said. His gaze remained locked on his slain friends, consumed in a solemn trance.

Gaelenn reached for Rin's shoulder in solidarity. But his pity soon gave way to anger, recalling how close he had been to his own death just a day before and how those at Key Rock had not been so lucky. The ends of his mouth twisted downward and desire for vengeance filled his soul again. He willed himself calm, shaking his head to rattle it back to the present. A deep breath preceded a slow, deliberate exhale. The room came into focus.

"What is this place? The ground isn't earth. Not stone either," he said as he bent down, ran his hand over the floor, and wiped away a thin layer of grime. "Polished smooth."

Then he found a groove, perfectly straight, leading to other grooves, and soon he was on all fours, using every one of his fingers to trace the impeccable diamond pattern imprinted in the tile.

"This is better craftsmanship than I've ever seen. Even guild masons aren't anywhere near this skilled," he said, his voice absent in thought.

Kell, also stewing, peered down to study the pattern. His eyebrows arched in honest surprise and he, too, spoke without thinking. "Even *I* couldn't make marble like this."

"The walls, too...what is this made of?" Gaelenn asked. "Not iron, not clay. Not brick. Too smooth to be stone. How could something be so...flawless?"

"They made it back in the Priestess' day," Rin said, interrupting their trances. "Kind of a lost art. We have a lot of it up at home. Stronger and lighter than rock or iron. Lasts forever, or so she says. Can be made to fit any shape you can imagine."

Gaelenn was too puzzled to notice himself resting his hands on the small, cylindrical table rising straight from the ground in the exact center of the perfectly circular room. Its unnatural coldness suddenly came to his attention when he kicked its base absently.

"This is stone...isn't it? Obsidian?" he said. "Polished. Immaculate."

He leaned over to survey it more closely, starting with the gently curved edges. His palms traced its circumference, admiring its perfection. His face came so near that he found himself staring at his reflection in the infinite blackness of its surface. Only a few thin smears of recently-dried blood marred the image.

"Looks like...hand prints," he said, and pressed his own palm against one of the shapes to make sure. Immediately, a dim red light shot out directly from the surface of the table into Gaelenn's eyes, and then a calm, crackled voice echoed through the room in a barely understandable accent.

IDENTIFICATION CONFIRMED. UNLOCKED.

A voice in a strange, barely intelligible dialect spoke out and the table blinked to life, filling the chamber with the same blue light that had filled the Priestess' room above the Ash Cliffs. The bodies against the side wall seemed to float, as if in the sea, but nobody paid attention to them now. In the middle of the table, the image of gentle rolling hills and blue skies stared with perfect vividness—except for a bloody hand print with two missing fingers—at the three men crowding around. Gaelenn reached for the bottom of his tunic and wiped as much blood off as he could.

"What did you do...?" Rin started, but saw the answer in Gaelenn's face. He had no idea, either.

"Don't move," Gaelenn said to the others, spreading his arms out to keep them from approaching.

"Gaelenn, you saw the Priestess use one of these. You, too, right?" Rin said, pointing at Kell. "The one she keeps in her quarters. Probably not that dangerous."

Gaelenn and Kell glanced at each other and back at Rin, then relaxed just enough to holster their weapons.

"So, what does it do?" Kell asked.

"I don't know. Lots of things, I think," Rin explained. "The Priestess is glued to hers. It lets her communicate somehow even when she's alone. She talks with people in other rooms and even buildings just by speaking through it. Like a conduit."

He waved his fingers in the air, casting mock magic. "Or when she needs to know something important, she touches it again and poof—she knows. Some of our people think it's the source of her power. But..."

He frowned. "Honestly...I never imagined there were more of these things. And here. All we've ever been told is to watch over this area. I had no idea this was here."

Gaelenn made a slow, acknowledging nod, and followed it with a pensive breath. "But it *is* here. Why would Anwir kill to find it? My mother's amulet... Livvy—er, your Priestess—seemed to be concerned with that, even though she called it a 'ruse.'"

"I wouldn't know. And I don't know where to begin knowing, either," Rin said, cocking his head to one side. "You'll have to ask *her*. Shall we?"

He gave a last, heavy look at his fallen comrades and turned away toward the entrance. Dusk was calling. "He must have known what was inside. Maybe you're right. Maybe he tried to use that amulet."

"Well, she said the amulet was only a ruse. I hope that ruse worked," Gaelenn said.

Rin sighed. "Right. Speaking of—let's go back home. Nothing more to glean here. Like I said, only she could know what he was doing. She's the only one with answers."

"No. Sorry, Rin." Wiping the dirt and blood from his hands onto his pants, he continued, "I need peace more than I need answers at this point. And I need my freedom to earn that peace."

He glanced at Kell, whose chin bunched up within his beard, and nodded. Rin looked between them, a dark lining forming around his eyes.

"Well, then, I guess your quest is at an end," he said, and tacked on an exaggerated, dramatic sigh. "I don't know what kind of chance you'd stand—if you could even get to him."

Gaelenn pressed his lips together, looking at Kell. "The two of us might stand a chance."

"Even if you did, how could you hope to find him? And then, get him alone?"

"I thought... I don't know. But maybe I can. First step is to find him."

"How?"

"I've been doing this a lot the last seven years, actually," Gaelenn said as he replayed the previous day's scene in his mind, struggling for details that he might have missed. "Well, he and his two friends called themselves 'Triumvirs.' A title. Leaders of something, somewhere. Had this sword."

He brandished the blade at his side, trying to catch the diminishing rays of light from the outside—and from the table, still lit. "Wore a green mantle. Purple band. The colors were Maynon Ohzan—thought maybe they were soldiers from there. Oh—one had a pack with a gold symbol on it. An eye and a scythe. Have no idea about that. Do you?"

Rin smiled, almost exasperated, as if there was an inside joke he was not privy to. He arched an eyebrow. "I refuse to believe that—"

But before he could continue the room spoke once again.

SEARCH COMMENCING. PLEASE WAIT A MOMENT.

The table below them began flickering with little squares, each one an image depicting similar symbols, accompanied by illegible script. All eyes followed.

"Can you read that?" Kell asked Rin.

"I'm afraid not, but I've seen it before...on the Priestess' table," he replied, whispering in reflex. "This symbol isn't exactly some sort of secret to us."

"Look at that!" Gaelenn exclaimed, reacting to the flurry of movement on the table's surface. Pictures of men and women in green capes flashed by. Impeccable images—not paintings, but real images, just as in the Priestess' room—popped up over each other at a furious pace. Their subjects donned fine leather just like Triumvir Anwir, and some even wore fabulous full-plate armor. But their clothes evolved slowly, morphing through countless iterations until they were simply splotchy-patterned uniforms in the same green color but with no iron, just padded cloth that fit its owners' bodies as tight as their own skin.

The weapons began to change, as well, from knives, swords, and spears to blunter weapons and then to small, unrecognizable black machines. The three men gathered around with furrowed brows, unsure whether they were looking into the past or the future.

"Are those supposed to be weapons? How would you kill somebody with those things?" Kell asked. "A good hammer would smash one of them to pieces!"

"Some sort of...projectile. Like an arrow with no shaft," Rin replied. "I've heard a bit about them. A bit."

At length, the moving painting froze and lingered on a final image: a woman and man wearing tight-fitting trousers and long boots and coats patterned in that familiar green but dotted with random touches of brown. They wore vests with pockets and packs snugly attached to their backs and legs. At their sides they held those crude, black, menacing weapons. Their helmets, which covered only the tops of their heads, were not made of iron.

Right in the center of them was the symbol Gaelenn was looking for: the eye and the scythe.

"That's it! That's the symbol on Anwir's bag. Where have I seen it before...?" Gaelenn asked, mostly to himself.

Rin, his voice half impish and half grave, answered him: "I was trying to tell you, I thought everybody knew that symbol. It's worn on the crowns of the three rulers of Maynon Ohza—the Triumvirate. And before that, it was the Eye's."

CHAPTER ELEVEN
The Eye and the Scythe

"So you really didn't know about them," Rin said, his voice now completely low and serious. "I thought you did. You've traveled enough."

"Right—traveled far and wide, but not so much *near*. I've stayed clear of any fighting, at least on this continent. Up until these past few days, at least."

Rin sighed and let his frustration and surprise dissipate. "Anyway, it's the symbol of the Triumvirate these days. The ones behind all this destruction. And...well, now you know who's behind *them*."

Gaelenn looked up, confused. "The 'Eye,' right?"

Rin nodded. "The Priestess will want to know that it's the Triumvirate that are the ENs. She already figured out the Eye's behind what's been happening at Maynon Ohza, but I suppose it's going to be more complicated now. The Eye controlling three ENs who control a nation—this is a new twist even for her, I'd guess."

"Yeah, they're the ones who destroyed Key Rock, all right. I saw that symbol then," Kell added, eyes and mind out of focus with the others. His beard bushed up around his mouth, but he resisted the tide of emotion from advancing any further and opted for silence.

Rin took over for him. "The symbol is old. Very old. Think thousands-of-years-old."

His flair for the dramatic worked its way to his hands, punctuating his speech with exaggerated gestures. "I've seen real pictures in books up at home. We learn a little about that stuff when we're younger. But I wasn't so great with history, myself."

Gaelenn was almost relieved to see the confusion hanging from Kell's drooping brow as well. Both were lost.

Rin put his hands on his hips and stretched the stiffness from his torso. "I'd have thought the Priestess would tell you about that first thing. Well, let's see: every so often there's a big war. She calls them resurgences."

"Okay," Gaelenn said. "Anything else we should know before we go start the next one?"

Rin caught himself laughing, his internal brightness fighting against the growing darkness—and the growing stench. "Well, we didn't exactly learn it at school, but the ENs—like your Triumvir—apparently used to be on our side. They were supposed to be the saviors of humanity or something. If the Priestess was surprised to hear that they're back and on the wrong side, she'll be blown away when she hears that they're the ones running the show. Or the Eye's show—whatever. The last time anybody heard about one was at least a thousand years ago."

Gaelenn looked down at the table, which had gone black, the bright tapestries that colored it moments ago disappearing somewhere below its surface. He ran his finger once more over the remainder of the bloody handprint. "What is the Eye, really?"

"You really should have spent more time with the Priestess," Rin said. "I don't think I'm capable of explaining it. I barely know myself. Are you sure you don't want to come back with me?"

Gaelenn let out a frustrated sigh. "I can't. I'm sorry."

Kell nodded solemnly in confirmation.

"I could use a little vengeance myself," Rin said, his eyes drifting to his fallen comrades. "I would guide you to where you're going if I could. But

I have to go back. Are you sure I can't convince you, just for a little while? Could really save my neck."

"Not a chance," Kell said. Gaelenn concurred.

"Well, I tried. At least I can tell the Priestess that. If *she* couldn't convince you, there's no way I can. But before you go running head-first into that hellhole of an empire, take another look at this room," Rin said, looking Gaelenn in the eye, echoing a small amount of the desperation that Livvy had shown. He pointed at the blood and the bodies. "We share the same enemy. It may have been your EN friend who did this, but now you know who's pulling his strings. If you think you're a match for something you can't even see, you're probably wrong. Keep that in mind."

Gaelenn nodded and turned, walking over the earthen rubble and out the door as he spoke, "Well, one step at a time. If Kell and I succeed, I'll come back."

"Aye," Kell concurred, and he and Rin followed Gaelenn out into the twilight.

"I'll have a team come back for my guards," Rin said, nodding toward the legs of the bodies through the open door. "And I'll give the Priestess your news."

The three gathered in a circle and each waited with blank expressions for another to lead off. Nobody knew what to do next.

"You could come with us, Rin," Gaelenn mused after a time. "We could use you. You're going to get in trouble anyway, right?"

Rin smiled suddenly. He was himself again already now that death was not lying at his feet. "What, and leave my girl behind? Never."

He slapped Gaelenn's shoulder.

"And the Priestess doesn't work that way. There's no torture at Last Retreat," he said. Unable to resist the chance, he added with a thick, melodramatic flair: "That I know of."

"Last Retreat?" Kell asked.

"That's what we call home," Rin answered with a wink.

Gaelenn looked straight into Rin's eyes. There was the slightest hint of color in his irises that sparkled a little when the moon hit them between the leaves' shadows. In his pure-white eyelashes rested dried tears.

"I'm sorry for your loss," Gaelenn said. Kell agreed with a bow of his head.

"I am, too. These were valuable soldiers...and good friends. Listen," Rin said, pivoting. "I don't know exactly what you plan to do next, but I might be able to help a little. From here, Maynon Ohza is directly north. Far north. The Empire is there, so I'm sure your Triumvir is, too. There's your vengeance, I guess. I know I can't convince you not to go, but I just want you to be careful. If anything happens to you, it's me who'll have hell to pay. Just...make sure you understand that you're chasing an EN—maybe three of them, for all we know."

"If Kell's learned to fight, I'm sure we can take the one together. Don't worry about us," Gaelenn said, elbowing his old friend.

Kell grunted, crossed his arms, and made a self-assured grin under his beard.

"And maybe, if luck's on our side, we'll find out something useful to your Priestess."

A shadow passed over Rin's face. "Yes, she does need all the help—and luck—she can get. I'll see you again soon. I can feel it."

They all nodded and waved goodbye. Rin watched the two silhouettes fade into the forest northward, swallowed hard, and sighed.

"Damn, am I in for it."

CHAPTER TWELVE
The Air Stood Still

"So." The weight behind the Priestess' stare might only have made sense to someone else who had lived for 20,000 years. Rin was not even close to understanding it. But he was nervous.

"So," she repeated, waiting again for effect, knowing that an answer would not come. "The most important, indispensable person to our entire cause somehow miraculously falls onto our lap after being thought dead for years, is then barely rescued from the clutches of the enemy who only now probably knows his true value and will be looking for him, and finally, by the grace of whatever god there is, comes willingly to our home and is willing to learn—"

Her temper flared, flushing her entire face with red heat, and her young lips wrinkled up into a bare line. She took a deep breath before finishing her thought. "And you break him out on the very first day he was here! As if we were going to treat him like a prisoner!"

It was hard for Rin to feel truly afraid of the figure in front of him, much smaller than himself, as she berated him. Still, he had never been yelled at like this by her—nobody had—and he was not sure what she was capable of in her hysteric state, so he simply stood and absorbed it.

"Do you understand at all what you've done? Everything we've been doing—I've been doing—for thousands of years hangs in the balance, and you don't feel that it's fair that he be held against his will, is that it? I didn't even have a chance to convince him to want to stay! Who are you to say that after he knew all the facts he wouldn't want to stay here and help us?"

Her chest heaved up and down as her lungs struggled to catch her breath. With conscious effort, she settled herself and punctuated her tirade with deadly calm.

"And not just that, but you send him to the most dangerous place he could possibly go. Into the lion's den, and not even with a proper guard. With only his childhood friend to protect him. He has no idea what he's walking into."

Rin waited to make sure the speech had finished. He raised his brow, looked down for a moment to gather the courage he needed to speak, and then returned the Priestess' stony gaze.

"I just don't believe it should be done if it's not done the right way. I am sorry, Lady. But I couldn't stand by and go against what we have always learned—what you have always taught us."

The truth in his words cut into her like a cold knife. Her shoulders fell, both her bravado and her last hope, gone.

"You're right," she said. "You're right."

She bent down over her table and let her hair fall in front of her face. "But sometimes we just don't have any other choice—imagine your life from when you were born until now. How long does that feel? Think about living to one hundred, and how far away that sounds, how long that would be."

Her voice grew louder with each word.

"Imagine living that over and over a hundred times, two hundred! Imagine that all of that time was dedicated to a single purpose; every day was dedicated to fighting a battle that nobody else knew was even happening." She looked up with her pale, blue eyes—the same color as the light globes outside, Rin noticed for the first time—and showed him the tears she was fighting back.

"And then, in the end, the one thing you had been building up to for that entire lifetime of lifetimes was taken from you. What would you do to get that back?"

The air stood still for a moment.

"But, you're right. You're right," she continued, stretching upright, "even if it was perfectly planned, and it wasn't, not by a long shot—but even if it was and even if our cause was the purest thing in the world—and it is!—it would only prove my unworthiness to be its champion."

Rin stood on the balls of his feet and rocked uneasily. "I can't really even begin to imagine what it has been like for you, my Lady."

"Start by imagining how long ago the luster of being called 'my Lady,' 'Priestess,' or 'your Grace' must have worn off," she snapped, then immediately calmed herself with further effort. "I'm sorry. Go on, it's your turn to speak."

"Um...Madame Priestess...Lady?" Rin had talked with her so many times before, but never so candidly, and rarely one-on-one. He swallowed hard and forged a bit of fake confidence into a smile. "We've always been told here at Last Retreat that we're different, we're special, we're fortunate. We're given an education from when we're young and taught letters and numbers and history—most importantly, history. And when the time comes, we can share our knowledge with a free world."

A more honest smile broke across his face as his passion overtook his nerves. "From what I gather, we're the only place in the world that has that. And that's what makes us special. Outside it's a brutal and uncivilized world, but up here we have laws and we have justice. We have peace. We have rights, and equality! That's what we've learned from you."

Livvy stared straight through Rin to the wall behind him, expressionless, repeating his speech in her head. Her chest swelled and then pushed out a loud sigh. Rin had won.

"That's right," she said. "We must—we have a purpose. The most important purpose any group of people ever has. We are the torchbearers."

He nodded, though he had no real understanding of the depth of her words.

"I can't really imagine what it feels like for you, but I know it must be hard," he said, reading the conflict on her face. "Gaelenn is a good man. I'm sure that when he understands what's happening and he sees it for himself, he'll come back to us on his own, and then you won't have to worry about it."

"Let's hope so," she said, and tried to force a weak smile. "Do you remember in your history lessons that since the first one ended, there have been four other major conflicts—events?"

"Yes," Rin replied quickly to the sudden change in conversation. "Well, actually, I thought it was three."

"Four," she corrected. "And we are on the cusp of the next. Each of the last four brought us to the brink. Every time, civilization has had to start back from scratch, or almost scratch. This will be the last one. Either we win, or the enemy does. So, I hope you forgive me for not quite being myself lately."

"Forgive? Of course there is nothing to forgive!" he said with a smile that surprised even himself, as nervous as he was. "But, um, by the way, Lady, we also sort of figured out that the ENs are the Triumvirate. Has that happened before?"

She hardened at once, the wheels in her head spinning at incomprehensible speed, then tapped her table a few times and made its images dance under her fingertips. "No, it hasn't. I have a mission for you. Another message. Please prepare to leave right away."

"You're not punishing me?" Rin responded in shock.

"There will be a time for that, if we're lucky. Right now, I understand why you did what you did, and that's enough."

Livvy looked straight into his eyes. "You proved yourself resourceful when you found Gaelenn the first time. Do that one more time for me. It's more urgent now than ever."

The door opened and a guard strode in and placed on the table a small piece of paper along with an inkwell and quill. Livvy picked the objects up and smirked.

"I haven't done *this* in a while," she said, pen in hand, and laughed, but the joke drifted past a confused Rin.

All he knew was that she was capable of going from almost screaming to giggling in a matter of minutes. She scribbled a note and rolled the paper up, sealing it with a ribbon she pulled from the sleeve of her dress.

Standing up, she handed it to Rin and said gravely, "Travel as fast as you can. Go alone. Find him and put this into his hands yourself."

CHAPTER THIRTEEN
THE ROAD NORTH

JUST AS RIN HAD promised, the road was long. Kell and Gaelenn traveled for days, just out of view of all the main paths though not a soul was seen anywhere. They crossed cool rivers, hunted beasts, fattened for the coming winter without humans around to hunt them, and camped without fire unless absolutely necessary. Until this moment, they had seen nothing and come across nobody.

"Rin did say far north. Did he say dangerous? I'm pretty sure he didn't," Gaelenn said. "He could have mentioned it."

"Well, what do you want to do?" Kell asked in his usual gruff manner.

Their backs were against a stone wall surrounding a ruinous watch tower, abandoned and reclaimed countless times over countless years—a patchwork of rotting stone, mortar, and wood, surrounded by a thick, ancient wall. Currently, it was inhabited by a number of moody guards.

"Wonder why they're in such foul spirits?" Gaelenn asked as he grabbed onto the stalk of one of the tall, tree-like weeds that gave them just enough cover to go unnoticed in the dark.

Kell ignored him and pressed again. "Well, do we knock them all off and liberate some clothes, or do we continue on our merry way? How many are there, you think?"

"Can you fight? Really fight?" Gaelenn asked. He gave a sly grin that Kell could only see half of. The blacksmith's beard parted in a toothy, moonlit smile.

"Just you wait and see," he said. "I still think we should go for it—you'll stick out like a sore thumb in Maynon Ohza with that shirt."

"Fair point."

Some camouflage for the trip ahead had had brought them this close to the tower. Looking down, Gaelenn considered his crisp, new, well-fitting leather jacket and tunic, perhaps inconspicuous in a port town like Key Rock but out of place so far from the sea. In the hot, tree-less, and presumably soldier-ridden expanse around the former kingdom of Sithica—now known to all as Maynon Ohza—it was much safer to dress the part. A loose robe with a cool hood to keep out the sun—and unwanted glances—would go a long way.

"Okay," he said to Kell, whose own hooded over-cloak would not trigger as much as a batted eye. "But we only get one chance at it. We don't want news of our arrival to precede us."

"Yup," Kell replied. "Been looking forward to putting on a show for you. Least I could do for you after eating all the critters you've killed on the way here. I told you, I'm just not a hunter with these heavy boots. But put a hammer in my hand and watch me dazzle your eyes!"

He almost laughed out loud, wiggling his fingers in front of Gae-lenn's eyes in a mock demonstration of his battle prowess.

Gaelenn gave him a half-entertained, half-suspicious smile. "When did you get a sense of humor?"

The past few days were spent catching up, when they could, on Gaelenn's travels and Kell's failed courtships.

Well, Gaelenn thought with a chuckle, *Kell's attempts to try talking to women.*

They spoke of that and all the days in between and the invasion and destruction and the dying until they just stopped talking altogether. Their wounds were too fresh, and at the moment, they had other things to worry about.

"So, when do we run in?" Kell asked.

Gaelenn shook his head.

"After we get a good look inside," he said, and probed the wall for a foothold to climb with. "We don't know how many are actually in there. And I thought I was the impulsive one."

Immediately after speaking, he found a crack wide enough to see through, but in the dark his eyes were useless. Instead, he set the side of his head against the wall and listened. Soldiers. Dozens of them, murmuring, stewing in their discontent. Preparing for some event—and not happy about it. Then, after a few minutes, movement toward the wall. Gaelenn pressed his ear harder. Voices came through.

"Sir Anwir returns tomorrow morning. He has sent word to apologize for his delay, and for us to make preparations to depart immediately after. We are keeping the prisoners on their carts until then but they've started to get sick and the asses refuse to get close because of the stench, so—"

The report was interrupted by a bored, hateful voice.

"Spare me the details. Run the cart through a river for all I care. It's Anwir who wants this show, he can deal with it."

Gaelenn recognized it immediately, still fresh in his mind. Triumvir Visha.

"But, my Lady Triumvir, I—"

Instantly, the crack of a whip choked away the voice in its throat. Its owner gasped for breath, a wheezing hiss bubbling in his mouth. Gaelenn stared at Kell, eyes wide and jaw clenched. He brought a finger to his mouth. *Shhh.* They were outside the EN's sleeping quarters.

"What did I say?" she continued, at once threatening and disinterested, her voice tunneling through the stones.

The soldier's body fell limp to the ground.

A deep grunt shook the wall; its owner woke from slumber. "Mm?"

"Yajuu, my friend," said Visha, "I apologize for waking you. I fear I have let my annoyance get the better of me. This one is dead. I whipped too hard again. Might I bother you to toss him away? I wouldn't want to send a panic through camp."

The slow creaking of wood scratched at Gaelenn's ears. Even Kell tilted his head with the unnatural noise. Heavy footsteps lumbered toward the wall, and another quick, deep grunt foreshadowed the crashing of the dead soldier right at the visitors' feet. It rolled several yards.

Kell bit his knuckles, and he and Gaelenn nodded to each other.

"Thank you, my friend," Visha said, placating. "But, since you're awake, would you mind keeping me company for a while? You know I can't sleep at this hour."

The giant exhaled loudly.

"Fine," he said in her language rather than his.

"I'll only keep you a few minutes, I promise."

"Mm."

The conversation paused briefly and Visha continued, her voice lower. "We have not had the chance to talk alone for some time, which I regret. Have you decided? Anwir plays a dangerous game."

"Mm."

"Our master would not be pleased."

"Mmmmm."

"If we were to expose him, we would be rewarded. But if we join Anwir, is the reward not that much greater?"

"Mmmmmm!"

"Indeed. Or...perhaps we can play both games. Why bet on one winner when you can bet on both and never lose? What do you say?"

The giant laughed in his throat. "Yes," he said.

"Good, it's settled then. We must both play our parts for this to work, as we have discussed. Upon our return, I will shadow him everywhere until we find some leverage—for our protection against master. If the worst comes to pass, we'll feed him Anwir and reap the rewards. As for you—earn Anwir's trust, for both of us. Be a good soldier. Volunteer to take over his next expedition. Whatever you can do to get him to let us in on his little secret. I suspect that little game is the one with the bigger payoff."

"Mm," Yajuu mumbled in apparent agreement.

"I am sorry, my friend," Visha said, her voice giddy and all the more sinister for it. "I have kept you from sleep. Forgive me; good night."

"Good night," the giant replied, crashing his weight back onto his wooden cot. The ground shook.

Kell shrugged at Gaelenn. *What?* He mimed.

Gaelenn just shook his head.

The friends crawled away from the wall toward the still warm body of the soldier. The ground had soaked up most of the blood, but the hooded cloak, which was perfect cover for their trek, glistened crimson in the starlight. It would still have to be washed in a stream before it could be worn.

Gaelenn grimaced and they unwrapped it from its grim host. Slowly, silently, they inched away from the tower, taking great care not to step on any twigs or dried leaves, knowing that death lay right beyond the wall they were leaving. Before they entered the cover of the trees, they looked back.

Against the brilliant canvas of stars the tower's dark silhouette loomed, and perched on its surrounding wall, a dark, feminine figure watched them, her eyes catching the moonlight in an evil glimmer.

They ran into the night, haunted by Visha's laughter echoing behind them.

CHAPTER FOURTEEN
MAYNON OHZA

THE JOURNEY TO MAYNON Ohza was tense after the brief terror at the tower. Days passed on their silent journey until Gaelenn and Kell could see the palace through the tree line, its surrounding town sprawling in the middle of a great, dusty plain. The only feature for miles was a small outcrop of hills in the northwest that rolled into the northern peaks and eventually Sapphire Mountain.

The two men had run all night and into the following day until they were sure they were not being followed. Paranoia, phantoms, and fear had been their companions. The hooded cape they acquired was perfectly plain and concealed Gaelenn's attire just enough after a thorough cleaning, but even so they took no chances and moved slowly, carefully, and out of sight.

"From now on, let's keep to the shade," they had agreed, and gone silent.

A cacophony of bells rang out as they finally passed the trees and made their way to the city gates.

"Noon?" Gaelenn asked.

"Must be," Kell said, and looked up at the sun. Just in case, both of them moved a step slower, less conspicuous.

"Listen to those things. They could use a couple wrings from my hammer for tuning. Awful sound," Kell said.

"You're kind of a funny guy somewhere in there, aren't you?" Gaelenn replied, his voice gravelly from days of disuse. As they walked, he sized up his bear of a friend: stout in limb and trunk with streaks of grime decorating his hands and clothes; he loved his ale as much as he loved his smithing hammer.

Gaelenn smiled, the thought just now dawning on him that he had missed his friend greatly. No thought was given to the chance that this might be his last smile for a long, long time.

A makeshift town overflowed from the walls of the city of Maynon Ohza like water spilling from a flooding well, unable to contain the massive populace within. Huts and tents and roads stretched for nearly a mile in all directions, filled to the brim with all manner of merchant, brigand, and beggar. Guards patrolled the stinking streets, wandering about, pretending to uphold laws that, in such a fetid heap of humanity, were merely rumors.

In the distance, inside the twenty-foot-tall walls of the city, its central palace pierced the sky with menacing magnificence. Each curved spike on its battlements shone like a mirror, making it look as if the ribbed spine of a giant, dead snake had been set there and polished. Nearly a dozen tall spires towered over the rest of the city, setting much of the town in shadow. The two friends used the shadow to their advantage as they neared the outskirts, taking care to cover themselves where they could and trying, as much as they could, to act like they belonged. Reaching the first row of tents and streets was not a problem as they were surrounded by a vast swarm of humanity as soon as they reached the first line.

"That was easier than I thought it would be," Kell said, his eyes darting between each passing footstep, nerves holding his gaze from faces.

Gaelenn raised an eyebrow and adjusted the hood over his head. "I get the feeling that could be the last thing that comes easy. Do I look okay?"

Kell peered out under scrutinizing eyebrows.

"You've never looked very good, tell the truth." The grinning teeth under his beard caught a glint of the sun. "But you don't look odd."

"Thanks. I feel much better now." Gaelenn felt Kell's powerful hand on his shoulder, and he absorbed the security it gave him. He knew that, just as he always had, he could count on his friend. "I guess a smith wouldn't be out-of-place anywhere."

The usual black of the tips of the blacksmith's fingers had almost turned green from the journey through the woods, and the handle of his hammer, almost as heavy as the head itself and in perfect balance, swung from side to side from his belt. There was nothing about him that would not have been normal in any place in the world that Gaelenn had ever been, and he had been from one end to the other over the past seven years. His eyes studied the people around him. Poor, wrecked souls.

"Look around," he said to Kell as his focus drifted outward. "Something is off."

Droves of men and women and children lived in makeshift squalor, huddled together in rags and robes and utter poverty. Rich merchants lorded over the rabble with chins high in the air, clothed in delicate silk. They were not all the same; there was a hierarchy to the level of people kept from the inside the city.

"Are these refugees?" he asked. "They don't look like citizens to me. Maybe I wouldn't have looked so out of place after all if we hadn't got this hood."

"So many people," Kell said. His eyes now could not help but jump from face to dirty face. "I never knew...is this how the people here live?"

He had never left the peace of his small home before being driven to Last Retreat, and without any reference he never truly knew what life was like outside its borders.

"Not the way they live inside those gates, I'm sure."

Gaelenn, on the other hand, was used to filth and sickness in his travels. He pitied the surrounding masses, his eyes downcast and soft. But this was a new level of destitution—and of desperation.

"Look at these people. They're not from around here. They were driven here. They have nothing," he said.

The closer he and Kell got to the city walls, however, the more the conditions improved. It was as if the longer a person was here, the better their position—the more Maynon Ohzan they became.

It was nearly half an hour before they navigated to the town gates, and the quality of life was not the only thing that had improved that close to the city—the guards had gone from mere grunts to upright, polished soldiers. And judging from their sneers, they were looking for whatever trouble they could find. Suddenly, the pair of intruders looked—and felt—dangerously out of place. They sped to the main city gate, which stared out at the slums from the southeast, huge and menacing.

"Who'd have thought they'd need an army to guard a door?" Kell mused. Ten guards stood almost shoulder to shoulder at the massive main gate, barring entrance to everyone, allowing only other guards through and the occasional merchant after strict examination of some official document or another. Other armor-clad soldiers lurked nearby with eyes on all who approached. Dozens of citizens were turned away less than politely. The two men stood as far out of scrutiny as they could.

"There has to be a way in there somehow," Gaelenn said. "But I don't think we're going through the walls. Or over them."

His eyes followed the towering, sheer stone to its apex.

"Or under. We have to find some other way." Kell peered through the slit in the gate to the town proper. "Looks like a proper city in there. Fancy buildings. What exactly is the plan if we make it through?"

"I'm not sure," Gaelenn responded too quickly to inspire any confidence.

He pointed to the spikes, which were just visible from the top of the palace. "So I suppose we'll sneak through here, and then into the palace, and, I don't know...see where that takes us. If we can corner one of those ENs, maybe the two of us together can take him. Or her—remember the woman at that tower."

Kell shivered.

Gaelenn shot him a wide-eyed glance. "I certainly wouldn't underestimate her."

"Neither would I. That voice will haunt me. So our plan is to wing it?" Kell put his hands on his hips and his mouth disappeared completely beneath his beard. "That sounds a lot like you."

The pursed lips on Kell's face were enough for Gaelenn to glean the futility and pointlessness of his quest, but he offered a response anyway. "Well, got a better idea?"

"Seems we've got a lot to think about."

All humor left Kell's face and he turned away from the hopeless situation in front of them, leading Gaelenn back away from the gate. Not far away they found a clearing near the main street to the gates. Hundreds of people gathered and lounged drunkenly, serviced with food and ale by several stalls around its edges.

"I could use a drink," Kell said.

Gaelenn nodded. "And a meal," he replied.

"With what money?"

"Maybe we should have borrowed some from Rin. Or Livvy. Looked like they had enough gold up there to spare."

"Wait! Got an idea. Not to worry," Kell said and walked straight past the end of the recreation area toward an alley lined with bazaars. "Let me show you how it's done."

"How what's done?" Gaelenn asked, lost.

But Kell brushed past him without answering. He studied the innumerable trinkets hanging by strings in the surrounding bazaar and the wares that, depending on the shop, were either neatly arranged or piled up into indistinguishable messes. He found a satisfactory booth, examined its owner—an old man with a white beard, sun-lined face, and wisdom in sunken eyes—and opened his jacket to unload a leather sack onto the table. A hammer, a chisel, several punches, tongs—an immaculate goldsmithing kit lay glistening on the wooden shelf of the shop. Among the tools fell rings, small jewels, and intricate filigrees in gold and silver.

The old shopkeeper's thin, clean hands latched onto the goods, one by one, and held them up to marvel at their form, light reflecting off them into his eyes, which shone like little black pearls.

"Peerless. Perfect. Incomparable! How did men such as yourselves come upon such...treasures?" he asked in a shockingly posh accent. He had seen money at some point in his life.

Kell leaned back and crossed his arms and gave a pride-consumed grin from ear to ear. He cleared his throat to speak.

"Oh, let's just say we acquired these recently," Gaelenn butted in, taking the baton from his friend. "The previous owner had no more use for them it seems."

He used an obvious, sly fake accent and winked, yanking the smile from his friend's mouth. The blacksmith huffed and scowled.

"Simply marvelous," the merchant repeated. "The gold accents, the immaculate craftsmanship. And...is this silver plating? Surely by weight alone they must have cost a fortune."

He raised a knowing brow at the men across from him. "How ever did the owner keep it from tarnishing, I wonder?"

Kell's eyes bulged out as if the secret was trying to bash itself out of his face, but somehow he kept himself from blurting it out.

"I'll give you thirty-five for the set," the merchant declared in a suddenly dry tone. Business had begun. He inched his hands toward the tools.

Gaelenn scoffed. "Thirty-five? Are you trying to cheat us? These are worth a hundred!"

The burly arm of the blacksmith found its way around Gaelenn's neck and pulled it to where the shopkeeper could not hear. "You crazy? Thirty-five *what*? Do you even know? Just take the money!"

"Let me take care of this." Gaelenn bumped his elbow into the middle of Kell's belly and looked over his shoulder at the expectant old man. "This old guy wants to barter more than he wants the stuff. If we didn't oblige we'd look suspicious."

"One hundred. Won't accept less," he said to the shopkeeper.

"Now, now! Not to be hasty! These are fine specimens, of course! But where am I to find the right buyer when I'm outside the gates?" he replied with a satisfied smile.

Bargaining always puts merchants in a good mood, Gaelenn thought.

"I might possibly be able to give you forty," the old man bargained.

"We're going to the next shop without seventy-five. Do you know what we had to do to get these?" Gaelenn's hand found the hilt of his sword and bent it to catch the light.

The merchant flinched.

"That sword...," he wondered aloud. A dark cloud briefly passed across his face before he woke himself with a start, as if from a daydream, and returned to bargaining. He smiled, his mouth full of teeth, and silently pulled out six cards of thick paper from one of his long sleeves, counted them carefully, and set them on the counter. "Sixty. Final offer."

The number ten was written on each of them in the common tongue, along with drawings of eyes and scythes. Gaelenn grabbed the stack, faked a dissatisfied look at the merchant—who looked quite pleased in return—and left, dragging Kell at the elbow to keep him from making a scene. They disappeared in an instant into the crowd.

"Well, however much this is, it can at least buy us food for a day or two," Gaelenn said after looking over his shoulder to make sure they were out of earshot.

"Mmph." Kell merely grunted. "Paper cards instead of gold and silver. Pa'd roll over in his grave."

They made their way back to the clearing and laid some of their windfall on a random counter in exchange for two massive bone flagons of ale and two skewers of meat. By sight alone the charred flesh should have had the two men retching but the savory aroma that drifted from them drowned out the putrid smell of the city and they ate with relish as they lounged on the bare dirt.

There was a lot of that—dirt—around. And plenty of blowing dust and smoke. Not a tree nor even a single stalk of grass, they noticed with wandering minds, was anywhere to be found anywhere within the confines of the town. Only a few dead and trampled patches of weeds told them that the surrounding town was much newer than the ancient city within. Perhaps only years or months old.

As soon as their stomachs were full and their curiosity of the city sated, reality came back around. They needed to get inside those gates. They could decide what to do next after that—if they could even make it that far.

Kell stewed by himself in deep thought, his heavy brow consuming all but the very bottoms of his eyes. Gaelenn held a casual gaze and focused on nothing in particular, using his ears as his eyes. Hundreds of drunkards and revelers laughed and shouted and whispered juicy rumors among themselves; it was the whispers that he latched onto.

"Have you heard? So-and-so is sleeping with the lender's wife."

"Somebody was caught stealing from a guard. Killed 'em right then and there!"

"The Triumvirate's coming back! Wish they'd just stayed abroad."

"It'll be a big scene tomorrow, I tell you," they whispered.

On and on the voices gossiped into the night. There was one rumor that dominated them all: tomorrow something big was going to happen: the parade. It was the same thing Gaelenn had heard in Key Rock and at the tower. They were coming back, victors over the whole continent. Not a single city had survived; Triumvir Anwir and the others, Yajuu and Visha, were to have their victory march with a huge festival in tow.

Hundreds and thousands of people were to gather and pay homage to the genocide, and in the revelry, the two friends suddenly foresaw some chance to sneak into the city, remote as it might be. Gaelenn leaned close to Kell and spoke just loud enough to be heard above the din. "Whatever is happening tomorrow will give us a ticket inside those walls. I'm telling you."

Kell dipped his head. "We'll see."

Gaelenn replied with silence. He could only hope. A gigantic swig of beer killed one of the fears that had twisted into a knot in his stomach. Another drink killed one more.

Kell joined in. By the time they drifted into slumber in comfortable anonymity, neither had any fear left in them.

Not until tomorrow.

CHAPTER FIFTEEN
The Parade

Drums thundered low and horns blew, breaking the peace of the morning. The crowd in the square, listless and hungover, slowly stirred. Gaelenn and Kell sat up and wiped the dried, cracked sweat from their faces.

"Be alert," Gaelenn mouthed and pointed to his eyes with his first two fingers.

The crowd was already on its feet, swarming to the main street like bees to honey. It was a parade, after all, and a momentous one at that. A dot in the distance to the south grew to a cavalcade within minutes, accompanied by the steady and growing beat of drums. Horned instruments blew so hard that Gaelenn and Kell could not help but wince in pain, their ears overwhelmed.

"Shouldn't have had so much to drink last night!" Kell shouted.

But it was nothing compared to the noise once the victory parade finally arrived. Huge carts pulled by servants, both human and beast, plodded in and out of view in an endless, staged celebration. The crowd cheered and shouted praises at the thousands of warriors in full regalia and their squires and slaves. Guards who, by the looks on their haggard faces must have been just as hungover as Gaelenn and Kell, quickly silenced dissenting jeers.

It was the war machines, though, that stole the show. Massive contraptions five times the size of a human, barely able to fit between the main city gates, menacingly spiked and armed. They rumbled along on wheels of wood and iron.

"Where are they going to fit those once they're inside the gate?" Gaelenn asked Kell. "The city must be massive!"

Trebuchets, horses with armor, and battering rams slathered in oil were flanked by soldiers marching in perfect unison. Barred carts packed with war prisoners collected curses and spit from the crowd along with a few rotten vegetables, the faces inside full of shame and horror, fated to certain torture and death.

Gaelenn caught a face in the last cart staring out at him—a toothless, knowing grin. He did not run or hide but looked straight back at the pirate captain that had strapped him to the front of the ship what felt like years ago by now. Dried blood covered his face and neck and he was past the point of raving, beaten and broken, but he was mad nonetheless.

A just fate, Gaelenn thought, though somehow he struggled to feel more anger than pity. The next round of horns sounded and more soldiers and flag bearers passed through.

"Victory!"

"They're back!"

"The Triumvirate!" the people screamed.

At the foot of the road, three warriors in elegant, green cloaks and purple armbands walked triumphantly over the flowers and wreaths thrown at their feet: the giant, the woman—and *him*, arm wrapped in a sling. A huge banner hung above them bearing the Eye and the Scythe, held up by a half-dozen squires struggling to keep the massive poles upright and moving.

Gaelenn shot downward and out of sight, jerking Kell down with him by the shoulder. The crowds screamed in god-like worship. Some jeered and were quickly removed by the guards. Anwir drew a staggering applause, the de facto leader, or perhaps it was his injury that had stirred them to their fervor.

"It's him! Stay down! I don't think he saw me. But that was him!" Gaelenn said.

"Who?" Kell screamed back. "The one who tried to kill you?"

Gaelenn stretched his face into an obvious *yes*. "Anwir!"

He clutched his chest as if it would help to control his heart. Following the Triumvirate's dramatic entry into the city, which was the highlight of the parade judging by the crowd's reaction, several more cavalries and infantries and artillery and war machines rolled along the wide street. But the orgiastic chaos festered until it threatened to explode, leaving the guards unable to contain it. Screams lashed out as hundreds of onlookers spilled into the street where the parade was reaching its end. They mobbed the marching soldiers, placing bows around their necks and kissing their cheeks. In an instant, it was impossible to tell who was supposed to be in the parade and who was not.

If there was any time for action, it was now. Gaelenn set his jaw and yanked Kell straight into the writhing ball of humanity right on the main street—and quickly approaching the main gate. Thousands of revelers slammed into each other and into the soldiers—some finding the wrong ends of their weapons—and the entire mob lurched forward to and through the great gate.

"We're going in!" Gaelenn yelled as they passed the gates into the city, riding the wave of bodies.

As quickly as the chaos had broken out, it died; the drums ceased and the giant gate slammed closed, leaving a mob of peasants scattering like roaches from candlelight. Spears closed in from all sides.

Two arms hung limp from the paper-thin crease between the massive gate doors, crushed either before their owners could make it in or before they could escape. Even though the music had died, the thick wood only half-muffled all the guards' shouts and gleeful and panicked screams of those who had made it inside in one piece. At least two hundred of them had managed to make it through, along with Gaelenn and Kell. The number was dwindling fast.

Kell sucked in a great swath of air and bolted after Gaelenn, who was already on his way to the nearest alley.

"Wait for me!" he shouted. His beard parted in two from the air beating against it.

A whoosh of air preceded the low, woody sound of a thick club just over Gaelenn's head, the first of many blows from all angles that he ducked under or dodged. It was not the first time he had been chased in his seven years of wandering.

Kell, who was running for his life for only the second time, was very efficient at catching the blows he might have avoided. One guard nicked his thigh, triggering a grimace, and another smacked him clean on the side of the head with a thin bat. He covered his blood-gushing ear and stooped over to run closer to the ground, lumbering like a massive, injured sow.

"Lesson learned!" he said to himself as he hunched over and ran with his knuckles dusting the ground for balance.

Gaelenn glanced back at his friend's awkward gallop and made a mental note to give him a good ribbing about it later.

They disappeared around a corner into a narrow alleyway along with a few others who soon found other random corners to escape to. The sound of whips and chains from the gate area echoed between the walls—only a few dozen escaped unscathed, and those who did not were being dealt with. Gaelenn and Kell kept running.

"There's no way...anyone...will find us now," Kell said between wheezes. After a minute's sprint they slowed down to a jog and then finally a brisk walking pace.

Gaelenn pulled his hood back over his head. "Act natural. Stop limping."

Kell tried to respond but had no his breath yet to speak with.

They pushed deep into the city through the twisting alleyways, meeting few others except for the occasional house servant carrying laundry or large jars above their heads. The walls stifled any breeze from penetrating and despite the general cleanliness of the streets and random wafts of incense, the air smelled just as rancid here as it had outside the tall walls.

"Where to?" Kell asked when he was able to speak. He pulled a cloth from his belt and rubbed the blood from his ear as they rounded another nameless corner to a more populated street.

Gaelenn spoke in a low voice. "Let's work our way to the palace, find our way inside maybe. Do a little eavesdropping."

He slapped Kell's belly with the back of his hand. "Nice job, by the way. I think we're getting pretty good at this stuff."

Kell bent nearly all the way over to catch his wind again.

"That may be true," an amused voice came from behind them. "But you definitely need to work on your sneaking-around-once-you-get-in skills."

They froze.

A hand landed on each of their shoulders and a body popped between them with a smiling face.

Kell grunted. "Oh, you."

He and Gaelenn released the handles of their weapons.

"Really, you ought to be more careful," Rin said. His hair was freshly dyed and hung slightly in front of his face, covering much of the lack of color that his dark hood did not.

Gaelenn was relieved to see a familiar face, and squeezed Rin's hand just a bit before he guided it off his shoulder.

"What's with the covering?" he asked, gesturing toward the hood.

"They don't take very kindly to strangers inside of these walls. If somebody saw my eyes, I'd be dead. Anybody with a different color is a target. Notice the variety outside compared to within? Natives inside, refugees outside."

He bounced his gaze around the citizens of the city.

"And you wouldn't want to see what they'd do to a woman who was out alone. My girlfriend has a bone to pick with them, actually. Yes—much, much better not to attract any sort of attention at all."

Stretching his own attention out to the crowd walking the wide main street, Gaelenn had to agree. The men, dressed in elaborate and shining robes, walked with gangs of women dressed in plain colors, wrapped to their chins in thick layers of fabric and donning wide-brimmed hats. Sure enough, everybody around had the same light brown eyes and dark, grayish skin. The few foreign-looking faces were alone and very conspicuous, eyes following them, leery and mistrustful. Gaelenn pulled his hood further down, making sure it covered his green eye well.

"You ought to be more careful, too," Rin said. "A dangerous place for you, in here. If I can find you, I'm sure others could as well—if they were looking for you. And you know they just might be."

He kept his eyes on the road but spoke low and aimed his mouth at Gaelenn. "And really, what do you think you're going to find inside the city? Your EN? You're not thinking of going into the palace, are you?"

"I don't know—we were thinking about it. We followed the Triumvirs into the city," Gaelenn said with gravity, but followed it with a smile, suddenly relaxed. "It's good to see you, Rin."

"I have to say you've got a singularly bad plan," Rin laughed quietly but in his usual carefree way. "I did come on serious business, though."

"What, news from your goddess? Let me guess, you're here to arrest me and take me back?"

"*Priestess*. And hey—I'm the one who broke you out of there."

"Yeah, and why did you do that, really?" Kell said from the other side of the line. Rin's impervious good mood somehow always made the blacksmith's worse.

Rin turned to him with a wide smile. "Did I do something wrong? It's not that I disagreed with the Priestess—I just disagreed with the method. Nobody should be held against their will."

He shrugged his shoulders and pulled a small, rolled paper from his jerkin. "I'm pretty sure that you would have stayed if you knew more. She thinks so, too. This is for you."

He passed the letter to Gaelenn, smiling. "I sure caught hell. Lucky for me, I'm the only one in the world who knew where you were going."

"I'm still not going back until we've—," Gaelenn said, pointing at Kell, "gotten some peace. What they did to my mother, to my hometown. Kell's family. Even my father's death is somehow related. Must be."

He hid the small, rolled paper under his shirt below his collar; there was no need to bring it to his nose to sense Livvy's perfumed scent on it, and he blushed.

"I wouldn't have minded staying under different circumstances," he said, closing his eyes to shut out the rushing feelings.

Rin glanced sideways at Gaelenn's longing face and raised a teasing eyebrow. "She tends to leave an impression, doesn't she? But didn't you insinuate that you were upset about having to stay there with her? I'm confused."

"It's...complicated," Gaelenn said and smiled back.

The Lieutenant Captain's grin widened. "I'm not sure what she wrote, but you might need a minute. Let's find another alley and get out of sight. Is that okay with you, smithy?"

Kell's mouth sunk deep into his beard. "You talk too much."

They dipped into a thin path among some off-white, plaster houses and continued until they found an empty clearing behind a mess of buildings. There were only two ways in or out: the way they came and another narrow gap on the opposite side. Rin checked around to make sure they had not been followed.

"Can never be too safe, yeah?" he said. "Not that I expect anything, but we weren't exactly welcomed into the city with open arms. Better to keep a watch out for guards."

Gaelenn clasped the rolled-up paper at his chest. "Give me a minute."

"Come on, smithy," Rin said. "You heard him. We'd better scout out this other alleyway, just in case." He led Kell toward the opposite side of the small yard and around the corner.

Gaelenn watched them pass out of sight and spun around to unfurl the tiny letter. The binding lace was so delicate that it needed only the barest nudge before it melted off like it was not even there. His mind and heart twisted together into one big knot. *How could she be so ruthless, and at the same time so...delicate?*

A few covered earthenware jars that made inviting seats were lying against the walls but he ignored them; nothing could make him sit down, just like nothing could calm his shaking hand. He pulled the bottom of the scroll gently and read.

> *Dear Gaelenn,*
>
> *I am sorry for the way your visit had to end. When you have been fighting for as long as I've been fighting, it's easy to lose your focus from time to time. I hope you can forgive me. I did have a million good reasons to want you here with me, though! Not the least of which is that you are in grave danger when you are away. Please, not just for my sake, but for everyone's, stay safe.*

The man, the EN, who caught you is not totally human. Not in the way you think. Even with the help of your friends, you are no match, for he carries with him some of the power of our enemy. An EN is a dangerous, unpredictable, and formidable foe, and in wars past, single ENs have leveled entire legions. So, keep as far away from him as possible—please!!

You may have a chance to get the revenge you seek someday soon. I promise you I will help. Until then, I beg you to be cautious and not run blindly into danger.

Also, there might be a way for you to help yourself gain an advantage, or at least some protection. Long ago, our home here, Last Retreat, was but one of many places on this continent and around the world from where we fought against the Eye in secret. Now it is the only one.

After the last major conflict, we lost the others, but it's possible that there are still some places, some machines like you saw here with me, that you can put to use. The nearest one is in the palace at Maynon Ohza, but it's in the hands of the enemy and far too dangerous (do not try!). Instead, make your way up the west side of Sapphire Mountain.

You will find a friend there. I trust you.

Always,

Livvy

Gaelenn reread the letter three times before he had calmed enough to breathe at a normal pace. Then he rolled it up and placed it back under his tunic. His fingers traced the ribbon laying in his palm for an extra second and wove it around his wrist into a knot, stuffing it under the base of his leather arm guard.

"Good news and bad news. Let's get moving," he said and set off to catch up to Kell and Rin.

A metal cry rang out just before he turned the corner into the alley. He had no time to react to it, but he could feel it. From his shoulder, a sudden and immense pain shot through his body like a bolt of lightning. He looked down at the thin, bloodied, rapier-like blade skewering him, pinning him fast to the wall. The pain and terror forced his mouth open in a mute cry, but he could breathe neither in nor out.

At the other end of the thin sword, so similar to the one at his side, was the face he knew all too well: the first Triumvir of Maynon Ohza, Anwir. He wore a grin so twisted it bent the air around him.

"Hello. Good to see you, friend." His voice was venom.

Gaelenn looked down again at the blood dripping from the wound; it had severed an artery in his shoulder and would begin spurting profusely as soon as its plug was removed. Death would follow in minutes.

"You know, I thought that was you back there. It didn't take as long to find you as I expected. And I didn't even have to go out!" He cackled at his own deadpanned-joke and waved his bandaged hand in Gaelenn's face. His lips were twisted and fanatical. "Lucky me."

Gaelenn tried to move, but the shock of pain kept the left half of his body still. The thin blade impaling his shoulder might as well have been a magic spell, as adamant as it felt. He used his good arm in an impotent swing, but the man simply turned away and laughed further, so he grabbed onto the bare blade instead and squeezed. The pain in his left side eased initially with the fresh cut to his fingers and palm. Kell and Rin were nowhere to be seen or heard.

"I don't know what you want, but I don't have it," Gaelenn said, managing a breath. "And you're going to get what's coming to you for what you did to my home. My mother."

He thought for a sliver of a moment, without meaning to, of her: that gentle, loving, and wise woman, so strong when his father had gone away. For seven years he had promised himself that he would return someday, whether he found his father or not. That day never came. She had been torn from the world—from him—without a goodbye. Even the small amulet she carried and coddled tearfully at night when Gaelenn was sleeping was lost. Her tears became his and he stared into the green man's eyes. The sadness turned to anger and the pain in his shoulder evaporated.

"Silly to resist," the man said. "What I want is *you*."

Gaelenn's jaw clenched hard and his eyes shot daggers of hate. His upper lip twitched and his legs drove him forward, sliding his shoulder along the long blade, leaving a shiny, bloody streak where his body had been. The man smiled in perverse satisfaction.

"That's the spirit," he purred, encouraging the challenge. "The more you struggle the easier this is for me. Now, let's come quietly, yes?"

He pulled out a small, dull-looking dagger and gave it a menacing flick toward the other shoulder, but Gaelenn pushed forward. The small blade, rusty with dried blood, had felt the inside of a body before—perhaps a favored device for inflicting pain, eager to fulfill its job once more.

"This will just help you sleep. Don't worry. And don't scream. You're going to help me whether you want to or not." It wasn't just dried, rusted blood on the knife—it was some kind of poison.

Gaelenn studied the intent in the Triumvir's eyes and watched in a trance as the thought traveled through the nerves and hit the sinews of his arm, which buckled and sprung forward. It all happened in a split second, but it felt like an hour. The tiny blade began its sluggish journey, and Gaelenn watched it come in slow motion. It was so absorbing—perhaps his last moment alive—that he did not even notice the black shadows come to life in the background.

With barely the sound of a gust of wind they swarmed the green man and all of his limbs at once and let out a collective cry that Gaelenn somehow thought sounded like, "Evil!"

Before the knife's blow could land, the shadowy ghosts grabbed his arm from behind and pulled him away. Despite Anwir's inhuman strength, he sank into a mass of bodies that overwhelmed him with sheer numbers. It happened too quickly for Gaelenn to notice that the sword that had been stuck in his shoulder was replaced by a steady spout of blood. His knees wobbled and he staggered back into the wall.

"You hurt, but you will live," came a woman's rushed voice. Through his blurring vision he could make out nothing but her heavy eyes, outlined in black. She grabbed the inside of his good shoulder and slid her body under it. She was strong.

But Gaelenn was weaker by the second.

"You will stay with me. Use your feet," she said, then, to some of the other robed figures, "Hurry, you will help me."

Three or four other robed figures swooped in as all of Gaelenn's weight pressed into her, and between them they bore his body two inches off the ground and took off. He tried to move his head back around to see what was happening, but everything was a blur of black and blood red. Strobes of light and dark played across his face and lulled him to sleep.

In all his travels, the one thing the wise people of the continent had always, invariably told him when he asked about death was that your ears are the last thing to go before you die.

They were right.

He just wished that the last thing he ever heard was not Anwir's blood-curdling scream of rage.

CHAPTER SIXTEEN
BLOOD IN THE ALLEY

KELL AND RIN SPUN around, their hairs collectively on end.

"What the hell was that noise?" Rin asked. The cry had snapped them back to the present.

"Shit," Kell muttered in response to the shout. "Gaelenn. We'd better get back."

They acknowledged their stupidity with a panicked glance between them.

"How did we get so far away?" Rin asked, and they sprinted back to the alley.

A phantom clad in black between the houses had lured them from where Gaelenn was waiting, and when they thought they spied the giant Triumvir walking by, they had not been able to resist the bait. It had not yet dawned on them how pointless—and dangerous—it was to leave their friend alone. But they felt it in their racing hearts now.

"I haven't...run this much since...Gaelenn used to have us all race...when we were kids!" Kell squeezed out words in spurts. "He's going to have...a good laugh at this."

When they turned the corner to the clearing, all they could do was gasp—they were no longer in an alley, they were in a slaughterhouse. It was hard to believe it was the same place from just minutes before; shredded black robes covered the ground where streaks of blood did not, and not a speck of dry dust remained. The yellow plaster of the walls would not see rain in time to wash off the drying crimson, and the smell of fresh death wafted from piles of bodies littered about. Kell swallowed to keep down the bile pushing up his throat, not sure if it was from the run or the sight of the blood and bodies.

Rin bent down over a group of corpses. "We were only away for two minutes. Three, max."

"Where is Gaelenn?" Kell asked, desperate. He placed his hand on his forehead but there was no sweat. Panic had no time to set in.

"Stop there!"

From the opposite side of the small clearing, a band of guards filed in and inspected the scene of the massacre with unbelieving eyes.

"What is this?" the man in the center demanded. He stepped forward and the other four formed up behind him in the shape of a V and pointed their spears from behind their shields. Bodies and pools of blood laid between them, flies beginning their feast.

Each side sized up the other in silence; Kell and Rin had drawn their own weapons without thinking and their eyes jumped between themselves and each guard, their heads refusing to swivel for fear of attack.

"Where is he?" the head guard shouted, sending echoes outward from the alleyway that buzzed as they passed outward.

"*Where is he?* You tell me!" Rin said. He pointed right at the head guard's face. The taunt risked escalation, but he did not care. Two-on-five was terrible odds, but he was now spoiling for a fight as much as he was for answers.

"Tell *you*...? One more time—where is the Triumvir?"

Rin replied with a vexed stare.

The guard had put up with enough. "Put those weapons down. You're coming with us."

"Where to?" Kell said, more a challenge than a question. He raised his heavy hammer until it was next to his face, and Rin, a few paces behind, drew a crossbow from under his cape and pointed it at the right-most soldier.

"We are the personal guardians to the Triumvirate and the head Triumvir, Sir Anwir," the guard said with an almost disinterested gaze. "He came this way. We know it. Do not throw your lives away. Put down your weapons. You will come with us, and we will talk. In the dungeon."

A beam of light shot through a crevice in the buildings and caught his ornate breastplate, which glittered like fire.

"That armor looks expensive enough for us to believe you," Rin said. "But...I'm afraid we cannot acquiesce. We've got to go find our own friend. Good luck finding yours."

The thick, stinking air and bloody dust held them apart for a moment. For ten seconds they paused, everybody waiting for somebody to make the next move.

"Arrest th—" the lead guard began, but his sentence was interrupted with the sound of a body crashing into the ground. The furthest guard lay crumpled, a crossbow bolt jutting from his neck and his blood shooting into the air like a geyser. The crossbow itself followed, hitting the next soldier in the face as he struggled and failed to catch it in time with his spear. Before he had time to recover, Rin had lunged at him with a pair of long daggers and stabbed at him relentlessly, targeting every chink in his armor.

"I like these odds better!" he said to Kell.

His blades whistled, stinging every open crease like a barrage of furious wasps. The soldier tried in vain to keep up, but his cape was more red than green before he hit the ground, dead.

Kell watched it all happen for a half second, incredulous, before he leapt into action himself. Not to be outdone by Rin, whose fighting skills sparked a tinge of envy, he threw himself into his heavy hammer and lunged at the remaining combatants. Well-trained and battle-hardened, they immediately regrouped and formed a single organized unit, two in front and one behind.

Brute strength and cunning made up for the blacksmith's lack of knowledge of battle tactics. When the front-liners shot forward with their spears he leaned aside and snapped their wooden shafts in a single downward swing of his hammer. They reached for the shorter weapons at their belts but it was not fast enough—the next swing of Kell's hammer caught one of them in the ribs and jerked him into the other and they flew into the wall together, dazed and incapacitated. A satisfied grin stretched the hair above Kell's mouth.

"How do you like that, *Lieutenant Captain*?" he said to Rin.

"We need to be looking for Gaelenn, blacksmith, not comparing sizes—look out!"

The head guard thrust his spear at Kell and caught a bare spot on his upper arm, leaving a straight line that bled over his long elbow sleeves. There was no time to feel the pain; the soldier tossed the spear in favor of his sword, which he drew high and swung down in one smooth arc.

The smith's hammer met it an inch before it split his skull in two and he gave a victorious, "Hah!"

The guard, however, was quick to recover. His hands still rang from the rejection, but he pressed his attack with a flurry of single-handed swings, using his other hand to hold his shield close to his body. Too close.

Kell found an opening and slammed his hammer into the exact center of the triangular shield. Strong though it was, it could not absorb the blow—a hole bent inward and broke the guard's hand into mush. A pained shout burst out of his mouth and the shield fell to the ground and spun like an inverted top.

The blacksmith's hammer surged head-first into that obnoxious chest plate and bent it inward until it pushed the air out of the guard's lungs;

the pure unorthodoxy of the move had struck him with nothing ready in defense.

His breath never came back. He fell backward and Rin swooped in and stabbed him in mid-air in one of the small openings under his arm. Writhing on the ground for a few seconds before death took him, his eyes looked between his executioners in wide shock.

"About time!" Kell said and turned back around to get a better assessment of the fight. The two soldiers he had knocked into the wall were coming to.

"Kell!" Rin said. His voice was urgent but muffled. Better to attract as little attention as possible, even though he was sure that somebody had to have heard the clanging metal and shouting. It was hard to predict how well these walls could broadcast sounds.

The guard who took the brunt of Kell's hammer stretched his arms to unbuckle his own mangled breastplate so he could breathe and move, and his last remaining comrade maneuvered in front to give him time. Sweat dripped from his nose and he had not even swung his weapon yet.

Rin swung a dagger at the air. "Where is our friend?"

But the guard, holding his spear so far in front of him that the tip bent down, responded with silence. The other, finally free of his armor, spoke for him. "If there's another of you, good—you'll all hang together."

He spat blood at his feet and doubled down. "Where is Sir Anwir?!"

Kell and Rin exchanged another sidelong glance. More silence.

"Well, this conversation isn't going anywhere," Rin said before launching into a fresh attack. Kell started more quickly this time, swinging his hammer in concert with the storm of blades. The Triumvirate Guard, a feared and famed battle unit, were nonetheless no match for the simple blacksmith and his pale friend. Victory was in hand.

Then, a fist larger than a human skull came out of nowhere and smashed into the side of Kell's head. His nose and mouth gushed with blood before he even hit the dirt. Rin saw the flash in the corner of his eyes and turned around to find his entire field of vision eaten up with one giant man—the green giant from the parade, Triumvir Yajuu.

He stared down with a devil's grin and bloodlust in his eyes, growling low. The two guards moved in closer and Rin craned his neck to the side to spy a fresh battalion of soldiers coming through the gap between the giant man's bare arm and barely-armored body. Muscles bulged out of every gap of cloth and leather—either he had no need for the steel armor worn by the rest of the Triumvirate or no smith could make a set large enough to fit him. The leather popped and buckled as his fists hardened.

"Oglahk ahmdor," he said through his teeth.

Rin swallowed and shrugged. "Don't get you, mate."

"Shee fall ahmdor, Sir Yajuu." A soldier behind cut in, translating something.

The giant glanced at him, then turned back to Rin and pointed at his face. He followed the taunt with the unsheathing of his massive axe.

Kell found his feet and picked up his hammer. Blood ran over his mouth and down the middle of his beard, complimenting the cuts on his arm and ear.

"We're in a bit of bind here, if you're done resting," Rin said.

Kell shook the buzzing from his head. "Whaddawe do now?"

"Anyone in the alley there?" Rin responded between set teeth.

"Nope."

"Then...run!" Rin flicked his smaller knife at the giant's foot, and although the attempt did not hit home, it did force the huge legs to hop backward. The giant's great arms spread apart for balance and blocked the other soldiers from giving chase just long enough for the two foreigners to escape.

Blessed with a split second's time, Rin and Kell took off into the alley, bounding through the maze.

"Just once I'd like not to be running away from certain death when I'm with you guys!" Rin said.

"Can't you practice that wit...when we're not...about to die?" Kell yelled, his breath failing him.

The giant's footsteps thundered like a bull's just seconds behind them, so they did not dare slow down, but it was clear they had no idea where they were going. They might have been running in circles for all they knew. But when they rounded the next corner they were greeted by a straight path, ten yards long, and an open doorway at the end. In front of it stood a small girl holding a loose sack who beckoned them in.

Kell and Rin were not in a position to refuse.

They dashed into the black hole and it shut fast behind them, the girl outside. In pitch blackness, they listened to the small footsteps scramble off with the sack flailing about in noisy diversion. They held their breath when a few seconds later the house trembled under the heavy pursuit of the green giant and the pitter-patter of the remaining guards and soldiers after him. Safe—for the moment. Their lungs burning, Kell and Rin finally exhaled and gulped several grateful mouthfuls of stale indoor air.

Odd. There were no windows at all—everything had been boarded up—and the only thing they could see at first was a tiny hole to the outside. A minute later, an old, wrinkly eye met the lone beam of light coming into the room and peered outward. The hole closed as soon as the eye's owner was satisfied that the chase had led elsewhere.

"Who are you?" Rin asked. There was no echo. "Why'd you do that for us?"

A lamp came to life in the middle of the room and illuminated an old, serene face in its yellow glow.

Kell gasped.

"You bought my tools yesterday," he said.

"That I did!" the old man laughed. "I know craftsmanship when I see it! Beautiful indeed—I already sold them off for five times what I paid you for! I suspect you didn't know much what they're worth here. Nor did you care, am I right?"

His face lurched over the lamp for effect.

"For there are bigger concerns on your mind, no?" Mimicking the hulking gait of the giant with his first two fingers, he added, "Very *big* concerns. Ah, I see you have replaced your friend as well! A better barterer, perhaps?"

Kell snorted.

Rin brushed the hair out of his eyes to study the round lamp, which stood in the middle of a small wooden table, and touched its flicker-less glass surface. Cold.

"Is this...?"

"Oh, a nifty little trinket, don't you think?" the shopkeeper said. "No oil, no flame! I just touch it in the right place, and I control it. Like this!"

He flicked it on and off a few times.

"We got it." Kell said. It had definitely come from Last Retreat at some point.

"Though, much like you, I suppose the seller was not so concerned with the price! 100 Daetells, and no more! If I remember correctly, she looked something like your pale friend here. A relative, perhaps?" His thick eyebrow arched upward. "Many interesting things are to be found outside the city walls these days. So many...*interesting* people finding their way here."

Thousands of trinkets and bobbles lined the walls that Kell's eyes had now adjusted enough to see. Rin had noticed them before the lamp had even turned on.

"As for why I helped you, well, why not? Filthy foreign beasts must have some evil reason to be chasing you! I hope what you've done was well worth it." He winked and smiled again, not unlike a much-older Rin. "Not everybody here in Maynon Ohza is happy with this 'Triumvirate.' *Liberation*. Bleh. Nonsense! Things might be good for a peddling man such as myself nowadays, but life sure was easier before you had to board up and soundproof your house!"

Kell and Rin looked at each other from the sides of their eyes. The old man certainly had a flair for the dramatic.

"So...they're not from here? I always thought the Triumvirate was from Maynon Ohza." Rin said.

Kell stopped wiping the blood from his face and arm just long enough to shoot a questioning glance and Rin made a small shrug. "Is this the time for questions?"

"Might as well ask," Rin shot back.

The old man fussed his brow and shook his head. "Oh, no no no! Came from across the sea some years ago! Life before that wasn't perfect. But it was peaceful enough. Not like now! Now we have beasts, yes, horrible beasts who rule over us! Come from some accursed foreign land with strange magic!"

He punctuated his exaggeration with a slap on his thigh.

Kell stuffed his bloody rag back under his belt. "What magic?"

"Unnatural strength. Unnatural!" the shopkeeper said with an involuntary quiver. "The big one—they call him Yajuu—personally executes criminals. But not with any weapons, no. Crushes their skulls in one hand! And, rumor is, *eats* them. Comes from an old society of cannibals. And the woman..."

His old, knotty finger trembled as it made a small arc in the air. "The woman...I saw her jump over the city wall one night!"

Both of the visitors scoffed.

"I swear! Has an appetite for destruction and sins of the flesh that would make a demon blush. They say that she is the cruelest of all of them. And the most devious! Mercifully, she lacks the lust for power of her brethren. Her name is Visha. Just don't get caught outside the gates at night, trust me. Or inside them if you're alone!"

Rin nodded. "And what about the other one—there are three Triumvirs, right?"

His boisterous personality was intact but his voice grew low. "Best not speak of Anwir. He's the sole reason that we hide and rebel in secret. His eyes are everywhere. Who knows, maybe even here."

"Fine, but—"

The door creaked open, startling Kell and Rin. The small girl returned and squeezed through.

"I'm back, grandpa," she said with a proud smile. She must have been seven or eight, her innocence long replaced with street-wise brown eyes.

"Well done, well done, my little princess," the old man said. He rewarded her with a warm smile and a pat on her head. She scurried past him further into the house where the lamp's light did not reach. Turning back to Kell and Rin, he whispered, "Little ears are invaluable—invaluable! Secrets are worth much more than hammers, yes? Especially these days."

"Right. We really must thank you for your help," Rin said. "But maybe it's time for us to get going. We don't want to cause you any more trouble, and we need to be looking for our friend."

The old man lifted his forehead high into a mess of wrinkles. The white puff of hair on his skull crawled back behind his ears. "Yes, yes, my granddaughter was watching. Before you depart, maybe I can help with a little information! Consider it my contribution to your trouble-making!"

He winked once more—how old men love winking—and continued in a graver tone.

"Your friend may have been taken by the Disciples of the Eye. A cult, yes. A fanatic, frightening cult. They are like shadows...and there were a lot of shadows around just before you arrived at my door."

"Do you know where we can find them?" Rin asked. He was at full attention now.

"Nobody knows where you can find them. Not even an old rumor-monger like me."

Kell blew a stream of air from his round cheeks. "Well, let's go then."

"Oh!" said the old man, standing from his stool. "Take a little food. A last token from me."

He handed a small loaf of meat-filled bread to each man before they walked out the door. "It will soon be dark—take care. Do not venture far. Triumvir Visha has been known to pluck men and women from even the locked houses inside the walls at night and take them as playthings to be tortured. Watch each other well."

"Thank you." Kell and Rin gave shallow bows.

"If you find your friend anywhere, it will be in the shadows. But there is danger there on all sides. Beware."

CHAPTER SEVENTEEN
The Disciples of the Eye

He did not know how long he had been awake, but it was not until he was already standing when Gaelenn finally gained control of himself. Metal clamps chewed at his wrists and bound his arms to his waist, and all he could see were large holes in the ceiling that illuminated the brick-and-dirt ground in moonlight. It was night, but he could not be sure whether he had been out for hours or days.

He stretched his head back to inspect his aching shoulder, wrapped up in bandages, and from the fragrant smell Gaelenn could tell that it was packed with a smattering of herbs. But there was also the scent of burnt flesh and a throbbing pain emanating from deep near his bones. He knelt down to rest the elbow of his lame arm on his knee to relieve some of the pressure. A grunt slipped out and he sucked in air between his bared teeth.

At the sound, a figure stepped into the light, its bare feet tapping on the brick. From the shins up, its body was clad in loose black robes and its head completely wrapped, showing only two deep black eyes.

"Thanks for the help," Gaelenn said.

His dry throat almost made him cough, but he was able to stifle it.

"Do you mind taking these off?" he asked, lifting his wrists up to where the figure could see. They stopped with a jerk—a rusty chain he hadn't noticed pinned them fast to the ground. Gaelenn winced. No response was given.

"When am I not going to be a prisoner anymore?" he asked himself and wondered whether the past week spent so often bound was some penance for the last seven years of roaming the world so freely.

The figure moved a step forward and unwound the wrap on its head.

"You, look up," a woman's voice commanded.

Gaelenn acquiesced, having no reason to resist. But in minor protest, his way of looking up was closer to rolling his eyes.

"You, what happened to your eyes?" she said.

"What about them?" Gaelenn said. He dropped his eyes and tried to use his forehead to shield them. Anything that called attention to them felt like it should be avoided if at all possible after his encounter with the Priestess.

"You, stand up."

Gaelenn squinted. "Pretty bossy, aren't we?"

He placed her accent to the lands of the far western reaches of the known world, her words severe and halting and imperious. He might have been able to understand her in her native tongue, he thought, having picked up a casual ability in a smattering of languages on his travels. She grew conscious of the idiosyncrasy and corrected it.

"Stand up!"

Gaelenn stood up and looked into her face, which had by now been stripped of its black cloth covering. Underneath was a youthful face which, despite its darker hue, was unblemished by the sun and perfectly smooth. It was also quite beautiful, he noticed, with a long nose and large, round eyes capable of catching a tiny ray of the moonlight above and amplifying it. In fact, he could hardly see anything at all except for the white globes in her eyes. Everything else went dark.

"Did you poison me?" he said and staggered forward against the chains. His balance left him and he was a half-step from falling completely.

She helped him keep straight and backed away again. "You have not been poisoned. You simply bled too much. Our healers have skill. Soon you will recover."

After a few deep breaths, he could see the light again, although it was still dim. It was the smell of salt on the woman's hands that woke him up and brought him back. It also took him back for a moment to the many moons he had spent across waters in a place so far away that they simply called it the "West Across the Sea," for lack of a proper name. A place where the salt was everywhere: in the food, the wind, the sea, and the people. It was one of Gaelenn's favorite places of all before the last of its coastal towns was snuffed out and it was destroyed forever.

"You're from Igtao, right?" he asked.

She took a half step back in surprise but ignored his question and fetched a clay jug of water, setting it on the floor next to him. He picked it up and drank deeply, tiny streams of water working their way down either side of his face. A great, relieved sigh burst out of his throat, followed by a rumble in his stomach. The cool liquid had stirred his hunger. The woman pursed her lips and pulled a small loaf of leaf-wrapped bread from her robe and gave it to Gaelenn, who shoved it into his mouth and swallowed faster than he could chew. Anything would have tasted good as hungry as he was, and this was sublime. He struggled between bites to speak again.

"You can call me Gaelenn instead of 'you,' if you want. What can I call you?" he asked.

"You—" she caught herself, paused, and continued, "there is no need to call me anything. Eat, and rest."

He did as she bid and sank to the floor when he was done.

"I think you do have poison. Or magic," he said in a stupor of exhaustion. "And now you've put a sleeping spell on me."

He fell on his good shoulder, rested his head on his arm, and slept. At least he was not dead.

IT FELT LIKE YEARS later when Gaelenn's eyes finally opened again. He grimaced and stretched his shoulder through the pain to force himself awake. A filled jug of water lay near his face. It was glazed brown and rather crude, made from patchy clay. Color—he could see color. It was daytime.

His eyes moved sideways before his head bothered to rise and he looked up toward a hole in the ceiling. He still could not see the sky, though, thanks to the depth. He was dozens of feet, or maybe even yards, deep under the surface. But the hole sent a focused pillar of light to the floor that was so bright that Gaelenn almost had to squint to look at it. He sat up, coughed, and took a fresh drink of the water. It tasted much worse than it had the night before.

Again, deep in the darkness, someone took notice. The woman he had talked to before, or so he guessed by her bare, feminine feet, wrapped tightly just above the ankles, stepped into the beam. She had replaced her hood and now she was harder to see and to read.

"Good," she started—yes, it was the woman. "You are finally awake."

She walked up to him and with an old key from her pocket, bent over and opened the lock on the floor that had been tethering the hand-clasps to the ground.

"That feels a bit better," Gaelenn said. "These next?"

He raised his wrists.

"You will keep them for now," she said, her delivery less severe than before but still less than friendly. "You have been sleeping for many days. Now it is time for you to talk."

"Days? Well, sure. I'd rather talk than fight, so that's good for me. Any way we could do breakfast first?"

The woman handed him a piece of the same bread and he again stuffed it down his throat, finishing with a last swig of water. She kept a patient eye on him and when he was done continued her instructions.

"Follow me and do not lose the way. It is dark down here and difficult to see."

"Down here? So we're underground. Where exactly?" he asked, and thought without speaking, *Sewers, again?*

She turned toward the darkness and her voice echoed back. "We exist in the places that the world above has forgotten. Please come. No more questions for now."

"Wow, she said 'please,'" Gaelenn said under his breath, trying not to be heard. He followed her, keying in on the movement of her robes as they swung to and fro in the thick air.

They worked their way through a half dozen corridors in a straight line, and then turned a corner and received the gift of light; an old-fashioned torch burned in a brazier and threw orange on a skeletal iron staircase leading up. The woman climbed it and its joints buckled and creaked. Gaelenn followed after testing the first step with his feet, but paused before they reached the top.

"There's no way out up there!"

The walls were close, and his echo came back and stung him in the ears. The woman turned her head around just long enough to give him an annoyed look before continuing on her way. At the top of the rickety staircase, she knocked twice on the ceiling and a hatch opened above her. They climbed up and out, one by one, into a perfectly circular room lined with torches around its edges. It was the same room—or perhaps a dirtier, older copy—as the one Livvy had shown him at Last Retreat, and a larger version of the one in the Windy Woods.

Black-robed figures lined the room at regular intervals, and in the center was a crooked table that looked like an older, evil twin of ones he had seen before. The same round walls circled around, made of that ageless material, here somehow aged, and the same smooth floor. It reflected the torchlight like a mirror, except for the area around the hatch, which was remade of stone and pasted with grime and the history of human touch. It was an exact replica, but used.

A voice next to the table spoke to him. "You were assaulted by the Triumvir Anwir, but he did not kill you. Why?"

"Straight to the point," Gaelenn said.

It was another woman—an old woman. She had escaped his notice from behind the table, but when he moved his head from side to side, he could see the light from the fire dancing on her hooded face.

"I...don't know. I have no idea."

"Be honest and plain. His enemies are our friends," she said. Her voice was old and hoarse but full of conviction and allure. "So, we are allies. We are friends."

Gaelenn looked back to find that the woman who had led him here had disappeared somewhere along the edge of the room with the other shadows. He could see only countless bare legs and feet of men and women under the standard black robes and leg wraps.

"Friends imprison friends in dungeons?"

"We must also protect ourselves. You understand."

The smell of incense seemed to intensify, triggering a throbbing pain between Gaelenn's temples. He rubbed them and then his shoulder. "Why would that lunatic have anything against me? I really don't know. I'm the one who was after him. I have a score to settle."

"Score to settle? All of us do. But you cannot beat him. No one can," the woman said. There was no emotion in her voice, just a matter-of-factness that unnerved Gaelenn. She walked around the table toward him and unwrapped her veil, then held her hand out and collected a torch from another cultist. The wrinkles on her old skin cast deep shadows over her face and her sharp eyes pierced the darkness and the light.

The torch jumped closer to his face, almost burning the whiskers on his chin and pushing him back a step.

The old woman held the flame steady for a few more seconds so she could stare into Gaelenn's eyes. When she was satisfied, she handed it back to its bearer, who stayed.

"You bear a mark in your iris," she said. "You have been touched by the Eye."

Gaelenn thought back to his short time with Livvy. Maybe he should have stayed longer with her after all; nothing added up yet.

"What 'Eye?'" he asked.

"Surely, you must know the Great Eye. Your birthmark proves it, for no one is born with such a scar. Your encounter with Anwir proves it, also. Else he would have killed you, rather than try to capture you."

"I can't answer for his motives. And..." Gaelenn pointed to his eyes. "No 'Eye' did this. I can guarantee that."

The old woman's ghostly gaze penetrated him; she searched his face for deception, and finding none, she drew closer to him and spoke lower. "Perhaps you do not know. Perhaps you hope to deceive us. But *we do know*. You carry with you a key, do you not? We have known this for time immemorial—that some exist who possess the gift of communion. Prophets. Like you."

"*Prophet?* Gift of what? Before we go any further, you have to at least tell me who you are." Gaelenn tried to cross his arms, only to wince as the clamps dug into his wrists.

"We are the Eye's Chosen—the disciples of the Great Unseen Eye," she responded without pause. It was not the first time she had given this speech. "The people of Maynon Ohza are oblivious to their god, the Eye! And yet he watches over us. And the world. The great and terrible and merciful Eye!"

She grew more animated as her fervor boiled, her arms flailing above her head like tentacles.

"And directly in our way," she spat at the name, "is *Anwir*, the blasphemer. Your enemy. Our enemy."

Gaelenn looked around at the other cultists. They stood like statues and hummed in unison at every mention of the name *Eye*.

"I thought he was part of the Triumvirate. I thought he was a servant of your...Eye."

"He lies. He lies!" she shouted into Gaelenn's face as if she herself had been wounded, not him. "Yes, he claims to serve our God. And he was blessed with great power by that same God. But we, the Eye's Chosen, have watched from the shadows for centuries. We know all in this world. From us there are no secrets!"

She grew a great breath. "And we know his treachery! He was given the greatest gift of all: a seat next to God as his hand upon the Earth. One of three among all the thousands. And yet—he desires the Great Eye's power for himself. Something he can never have!"

The air left her lungs in a great burst; her speech was finished.

Gaelenn stared at her. "Okay, so this Anwir is a bad guy. What does he want with me? If you can't defeat him, and I can't defeat him, why did you save me from him? Why bring me here?"

The lead cultist hesitated, drawing up her beady eyes to his.

"We cannot commune with the Great Unseen Eye as we once could," she said, the strength in her voice ebbing. She turned and walked toward the table and embraced it with both hands.

Gaelenn watched her with one eyebrow raised. It was only natural that someone with such alluring showmanship be surrounded by an army of zealots, but it also meant that not all of what she said could be trusted.

"Someone—or some power—has sabotaged us. Our shrine no longer functions. The Eye has left our temple." The woman was almost on the verge of tears before whipping herself into a frenzy. "At first, we thought we had been forsaken. But it is not so! *Someone* has done this, and purposefully."

Her hand reached to the other side and pulled open a small slot in the crooked table to expose the frayed end of some kind of metal wire. The cultists hissed. "But we will not lose faith! We pray every minute of every day for forgiveness. We pray the Eye will see the treachery of the false prophet, Anwir! The worm. We know it was him!"

"How do you know he did this?"

"We have faith. And we know all."

"And how do you know he plots against your god?"

"He has conspired privately against the Great Eye. We have seen it, truly. Our shadows have heard his words. He plots against our God in the darkness, where only he knows the Eye cannot see."

Her fists shot to the sky in anger. "And when he convenes with the Eye in their palace, he professes his love and obedience. Lies!"

The performance ended and she drooped her arms over the table in a final, melodramatic flutter. For a full two minutes, the cult leader lay motionless. Everything froze—no one came to rescue her from her swoon. Nobody even asked if she was okay. The only movement in the room was the small plumes of smoke from the incense and torches that trailed upward into the darkness. When at last she came to, her finger shot straight to Gaelenn's face, followed by her weightless body as she began another dramatic waltz toward him until she all but poked out his dazzling green eye.

"You have been touched. You have the gift. The gift of a prophet," she said.

Gaelenn neither blinked nor stepped away.

"I don't know any gods," he said. "And I don't have any gifts. Plenty of problems, it seems, but no gifts."

"You do have a gift, whether you understand it or not. And with it, you may earn your freedom from Maynon Ohza. It is too dangerous for you alone. The palace is impossible. One step outside our protection and you will be found. You know it. Thus, we have a proposition for you."

His lower lip curled up above his teeth; sycophants were not known for good deals or fair terms. "What do you want with me?"

"We will lead you to your freedom, and your friends."

"In exchange for?"

The old woman's shrewd gaze flashed at Gaelenn, her eyes catching the gleam of the torches and becoming globes of fire.

"Nobody knows what the Great Unseen Eye has given you. But in time you may come to realize," she exclaimed, charged once again with excited fervor.

"And yet, the traitor Anwir will hunt you down for his own nefarious purpose! What he is planning is secret from even us. Perhaps he will use you as leverage over his master. Perhaps not. Nonetheless, it is certain that you cannot stand against him. But you can help us! And help yourself!"

Her performance picked back up and swept her about in a meandering, barefooted dance around the center of the room.

"There is nothing I can do, I'm afraid. Please...you must let me go." A bead of blood that trailed from his wrist to the tip of his fingernail dropped to the floor, and Gaelenn watched it fall and splatter. "My friends will be looking for me, if they're still alive."

He took a single step out onto the white part of the floor and several robed cultists rushed him from the room's edges and pushed him back to the small stone area he had been standing. One of them fell face down with a towel and scrubbed where his feet had been, as well as the blood over the stone area, before withdrawing.

"My boots aren't that dirty—" Gaelenn tried to protest but was ignored. It was sacred ground. He looked back up and pleaded with the decrepit old woman. "Please."

"As I said, worry not. Your friends are alive. We have made sure of that, though they *were* hunted. We will take you to them, and safely out of the city. Providing you accept our terms."

"I told you there's nothing I can do. Let me go, and I'll leave this city behind. This man will never be able to find me," Gaelenn said.

"Do not underestimate him! For he will find you wherever you go. He will hunt you, and he will take you before the Eye for his own evil purpose. To your loss and ours," she said, her eyes wide and unfocused, as if in a trance. "We cannot simply let you go. It is impossible. No; the only way out for you is with us."

A long breath hissed out of Gaelenn's heavy mouth. The irons dug further into his wrists and he contemplated the chances of escape with a downward stare. There were none. He had no choice.

"What are these terms?"

The cultist brightened—or seemed to burn brighter—and spun around.

"The simplest terms!" she said. "All you must do is to use your power to open a temple to us. After that, you are released from your bond. It is simple, is it not?"

"You mean, unlock one of these...shrines?" Gaelenn's blood-dripping palms pointed toward the mangled table next to the cult leader. "I'm not sure that I can. And even if I did, what do you plan to do with it?"

"What we do is our concern!"

She whipped around to face her prisoner.

"But...as it also benefits you, I will tell you. We will simply commune with the Eye and expose the Triumvir's treachery. Then our God will deal with him, and you may walk free without *burden*," she said, jerking the last word like a hook in a fish's mouth.

Gaelenn's head turned slightly to one side, but his eyes remained fixed on the woman.

"But I don't know how to do it."

"We do. We will guide you to the Sapphire Mountain, where a temple rests. Do you accept our offer?"

"I can't guarantee the safety of your guides."

"Our guide will be quite safe from you or anything else. Do you accept our offer?"

"There's no guarantee I'll be able to unlock your temple."

"Our faith will open the way. Do you accept?"

The air came out of Gaelenn's lungs all at once. He looked down again at the irons pulling at his hands. Already deep scars had worn into his wrists; within a day the clasps would hit bone.

"Escort him back to his room," the woman instructed, her patience spent. Several shadows drifted toward him.

Gaelenn lifted his head up and looked at her with glaring eyes.

"Fine. I accept."

The shadows stopped.

Torch flame circled her pupils like wreaths, and her head tilted up slightly in victory. Gaelenn could see the edges of her lips almost curl up into a smile.

"Good," she said. "Very good."

Yes, very good indeed, Gaelenn thought, *that I was heading there anyway.*

CHAPTER EIGHTEEN
SHADOW

"WHAT ARE YOU TWO doing here?"

The words burst out of Gaelenn's throat before his brain had a chance to think. The puzzled brows on Kell's and Rin's told him they were thinking the same thing.

"Looks like I'm not the only one who doesn't know what the hell's going on, then," Gaelenn said.

The three friends embraced and shared speechless looks of relief as the door behind them eased shut until it was flush with the stone around it.

"Hidden doors. Clever," Gaelenn remarked and then turned back around. "Where did you guys go?"

After he had struck his deal with the cult leader, he had been ushered through the maze of underground tunnels, rearmed, provisioned, and sent on his mission. The wounds on his wrists were cleaned and wrapped in herbs and bandages, his arm guards were replaced, and his captors had even returned the lace from Livvy's letter. At his side, his sword hung downward, returned to him without a scratch. Night had taken over the day, and its shadows concealed his new companion: the cultist who had taken care of him while he recovered.

Only Rin's eyes, adapted to darkness, were keen enough here.

"Got a new friend? Or hostage?" he asked, leaning around Gaelenn and looking her up and down. His face went bitter when he got to her bare feet.

"I think we should leave. Now," Kell said.

The woman spoke in a low whisper. "You will be quiet and follow me. It is dangerous above ground, even at night."

She seemed perpetually in shadow; even when she stood right in front of the group, they had to squint to see her. She dismissed their stares and repeated herself before darting away. "You will follow me."

So they followed.

Rin rivaled her stealth marvelously, Gaelenn kept low and silent, and Kell, despite a brief stutter step whenever he made eye contact with the woman, did his best to keep quiet and not get left behind. Guards patrolled the main streets and lit torch posts in their evening rounds, visible in slices between buildings from the side routes.

"I can't see anything," Kell whispered, a few yards behind the pack. Without the sun, the dense alleyways were a black labyrinth. "Where are we going?"

"Shhh," Rin scolded. "Is that what you call 'being quiet?' Quiet as a horse, maybe!"

The woman jerked her head around as she plowed forward. "You will be silent! You may criticize one another when we are safe!"

"This lady needs to work on her speaking manners," Rin said.

Gaelenn responded with an apologetic shrug and a half-smirk, and then looked up and mouthed a question. "Where are we?"

Where he expected the great city wall, he saw only the full moon on its journey into the night sky. At least, he thought he had only mouthed the words—the woman stopped short and turned her whole body to face the men. She put a finger over her lips and pointed behind them with her covered chin. When Gaelenn returned a confused glance, she lifted her head higher and flashed the whites of her eyes.

"Turn around."

Above the huts to their rear, the stars were cut off by the shade of the city wall, its curled spires illuminated with dim torches. Atop the palace in the distance, countless scythes reflected the moonlight like rows of dragon's teeth.

"We've been outside the city this whole time?" Gaelenn asked. The Disciples of the Eye must have had tunnels underneath the entire city and beyond—convenient for a secret cult.

Kell slapped him on the back and nodded.

"Keep moving," he said, returning his gaze to the woman, where it refused to leave.

The houses and huts dwindled to hovels and tents until the four reached the edge of the town, where the woman looked out. "We are safer out there than in the city. But we are still not truly safe. We will travel until morning. You may rest then."

Rin grumbled in protest and Gaelenn rubbed his wrists, but Kell gave an agreeable grin and followed at the woman's heels after a quick squeeze on his friends' shoulders. His mood was so bright that he did not notice Gaelenn wince in the darkness.

But it was not that blacksmith's strong grip on the wound at his shoulder, still fresh and painful—it was because he knew where they were being led. Tonight it glowed like a ghost on the horizon, just as it had every night in Gaelenn's youth. Sapphire Mountain.

CHAPTER NINETEEN
FRIENDSHIP AND DUTY

THE SUN COULD NOT rise fast enough. The quartet had kept up a dogged pace all through the night and had long ago lost sight of the glinting palace and its town. Rocks and cliffs surrounded them, dotted with bunches of trees and tall bushes.

"You may rest now," the cultist said as they came to a clearing just large enough for a few men to stretch out. She walked to the edge, checked the surroundings for safety, and laid down under a low-hanging branch.

"You will want sleep. No fires. We cannot be sure where our enemy's minions watch."

Gaelenn, Kell, and Rin slumped to the ground at the other end, facing each other.

"Our? She's on our team now?" Rin asked.

"So," Gaelenn said. "I guess we have some catching up to do. Or maybe I have some explaining. How long were you guys looking for me?"

"What do you mean, 'how long?' What happened to you?" Kell asked with an irritated frown.

Gaelenn stretched his leather shirt down and exposed part of the bandages on his shoulder.

"I had a run-in with our friend, Anwir," he said. "And I guess it took me a bit to come to—two, three days?"

"It's been a week!" Rin snapped with a mix of exasperation and relief. "We looked for you everywhere! Almost got caught five or six times. We had a few run-ins as well."

The three recounted their adventures—Kell and Rin had scoured the city after their scare with Yajuu, raising suspicion and growing desperate. They had been stalked for the past three nights by the shadow of a woman, who cackled down at them from the rooftops, only to vanish when they tried to pursue. Sleep was dangerous, and to be stolen only when necessary. On the final night, they had been surprised to be approached by a different shadow—a figure robed in black—and instructed to go to a certain location, where Gaelenn magically appeared.

"And you made a new friend. What's this about?" Kell asked. As much as he tried, he could not contain the excitement in his voice.

Gaelenn easily saw through the fake mask of distaste, having known Kell since before he could remember. He made a sly grin, musing, "Why so interested?"

Rin laughed.

"Interested? This one's had eyes for just about anything on two legs, never mind looking for his best friend!" He slapped Kell on the back.

"Not this again," Kell said.

"Silence!" the woman said through closed eyes. "If you must speak, you will do so quietly. These rocks guide voices far. I insist you eat and sleep."

Gaelenn shrugged. He pulled a piece of flatbread from the bag that the Eye's disciples had wrapped around his neck and ripped it up to share, and the three men ate over more stories before drifting off under a sparse canopy of leaves and rock. Late the following morning, when the sun was deep into its daily ritual, the woman poked each of them awake with a stick.

"It's time to move again," she said, and they rose and continued.

Once he walked off the stiffness of sleep in his knees, Gaelenn rushed up until he was shoulder to shoulder with her. "I'm not sure if I should be thanking you or cursing you for taking care of me back in Maynon Ohza. But why don't you tell me your name so we can at least talk to you if we need to?"

She gave him a sidelong glance through the slit in her veil.

"You may—" she began, and then she remembered her idiosyncrasy again with a blink and corrected herself: "I am Aydya."

Gaelenn nodded.

"Okay, Aydya. I'm Gaelenn, and this is Rin and Kell," he said, pointing to them in turn. Kell made an embarrassed smile under his beard.

"Now you've got to tell them where we're going."

She looked forward and contemplated the question or whether she would answer at all. Eventually she did, but only with her hand, which pointed straight ahead. In the distance, the snowy twin peaks of Sapphire Mountain, a single mountain split in two by its great blue jewel, glistened in the encroaching twilight like a million candles blowing in the wind. The travelers were just close enough to see the sparkles in its depths.

Gaelenn turned and faced his friends.

"That...letter told me that there are two places we can go," he said, avoiding Livvy's name in front of Aydya. "One was the palace at Maynon Ohza—that's out of the question—and the other is at Sapphire Mountain. Aydya's taking us there, I think. Right?"

"Yes, and we must hurry," she confirmed. "Traitor Anwir might not know where we are, but he is surely looking for you. And if he is looking for you, he will find you. It is only a matter of time."

She stared at Gaelenn before addressing the others.

"We have yet some days and nights ahead of us." The conversation ended.

Though for the most part the group rested during the daytime, the nights stretched on and on. The terrain did not help their progress, changing from rocky wastelands to dense, mountainous forests to swamps, which were treacherous to cross at night. Their only solace was the moon, which was full and bright, and Sapphire Mountain itself, which spread its hazy blue shadow for countless miles south.

"At least we have food," Rin joked one morning as they sat down to their one sparse daily meal.

But aside from a few comments here and there, there was very little chatter among them. They were too tired even to think about what waited next, and it was a waste to move lips to speak when their mouths were too busy grasping for breath.

Driven by zeal, or perhaps less burdened by heavy clothing, Aydya did not share her companions' struggles. Or, maybe, she was simply better at hiding her suffering, as fanatics often are. Many nights into their trek, they followed the mountain line up to such a height that when they passed into a clearing, the whole of the country to the south bared itself to them in a vast panorama: the entire valley was aglow with starlight and the rivers and lakes gleamed and shimmered.

"What do you think is happening there?" Gaelenn wheezed, pointing at several pocks of fire far away. They were only little points from this distance, but up close they would have been massive blazes.

"Not just there," Rin said with his finger darting from dot to dot. "But there and there. And there. The whole country is burning."

They continued on in silence. Just before daybreak on the sixth morning, the four companions sat down to another sparse meal of some sort of rodent that Rin and Gaelenn had managed to catch during the night and risked a fire to cook. Nobody complained about the stringy, tasteless meat—they smiled in thanks that it was not yet another meal of stale bread. Even Aydya accepted her portion with open hands.

Kell watched it disappear under the black cloth at her mouth and smiled, but blushed and diverted his gaze when she caught him. Gaelenn and Rin shared elbows and chuckles.

"The Captain back at Last Resort, that's your woman?" Gaelenn asked Rin. It was the first conversation in days.

"It's much more accurate to say I'm her man," Rin laughed. "Now *she* is a woman. Astrid is her name."

His eyes glazed over, unfocused, as Aydya's narrowed ever so slightly. "Miss her?"

Rin sighed. "Like the night misses the sun. But truth be told, she's also the reason I'm not at home."

"What?" Kell said. His jaw was slack and water dripped from the ends of his mustache. "What kind of nonsense is that?"

"Oh, I wouldn't expect a brute like you to understand the subtleties of love, blacksmith. When you've got a woman like that, it's not easy."

Kell rolled his eyes.

Rin chuckled, continuing, "She's just...she's amazing. She's the smartest and the bravest we have. She's almost too amazing."

His effervescence went flat.

"Because, honestly, next to her, what am I? Her funny sidekick? Some kind of errand boy?"

Gaelenn studied Rin's lost stare and nodded with him.

"So, you know, I thought I had to do something on my own. Forge my own path. Make a name for myself. Don't tell anybody else this, but ironically—it's all for her." He slapped Gaelenn's back. "And then you fell into my lap, and here we are! No place I'd rather be."

His mouth spread wide in a toothy smile; sadness and self-reflection for Rin were but passing phantoms over his face; they were gone just as soon as they had come. But Gaelenn looked deep into Rin's eyes and felt the pain that they hid, and smiled—not because he was happy but because he understood. It wasn't easy to live in someone's shadow, whether it was your best friend, your partner—or, hardest of all, he thought—your father. His eyes widened for a split second before he could hide his internal revelation.

In Rin he saw much of himself. They looked different, true—Rin's eyes were colorless, his skin translucent, and his straight black hair was so long it had to be tied behind his head—but inside they were the same kind of person. The same thing drove each man from impulse to impulse. Gaelenn loved his father but was overshadowed by him. It was the same for Rin and the Captain of Last Retreat. They had a need, deep down, somewhere, to prove that they were enough.

The knot in Gaelenn's heart that had twisted it for years seemed to loosen a bit. He understood himself better. Here, in front of him, he gazed at a man who was more him than he was. That was why he smiled: he had figured a part of himself out. He had also found a comrade in recklessness. A tear surprised him and attempted to work its way out of the corner of his eye, so he feigned exhaustion and rolled onto his back to rest.

Nobody noticed, thank the gods. And now he had two best friends.

The sun rose and began its slow ascension over the next hour, and there was little rest to be had. Sapphire Mountain loomed large overhead, towering above the group, the shadows of its spires threatening to wake up the famed orb. Aydya rose and checked the camp area as she usually did, and then paused, huffed, and unwound her headdress.

Rin nudged Kell's leg.

Waves of black hair cascaded down to the middle of her back when she pulled off the last wrapping. Gaelenn, alerted by the trance in his friends, raised his eyes. The morning sun hit at just that moment and lit up her eyes up like amber, and the three men—even Rin—basked in her beauty.

She turned around and shot sharp glances at each of them. "It has been many days since my face has tasted the sun."

"Then why is your skin so dark?" Rin asked.

Gaelenn answered for her. "She is from a place where the sun is god."

He nodded at her but received no gesture in reply.

"Not my god," she said, and looked up at the spires of the mountain. The subject was finished. "We are not far now."

"Do you know where this place is? It's a big mountain," Gaelenn said. "I hope we don't have to go all the way up to the top."

"No, we do not." Aydya shook her head. "We, the Disciples of the Eye, know where to go, though none of us has ever succeeded in getting there."

"What does that mean?" asked Rin. His smile went sour. "Don't tell me there's some dragon or something guarding it."

The woman pressed her palms flat together, brought them before her face, and closed her eyes briefly as if in prayer. Then she slid two curved blades out of her sleeves and laid them on the ground before her.

"Dragons do not exist. But some things are much, much worse."

CHAPTER TWENTY
TWISTED METAL

SIRENS—A STRANGE, ALIEN SOUND like a thousand bells ringing all at once burst out from a few hundred yards up the mountainside.

Aydya shot up to the tips of her feet and scanned the mountain up and down. "The fire, they must have seen the fire!" She swooped up her knives.

"Eefrah!" she cried—some sort of curse in her native tongue.

"What's going on?" Gaelenn and Kell said in unison.

Rin ran toward the origin of the alarm, drawing a crossbow and his long dagger. It was an odd moment for Gaelenn to notice that the white roots of his hair had started growing out.

"Silent! Fall back!" Aydya insisted in a half-yell.

The four inched backwards together, facing the mountain.

"What's happening?" Gaelenn asked again.

Aydya's eyes were wide open in terror. "Something guards our destination. I do not know what, only because none of my Order has ever survived to tell."

Her bottom lip quivered as she spoke.

"Isn't this something you should have told us before? We could have made a plan or something!" Rin said.

"There is no planning for the unknown!"

The sirens screamed for almost a minute longer and then, without warning, ceased.

Kell looked at the others. "Danger passed?"

A frozen minute passed.

BOOM

The ground in front of them burst open in a flameless explosion, showering the four companions in earth and rock. It was a warning for what was coming.

BOOM BOOM BOOM BOOM BOOM

Trees and rocks split open around them at each thunderous beat, pulverized by invisible blasts and piercing whistles. Gaelenn, Rin, and Aydya scrambled on the hill to a cover of trees, but before Kell could reach it, his path disappeared in dusty smoke. Jerking himself backwards, he spun around and found shelter on the other side, waiting until he arrived to check his legs and arms to make sure they were still intact. Somehow, he was still whole.

His three companions, their faces blackened and scratched, checked each other as well. Safe. The ground stopped exploding along with the heart-rattling thuds, but they were not about to stick their necks out now. Gaelenn waved at Kell across the hill to get his attention, pointed at himself, and motioned his head toward the direction the explosions seemed to come from. It took Kell a few seconds to understand. He nodded back.

From the side of his mouth Gaelenn said back to Rin, "I'll try to run up a ways. Maybe I can draw away some attention. When I go, check around to see what the hell is happening!"

"Don't you think we should talk about—"

"We will watch," Aydya cut Rin off.

He shrugged his shoulders and Gaelenn dashed out from their cover and up the hill. The explosions had stopped, but in their place, lines of smooth, arrow-like projectiles fired from afar and planted themselves into the ground, following him up and up the mountain. One stumble and Gaelenn would be impaled.

Kell, Aydya, and Rin used their respite—no spears or arrows landed as far back as they were—to look around. The only thing they found was that they could no longer see Gaelenn.

"Look!" Aydya shouted, pointing deliberately at something in front of Kell.

Rin followed her arm and found it.

"There!" he shouted, trying to get the blacksmith's attention. "Smithy! In front of you! It's too far from us!"

A coal-black, bent iron tube was hiding in an out-of-place overgrowth of bushes. Kell looked up from the opposite side of his tree cover and, squinting, just made out its edges thanks to a tiny line of smoke climbing from its mouth.

He pulled the hammer from his belt, swung around the trees, and with a mighty downward swing he buried the tip of the tube inches into the ground. The wrenching sound of steel echoed out, and he let loose a primal scream from his gut. His bottom teeth stretched over his mustache, bared with fury. In triumph he looked up to find Rin and Aydya, but another pipe just above them caught his eye first, and it was rotating toward them.

"Rin!" he yelled, but he did not need to point.

The Lieutenant Captain jumped and ran around the trees and Aydya closed in from the other side toward the automated menace.

"Watch out!" Aydya said to Rin, who dove to the side just as the mouth of the barrel revealed to him the fire it hid inside. A solid projectile rocketed just past Rin's ear and pushed him against the half-rock slope. His eardrum burst and erupted in blood.

Kell closed in on the weapon with his hammer high, ready to strike when the steel pipe turned and bore down on him. He looked straight into its mouth, black except for the thin stream of gray smoke, and then, deep inside, saw a small blue fire ignite. But no projectile or magic shot out of it this time; a stone the size of a skull closed it shut from above before it had a chance.

Aydya stood above it victorious, and for the first time, Kell and Rin saw her grasp for breath.

"Shit. Thanks!" Kell said.

"Where is your friend?" she asked, scanning the hill above them.

Rin stumbled onto his feet, groping the terrain with his free hand. The other hand covered his ear, which had stopped ringing and gone numb. All three looked, but there was not a single trace of Gaelenn except for the lines of arrows in the ground. They all ran up as fast as they could.

"Up here!" Gaelenn called. Kell and Rin dropped to their knees instinctively while Aydya ran up to him.

"I stopped the arrows," he said from around a corner. He popped out from behind a large boulder and held up his sword. "This thing is pretty nice. Sharp as a razor!"

Rin exhaled. "We're coming up," he said and rose to his feet with Kell.

A shudder went through the earth and knocked him back down.

"Wait, stop! Hide!" Gaelenn shouted down.

The trees were too sparse now to be suitable cover, so the three stragglers ran into a crevasse and inched their way up the hill.

Rin was the first to notice a pattern: "The canyon is funneling us up to a point. This can't be good."

"Yes. And we are almost there. I fear the final trial awaits," Aydya said.

The sound of grinding metal rebounded through the twisting channel ahead and all the way down the mountain.

"Is that just my ear still ringing?" Rin asked. "Or can you hear that, too?"

"I hear it," Kell said. "Wish I couldn't."

Aydya faced the two men with a pained but solemn face. "It is our challenge. The guardian of this sanctuary. We cannot face it alone, and we cannot allow your friend Gaelenn to, either. We must confront it together."

The noise grew louder, with great aches and squeals, as it descended the hill.

"Whatever it is, it moves pretty slowly," Rin said. He pointed his good ear at the noise to get a bead on it. "I might die of the suspense before it gets here, though, damnit. What is it? A cartful of berserkers?"

"If it were only an army of men and women, the Disciples would have penetrated this mountain long ago," Aydya said, unamused.

Gaelenn shook his head. He was fifty yards above his friends and could still hear their bickering. But the march of the mechanized cacophony ahead drowned them out.

"What the hell could this one be?" he asked himself.

BOOM

Their moment of respite vanished. The wall of stone above Gaelenn's head shattered into a shower of sharp pebbles. Exploding rock stung his skin through his clothes as the walls behind him burst into nothing. Even if he somehow avoided the direct blasts, he knew, he would be buried alive in rubble in a matter of minutes.

The only way out was the open canyon, so that is where he escaped, coming into full view of a great, horrible metal beast, as tall as two men and three times as long. It was a scaly stone monster lined with razor spikes, and where it should have had legs, it crawled over the ground like a slug, flattening everything under its enormous weight. Hollow metal barrels poked out from under armored plates and aimed themselves straight at Gaelenn.

"Eefrah!" Aydya screamed just behind Gaelenn.

He did not dare look back at his friends, who had run up to meet him.

"Stop," he commanded. "You all need to run back down. Nothing we can do against a beast like this. Go!"

"To hell with that," Kell said, launching his hammer. It pounded through the air with a rhythmic whoosh and struck true on one of the monster's dozens of eyes and shattered it like glass. It *was* glass. The beast roared and crawled down toward the party.

"Nice throw—but I don't think the rest of our weapons are going to do much," Gaelenn said.

Rin stepped next to him. "Well, we're not going to punch and kick it to death. But we *are* going to try!"

He fired his crossbow, but it did nothing except knock off a little black rust. "Damn. If it didn't have all those thorns we might have been able to crawl up on top of it!"

Gaelenn shouted again, desperate to keep his comrades from further harm. "Run! We can't beat this thing!"

"We must!" Aydya cried back.

The monster lurched closer and closer and its symphony of iron grew so loud that they could no longer hear each other speak. When it passed out of the shadow of the mountain and into the blue glare of the gem in the mountain, it grew even more intimidating and spectacular. It was only a few yards away now and poised to strike.

Gaelenn held his sword in front of him and walked up to meet it. When he stepped into the unnatural light, his gray eye seemed to disappear, but his other eye sparkled in a fiery golden-green. All four of them dug in their heels, covered their eyes, and prepared their last assault.

The beast stopped dead in its tracks and went silent.

"What...?" Kell cried, weaponless, fists poised to strike, and looked around.

"Hey! Down there!" A shout came down to them from above, past the iron beast.

"Did you hear that?" Rin asked.

"Come on up! It won't bite," the voice said again. "Not anymore!"

"There!" Kell said. He motioned his bearded chin toward the distant figure of a man waving one hand from a door in the side of the mountain.

"We have passed the challenge." Aydya cupped her hands and prayed.

They stood for a few moments in disbelief before Gaelenn shrugged and looked at the others. "Well, that was a lot easier than I thought. Better be careful."

They walked up, taking care to give the dormant monster an arm's length of space. Just in case, Kell gave it a kick before prying his hammer free and joining his companions.

CHAPTER TWENTY ONE
A COUNCIL OF WAR

LIVVY PUSHED HER PLATE away from her, the food only half eaten. Her pursed lips were enough to convey her disappointment in herself for not finishing it; she had been through enough lean times to know how important it was to appreciate every morsel. Her mind was just too busy for her stomach to be hungry, a rarity for her.

"There's got to be a pattern somewhere," she said. "It's the Eye's nature. Maybe subtler this time, but it's there. It has to be."

A huff broke her thoughts as she circled back. "But it's just too soon. It's never happened at this stage before. Here, take another look."

She lit up her table with her fingertips and summoned a map.

"You've read your history, Astrid. What do you see?" Livvy never liked to dine alone, and today for breakfast she had invited the Captain of her Guard.

Astrid's strong nose hung over the screen, lined in the green of the land below. She tried to find whatever pattern the priestess was referring to, but it was not there for her to see.

"I'm sorry, Lady, I'm not sure what you mean."

"Here. Do you see how this one place," she said, pointing to Maynon Ohza, "remains untouched while everywhere else is wiped out?"

Her hand darted around the map to a number of gray spots. "Actually, Maynon Ohza is growing."

"I...see," Astrid said. She struggled to hide the distraction weighing on her brow. Rin had been gone too long, and she had to push herself to concentrate. She had gone to great pains this morning, as she did every morning, to present herself flawlessly. It was part of her duty to provide an example.

Livvy noticed the cracks in the seams of Astrid's psyche and kept close watch, but pressed on with her examination.

"Here," she said again, and touched the screen this time with two hands. The image stretched and grew under her touch—and then began *moving*, as if time was passing, the towns blipping out one by one.

Astrid gasped, having never lost the sense of awe of the priestess' magic.

"Look at these towns. Wiped out. Gone," she continued. "Almost every center of population—Haukney, Newmast, Mishim, Susano, little Key Rock—all of them stamped out. It's the same across the sea, too. Well, as far as my eyes in the sky can see."

Astrid strained her eyes, nodded, and said at length, "I'm sorry...honestly, I see no pattern."

With a whip of her hands, Livvy pushed the map through the table so far that the whole continent was visible. The long, thin landmass looked as if ash had rained on it, gray dots pocking its surface in all directions. The islands around and even the wasteland country to the east, where the only places suitable for living were right on the coast, were the same. The Captain watched and waited.

"This isn't the first time this has happened, as you know, Astrid. The whole world used to be habitable. People lived all around it. It's much bigger than it appears now." Her arms crossed and she tapped her fingers on her skin as she talked, hoping the oral lesson might stoke her own memory or imagination.

"Now, there is nothing beyond the borders of this map you see here. We've been herded in close by a cruel shepherd. I'm afraid he intends to slaughter his flock."

Astrid choked down the last of her food for politeness and clasped her hands together in the traditional gesture of thanks in Last Retreat. She, too, had no appetite this morning. Nerves always did it to her.

"I was taught many of these things during my education," she said. "But it has always been difficult to really grasp."

A kind smile crossed Livvy's lips. "Of course you can't understand. I'm sorry. It must be impossible to really grasp it. Let's try together, shall we? It will help me explain things more plainly. Well—the last time this kind of thing happened, it was quicker. Of course, this was…a few thousand years ago now. After which we came up here with your ancestors and established our new home. You know, this whole structure used to be a holiday resort for the rich?"

She almost laughed.

Astrid's nostrils twitched. She could say nothing. The Priestess had never been so frank and up front with her—or anybody.

Livvy caught herself from drifting with a brief shake of her head. "At the end of that particular age, the '*climax*' took a while after symptoms appeared before it really happened. Months and years—but it came. The time before that it was even longer, and so on. The first time, we barely even knew what was happening, it took so long to reveal itself."

She cleared her throat and found her train of thought before memories could overcome her.

"So we assumed it would be quicker still this time, based on that pattern. There's *always* a pattern. And all the usual symptoms are here. As far as I can see with this mess, though," she said, her hands spread wide above the glowing canvas. "This time there is no clear picture. No countdown. No pattern. And it's all happening too quickly."

She bunched her lips together just under her nose until they touched. "The Eye has definitely learned something new."

Astrid almost laughed despite herself; as old as the Priestess claimed to be, she had never let go of some childish tendencies. No matter what she did, she did it gracefully, almost cute. Next to her, the Captain felt like a brute. She bent down more deeply to look at the map to hide her embarrassment from showing in her cheeks.

"So," Livvy continued. "That's what I need your eyes to see. Fresh eyes. Military eyes, maybe. I need to see the pattern. Focus on the cadence, the intervals between these events. That way we might have a clue about how much time we have before...well, whatever it is starts. We need to know when it's too dangerous to stay here any longer."

"Stay here...? I see. I will try," Astrid said, ignoring her surprise to focus on the task.

Livvy spoke again, clarifying, "Look here—people have been funneled from abroad into our country. What my sky eyes can't see, our scouts have confirmed; the ports and islands and the entire seaboard of the eastern continent are being abandoned—or have been abandoned already. Every human being from every settlement we know of is being herded here to our continent, Sintarria. And once they get here it's more of the same. Every town, every village, every farm or dwelling or hut, no matter how small or remote, is trampled to dust. And every person who is not killed has nowhere to run. Except to Maynon Ohza."

Her eyes hardened. "So, we can assume two things: first, that Maynon Ohza is where our enemy has concentrated its essence. And we know that the new ENs—three of them, the Triumvirate—control things there and carry out the Eye's commands. Second, that the Eye knows we are close by, and its systematic elimination of all dwellings is meant to root us out."

A breath escaped from her lips along with her thoughts: "What a coincidence that we've been this close to each other all this time..."

Astrid looked at the priestess eye-to-eye. "So, you know where *it* is. *It* doesn't yet know where we are. And you know we can fight. Aren't we at an advantage?"

"No. No, we're not." Livvy was cold and honest. "We have a few thousand who can fight. The Triumvirate and their legions will have conscripted every able-bodied refugee into their army. And even if that were not so..."

Her eyes drifted past the guard captain, lost in horrible thought. "I fear that it might only take those three ENs, even without their armies, to kill us all and end everything we fight for. That might be an exaggeration, but not by much. And without our key—Gaelenn—under our protection, or at least somewhere we knew he was safe, we cannot make the first move."

"What can we do? What else are we waiting for?"

"Our only true advantage, as you said, is that the Eye does not know we are here. We think. Our..."

She paused to consider her words before continuing, "Er, the 'magic' we use to cloud its vision is and always has been a temporary solution, at best. Miraculously, it has lasted all this time. But just like the machine that snapped our line of keyholders—and triggered Gaelenn's father's exodus after it broke—it cannot last forever."

Her eyes seemed to pierce the wall in front of her, focusing toward the room behind the elaborate door upstairs.

"The Eye doesn't have the imagination, luckily, to think that we still have the ability to deceive it. We have spent countless resources purposefully perpetrating that lie. But our camouflage will only hold it at bay for so long.

Eventually, after it destroys every city, town, and village, it's going to start turning over all the stones. And we're on top of a pretty big stone."

"It couldn't possibly reach us up here! Not in force. We are well-protected." Astrid sat up straight, propped up on her pride.

Livvy bowed her head and closed her eyes; terrible memories flooded in. "No. There is nothing that the Eye is not capable of. We have underestimated it to humanity's cost before. I have. And I will never do it again. Right now, the only advantage we might have is if we can learn *when* it plans to strike before it does and defend accordingly. Or run and bide our time. So...we simply must know—we'll need all the power of our spies down on the ground. And we must work under the assumption that once it finds out we are up here it will come for us immediately. It is looking for me—for us."

She grimaced at the word '*me*,' knowing that her existence threatened the lives of the people she had loved and cared for over generations, and continued, "It knows we are here somewhere, and with three new ENs it will find out sooner or later. We need those three covered at all times, at any cost."

"I will assign our finest agents," Astrid said, and frowned. "I'm sorry, Lady, to speak out of turn...but one thing sticks in my mind. The enemy is using its army to wipe out the country. And willing and unwilling survivors are added to its ranks. I understand that."

She had forgotten her filter of decorum, and thoughts and questions were leaving her mouth before they checked with her brain first.

"That's right," Livvy said.

"So, their army is growing ever larger while resistance is waning."

"Yes."

"When it's conquered all of the continent and it comes for us, won't we be fighting against our own people? Or the people we are fighting to keep free?"

Livvy looked into Astrid's pleading eyes and studied them, but said nothing.

"And then, say they win. We lose. They'll have an army and no enemy. What will happen then?"

"I don't know. But it scares me, too. I don't know if I can answer your questions directly because...I just don't know. But I can tell you what's happened in the past."

The Captain gave a hesitant nod.

"The Eye...is pure hate. Time means nothing to it—it can wait, patiently, until civilization inevitably grows back to a certain point before it strikes. It has before, more than once. Every single time humanity stands back up to control the planet, the Eye poisons the well, so to speak, and subverts it."

"Poisons the well?" Astrid asked, confusion wrinkling the space between her eyes.

Livvy rubbed her temples. "It destroys us from within and without and sends humanity back to the caves. And every time, we come back weaker. Rebuild slower. After me, there will be nobody alive left to know the Eye even exists. There may be no coming back, no fighting back without knowledge of what's happened in the past. We will be completely under its control—if it even *allows* us to survive."

Astrid paused to think, her gaze lingering on the map below her. "But how could it wipe us out, just like that...?"

Livvy just shook her head. "In the past? There were a lot more people in the world, and its plans were more insidious, less direct. But it played its hand masterfully. Now? With the ENs at its command and the entire world population on one small island, all it needs to do is snap its fingers."

"You also said that if we lose you, we've lost the war?" the captain asked with a slight crack in her voice.

"Well—that's why we have Gaelenn and his lineage. I wasn't supposed to live this long. I was only supposed to keep our past from being erased. To keep the hope of humanity alive. There used to be a hundred of us. Now, there are two, and I'm the only one who hasn't given up. Of course, we have tried, many times, in fact, to bring the truth to the masses. But I've found that most of them are not capable of understanding. We can't seem to progress civilization far enough to be able to understand before it's subverted. Because what I have to say about the truth of the past scares them. The enemy indoctrinates them well. I and those like me have been labeled as false prophets or witches. Been hunted. And the longer time goes on, the further truth becomes legend, and legend passes into myth, until it's forgotten completely. Like it is now."

Astrid had held her breath over Livvy's entire speech, but suddenly blurted out, "Witch? Never!"

"Thank you. But this is a true story. Very true."

Astrid spread her hands on the table and pressed them so hard that they turned white. "But...!"

"I know! I know. But Astrid, you and your people have been educated from birth. What I tell you about the world is acceptable to you because you were born into the truth. Others live in a harsher world. They can't understand my message, let alone accept it."

"Barbarians..."

"Yes, some of them. If we must—if it means that humanity and our history will survive—we will defend ourselves here against the Eye and its army. Some will die. I wish it didn't have to happen that way. But the army of Maynon Ohza isn't about to lie down when we tell them they're fighting on the wrong side. And we aren't going to lie down and die, either."

The gaze of the Priestess drifted off, glazed over with tears that she forced back. "But at the same time, we must pity those people. We have to understand their sacrifice, even if they don't themselves. Because it's not their fault. It's the Eye's. Your people here at Last Retreat are the descendants of believers. The only believers who survived the last conflict. We have lived up here, together, where you have upheld your old customs for these thousands of years."

Livvy could barely contain a slight laugh, even though her eyes were still wet. "When we first got here, your ancestors had jet black hair! And look at you all today. You lost the color but keep putting it back in!"

The Captain blushed and crossed her arms.

"I'm sorry, I don't mean to tease. Everything seems just like yesterday to me."

They sat in silence for a few minutes and stared at the map of their dying world while Livvy dried her eyes. The gray craters mocked them. The pattern eluded them.

"Priestess," Astrid said at length. "This map. Can you...show me...the changes?"

Words came out of her in bursts as her mouth tried to catch up with her mind.

"I'd like to see the *movement*. With your...magic." Her hands waved around in stiff imitation.

"You know it's not true magic, Astrid." Livvy said. "But let me see."

She tapped and waved her hands around the table's surface. In a few seconds, the map blipped back to when the cities were still alive, and then she set it in motion with the flick of her finger. The living, green continent writhed like a living thing; it was a heart that beat with each season. But it was dying. The death and destruction were the only things that Livvy could see, and she wept. She grew so despondent that she almost didn't hear Astrid's growing excitement.

"Priestess, Priestess!" the Captain said again.

Livvy snapped to and watched Astrid's arms spread wide, making circle after circle in the air with her fingers, each one smaller than the last, until they reached a point. Then she started again with a slightly-less-wide circle and came to a point, and over and over again.

"Do you see it? It's like a rhythm. The changes begin on the outer-reaches, past the seas, and then come toward a point. And then it starts back at the edge again, a little further in, and moves inward. Again and again, and each time it starts closer to the center. I'm sure I see it."

Livvy tilted her head to see the whole map from different angles. "Hmm."

She moved her chair in closer to the table, stood up on it, and bent over so her face was directly above, just far enough away so she could touch it. The map reset and cycled through from the beginning. Land morphed from green to red to white to brown, over and over and over. The gray dots multiplied. There it was. The pattern.

The country was being swept like a dusty floor. Each time a wave reached Maynon Ohza, another started at the edge of the map and squeezed more life out of the land. The first wave was the largest cities. The next, towns. And then villages and farms and houses, all the way down to the tiniest little dots that must have been nothing more than shacks. It was wringing the life out of the world and putting the leftovers in one, single place. And now it was almost back to Maynon Ohza again.

"You did it! There's the pattern. I knew I was missing something." She stepped off the chair but kept her eyes on the table.

"It is subtle and slow, but unmistakable," Astrid said. "Can you tell the time frequency?"

"Yes. So the Eye does have limits to its creativity, after all. And," Livvy said, stopping the motion of the map at its most recent point, "we have the countdown. Now."

"Lady?"

"That tricky bastard," Livvy cursed. "Yes, a countdown. And time is almost up."

Astrid, having never heard the priestess swear before, blushed again and looked away. "Based on the...past, how long do you think we have?"

"Let me have my machine analyze that. But just eyeballing it, I'd say it's imminent," Livvy said. Her voice trailed off, speaking to herself out loud in deep thought, and her neck craned backwards. She traced the little dancing cherubs and angels painted on the ceiling. They were always there to distract the mind when it was too painful to think.

"It could be any time...any day...any hour."

She snapped her head back straight. "My god, what am I doing? There's no time to sit here and ponder. There are no more cities to sweep—our time is up! Astrid! Go find your boyfriend and Gaelenn. I don't care if you have to paralyze them from the neck down—bring them back here as fast as you can! We can't afford to have them trotting around the continent when it's about to fall apart. If they're in the wrong place at the wrong time... We need Gaelenn where we can protect him. We can worry about the morality of it later. And we need Rin and every able-bodied soldier we can muster because if we don't get ready to leave in time, we'd better be ready to fight!"

The Captain sprang up to her feet to take the order.

"I will do it," she said with a solemn salute. "I swear."

"Good. Then we'll plan either our defense when you get back or our escape. Hurry! Take only your fastest and bravest."

Astrid bowed.

"I understand," she said as she turned to leave. She looked back. "Actually, may I ask something, Lady? The thought has bothered me for days."

"Of course."

"What is it about Gaelenn that we need so badly?"

Livvy did not hesitate and did not translate. "His iris displays his decoded genome, which is the password for our database archive. And only half of it can be unlocked unless we can find or make another optic translator."

Astrid squinted, blinded by incomprehension rather than light.

"We need him, his eye, and his blood," Livvy explained. "Oh, and Astrid—"

The lilt in her voice returned. "One more thing before you go. I'm only joking about the 'paralyze them' thing. Just bring Gaelenn and Rin back. Start at Sapphire Mountain. Go as fast as you possibly can."

CHAPTER TWENTY TWO
The Hermit

Gaelenn and Rin were the first to walk up to the door. Kell followed, hammer in hand, and Aydya tagged along a yard or two behind. She was the only thing on the mountain that was not bathed in blue; her black robes absorbed and negated the light from the massive translucent sapphire stone, and it made her stick out even more than usual.

Her discomfort gnarled her mouth into a straight, pensive line. Or maybe it was the man ahead of them. He stood next to a human-sized hole in the side of the mountain, crossing his arms, waiting patiently. His body was well-hidden in drab, loose-fitting rags strewn about randomly that belied the wisdom of his dark brown face and almost golden eyes. A blowing wisp of short, silver hair sat atop his head like a small crown. From under a severe brow he pierced each traveler with his gaze as they approached, but he did not speak until they were within a whisper's reach.

"Ricar's son," he said in a smooth, low voice. "I thought so."

Gaelenn's three companions glanced at him and he gave confused looks back. "Who are you?" he asked.

"I'm Dean." Satisfied that the four were no threat, his arms fell free, revealing a small obsidian box in one hand.

Some kind of magic for controlling other things, perhaps, Gaelenn noted.

Dean waved them gently into the door. "Well, come on in."

"You first," Gaelenn said. He and his friends were still on edge, and looked it. They were running on pure adrenaline.

The old man acquiesced with a shrug of his shoulders and disappeared within. Kell went in, and then Aydya, and finally Rin and Gaelenn.

"Not a lot of words, this guy," Rin remarked before he passed into the side of the mountain.

They followed Dean through several small rooms and corridors that bent at hard angles, punctuated at each end by portal-like doors that forced them to bend down slightly to cross. From the ceiling hung a smattering of orbs not unlike the lights at Last Retreat, but cruder and yellow. There were several hallways, a makeshift bedroom, a sort of larder or kitchen, a workshop full of scraps of iron and trinkets, and, at the very end, another perfectly circular room with that now-familiar table in the center.

The man walked right up to it and invited the others to follow with an open hand. "Welcome to my research facility."

The four of them looked back at him expectantly.

"Seen one of these before, then?" he asked. His accent was slight and hard to place for Gaelenn—much like Livvy's, his voice carried the weight of years that his face did not.

"What's a 'felicity?'" Kell muttered.

Dean cocked his head back. He had heard the question a thousand times. "'Fa-ci-li-ty.' It's what these places used to be called before they became 'temples' to everybody. So, let's see. Ricar's son. That's easy, nobody else I know of with only one green eye."

He closed one of his eyes and then the other, as if he was making sure one of them wasn't tricking him. "A local boy, maybe an old friend, a tinkerer or smith of some sort."

"Boy?" Kell said, but his protest fell lame.

"Ooh, a *Disciple*," the older man continued, plastering a thick layer of fake enthusiasm on the last word, but only with his voice. His face remained as dry as it had been since they first saw him. "Interesting. This may be the first time that one of you has ever seen the inside of this place. Usually you only get to see the sole of my boot."

He smirked with satisfaction and leaned against the table.

Aydya leered at him.

"And, last but not least, a guard from Last Retreat. Wow. What a gang," he said and then added, "Tell me, how is the 'priestess' doing these days?"

Rin flinched. "How do you—"

"...Know all this stuff?" Dean finished the thought.

"First you tell me what I don't know: what you're doing here. Then we'll do this," he said, wagging his finger between his chest and his visitors.

Gaelenn would not wait. "How do you know my father? When did you last see him?"

Dean's palms floated up in a sign of peace.

"Hey, let's slow down. But I'll play; it was years ago. We used to be good friends," he said.

Gaelenn's fists unclenched.

"I was there when that happened to your eye. Your parents hadn't even decided on a name yet, you were so little." A warm smile finally passed the old man's lips, which were somehow older than the rest of his face. "But that doesn't tell me why you're here, or how you found me."

"We didn't come to find you. We came for that," Aydya spoke out, pointing at the apparatus hanging from above and the machine below it.

Gaelenn stayed silent. He alone knew the content of the Priestess' letter.

The hermit used his hip to bounce away from the table. "Oh, I know *you* would love to use this. But what *I* need to know is how you convinced this group to come with you."

"I'd like to know, too," Rin said. He walked around, tracing the edge of the room with his hands and examining the walls.

Kell puffed out his chest and crossed his arms to make himself look more intimidating. The 'boy' comment had wounded him, but he added little more than a few grunts and growls to the conversation.

"It wasn't just her," Gaelenn said, tilting his head to Aydya. "The Priestess told me a friend might be here. Somebody who could help. I guess that's you. I don't know where else to go. My father's long gone. My home, my mother—this whole country's being destroyed. I'm going to do whatever I can to stop it."

"You forgot to mention you have an insane butcher after you," Rin added.

The old man's hand reached up and held Gaelenn's shoulder.

"I'm sorry to hear about your mother," he said. "She was a good woman. Made a lot of sacrifices for the greater good. But no—nobody's going to be using this facility. Tell you what, you all look like you could use some rest and some food. We can chat more after that."

He led them back through the hallways to the kitchen area and sat them at a square, wooden table, then served them some dried meat and nuts from large wooden bowls and air-tight jars while making random comments that they barely noted. "This place has been here since the beginning. I've seen what's been happening down in the valley. There's nothing more that can be done. I'm sorry."

When they had eaten their fill, the four laid their heads on the tabletop one by one and slept. And Dean kept on talking.

CHAPTER TWENTY THREE
THE LABORATORY

A FEW HOURS PASSED before Gaelenn woke up. Not that he could tell what time of day it was; there were no windows anywhere. Rin and Kell were sleeping exactly where they had fallen, and Aydya was nowhere in the room.

"She's in her 'temple,'" Dean said from behind, noting the alarm on Gaelenn's face. "Trying to do whatever those dirty freaks do there. Nothing she'll be able to break, though—the station is locked and will remain locked. Thank God. Thank *me*."

Gaelenn rubbed his eyes. "Locked? What do you mean?" he asked and swiveled around on his thigh until they were face-to-face.

Dean, sitting on a stool by the wall, leaned forward and rested his elbows on his knees. He peered straight through Gaelenn. "How much did your dad teach you?"

"Reading, writing...," Gaelenn said. "He wasn't around much. Who are you?"

The old man seemed to contemplate the question before giving another heavy nod.

"I didn't think so," he said, and followed it with a dark sigh. "We'll get to who I am later. So, you don't know what happened to you? Your iris?"

"Sort of. Livvy—the Priestess—uh, the leader of Last Retreat, said that something broke before they could finish what they started."

"Not 'priestess.' Still going by 'Livvy,' I see. And that's right," he said. "I was there, too. Actually, I was the one performing the operation."

His words came out slow and heavy. "That's when everything changed. The beginning of the end. Now we're right in the middle of the end, I guess. It's only a matter of time."

"I don't—what do you mean, 'the end?'" Gaelenn asked. "End of what?"

"Of us. Our fight. And with it, humanity." Dean's dejection was so profound that he seemed to sit in a halo of darkness and the room's light did not reach him. "I'd fixed that machine a thousand times before. Always came back. Not this time. The laser had degraded so badly that the machine wouldn't even recognize it..."

"What?" Gaelenn asked. His eyebrows weaved up and down in a zigzag.

"Oh," Dean said, resetting his expression. "Whoops. Forget it. Anyway, after that happened, I left Last Retreat to look for another working facility or material I could use. Your father came along with me for a time, too. We didn't find anything."

"What's wrong with this place? The one you have here?" Gaelenn asked.

"Well, for one, it's not the right kind. It's just for data storage—keeping records."

"It looks the same as the three others I've been to."

"These places all look the same," Dean said. "Number two, like I told you, it's locked. With your father gone, the only human alive with the key is you. Though even if he was here, who knows if he'd be helping us or fighting us..."

Dean curled his bottom lip inward at the jolt in Gaelenn's spine. A careless remark from unpracticed conversation. "I'm sorry, boy, but I'm sure you know. He's gone."

Gaelenn looked at the floor. "I know. I chased his ghost for seven years. I've accepted it."

Dean let the moment work out its tension before starting again.

"So, what I mean is there's only one key left, and no backups," he said, pointing straight at Gaelenn's green eye.

"It worked just fine in that rotten mound outside of Last Retreat," Rin said through a yawn. "After that freak who's after you was done with it."

Gaelenn started and bent his neck around. "When did you guys wake up?"

Dean refused to let the topic change and sat up, demanding, "How did what work? What freak? What happened?

His eyes bored so hard into Gaelenn they looked like they would come out of their sockets and hit him.

"Well, I don't know much," Gaelenn said, shrugging his shoulders and shaking his head. "I just looked at one of those altars, just like that one you have in there, in the woods between Last Retreat and Key Rock. A voice spoke out to me. And there was somebody there before us with my mother's amulet. He may be after me."

"Most definitely is," Rin said.

"Fine. Anyway, we saw some lights, and some...magic inside the table showed us the strangest images. Nothing we could understand. That's all."

Dean's eyes moved around in their sockets like he was dreaming with his eyelids pulled open, retracing years. They stopped on Gaelenn for a split second. He collected what he could of the saliva in his dry mouth and swallowed, but the butter in his usual voice came out like gravel. "Damn. Damn."

"Damn what?"

"Nothing." The old man sighed. "Never mind. Well, the place you went to was just a remote backup anyway. There are a few of those around what's left of the world. We built things to last way back when. It was an obsession for some. That's why some of these machines still exist. Sometimes I can't decide if it was providence or the work of the Devil."

He trailed off again.

"I still have no idea what's going on," Gaelenn said.

Dean snapped to and attempted a clearer explanation. "The machines. Some of them still exist. But getting them to work is a different story. That one I have here still works. Fine. Too bad it's the wrong type. Next I want you to tell me about this person who's after you and tried to use that facility."

"Wait—wrong type?"

"That's right. Like I just said, it's just a little backup of what we already have at Last Retreat. After what happened to you, we spent all our time looking for an operational facility to fix your eyes. Man, all of that anguish and uncertainty...that's when your dad got his crazy ideas, and when he met..."

"Met who? What ideas?" Gaelenn asked, suddenly fuming. He stretched his patience to its limits, took a deep breath, and regained control over himself. "Forget it. I don't want to know."

"That's right. Good. It doesn't matter anymore. We can chat about it later if you want. Now, the facility in *this* place, on the other hand..." Dean's eyes clamped shut, and he sucked in the dry bunker air through whistling lips.

"This place what?" Kell asked. He ran his fingers into his beard, engrossed but oblivious.

"This place is *live*."

Rin jumped to his feet and dusted off his bottom. "Alive? What does that mean?"

"You all could wait until I'm done explaining, right? Leave the dumb questions to me," Dean deadpanned. The thin mustache over his upper lip bent to the side of his face. He held one elbow inside the other, stretched across his thin frame, and cradled his chin in the circle of his finger and thumb.

"This is a Level 1 facility. Which means it's fully online. It's a complete archive. It's got all the goodies that we're missing at Last Retreat—except for the way to fix your other eye there, of course. Trouble is, being live, the minute we fire it up, the Eye's onto us. Ka-boom."

"What—" Gaelenn said, but caught himself before finishing his newest dumb question.

"I'm sure you heard of the Eye from your priestess. Yeah? Anything that's online, except for the stuff we have protected at Last Retreat, is the Eye's domain. It means anytime, anywhere you open it up, you open up a portal right to the sucker. And that thing is bad news."

He snapped his fingers hard and the click echoed through the bunker's chambers. "Okay, I'm open to dumb questions now."

"How would anybody know?" Gaelenn asked. "What would doing one thing here have anything to do with what happens somewhere else?"

Rin stood up. "You've seen the magic on those things. You shouldn't doubt what else they can do," he said.

"Your pale friend is right," Dean said, "except it wasn't called magic when I was young."

"When was that?" Kell asked.

"When I worked with your priestess' parents."

Rin slammed his fist down on the table without thinking. "With her parents? I don't believe that for a second! Don't you know how old she is?"

"I sure do. And it's true," the old man explained. "We all worked together, ages and ages ago. We spent a lot of time together, she and I—and others."

A cryptic tone twisted his words.

"I never heard or read about you or any others, and I've studied history. *Real* history," Rin said. "The Priestess is the only one gifted with eternal life."

"Eternal life?" Kell said, choking on his own breath.

Gaelenn nodded at him.

Dean's face broke into a half-smile. It was not from happiness—it was the smile of a grownup amused by the naivety of a child. From under his rags, he pulled the small black stone he had held when they first met him and touched it just like Livvy always did with her own magic table.

"You guys were this close to being blown the hell up by this thing when you were walking up that hill. Bringing that cultist with you. Shake my damn head," he said under his breath as he swiped.

When he found what he was looking for he held out the object to the three younger men, who huddled around it. By now it seemed natural to Gaelenn that the tiny obelisk would show an image with such intense detail, but just a few weeks ago that it would have felt that they were staring into another dimension.

In a way, they were: it was a picture of Livvy, exactly as they had last seen her. Except for her beaming smile. Less weight pressed on her shoulders. A man stood behind her, tall and old and gray, holding her with one arm. To the side was a woman, standing proud, with brown hair tied up tightly behind her head. And to the other side was a copy of the very man in front of them. Dean's wide smile in the magic stone was the only difference between that version and the one with them now. He was actually happy back then.

"What the...?" Kell said in a drawn-out gasp.

"You didn't get to see these things up at Last Resort?" Gaelenn asked.

Banging from somewhere in the adjacent rooms shook the walls.

"What in hell is that noise...?" Dean sighed. "Before I go educate your lady friend as to the correct use of this facility with the back of my hand, tell me why you brought her?"

Gaelenn shrugged. "It was the only way her group would let me go—if I brought her here and let her talk to the Eye. I was rescued by them...or imprisoned, I'm not sure."

"Well *that* won't happen." Dean said with another sigh and stood up. "Let's go see what she's up to. That sound's coming from the main room."

He bounded out of sight while the three younger men struggled to keep up—Dean was sprightly for an old man. They found Aydya tapping the mid-room table in random places with a wooden hammer she had taken from Dean's workshop.

"It's not on."

Dean's dry voice caught her by surprise and she nearly dropped it. "And you couldn't use it if you wanted to, anyway."

"I know how to commune with the great Eye," she replied with snake-like eyes. "I have to warn it."

Dean raised an eyebrow, unconvinced and unmoved. "You Disciples don't know what you're dealing with. It's the same every damn time."

He shook his head. "Human nature, maybe, to worship your oppressor."

"Oppressor?" She spat venom. "The Eye is our liberator! The rule of corrupt men will soon come to an end. You will make this portal move."

"I will not," Dean replied, almost amused.

The black-clad woman turned to Gaelenn, her eyes swelling with unshed, frustrated tears. "You have sworn to us to open the portal!"

"It was either that or stay in her dungeon," he said, turning to Dean. "But I did promise to try to unlock the thing. I kind of owe them one for saving me."

"Saving you from what?" Dean asked.

"Ah," Rin answered for his friend. "That lunatic who's after him."

"What lunatic?" Alarm bells rang in the old man's head and drew his eyelids high. He answered himself before the others, who were alarmed themselves at his racing tone, had a chance to answer. "Someone who seems to have magic powers? Inhuman strength?"

Gaelenn collected the thoughts from his companions who stood with slack jaws. "Right. One is after me, I think."

"ENs...great. One...?"

"Of three that we know. At least one is after me."

"Three, then. They don't come in singles. We wouldn't be so lucky, would we?"

Dean bowed his head until it almost touched his chest. "I'd almost say if it's only three of them we're lucky. In the past it was always more. But even one is enough to push us to the brink. Listen—this isn't the first time we've faced this."

Gaelenn crossed his arms. "You know about those things? Livvy said something about them to me, too. But she only told me to keep away."

Dean chuffed.

"Now that is some sage advice. These things aren't your normal, every-day humans. They are created and controlled by our enemy. Your 'Great Eye,'" he said, pointing at Aydya, "to do its bidding."

"This I know," she replied.

He turned to Gaelenn and continued. "If this thing is after you, I'd say it means it's discovered who you are, and that means that the Eye knows, too."

"The Great Eye is no enemy!" Aydya protested. "The enemy is the traitor Anwir! He plots against the Eye."

"Say that again?" Dean's ears stretched backwards. "*Against* the Eye?"

"Anwir works in secret, in the shadows where the Great Eye cannot see, to overthrow him. Only we, the Eye's Disciples, know of his treachery. We have ears in the palace. This is why we must activate this portal. To warn him."

Dean stewed, tapping his foot. With his thumb and finger he traced his peppered mustache from its center to its ends, over and over, pondering Aydya's words.

"Well, this is a new one. Hm," he said.

"New one? What does that mean?" Gaelenn asked.

Kell grunted in agreement.

Rin answered for Dean. "This isn't the first end-of-the-world. And this race of super-humans has been around for a while. At least that's what our old texts taught us."

"That's right. But this...this might be the real deal," Dean said. "The actual end. Our line of keys is broken since we can't decode them even if you start having kids."

He pointed to Gaelenn. "There's only one remaining hideout in the entire habitable world. Up on that death trap of a mountain, Last Retreat—sure is ironic that you can't retreat from it. And worse, we have no weapons to fight back with against three ENs. There's not a person alive who could take on one of them. I mean, that's why we made them in the first place."

Gaelenn staggered. "Stop. I don't understand anything. Here's the dumbest question of all: what's the difference between your facility here and the one at Last Retreat? I know they're 'separate,' whatever that means."

The old man pondered the question, leaning his body against the center table, his eyes on the blank ceiling. "Well, the ones we control have history from our perspective. The records that we need to prevent something like the Eye from just popping up again. That's if we're able to stop it and get to a point of civilization where we can prevent it. You see, we've won four times against it. But really, we've lost. Because that thing is a cancer. You kill it, and it just comes right back. Give or take a thousand years or two. From what I see, we won't even get the moral victory this time."

He pressed his palms against the table's cold surface until he was resting his whole body on it; reliving the last 20,000 years took its toll on him, too.

Gaelenn's eyes went bright, the beginning of an idea working its way into his brain. "What about the live facilities like this one? The ones the Eye could...infect? They hold our history. And I suppose they hold history from its perspective, too, right? That's gotta be dark."

Silence in the room held for a full minute, the implications reverberating between those present. He continued.

"So if the Eye controls this one and has its own history inside—the things it doesn't want people like us to know—does that mean it has its own secrets there? Like, knowledge about itself? Could we use that against it somehow?"

A spark exploded in Dean's old eyes. "Use it against itself...use it against itself... My boy, that's an idea."

"It is?"

"I would never have thought of it in a million years. Oh, Elizabeth is going to kill me for not thinking about it. Or maybe kill you for actually coming up with it, I'm not sure which."

"Elizabeth...?" Gaelenn looked at him sideways.

"Maybe it is time to turn this thing on after all and see what happens. Sew a little chaos. I'm not even sure if it really works, to be honest. Haven't run a full test in centuries," Dean said, half-closing one eye at Aydya. "You might get your wish after all."

Her chest swelled up with air and importance.

"Now, Gaelenn," Dean said. "It won't be easy. Or comfortable."

"I'll do it," he replied. Thoughts of Livvy filled his head and lit fire to his zeal.

"Yeah, I can see that you're eager to do just about whatever I say. But your friends can't help you." He said, nodding at Kell and Rin, who looked gave each other suspicious looks.

Gaelenn set his jaw. "I'm not dumb. Or weak."

"I know you're not. But this is different. As soon as the Eye feels that you're connected, it'll have free access to you. You'll see what it thinks, and it'll see what you think."

"I have nothing to hide from it."

Dean shook his head. "Not that you know of, consciously, no. You'd be surprised. One other thing: it's not going to be easy to find what you're looking for. You're going to have to go down some dark tunnels, I'd guess. What you want to know is what the Eye is planning *now*. That's what we want to know—that's what we're missing. Stay away from anything else you find. Believe me."

"I'm going to tell you what I told the Priestess," Gaelenn said without expression. "I'll do it. I'll do whatever I have to—I can't sit around and do nothing. I can't. I'll try to find out what I can."

"After you open this, you'll see things her way, I'm afraid," Dean said with some pain in his words. "I guarantee it. Let's get another bite to eat. You're going to need your strength."

He spent the next few hours performing odd rituals on the table with a box full of alien instruments. Gaelenn and Rin sat at the edge of the circular room and watched, nibbling on bread and the last of their own dried meat and some of Dean's. Aydya passed the entire time on her knees and threw intermittent glances of disgust between their boots and the floor, and Kell, when he was not looking over the old man's tools, kept his eyes on Aydya.

They couldn't see it, but the sun had almost risen again by the time Dean had finished his preparations.

"There. We should be ready to start," he said, breaking the long silence. "Are you really sure you want to do this?"

Gaelenn stood up and stretched the stiffness out of his knees. "Yes. I'm ready. But I'm not going to promise you I'll run back to Last Retreat and hide out with the Priestess."

"I don't think there's going to be time for thinking once you're out," said Dean. "You'll be down and out for a while. Again, when you unlock it—*if* you unlock it—then our cover is blown. The enemy will know you're here. It will come after you physically, not just in your mind. When they get here, I'm pulling the plug. In the meantime, I'm going to re-set our defenses here. We might need a way out, depending on how long they take to find us."

"Got it," Gaelenn said.

"You there, lady in black," Dean said, pointing his chin at Aydya while his hands were busy putting the finishing touches on the apparatus.

"Yes. What?"

"If there's enough time left over, you can have a word with your Eye."

Aydya made a shallow bow, keeping her eyes on his.

"I'll have a visual up while it happens. We might be able to see a little of what's going on inside," Dean said.

All four of the visitors looked around, puzzled, before he addressed them all. "Nevermind, you'll see soon enough. The rest of you, you said you came right after you picked this woman up, right? How long did that take you?"

"Six nights," Aydya said. "As fast as we could push."

She shot a quick glare again at Kell, forcing a rush of blood to his cheeks that matched the color of his beard.

"Then let's be safe and say it will take them half that to get here. We'd better be long gone by then, or we're all dead," said the old man. "Gaelenn, you'll be tied down the whole time. We'll be feeding you water and food directly into your blood with these tubes. But don't you worry, it won't hurt a bit."

In his voice was a void of emotion, almost hollow, that reminded Gaelenn of the way many old souls almost welcomed death, hoped for it.

He motioned toward the table and Gaelenn laid down on it, instinctively, face up. With a swipe on the black stone from his pocket, the table transformed, becoming something more like a laid-back chair. It fitted itself to Gaelenn's body, cradling him. Despite its age, not even the sound of grinding stone came from its invisible joints.

Even without restraints holding him down, Gaelenn found it hard to find the will to move or even to adjust his posture. From the ceiling, a light he had not noticed descended on a string toward his face. Dean stabbed his arms with strange, needled tubes and, finally, wrapped his limbs to the table with fuzzy, somewhat scratchy, black straps.

"When you wake up, you're going to be more than yourself. You'll be carrying a lot more memories than you might like," Dean said, shaking his head. "I'm not sure if I hope this works or that I hope it doesn't."

It was the closest thing he ever got to a joke.

Then, Gaelenn's world went black.

CHAPTER TWENTY FOUR
In the Eye's Mind

Gaelenn's heart jolted in his chest. His whole body shook, drenched in sweat. He jumped upright, eyes as wide as saucers and his mouth gaping open, gasping for breath. But he was safe in his old straw bed in his own home—*home*. He could see it, smell it, even taste the dust in the air. His mother was breathing softly in the next room and he forced his heart calm.

He looked around. There was a small window in his room up toward the roof, allowing the brisk air to flow in and dry his forehead. For the coldest months of the year they kept the hole closed, but now it was summer.

A cool beam of moonlight shot through the dark onto the smooth part of the stone floor and little bits of dirt danced at its edges. Gaelenn swung his feet around and pressed them against the rock and absorbed its coldness. He smiled—it felt good. In fact, he could feel everything in his room. He clenched his eyes shut to make sure, but the distinct detail of every inch could not escape him. He could see without seeing.

Where am I, really?

The answer was clear as soon as he imagined the question. *This is the day I left home.* He stood up without willing it, not entirely in control of himself, as if he were watching the scene play out in his memory. Walking to the small wooden table next to his bed, he sat down and silently removed a parchment from its drawer. It was the letter he had written to his mother.

Mother,

When you wake up I will be gone over the sea. I'm sorry I couldn't tell you, but I must go away. I have to find Dad. There's so much I have to ask him.

I'll come back someday. I'll bring Dad back, too. I love you.

Gaelenn

He slid the letter away, just as he had on the same day so many years ago, where it would be found at daylight and put on his old boots and strapped on his pack of supplies. He knew that his mother would find it too early and run in tears to the docks and see him off there. At the door, he looked back once more at the foot of the bed where his mother lay sleeping, turned, and left.

But only his body that went out the door.

His mind stayed and watched the door close. Not a moment after, his mother sat up in her bed and wept, totally aware and completely crushed. She had already read it. Her heart was broken in two—the two people she loved most had walked away from her. All she could do was squeeze the amulet and the letter to her breast and whisper into it.

What she said was the only detail Gaelenn could not catch, and in the next moment, she ran out the door and his mind was no longer there.

He blinked without blinking, and the next scene appeared, more vivid than he imagined was possible. He could touch it and hear it and smell it more intensely than he had ever experienced anything before, in real life or in dreams, and it was terrifying.

High above a plain in a vast valley, suspended in the sky, distant, tall mountains and forests surrounded him below, and the sea was at his back. In the distance ahead the giant gem in Sapphire Mountain glowed through a sliver of the rock—he must have been looking at it from the north, where he had never seen it from before. He looked down and found that he was directly above a needle-like tower, impossibly tall. If he could kick it, he might knock it over, but at the moment, he had no legs, no body.

Though he did have eyes. A pain came to them and like a sharp speck of dust and blocked his vision in one place. He had to strain to focus on it. On the land between him and the mountain, a massive stone and wood castle with crimson red spires cut through the sky. Tattered flags at their peaks whipped back and forth in the wind.

People appeared below and painted the green between him and the castle in silver and red; a bloody battle raged. Thousands upon thousands of soldiers in shimmering steel swarmed like ants against each other and their screams and shouts and the clanging of metal on metal sent up chilling vibrations to Gaelenn. It was a battle of such immensity and scale that he would not have believed it had he lived it himself. And here he was, living it.

He sharpened his eyes and the ground swelled up beneath him until he could see the faces of the men and women fighting passionately. Some wore green. Some wore purple armbands. ENs! They bounded around on the battlefield like gods, mowing down whole lines of warriors with single strikes. Not one of them fell, and the tide was turning. The enemy was losing its grip.

Then he felt *it*: a presence—someone, something—was *here*. Goosebumps crawled up Gaelenn's arms in some peripheral reality, though he had no body to feel in this one. The presence had no face and no voice, but it was all over the battlefield, and it was full of hate. It hated the warriors destroying its army. It hated the bystanders who watched the battle from afar, waiting to plunder the aftermath. It hated its own weak soldiers, even, and the people who huddled in within the walls of its castle.

But most of all it hated Gaelenn. It had found him.

The sensation permeated him, sending spikes of agony through his brain. He had never felt anything stronger or viler or more terrible. It fixated all of its wrath on him; its gaze pierced right through him and paralyzed his thought.

The only weapon he had to fight back with, he found, was his will, and he pushed and fought until at last he broke free. When he looked down again, he saw that he *did* have a body. Commanding his limbs to move, he found that they were his. They listened, and with each effort they became more willing and responsive until he reveled in their power and speed. In his mind, he imagined moving forward, and to his surprise he shot through the air like a spear.

The sun waned, painting the sky in pink fire, and the ground darkened with smoke and shadow and blood. A tiny dot of infinite light rose from the castle into the sky and paused. Then it exploded.

Gaelenn knew what it was. He knew he was watching some memory from the past that was not his. But he was *there*. He shot forward, resolute, ignoring the fear in his heart, against the Eye. A shockwave from the explosion deafened him. It was a force Gaelenn could not quite understand but somehow knew.

Here it comes.

There was no mistaking the malice shooting toward him at blinding speed. With his mind he tried to shield himself, but his will was not enough now.

It arrived, and in its wake brought indescribable pain. His skin burned and his mind ached and he reeled before gathering his remaining strength and willing himself forth. But it was only the precursor of the wave of death that spread from the castle and devoured everything in its path, including Gaelenn.

His ears were the last thing to go, as they had the last time death had found him. And all he could hear was the laughter of the Great Eye, destroyer of the world.

Time slowed down. Closer. Slower. That last moment before death, he thought, was more excruciating than death itself. And then he died.

The very next moment, he opened his eyes and was in another time and another place, in another great battle. Troops marched, clad in the same strange garb that he had seen in the obsidian crystal in the forest temple outside of Last Retreat. They died, too.

And then he was born again. Another confrontation, differing only in basic details: the location; the colors; the scale—but all sides fought and fought and died.

Again and again this cycle of death and war and struggle repeated itself.

Always, the lives of thousands upon thousands were spent in fruitless battles. The weapons they used grew more sophisticated, more elegant, and more brutal the further forward he went—or was it backward? Yes, it was backward.

Gaelenn found that with each second and each scene unravelling before him his understanding of what was happening multiplied; he was not just witnessing events, he was understanding the past. *Living* it. And so far, it was just exactly how Livvy had described.

Livvy! As if summoned at the very mention of her name, he found himself in the middle of a small room. Lines of perfectly straight bulbs—fluorescent light, he now knew, somehow—highlighted the fifty or so cramped faces in unnatural white light. They were planning their very first counterattack on the enemy. The Eye was watching them, spying on them.

Dean was in the middle of the room, arguing with youthful passion, and Livvy's parents sat across from him, debating the steps to come. Some faces he recognized from when the Priestess had shown him her images of the past, but most were foreign, with strange, varied skin and alien features. They all wore strange, utilitarian clothes on their bodies and fear on their faces.

In the farthest corner, almost hidden away, sat Livvy herself, exactly as she had when Gaelenn had first met her. The wall at her back seemed to glow a little brighter than the rest of the dank room, having caught the radiance of her youth.

Gaelenn's heart skipped a beat, and another.

Her hands were wrapped around the arm of the tall, black-haired man next to her who was engaged in the rabble. She was deeply in love, and radiant.

Around the room, they all spoke in a language that Gaelenn did not recognize but somehow understood, arguing over their plan, hammering out details in tactics and contingencies and potentialities. He was not really there this time; he was just a witness, as the Eye was once a witness. None of them could see him standing in the corner of the room.

Except Livvy. When he turned around again, she was staring straight at him, boring her eyes into him the same way she had when he they first met, almost twenty thousand years after. Six days ago. She stood up, dropped her hands from the man next to her, and without dropping her gaze from him, she spoke. The entire room went mute and bent their ears toward her to catch her tiny voice. "The most important thing of all is that we never forget how this happened in the first place. If we do, it will happen again. We can't forget. No matter what happens."

With that, Gaelenn knew exactly what Livvy was trying to do all along: stop the Eye's cycle of death and destruction. To do it, she only needed to keep the past alive until the world could make use of it.

Her words reverberated around the room and outward into the ages. The Eye was not there with Gaelenn now. He could not feel its presence, thankfully. But Gaelenn knew it had seen this play out a billion billion billion times since its recording 19,724 years ago. And each time it hated each person in that white room more. It hated Livvy most of all.

"Where is the Eye?" Gaelenn said into the void as the lights went dark. No one responded, of course. It was just a test to see if it was listening. No—he was right. It was off somewhere, making some plan that Gaelenn could not see. Something horrible. Something that was coming.

All in time.

...Time! No time! Gaelenn panicked, and his consciousness sped through his dream; he had to find more of the Eye's memories. They were the only thing that mattered now. They alone could tell him when the next cataclysm would come. Dean wanted to know. Livvy *needed* to know.

But suddenly Gaelenn lost himself. He was awash with unfocus. He had to find why the Eye was what it was. How it came to be. What it fears. *If I can find that, I can kill it.*

And there it was, again summoned by thought alone: the Eye. The true Eye—a huge construct, an ancient mind made of thin metal wires and perfect rows of perfect silicon, stretching for a mile underneath the ground. A perfect chaos made from imperfect beings. That was it: people, humans. Humanity gave birth to the Eye, and it feared and hated its creators more than anything.

Gaelenn reached his hand through a thin opening in the giant machine, his mind inside his palm. *It's here—the secret. The method of its doom.*

Almost... Almost...

Not quite.

No! Gaelenn's heart screamed. But the alarm had sounded. His body—his real one—was being dragged back to consciousness. He was not fast enough. He had failed.

Tumbling back forward through time, he woke up.

CHAPTER TWENTY FIVE
Scorched Earth

RAH-RAH-RAH-RAH

Before his eyes came back to him, Gaelenn could hear the incessant, deafening whine of the rhythmic siren. They pierced his skull with dagger-like squeals.

"Where am I?" he asked out loud in a dry, cracked voice.

A slap across his face jolted his eyes to life.

"Get up!" Aydya screamed. "We have no time for questions. We must go!"

Tears streamed from her eyes, pleading with him to hurry. Kell and Rin flanked her.

"We do have to hurry, so now that you're alive again, shall we get going?" Rin added with a bit more sympathy.

Gaelenn stumbled off of the table, feeling the aches in his muscles from extended disuse. "How long was I out?"

Dean swooped into the room.

"Twenty hours," he answered, still moving. He had a large sack strapped to his back. "That's the proximity alarm. They got here faster than I anticipated—must be a regiment from a nearby town or camp, or some kind of expedition."

"Twenty hours?" Gaelenn said, stupefied.

"So is this our last stand?" Kell asked. He was hovering close to Aydya, his arm close to her but not touching, indecision keeping it from comforting her.

"Is there another way out somehow?" Rin asked.

Dean let out a weighty breath and his eyes closed. "...There's one. Maybe."

"Maybe? I'm not sure that's good enough, old man."

"There's no time to explain. They'll be through the defenses before long," Dean said. "Come with me."

"What's wrong with her?" Gaelenn asked Rin, watching Aydya as they followed Dean out of the room.

Rin shook his head in response. "At first she was upset she couldn't use the machine the way she thought, kept whining that she'd failed. She watched everything. Didn't take a single break. She stopped praying halfway through."

What should have been a whisper was a shout; the alarm was now punctuated by the drumming of footsteps and explosions outside. Dirt and rock rained on their heads as the mountain groaned and shifted.

"Probably had to do with the paintings we saw," Rin added.

"Paintings?"

"The images from your dream. A bunch of them, and they even moved! Showed up on some of the black plates while you were under. Lots of fighting. Lots of death. The old man said they were some of the things you were seeing."

Gaelenn cocked his head, confused, but it was clearly a bad time to continue the conversation.

When they reached Dean's living space, he directed the group to get under the table. They did, one by one, exchanging confused but unquestioning looks. Dean followed them after gathering a few last possessions from his shelves. He would not be coming back.

Their heads almost touched huddling under the thick wood and the walls seemed to draw closer. Gaelenn had not noticed how stale and stuffy it was now that all the doors were sealed.

"There isn't really a way out, technically...yet," Dean said, and then paused before adding with a frown, "If we don't make it out of here, I'm sorry. Best close your eyes now."

None of them did.

The old man reached deep into a pouch at his belly and instead of the glossy black tool he had used before, he pulled out a crude-looking, rusty iron box with a painted red circle. Searching the floor, he found a shiny rope that evidently he had placed there some time before and, with two breaths to blow away the dust, used his deft fingers to braid it to his box.

He seemed to count to himself while stroking his mustache. 10, 9, 8... When he hit 0, his thumb pressed the circle and a massive quake jarred the entire mountain. The roof of the room partially collapsed. The chaos outside ceased.

"Sturdy table," Rin said between coughs. The dust falling through its cracks forced their eyes closed for a minute.

"Would you look at that—we didn't die. But we may yet if we stay here! Come with me, let's go!" Dean exclaimed and got up and ran back toward the facility room. Again, they all followed him as he began chanting, "50, 49, 48..."

"You're still counting!" Gaelenn shouted ahead as he crossed the portal into the temple room, but the path of his thought stopped dead—the room was flooded with sunlight. "What happened?"

All of them asked the same thing, in turn, as they came into what used to be a room. A gigantic hole where there was once solid rock wall led all the way outside. The table stood intact with the light swinging above it, covered in soot and chunks of mountain.

"How the hell...?" Rin added, spellbound.

"32... 31... We have 30 seconds to get out of here," Dean said. The alarms had stopped. "Go! Now! Through the hole!"

He stopped counting and they all dashed away, leaping and climbing their way through the broken rocky path. The blast had carved a great divot right in the side of the mountain. The old man had been busy while Gaelenn was unconscious.

At the end of the tunnel the mountain dropped precipitously. Dean waved Rin through, then Kell and Aydya, who, with trails of tears still carving through the dust on her face, took one look back at the table in the middle of the room and then descended. Gaelenn jumped over the others after a too-short check and barely caught the edge of a jagged stone.

"And I thought I was reckless!" Rin said, grabbing his wrist and saving him.

Dean swung to the side of the crater and held tight to the rocks and shouted, "Cover your heads," just before a second blast shot out directly from the facility room. The mountain vomited a huge cloud of rock and dust and the tunnel and the table and the home inside it were no more.

The four survivors cupped their ears to stifle the pain and ringing. When the last of the loose rubble had run down the side of the mountain, they climbed down to a narrow ledge below, where the mountain opened up to the sky and a fierce wind pierced their clothes and whipped at their hair. It was several seconds before any communication was possible; they needed time to recover their wits, and Dean, though not in pain himself, let them rest their ears.

"Are you ready? We need to go. Now," he said after his patience had dried up. "That probably just pushed them a little down the mountain."

Rin was still wincing. "Go where? Down there?"

He stared out at a wide expanse on the opposite side of the half-mountain from where they had come: a rocky and desolate plateau pocked with sparse dead trees and dried-up lake beds. Here and there brown covered the bare canvas, but compared to the fertile valley south, it was a yellow wasteland.

"Anywhere but up here—keep your voice low!" Dean warned. "It carries far over all this rock."

Gaelenn closed his mouth and focused hard on his ears, almost as if he were still in his dream. Sure enough, he heard a clamor coming from around the mountain from the southwestern entrance to Dean's cave, and it was growing louder.

"Are we safe here?" he asked Dean.

"I wouldn't count on it." The old man grimaced. Dust from the explosion had settled on his hair and mustache and the added gray made him look much older.

Or, thought Gaelenn absently, perhaps a few new wrinkles had really lined his face after what just happened.

"What will we do now?" Aydya stood up and issued the challenge to the men. Her tears had dried and her eyes now had the same hardness as the rocks around her.

Kell watched her strength in awe and grinned.

"Let's ask the man in charge," Rin said. "What do you say, old man?"

Dean was too occupied scanning the mountain with his ears at the moment to reply. His eyes squinted even though he was not using them, as if closing off one sense would enhance the other. "They're coming around, and fast," he said, and then shifted back to the original question. "What to do? Get as far away from here as we can. Without attracting any attention."

He swiveled around to face Gaelenn, glancing back and forth between the green and gray eyes. "You've got to do whatever it takes to stay away from them. No matter what. If we get separated, swing back around the mountain to the North and head back to Last Retreat. I hope you learned a few things on that table. We'll have to talk about it—later."

Gaelenn only nodded. When Dean looked away, he rubbed his forehead to make sure it was whole; it didn't hurt, but he felt broken. His head was swimming with memories, and almost none of them were his. "Dean, what did that thing do to me?"

The old man rested his hands on his knees and sighed, partially satisfied. "Good. That tells me it worked. I just hope you got some answers we can use. You okay?"

"I'm fine," Gaelenn said, unable to express the feeling; some memories were missing from where they should have been. Not that they were his memories to begin with.

Dean wrenched his spine straight and shifted his jaw to the side to chew on his tongue. "You sure?"

Just as the last word left his lips, a long spear whistled through the air and shot clean through the side of his abdomen, ricocheting off the rock under him with a bloody slap and continuing down the mountain. He growled in pain and bit off the part of his tongue he had been playing with; blood spewed from his side and his mouth.

"Go! Down!" Gaelenn shouted. He reached for Dean's arm to throw it over his shoulder but a barrage of arrows arrived and one nicked the exposed part of his forearm, forcing it back with a jolt.

Around the mountain, a battalion of Maynon Ohzans traversed the steep rock of that separated them. One soldier was twice as large as the rest and wore a purple armband.

"It is the giant, Yajuu!" Aydya reported, standing upright and staring wide.

Gaelenn's arm reached out for Dean again but the sound of another round of bow twangs stopped it from pulling him in; instead, he shoved him hard into Kell and Rin, and all three of them slammed against the rock wall behind them, shielded from the arrows by a sloping edge above.

Gaelenn dove down the side mountain in a leap of faith, choosing uncertainty over certain death. For a moment, he thought he had chosen poorly—his jump was too far. Beneath him lay nothing but air for hundreds of yards. He flailed his arms, scrambling to reach a ledge—and found a hand instead.

Aydya nearly tumbled down with him but braced her body by wrapping her other arm around a protruding boulder. She gritted her teeth and pulled as hard as she could, but the weight was too great for her fingers to bear.

It was, however, just enough to slow Gaelenn down and bring him closer to the mountain where his arms caught the ledge at her feet.

"You, up!" she demanded. After the first volley of arrows she had gone down and flitted out of sight. Unlike Gaelenn, she had been wise enough to look before jumping.

"Thank you," he said to her before pulling himself up to his feet. "Come on!" he then shouted upward, cupping his hands around his mouth.

The arrows were answer enough and rained down without pause. Kell's gritty voice came after a pregnant pause. "Not a chance!"

"If you stay up there you'll be killed, you idiots! The green giant's with them!"

Rin answered above the whistling arrows. "We'll find another way, then! The old man's not going to make that jump!"

"Quick! There's no time!" Gaelenn shouted again.

Rain started, reaching a deluge in less than a minute from close clouds and rendering the rocky ledges even more precarious. It re-wet the edges of the blood from Dean's mouth and he spoke weakly to Kell, who was bringing the old man's limp arm over his own shoulder and close enough to hear.

"There's another way down the mountain for us...tell them to escape north."

"Go!" Kell yelled down to Gaelenn and Aydya. His low voice was almost angry. "We'll get down on our own! Dean knows a way!"

Gaelenn bared his teeth, furious at his own helplessness. "There's no way back up, is there?" He asked Aydya, standing next to him.

She shook her head. The cavalcade grew ever closer—and louder.

He screamed again. "Come on! Jump down!"

But it was hopeless. The projectiles continued to streak across the sky, as thick as the rain. Aydya pulled Gaelenn's arm to her. The warmth of her body spoke to him and brought his senses back. "We must descend! They will find another way off! Come, quickly. Now is our only chance!"

She tugged his tunic and arms and moved him inch by inch. His eyes were glued above, but he moved.

"I can't leave my friends. Or that man," Gaelenn said in vain.

If it was not for the red around his eyes, Aydya would not have known he was weeping. She walked around and stood right in front of him, looked up into his face, and stared with soft, understanding brown eyes. At that moment, she was neither Disciple nor cultist. She was not the unfeeling fanatic that she had been during their journey together; she was a woman. And human.

Releasing his arm, she used her words to touch him. "Gaelenn. If your friends are meant to survive, they will survive. I do not wish them dead. But you must not be found. This is as much for your sake as it is for mine. Or theirs. Trust your friends. We must go."

It was the first time she ever said his name.

The roar above now drowned out the wind, which was much stronger here on the bare north side of the mountain. The fight had come to their companions. Gaelenn felt Aydya's words echoing again in his mind. "Okay," he tried to say back, but it came out mostly as a nod.

In an instant, Aydya grabbed him again by the arm and together they took a great leap sideways between the rain to a rock a few yards down, and then again, and again, grasping the mountain wall here and there to slide and crawl down where it was steepest. They descended as fast as their limbs and their grip would allow.

The jagged rocks above seemed to play tricks on Gaelenn's eyes. Every once in a while, when he looked up, he swore he saw a shadow tracking them down. It must have been the rain, because the shadow disappeared as soon as they had cleared the rain. After a few dozen minutes that felt like days, the furor above was distant enough to for them to talk. But they had no words to utter to each other. They stayed on their path.

"Whatever god or gods there are—I'd give my soul to bring my friends out of this alive," Gaelenn said, looking back up one last time.

Aydya looked only at him.

CHAPTER TWENTY SIX
DIVERSION

ROCKS CAREENED DOWN IN front of Kell, Rin, and Dean, following a fresh explosion and its rumbling quake. A normal axe would shatter at such an impact, but the one that caused this mess was large enough to win a battle with stone.

Looking up, Rin could just barely see the thrown weapon's crescent peeking over the top of the ledge that had protected them. He winked at Kell and rubbed his thumb over the ball he held in his hand. "Let's see what these things can do, yeah?"

Kell bent down so the wincing old man could hear. "Hope it works."

"They'll work," Dean said. He pulled out his little black obelisk and wiped it with the bottom of his loose sleeve. It was immediately covered in water again, the rain thick as soup. "I think I've lost too much blood. I can't think straight. Fire that thing up."

He motioned to the blacksmith's waist. Kell grunted. He unfastened his hammer, kissed it—perhaps for luck, but maybe for love—and pressed it to the new dark iron belt buckle at his waist. A light humming sound arose and within five seconds the head of his iron tool glowed red with intense heat.

"Give it to me," Dean said.

Kell offered the handle and Dean took it, lifted the end of his soaking shirt, and forced it onto the wound on his side to cauterize it. He let out a small growl but swallowed the pain and pressed it quickly again to his lower back, where the spear had entered.

The stench of charred flesh rose to Kell's and Rin's noses between raindrops.

"Charge it up again," he said painfully as he gave it back.

Kell pressed it up against his belt again and it got so hot and bright that the rain turned to steam even before hitting it, making it more like the fiery torch of a god than a hammer. He raised it up in a threatening pose, illuminating his face in the yellow-red light.

Rin pulled out his crossbow and smiled back at Kell and Dean, steadying his aim. "How long now do we have to hold them off?"

"Just long enough for those two to get far away," Dean said through clenched teeth. "I hope."

The ledge was easily wide enough for Kell and Rin to stand side-by-side, but they were vulnerable from above, so they stuck closer to the mountain wall and waited.

The arrows dried up; most of the soldiers had started the treacherous journey across the hundred-yard gap of sheer mountain that separated them from their prey and abandoned their bows. Not all of them made it, judging by the random, tumbling screams.

But Triumvir Yajuu did.

Before Kell and Rin knew he was upon them, he dislodged his enormous axe and jumped onto their ledge. He was so large that one hand still held onto a rock above. Rin and Kell would have had trouble have reaching that height with one on the other's shoulders.

Kell marveled at the mass of man before them, but Rin, always on the lookout for an advantage, shot a bolt at his head. The giant deflected it with an effortless swing of his axe and laughed. He babbled something foreign and pointed at them, their eyes now white with fear.

Dean, in the same incomprehensible language, spoke back. "Dee alm foo seek."

The Triumvir recoiled in shock before taking a more serious stance and lifting his axe.

"What'd you say?" Rin asked.

"Oh, just riled him up a little."

Rin could not see Dean's private grin behind him, but he could tell the answer was not exactly the truth.

"Was that wise?" Kell said and spat out the rain spilling into his mouth from his beard.

The giant swung his axe wide from the side with an accompanying roar. Slowed by the rain, it wafted high, but succeeded in knocking Kell and Rin backwards and off balance. Rin danced around with what room he had and bounced back, gracefully slashing at whatever openings he could find with his long-bladed dagger.

Kell caught his footing and launched forward with a wild swing of his hammer. It cracked through the air and left a trail of flame in its wake, hitting the giant's axe with a powerful blow and report. Again and again he struck as the smoke and steam built up around him and for a moment he was a god of fire—from hand to beard.

Rin continued his own attacks on the other side, forcing Yajuu to use both ends of his long axe to defend himself. The dagger was too swift for even the green giant's unnatural reflexes, and though at first he only found air, Rin eventually began slashing flesh. The giant's weakness was exposed—speed. They forced the massive hulk back, reveling in their advantage with raging smiles.

Triumvir Yajuu planted his feet and stopped to catch his breath between raindrops. His brow, taut with fury, almost buried his beady eyes.

He had only been waiting for his opening, lulling the two into his trap, and here it was. His axe swept around backward and its handle struck Rin's and Kell's chests, knocking them to their backs several yards away as if he had just swatted two flies. He reached to his shoulders one at a time and unbuckled his heavy, soaking green cape. The rain pushed it down into a heap and he spit at the ground between him and his enemies. Rain cascaded off of his bare head and rippling arms.

Struggling to sit up and still panting, Rin managed a laugh.

"Intimidating. Don't you think, Kell?"

Kell sat up on one knee. "Absolutely." He grinned; it felt good to finally fight again instead of run.

The monster's frown dug deep into his jaw as Kell and Rin rose to their feet. "You will come with me now," he said, this time perfectly intelligible despite a heavy accent.

"Hey old man, much longer? We just got an ultimatum. I think," Rin said out of the side of his mouth.

Dean hid his eyes to sneak a glance toward the dry side of the mountain. They found the tiny outlines of Gaelenn and Aydya.

"Just another minute or two," he replied.

Rin tossed his eyebrows up and shrugged. "If we must, we must." He lunged again at Yajuu in a renewed attack.

Kell followed with his swinging hammer, igniting the air in a brilliant show of light that helped confuse the huge monster. But every minute they fought was one minute closer to death. They were losing ground, and in another minute, they were sure to be corpses, but they fought on.

"Ready!" Dean willed himself up and stopped the fight.

"Finally!" Rin said. He and Kell darted back toward Dean. From there they saw what he saw: the encroaching Maynon Ohzans. At least half of them had already made it across, and as soon as they did, out came their bows.

Rin's eyes bobbed up and down from soldier to soldier. "That's fewer than fifty. Is that all of you who made it? Any more on the way?"

They drew their bows tight, waiting for Triumvir Yajuu's command. It did not come quick enough.

"Now!" Dean yelled.

Rin, his hand at his hips in mock pain, snapped straight, snatched a hidden black ball from his belt and flung it right at the feet of the green giant. It exploded in a blinding flash and left a plume of smoke that provided enough cover for Rin to throw two more of them at the legion above. The ledge shuddered under the fiery chaos. Yajuu crashed backwards into the ground.

Kell sprinted at Dean with the chaos they had created as cover. The old man was tapping his black stone, and the blacksmith picked him up by the shoulder. "You going to make it?"

"I've had worse. Let's go!" he said, looking over Kell to Rin, who had just arrived on his other side with a wide smile. "You've got two more. Use them!"

"Happy to oblige!" he cackled, tossing his last two magic spheres almost casually behind the soldiers. Several boulders dislodged and began bouncing down the mountain, bringing down waves of Maynon Ohzan soldiers with them. Falling screams punctuated the low rumbling until the lungs that screamed them were crushed on rocks below.

Rin and Kell secured Dean, who had spent the most frantic moments of the battle fastening a rope to a rock, and together swung across a wide, sheer mountain wall. When they found their footing on the other side, Rin held on to the rope just a half second longer to admire it.

"This stuff really is magic," he said, and left it to dangle, lifeless, in the center where nobody could use it.

They continued down along the western side of the mountain, descending as they jumped from ledge to ledge and then back around to the slope they had ascended more than a day before.

"Let them see where we're going!" Dean repeated each time they stopped to catch their breath. "Just like we talked about."

They were far enough away that by the time the remaining Maynon Ohzans had recovered and located them, the volley of arrows they loosed fell as harmlessly as leaves. Then the army rallied with several great, collective cries, and descended after the three men.

"They're coming!" Kell said, looking back at where the smoke was being washed away by the rain.

They had taken the bait, and Triumvir Yajuu was already leading the chase. The giant leapt from rock to rock, some of which refused to support his massive frame and crumbled to dust under him, but he crawled like a spider when he could not stand.

"I don't believe it, I hit him right in the legs with that thing!" Rin flung his arms in the air.

"And he's going to be extra pissed after that," Dean said with an involuntary wince. "Keep going! We've got to keep just enough space between us that by the time we get to the bottom those bastards'll know that we've gotten down but not where we've run off to. I didn't intend this to be a sacrifice, you know."

His eyes warmed up a bit and a wisp of a knowing smile blew across his face. "And hopefully there won't be as many following us by then."

On cue, the churning echo of grinding metal crawled over the mountainside. The three were now just coming into view of its source and stretched their necks to examine the crater in the mountain where Dean's door used to be. Right then, Dean's metal monster rumbled over a heap of rubble and pointed its long mouths at the chasing soldiers.

BOOM BOOM BOOM

It sang in thudding, baritone notes, over and over again. The soldiers began screaming and Rin and Kell—and even Dean if one looked quickly enough to catch it—grinned from ear to ear. Glad for the reprieve, they adjusted their descent just enough to handle the old man with a little less jostling, and by the time the steep mountain path gave way to a walkable hill, they were creeping along at a gingerly pace.

CHAPTER TWENTY SEVEN
THE WASTELAND

GAELENN JERKED HIS HEAD back around at the sound. He and Aydya were far enough away now that they must be invisible from where their friends were, thanks to the thick downpour wreathing the mountain. It was easier to see things at this distance looking upward with only wind instead of rain, especially when things were exploding. The mountain roared in agony with blasts of fire, and smoke that could not be extinguished billowed out and up.

"Damnit," Gaelenn said, grimacing. "What are they doing? We should have stayed."

Aydya's warm hands cradled his forearm. "Do not worry. I am sure they will survive. We must continue, at least until it is safe enough to circle back south. Perhaps around east, as your old friend suggested."

Gaelenn turned his gaze north and shook his head. "No, I'm not going back south. Not yet, at least. Damn, I hope they got out of there…"

Something he *knew* yet had never *seen* told him that somewhere in the barren wasteland ahead of them lay a critical piece of his puzzle. But, right now, he did not know which puzzle the piece belonged to; his mind was too fragmented and scattered.

The two had already come a long way down and were now treading along one of dozens of deep grooves in the hill leading from the mountain, carved long ago when rain and melting snow flowed more readily on this side of it. As soon as they had begun descending, the torrent had abated, though it was still showering the mountain behind them where the two spires had captured its clouds. The water on their clothes had long since sucked up the dust and turned it into caked mud, and there was no vegetation here to wipe it off.

Gaelenn, keeping a step behind, finally noticed that Aydya was wearing long, leather boots. *Strange, she was always barefoot before.* His thoughts rose from her feet to her ankles and knees and hips, and then with a shake of his head, he forced his train of thought to its end. After a long minute, he realized he had not stopped once in the past few weeks to recover. And think. Ideas and thoughts were luxuries in the face of action, and ever since he had been strapped up by those damned pirates, life had been full-go.

"I just don't know," he said neglectfully, followed by a deep breath.

Aydya matched his gait and lifted her eyebrows to a point and gazed at him, confused.

"Sorry," Gaelenn said, "I didn't mean to say that out loud."

She brushed it off and they walked for another few hours in silence. It was already dark by the time they stopped for the night.

"I don't suppose there are any animals to hunt around here," Gaelenn said. "Not that I have a bow or a spear."

Aydya set down a small cloth pack—she had not been carrying it before, either, Gaelenn was sure—and stretched it open. She pulled out a few pieces of dried meat and bread and handed them to him along with a skin of water. He drank before eating.

"We must not risk a fire," she said in a whisper, continuing after he had a few moments to let the food settle, "Why are we not to go back south? I must...tell my brothers and sisters about what happened. And you are now free from pursuit. It will be easy for you to remain hidden if you are careful."

Gaelenn turned his head at her hesitation when speaking of her fellow disciples, but ignored the sign for now.

"You can go back. You should—as soon as we know for sure that it's safe," he said. "I fulfilled my promise to your people. Now I feel like there's something up here I need to see."

Aydya's head slumped uncharacteristically, but she nodded.

"What happened while I was out? How long was it, again?" Gaelenn asked.

"Many things were said while you were sleeping," she said, looking at the ground with dead eyes. "Many things were seen. You were sleeping for a long time. Many hours."

She paused for a few moments to summon the energy to continue. "I begged the man, Dean, to allow me to commune with the Eye. But I learned things. I saw many images in the pillar from your dreams."

She swallowed slowly. "Things I did not know. I..." she said, her voice and trailing off with her thoughts.

"What did you see?" Gaelenn pressed, leaning closer to her.

Her head shook from side to side and her eyes went wide as she recalled her memory. Her lips moved but nothing came out, as if she were mouthing a curse or a prayer. At last stiff words trickled out.

"I...begged and begged, 'let me talk with him!' I needed to commune with the Great Eye—to warn it about the traitor, and...to ask if the images you made were true."

Gaelenn listened, his gaze pressing into her.

"Your friend, Dean, offered me the chance. And...I hesitated. I couldn't do it." Aydya said, and covered her face with her hands, slumping into the dirt.

"Why?" Gaelenn himself whispered now, careful not to push too hard. The moon appeared from behind the clouds and gave them sight; it lit up her black eyes like the blue globes from Last Retreat. Her great beauty was marred only by the troubled thoughts that beat at her brow.

She mouthed the word, "nothing," once before succeeding in saying it aloud on her second attempt.

"No, not 'nothing,'" she continued, "just emptiness. I saw...I thought I saw...no."

Her hand wrenched at her own throat as if she wanted to choke herself to death. Aydya held back her tears but they gathered at the ends of her eyes and threatened to fall. Her faith, the one thing that had held her together throughout her tumultuous young life, was shaken.

Gaelenn closed his eyes and sighed for her, relieved, in the pragmatic end of his mind, at her failure. But the sigh was also part of a struggle—he could not help but be moved by her earnestness; he felt her pain. "What else happened while I was...sleeping?"

She wiped her face, erasing the previous conversation in one motion, or at least pretending to. "There were many things. Your friends talked and rested and ate. The elder man was busy preparing for our escape. But...it was mostly waiting."

Gaelenn stammered up to his feet and stretched his legs and paced around as Aydya detailed what had happened: Dean had taught and given many things to Kell, "the bearded brute." And Rin, "the painted one," had asked so many questions about the temple that the old man had grown sore and silent.

They talked about how the three of them had agreed and planned that when the time came, they would do whatever possible to prevent Gaelenn from falling into the hands of the Maynon Ohzans—especially the ENs. Or the "goblins," as Aydya called them, lacking the vocabulary to express her hatred in more appropriate words.

They had agreed that if needed, she would escape with Gaelenn while the others drew any attention away. Rin had objected fervently, Kell had only mildly raised some concerns, and Dean, according to Aydya, was the main proponent.

Gaelenn nodded and kept his eyes from meeting hers. Dean knew more than just a little—about the ENs, Maynon Ohza, the Disciples—about everything. He knew, after what he had absorbed on the table on the mountain, that there was wisdom in the old man's words.

"I understand," he said. "Thank you."

He cleared his throat and forced himself to look at her. As soon as they had come down the mountain, he had noticed that Aydya's monochrome, black-and-white aura had transformed. She was full of color now; grays and browns and yellows and reds, all in a confused, all-too-human pattern.

Gaelenn stopped and looked up at the moon, using it to focus his thoughts, and drew a long breath of the cool air. "I know there wasn't much time, but why didn't anybody tell me any of this before we split up? We could have fought back, or at least escaped together!"

Aydya, who had been studying the rocks on the ground during her speech, traced the lines up to meet Gaelenn's eyes. "The bearded one insisted that if you knew, you would not allow their sacrifice. The man Dean agreed. It was necessary."

Gaelenn drove his fist into his thigh. Kell was right, of course. "But...!"

His bottom lip bunched up so hard over his teeth that it went numb.

"Do not grieve," she said. "Not yet. Your friends may be alive. The painted one is wily and skilled, and the man Dean is clever. The bearded one...," her nose twitched as she spoke, as if a foul odor crawled up her nose, "is at the very least strong."

Gaelenn found a soft patch of soot and crashed, planting all of his exhaustion into the dirt, and rested his head on his crossed hands behind him. "You're right. Thanks. For everything. Tomorrow you can head back to your home. Thank you again. For your help."

Aydya did not answer right away; she just sat, hugging her knees for warmth, and stared at him. At length, she spoke low, "I have no home now. I will go with you. As far as you go."

One last thought penetrated Gaelenn's mind before he drifted to sleep: were they now equal partners in this journey, or was he her new god?

CHAPTER TWENTY EIGHT
LEGION

THE TREES OFFERED ONLY a momentary respite for Dean, Rin, and Kell. As relieved as they were to reach cover, the military machine at their heels could cover a lot of ground, and they were only three men, one of whom should be dead.

"We need to rest—you need to rest," Kell said to Dean.

The old man shook his head.

"Maybe just a minute. I'll be fine with a little food," he whispered and winced again. "Reach into my sack and get me something."

Kell bent down and pulled out a few pieces of soaking flatbread, and Dean swallowed them whole. "This will fix me up."

Rin studied him. "You've got an appetite like the Priestess's."

"Well, see, we've got a few things in common, she and I. And that's definitely one of them." Dean pointed at the bag and back and forth between Kell and Rin.

"There's no way I could eat with that thing after us," Rin said. "How can you? I wasn't even the one skewered by a big stick just a couple hours ago!"

Dean shrugged and pulled himself up. "It's my curse. But it keeps me going," he said, rubbing his hand once over the already healing wound on his side.

Trees crunched behind them, further up the mountain, sending muddy snaps through the thick rain and bringing Kell and Rin to their feet with Dean.

"What in hell...?" Kell said over his shoulder as they pressed on.

"I told you. That thing after us isn't quite human," Dean remarked. His steps were already stronger.

Rin caught up to him, careful not to throw his voice too far into the woods. He nodded to Kell. "So, not human—then what is it?"

"Something bad, that's for sure."

"Come on, old man, I know you know something," Rin pressed.

They wove through the thin tree trunks in silence for a minute as Dean gathered his thought through grinding teeth. He stopped short and faced Rin. "Now's not the time. Elizabeth never said anything to you guys about the ENs?"

"Everybody knows the Triumvirate, but I didn't know about this 'EN' stuff until all this stuff started happening. What's so special about them? If we're going to be going to be taking you back to Last Retreat—we are, aren't we? We might as well fill the time enlightening each other," Rin said.

"You talk a lot," Dean replied, aptly deflecting the litany of questions.

Kell snorted and grinned. "He does."

The roar behind grew louder and whipped the group on faster, and the clouds darkened further and loomed low over the thin evergreen trees. But they did not dare stop to rest that night until morning broke, and then it was only for an hour. None of them had had a wink of actual sleep before they set off again.

When they were on the march again, though, the sounds not only came from behind them but seemed to close in from all sides. They ripped off a few pieces of spiced meat to break their fasts while they stumbled their way over the rough, soggy ground under the trees. Rin had managed to keep his mouth mostly shut.

"We used to call the ENs, 'The Legion,'" Dean said. It was the first thing any of them had muttered since the day before. "They don't exist anymore, or they shouldn't."

Kell and Rin drew closer to him to hear him over the rain, which had not ceased since they were up on the side of Sapphire Mountain.

Finally, the old man was ready to talk. "Or at least they don't exist in the same sense that they used to. Same name, different management, it seems."

"Huh?" Kell frowned.

"Figure of speech," Dean said. "Now they're just tools of our enemy. Anyway, you might call them human—or you might not. They used to be on the right side. Used to be *human*."

"Used to be?" Rin said, recoiling. "Well, if they *used to be human* then can we at least assume they're not immortal like you and the Priestess?"

Dean swiped at the air toward Rin, waving away the idea. "We're not immortal. You saw the spear yesterday."

Blood still clung to the ends of his mustache where the rain couldn't reach, and he looked down at himself to double check the stains on his clothes where he had been run clean through. The wound was now totally closed and a small, innocuous scar was all that marked his should-have-been mortal wound.

"Coulda fooled me," Rin said with a huff and raised brow.

He and Kell wore horror on their faces, but he laughed. "I've had worse."

His smile died as soon as he looked up with a sigh. "Those things exist because of me. They're my fault."

"Your fault? How?" Kell asked. He was gulping air so violently from their incessant exertion that anything beyond single words was impossible to get out. Their pace had increased, unconsciously, as the sounds behind them grew ever closer.

"I thought this stuff was in your history books," Dean said with a sidelong look at Rin.

"I'm afraid not. And I was quite an excellent student."

"Good student? Now why I am I finding that hard to believe," Dean replied. A retort from a tree snapping to the east reminded him to stay focused as they continued on.

"A long time ago, before the wars started, I was a damn good...'magician,'" he said, substituting a more suitable word for his audience.

"I was a master of potions, you might say. Did a lot of good work. When the first war came, humanity was hanging on by a thread. We were no match for what we'd unleashed. We were massacred en masse."

Rin and Kell walked, spellbound, on either side of Dean. Without noticing themselves, they had begun tiptoeing across the ground so they could hear him better, and for the moment they forgot about the danger behind and around them.

"We had no way to fight back—all of our weapons were turned against us. We were fighting with spoons while our enemy fought with bows and swords." He tripped on a dead log, consumed for the moment in his own story. When Kell and Rin helped him up, his hands searched for the scar on his side; it was already less conspicuous than it had been just minutes before. He nodded to himself and glanced at Kell, who, between deep breaths, maintained a deep crease in the skin between his eyebrows.

"Not really spoons, of course," he continued. "I mean they took all of our useful weapons away from us. We couldn't fight back effectively. Nobody could."

Kell looked forward again, apparently satisfied.

"And every time we tried to create a new weapon or come up with a new strategy, the other side would steal that and turn it against us, too. Nothing we did worked," Dean said, selecting his words with special care. "We made things that blew up bigger. And bigger. We scarred the planet. You saw the place we just came from, Sapphire Mountain. That kind of thing doesn't just happen in nature. We were the worst kind of desperate."

A few minutes passed before Dean picked up his mind's thread again, lost in memories.

"In desperate times, we make the only choices we think we have," he continued at length, "and we thought that if our enemy could corrupt anything we made, then our best option would be to turn *ourselves* into weapons. No way the Eye could corrupt that. So I used my 'magic' and...created the Legion. The ENs. Our ace in the hole."

Rin stopped cold. "You *created* them?" he shouted, stupefied.

Dean tilted his head at Rin. "Let me finish. And don't stop moving. Like I said, we never thought in a million years it'd be able to corrupt *us*. But as it turned out, the Eye only needed a couple thousand."

Rin's legs started churning again after a brief, stupefied pause, but his jaw muscles flared out from the sides of his head.

"At first, you know, it worked. We fought that bastard and beat it. We thought we won," Dean explained further. "We were wrong, but we thought that our long fight had ended. We came out of our caves and started to rebuild. It was supposed to be for the last time. But it had only begun."

Kell growled. "What had?"

"The Eye struck out again, and we beat it back again, and it came back, and on and on. We'd rebuilt, it would emerge, and eventually both sides dwindled to nothing. The world suffered. In the end, somehow, it turned our last and only good weapon—the Legion—against us. I still don't know exactly how."

"Are you...one of...those weapons?" Kell struggled to ask.

Dean shook his head. "No."

"Is the Priestess?" Rin asked.

Dean considered the question for a long time. "No, she's like me. We're no weapons."

"Gods?"

"Of course not! Don't talk stupid. If you need any proof, there used to be almost a hundred of us. Now there are only two," Dean said as he mimed the number two with his fingers. He fell silent and would speak no more, so they ran on, the lesson over.

The crash of a falling tree a few hundred yards to their west drove the three companions to the ground. They examined each other and then searched in the direction of the noise. Footsteps—hundreds of them—were closing in. Even at their torrid pace they had been too slow. Their stand was near.

Rin jaunted ahead and squinted in all directions, and then closed his eyes and focused his ears.

"This way," he whispered, and Dean and Kell followed him, keeping low to the ground, and headed southeast.

For an hour, they crept on as fast as they could manage without being seen, though they could feel the enemy all around them. Dean needed to stop once every twenty minutes for a mouthful of water and wet bread, and Kell used those respites to rest on all fours. Rin remained on the lookout.

Kell, during one spell, looked down at his heaving chest and noted all the weight he had lost over the past few weeks. A fifth of his body had evaporated away. He drew his fist in front of his eyes and sighed in thanks. The strength in his arms remained.

Rin's body, already lean, had leaned further as well, but the most shocking change was in the roots of his hair, which were growing in pure white, painting a skunk-like pattern atop his head. The rain pounded against their backs for hours and hours, and all of them, even tireless Rin, had come to the verge of succumbing to exhaustion.

"I can't...go...any...further," Kell sputtered, fell to the ground, and dry heaved. But there was no water in his stomach to wring out, so he rolled over and let some rain in.

They stared out at a vast clearing just in front of them.

"Just our luck," said Rin, resting cross-legged. "The moment we step out of these woods we'll be attacked. Well, old man, any more tricks up your sleeve?"

Dean shrugged. "Fresh out. Looks like we're going to have to run across."

Kell groaned loudly and rolled over. "Run?" But there wasn't enough fat on his stomach anymore to prevent a pained grimace, having rolled onto a sharp stick.

Rin stepped to the edge and studied the plain ahead. It was night again and his eyes alone were able to cut through the black swaths of rain.

"The grass is tall," he reported, "but it's not going to keep us hidden. There's a pile of rubble on the other side—maybe an old city, but it's hard to tell from here. And to the left—north-east—there's a hill, but we can't go up there. Too steep. There are some more trees on the other side of the ruins."

He rubbed his hands together. "Damn, the other side is a long way off. If they have any arrows left, they'll probably be able to reach us."

"Then let's hope their aim is off in the dark," Dean said. "Looked like there was only one of those ENs, right? And he can only do so much with two hands against three of us."

His deadpan voice grew lower. "What I mean is we have three chances to make it out of here and back to Last Retreat to tell them what happened. That's all that matters. One of us has to make it."

He analyzed Rin and Kell through half-closed eyes and assessed their constitution, then made a satisfied nod. "Good men. Let's make for the ruins. Try to lose them there. It's dark enough. We just need to be fast enough."

"No better alternatives," Rin said. "Right?"

Kell summoned his strength, using his hands to raise up his body, from his knees to his sides. The three of them crept to the trunk of the last tree that was big enough to provide cover and gazed out onto the grass swaying in the wild, wet wind. Moonlight drifted through slivers in the clouds and mingled with the rain, falling on each glossy strand.

"On my mark," Rin instructed with one last look around. "Go!"

They launched out at full speed, leaving three weaving trails behind them like shark fins cutting through the sea. They made it two hundred yards out when fiery torches cascaded out of the woods to their rear left—and right—accompanied by a din of shouts and battle cries. Directly behind where they had left the tree line, a great voice roared and each of the runners craned his neck around to see the pale outline of Triumvir Yajuu closing the distance in great, impossible bounds.

"We'll make it! Keep moving!" Rin yelled.

"Make it where?" Kell screamed.

"To those ruins! Keep moving!"

With plodding, high steps through the shin-deep, flooded plain, they closed the distance to the ruins outlined in the scarce moonlight. It was a once-great city with skeletons of buildings and keeps and walls still firmly in the ground. Moss had not yet lined the creases of the mortar between stones; it was a fresh Maynon Ohzan kill. But as they approached, pursued from all other directions, a blast of lightning illuminated the helmet and breastplate of the figure in glimmering armor directly in front of the ruined city. A tall woman stood, feet anchored in the ground, and drew a long sword from the scabbard at her belt.

"Oh gods, is that the woman? The Triumvir? Legion!" Kell said.

Rin threw his forearm over his eyes to see clearly, but had no answer.

Another warrior emerged from behind her, and then another, and another at each flashing bolt of lightning until over 30 armored soldiers had created a perfect line of wet steel. Like hunted deer, the three unlikely friends had allowed themselves to be flushed out of cover and into the open.

It was the perfect trap.

CHAPTER TWENTY NINE
EDGEBOUND NORTH

GAELENN STRETCHED HIS LEG and stepped over the mangled iron gate in front of him.

"Strange, it's bent *outward*," he said to Aydya. "Better be careful."

It was the first sign of life they had seen since they left the mountain and their friends several days earlier: an old, gated desert village. The place from his dreams—or, more accurately, his memories.

"So it is abandoned," Aydya said, scanning the buildings and rubble for life. The disappointment pulled at the ends of her lips. "As we thought from afar."

She had warmed to Gaelenn during their trek, day by day, and though he was still working on solving the veil of riddles she protected herself with, they had spoken more or less normally. Bond, even.

He glimpsed her black-lined, squinting eyes. She had not worn her hood despite the harsh sun since before they set out from Sapphire Mountain and her already brown skin had grown a shade darker. Zeal no longer burned in her eyes. In fact, aside from the knee-length black robe, she looked like a normal person. He snuck another look at her proud form from the side.

She might not even be a Disciple anymore, he remarked in silence.

"Is this the place you were looking for?" Aydya asked. Her hand covered her eyes from the piercing daylight as she gazed up at the top of the strange, impossibly tall cylindrical tower jutting out of the ground amid dozens of crumbling, slowly-rotting huts.

"Yes. I think so," Gaelenn replied, tired for the moment of speaking. He had spent the better part of the past day trying to make Aydya understand what had happened to him. But the results were mixed; having not experienced his new memories himself, he often found his meandering explanations left her more and more confused.

In the end it was better just to stick to the most basic details, like: "We're looking for a tower."

"Over here!" she said, without missing a beat.

Gaelenn kicked up a plume of dust, drew his sword, and dashed to the low wall onto which she had perched herself.

"Do not make such noise!" she scolded. "Look."

She straddled the mud bricks and pulled at a rusty chain hanging from a pulley a step away, which whined but eventually gave way.

"A well!" Gaelenn said, catching himself just in time to prevent shouting with excitement. He grasped the nearly-empty water skin at his side; they had not been able to refill at all and the dry air north of Sapphire Mountain had been attacking their throats ruthlessly. He sheathed his sword and helped her pull at the chain, moving it at double the pace. It cried and squeaked, and the other end eased out of the hole in the ground in turn.

"How deep could it be? Maybe the people here left when the water dried up," Gaelenn said.

Aydya shook her head between pulls. "No. A deep well is a good well. Where I am from, the sun never rests. If the well is shallow, the sun consumes it."

Gaelenn licked his wind-chapped lips with his dry tongue. "The people here seem to have left pretty quickly, judging by that gate. Could have been the water." He let go of the chain and nursed his hands.

Aydya picked up his slack, jerking the chain more and more furiously. Gaelenn half-marveled at her determination and half-pitied her stubbornness at what looked for sure to be a hopeless effort. But her last thrust whipped a drip of fresh water into Gaelenn's eye. The chain came up in two colors: orange as dust and iron gray—with water.

"You did it!" He rested his hand on Aydya's shoulder and reached out again to help her. They found an intact clay pot inside a hut nearby, fastened it to the chain with some of Aydya's rope, and drank deeply from the well.

"What luck," Gaelenn said.

"Perhaps something or someone is looking over us. Let this teach you to keep your faith. Do not give up so easily," she remarked as she delicately wiped the water from her chin.

Gaelenn let the streams flow freely and dry on his long stubble, savoring the water's coolness with closed eyes. *So, she did indeed keep her religion,* he thought.

Most of the huts had long collapsed, they found, but there were still a few with sturdy roofs, and they took a few hours to rest under one and eat. Gaelenn shaved off his beard while Aydya tended to her hair with a fine bone brush she kept in a concealed pouch. She sat on her heels, using one of the curved daggers she kept in her sleeves as a mirror, and Gaelenn studied her body from across the room. Her robe was beginning to tatter, revealing in pieces a single inner layer of skin-tight black covering. Curious at the how a material could be so tight yet flexible, he leaned his body a little closer to her. She caught him in her dagger mirror and retorted with a disapproving frown.

"Sorry," he said, "I just...I've been around the world. You're from Igtao, right? I think I asked you when we first met. You never answered."

She dropped the dagger and spun around on her knees. "Yes. And how did you know that?"

"Like I said, I've been around. When did you leave?"

"When my village was destroyed, I escaped. I was just a girl then," she said with a downward glance.

"It has been at least ten years. I do not know how many of my people survived."

"I have seen your hometown...I've been to all the great cities of your continent, Savyana—every one of them. I'm sorry to say it...but each one was just wiped clean off the map. All those great, big, beautiful spires Igtao was famous for...The endless street markets with all the wonderful spiced meats, the..."

Aydya's eyes closed tightly.

"...Well, pretty much anywhere I went to for the past few years was gone. It's not just Igtao," he said.

She opened her eyes and stared right through his. "Please do not speak of such things."

Gaelenn bowed his head low in apology. "How did you find your new group? The Disciples?"

She lifted an eyebrow, suspicious at the change in conversation, but answered.

"Survivors from my city and many others drifted for a time. In the end we came to the city with spires. It is now known as Maynon Ohza, which means 'Throne of the Eye' in an ancient tongue, did you know? Where all refugees go," she explained. Her words took on a profound weight, her S-sounds more pronounced than usual. She had started to let her guard drop, and her native accent seeped to the surface. "I did not find the Disciples, they found me."

"I don't mean to pry," Gaelenn replied. His face was solemn but he noted it was the first time she spoke of her order using the word 'they' and not 'we.'

She thought again before accepting his apology with a gentle shake of her head.

"I think that you have also lost much," she said, and suddenly Gaelenn was anxious to end the conversation.

He mouthed, "yes," and then sighed and rose to his feet, feeling the pleasure of blood draining back into them. "Well...are you ready? That tower is our destination."

He pointed his thumb at it but stayed focused on her.

"Yes," Aydya said, standing up. "Where you go, I will go."

Dusk had arrived, dampening the sun's power, but there was still enough light to walk easily. The two arrived at the base of the tower after a minute's journey and examined its smooth, perfectly rounded walls.

"It is like the inside of our temple!" Aydya said, eyes wide with surprise. She hesitated but ultimately decided that it was okay to touch.

"This is an older one," Gaelenn interjected. "Actually, I think they're all old."

He looked up at the spire, which stretched much higher into the sky than it had any right to. It was not thick enough, or at least it felt that way. "It looks like a stray breath would topple it."

But it still was not as tall as the memory implanted in his brain told him it should be. His fingers found and traced several deep grooves in its surface—attacks of some sort from long ago. But there was no rust. No paint. And no door.

"I've seen this tower before. I mean, I saw it in my...dream...thing. I can see it in my mind now as much as I can with my eyes. It was taller though. And there was a way in."

Aydya considered his words with her hand at her chin. Her head jerked up and down, and her eyes, unconscious of the white glare of the tower that should have blinded them, examined every inch.

"The tallest trees have deep roots," she said at length.

Gaelenn did not hear her at first. Religious zealots almost always spoke in cryptic idioms, and through his travels he had met many; it was a reflex to ignore them. But her words echoed in his mind. He pursed his lips for a moment before the light hit him.

"You're right!" he exclaimed, and ran all the way around the base of the tower with his hand stuck to it.

Aydya's mouth rose at the corners in a faint smile of vindication.

"That's the first I've seen you smile," Gaelenn said, returning, and she blushed and erased the emotion from her lips. "Now that I really think about it, the images in my mind of this tower are true. There was a settlement around it, but it wasn't like this."

He glanced at the broken wooden buildings. They were makeshift; not meant to last. "The buildings were bigger. Stone or brick or something more permanent. This tower and these shacks are from different ages altogether..."

He looked up at the tall, wind-blasted white walls of the spire. "There are no windows, are there? No way in at all...*wait.*"

He dropped to his knees and dug his finger into the hard dirt against the tower. "Except from underneath."

"Just as the tower in the Palace at Maynon Ohza!" Aydya squealed, her eyes alight. Her smile returned.

"I'd bet all my money on it," Gaelenn said, adding dryly, "not that I have any to bet."

They searched the buildings around for any lower levels or larders or trapdoors, but even without the sun to guide them, it was evident that nobody had ever tried to go under the tower.

"Let's rest." Gaelenn grabbed Aydya's shoulders, and she gave no resistance, but allowed his touch freely. "And sleep. There are some tools around. Tomorrow, we dig."

CHAPTER THIRTY
THUNDER AND LIGHTNING

"WHAT DO WE DO?" Kell shouted.

He, Rin, and Dean were bearing down on the wall of steel-clad bodies in front of them, sloshing through the rain and flooded grass as fast as their feet could unstick themselves from the mud. Behind them from all sides came the Maynon Ohzans and their leader, Triumvir Yajuu, though none of the three fugitives had time to look back to check. Their ears told them all they needed to know. Sudden, brutal, and close lightning highlighted the only possible ways to lose their predators: another forest, far off to their right, too far to provide cover for the trio in time; a steep hill and ledge, slightly closer on the left but likely impossible to mount in the storm; and the ruins directly in view—a great place to buy more time, of course, but currently guarded by the impossible line of soldiers. They were out of options.

"Shit," Dean said, "I don't think there's any choice. Up that hill!"

Despite his injury he moved faster than Kell and almost as fast as Rin. They leered to their left but Dean's foot caught a log hiding in the grass and he tumbled head over heels into the flooded ground in a great, muddy splash. He yelled in pain and grabbed his side. "You two better run! There's no time!"

"Not on your life, old man," Rin said, and he and Kell stooped to Dean's side to help him up.

Another blast of lightning hit a building in the ruins ahead and half a second later, the booming retort of thunder rocked their ears. Rin looked up, adjusted his eyes to the returning darkness, and shouted, "Run to the ruins! Run to them! Run through them!"

"What?" Kell snapped. Rain spun off his beard sideways at the jerk of his neck. "Crazy fool!"

"Trust me! Like the old man said, there's no time!"

They dragged Dean to his feet and with his arms around their necks moved forward as one. Their attackers had them surrounded, and they were walking straight into the trap. But the Lieutenant Captain's face lit up with hope.

"Rrrrrrrrriiiiiiiiiiiiiiin!" A bellowing cry split the air louder than the thunder. It came from the line of fighters ahead.

"What did I tell you?" Rin said to the others. "Just go!"

In a minute they were close enough that the more average eyes of the Kell and Dean could see the warriors clearly. It was the Priestess' Guard. In the center stood Astrid, like the statue of a goddess, donning a silver-plated helmet with long twisting horns and an ornate breastplate that gleamed with the outline of a star. Her tall shield caught the lightning's glare and seemed to hold it there even after it had struck, and her spear towered over her own substantial frame, set with a soaked, black flag just below the head. The rest of the warriors from Last Retreat held their own spears and shields perfectly straight, forming a phalanx of steel.

Astrid and the soldier next to her moved one step apart and created a break in the line just in time for Rin, Kell, and Dean to go tumbling through. As soon as they had collapsed into the grass behind, the line closed up again. She craned her head back and glanced at Rin.

"We found you," she said in a moment of rare and fleeting open emotion. "Lady be praised we were forced to take this route to the mountain due to the storm. Now, Lieutenant Captain, put on your helmet and take your place by my side! We've got a fight coming."

A guard in the unseen second line behind the main one fell forward and unwrapped the wet cloth around a pack holding a similar but less exquisite set of armor and helmet. Rin put one hand on the dome of the helmet, paused and raised his opposite palm in the air, and when he caught his breath, wheezed, "Give me a minute for hell's sake."

"I don't think we have a minute, Lieutenant Captain," said one of the second-line soldiers, peeking through the line at the torches bearing down.

Altogether there were around fifty of the Priestess' guard. Across the field, there were over a hundred sprinting Maynon Ohzans—and one mad giant. Kell struggled to his feet and wiped off his beard with his bare forearm. It was soaked again before his hand reached his hammer.

"Some of you'd better stay back here with this old man," he said.

"Do it," Rin commanded, and two of the soldiers helped Dean up.

"Take care," Dean said to Kell and Rin as he was led into the shadowy ruins. He tossed a small bag at Rin. "I lied—here's a couple more of those toys for you. And you, blacksmith—make good use of that belt. I'll show you how to *really* make sparks fly later. You just have to make it out of this."

Kell nodded and pressed the head of his mace against the belt. Steam burst out almost at once.

"You'd better make it, old man," he said, "because I'm coming to look for you when I get back."

He couldn't think of anything else to say, and lacking the breath to say it anyway, he kept his closing remark short. "Don't die."

Dean disappeared behind them with his escort of guards and Rin took one last, long breath before strapping on the hard leather cuirass—his own, light and flexible—as well as his helmet. A soldier handed him a long spear and he squeezed in next to Astrid. The armies were only a hundred yards apart. The line braced.

"Where is Gaelenn?" Astrid said through her teeth. "I was instructed to bring you and him back to Last Retreat."

"I'll let you know after we've crushed these assholes," Rin said. His free arm squeezed hers just above the elbow. "Just watch the big one."

And the battle began. The left flank arrived first. Screams on both sides climaxed just before the clash of iron sent chills through the bones of those waiting; it would soon reach them all.

The Maynon Ohzans were fierce, skilled fighters who grew stronger at the scent of blood, and their first strike was like a whip upon a mouse. They swiped with their maces and spears and landed a score of successful blows, knocking the defenders back.

And that was only the left flank—when the right flank arrived, the fight on both sides bent the line inward into a full circle. The Priestess' Guard was too far outnumbered. But not outmatched.

"Guard! Attack!"

Astrid's great shout penetrated the walls of rain, reverberating throughout the entire battlefield. Her fighters stopped their backwards movement—a cunning tactic to absorb the first blow like rubber—and snapped back with their long polearms, devastating the front line of the Maynon Ohzans. Dozens of the green-clad soldiers splashed into the marshy grass, dead or dying. Astrid's troops proved the more elite.

They pressed their advantage in skill with another counterattack, mixing in long blades for close-range fighting with a volley of arrows from the second line. Picking off their counterparts soldier by soldier, the women and men of Last Retreat let out a collective victory cry.

Rin darted out and swung his spear like a poet writing script on a parchment, with the skill and precision of an artist. He tossed Dean's magic rocks deftly, launching Maynon Ohzans into the air in watery bursts, creating holes that his comrades readily exploited.

Kell burst forth with his fiery hammer, a beacon of flame in the black plains, and the opposing soldiers fled his reach with panicked screams, thinking him a monster of old.

The attacking force was shocked for the moment, but not beaten. They dug in their heels and fell back on their advantage in numbers. With two of them for every one of Astrid's forces, they still had the upper hand. But the guardians of Last Retreat had Astrid. She stood her ground, the anchor of the battlefield, keeping her troops tightly knit and working in unison. Barking orders and inspirational cheers and calls, she was a maestro, orchestrating the fight in a great, exquisite performance of deadly harmony and beauty.

Her talent for leadership was surpassed only by her skill as a warrior. Left and right she spun, dodging blows like a dancer, swatting legionnaires to the ground like mosquitoes, leaping into the air when those all around her could barely move their feet.

"That's why she's the Captain!" Rin shouted to Kell. Both stood mesmerized by her brutal dance. The lightning seemed to land with each strike of her spear.

Kell worked his way closer to Rin. The rain pelted his eyes, and he wiped it away with his blackened hands.

"Wait. Where's the giant?" he yelled.

"Good question, no idea!" Rin said. "Can I panic yet?"

A massive lightning bolt struck a spear sticking vertically from a body, flashing everyone in a momentary frame. There he was: Triumvir Yajuu, finally approaching—and mad. His huge girth sunk each step into the ground all the way past his knees, so he had crossed the field at half the speed of his army. It would have been a stroke of good fortune for Astrid and her guards, too, had it not made his anger swell with each successive stomp.

The rain abated for a moment and silent gasps welcomed his arrival. Strobing, soundless lightning made his first swing appear to all around to move in slow motion. The silence broke with the screams of two Star Guardians—elite guards of the Priestess—as they flew over the heads of Astrid, Rin, and Kell into the steep pool of fresh marsh behind them.

The water cut short their torment by drowning them before the loss of blood from their severed torsos did the job.

Astrid swung around crouching, a tiger ready to pounce, and screamed a painful blood-cry. She leapt at him, catching the giant off guard, and with her spear slashed at his hand, forcing his axe to the mud. Still in midair, she drew a long dagger and aimed at his heart.

The speed with which he rebounded shocked her eyes into perfectly round balls of white—her irises were so pale that the only real color in them was the black of her pupils, dilated to their limits. With his other hand he made a great fist and smacked her into the ground just as she was about to land.

"Astrid!" Rin screamed, incensed. He cursed himself for using up all of Dean's magic rocks. "Damnit, why didn't I save one? Kell!"

The blacksmith, who had just branded the faces of a group of Maynon Ohzans, treaded the muddy water to Rin's side. "What happened?"

"The green giant! Let's burn him down!"

"With pleasure!" Kell said and leapt forward with a low roar. His red-hot hammer again ignited the air in a steamy trail of flame. Yajuu's own blood-red irises widened as his pupils shrank in the light of the mace, and he plod backwards, protecting his face with his arms when he was not using them to stay upright.

Rin took the opportunity to free stray spears from the ground and launch them anew, but despite the huge target that he made, the giant moved like a cat above his stuck knees. Speed was his weakness, but compared to an average fighter he was lightning itself.

He was, however, victim of the dark as much as anyone. He took a miscalculated step back and with a massive, suctiony *sloop* and fell right over a stray branch.

Kell's teeth glistened through his beard; he set his hammer with both hands above his head and threw it down right at the green giant's head.

There was no dodging the blow this time, the giant's gaping mouth admitted, so the only course was to bear the stroke with his hands on the head of the mace. He let out a high-pitched, blood-curdling wail, and the stench of charred flesh at once mixed with the smell of blood, causing some around to bend over heaving.

Kell pried the hammer from the giant's hands—the iron had bonded with the skin and had to be wrenched off with a jerk. Rin shot in with a spear in hand, eyes set downward with determination not to miss another throw and instead he readied himself to impale the giant directly.

Wounded and scared and focused on the incoming spear, Yajuu kicked his feet out of the mud and craned his torso up just as Kell brought his fiery hammer around for another surprise blow right into his chest.

SMASH

The wind in giant's lungs blew out in a great gust and he fell backward again onto the other end of the twisted log, launching it into the air in front of Rin, who was preparing his thrust, but the opportunity to skewer the giant was lost.

The log reached its peak in the air and summoned a fierce bolt of lightning. Rin and Kell were blasted onto their backs and thousands of splinters rocketed into the ground around them, a battery of whistles all splashing into the surrounding pools of water at once.

"Rin!" Astrid shouted again. Her helmet, disheveled, dented, and smothered in blood, mud, and grass, still somehow clung to her head and shook from left to right as she swooped to gather her lover in her arms.

"Shit," Rin said. "Not the ear again!"

Its wound, freshly healed, reopened and bled freely. He cursed but ignored it, taking Astrid's arm and using it to help himself up.

Kell followed a second later, shaking the daze from his head along with the water and grass in his beard. He spat out a mouthful of black mud.

"Cursed giant! C'mon, lovebirds, get on it!" he shouted to Rin and Astrid.

But they were too late; a group of Maynon Ohzans in their tattered, rain-soaked capes surrounded them.

Astrid swung her body around to get a good look at the predicament. She ignored her own pain—a bloody nose and swelling eyes—and counted the survivors in groups of five.

"One, two, three...is that all?" she cried. Barely fifteen of her guard remained standing. "Guards! To me!"

The clashing of iron dwindled and her army rushed to her side. Just sixteen in total. "Madame! Sir!" saluted one of the remaining ranking troops. Fresh lines had been drawn between the sides as they regrouped.

"Only nine of them, though," Astrid said, lifting her chin. "Warriors! Well fought."

The battered soldiers let out a bittersweet and prideful battle cry. Her affirming nod erased the sadness from their faces and she looked each of the men and women in the eyes. When she was satisfied that they were fit to continue, she swiveled her head to the Maynon Ohzans and their leader.

"Guardians of the Priestess!" she shouted, directing the words themselves at her own troops but their spirit toward the enemy. "You have fought bravely! Where once you were outnumbered you now have the advantage!"

Her taunts froze the Maynon Ohzans in place. A few of them looked at each other and saw only sour, injured scowls.

"Their mighty legions are soft! Perhaps they lost their fighting edge marauding helpless villages! Trampling tiny towns! Murdering innocent lives! Beating and raping helpless women—and men!"

Her speech hit with devastating effectiveness, demoralizing her opposition as if daggers twisted in their hearts. A straggler inched away and ran. Nobody tried to stop him. The adrenaline of battle overrode her caution and she continued her taunts and declarations.

"We will let the rest of you live today. Go back to your home and tell the rest of your rulers that on this day, the Army of the Star Priestess has risen to meet Maynon Ohza and the Eye. Though the hour is late, the battle has only now begun! We will come, and we will rid the world of your Triumvirate—and their god—once and for all!"

Astrid let the words hang in the air and savored their bravado. Her confidence bolstered the remaining warriors and lifted them up until all fatigue had left them. And now the rumor of the Priestess' existence—and likely Last Retreat itself—were compromised. But she could not back down now.

She drew a deep breath for her last proclamation. "You may drop your weapons, turn around, and go back to your city. Keep your lives for now." Her lips drew up in a sneer and she looked at them one-by-one, and fed on their cowardice and hate and fear. They were nothing now but a humiliated rabble. Astrid beamed, and broke them.

The Maynon Ohzan soldiers' eyes fell; they could sustain neither her gaze nor each other's. One by one, they threw down their spears and knives and swords and stood for a moment in shame before the Priestess' Guard. Then, as a unit, they turned around, their backs framed in a silent bolt of lightning.

The giant, Triumvir Yajuu, was no longer there.

The shame in their eyes turned to twisted gasps of horror. A great swoop shot out of the darkness from behind, severing the bodies of three soldiers in half. Not a half-second later, another three were hewn in two. And before the last three could even scream, their voices were silenced by the great axe which the giant had found to exact punishment on the traitors.

"Dak lamoot!" he cried in his foreign tongue, his voice like thunder.

Astrid, watching the scene with the others between the flashes of lightning, set her feet and spear.

"Get that giant green bastard," she said, and her army charged with a great, single cry.

Kell and Rin, who beamed with pride and awe, brought up the rear. Astrid pushed them all forward. From above, it must have looked like an arrow speeding toward its target.

Yajuu squeezed the shaft of his axe with his bloody, skinless hands, ignoring the pain, mad with bloodlust, and bent over to scream at his attackers. He raised his axe to attack just as they came within reach, and in the same instant his arms launched his axe into the air, Rin and Astrid both let loose their spears.

The giant could not dodge them both and his indecision ended his life.

The first one arrived, piercing the giant's great heart. His eyes popped out of their sockets with the instant shock of its very last beat. The second one struck even truer, right through his skull, and the soldiers, not leaving anything to chance, hacked up his defenseless body.

He fell, dead, throwing up one last splash of bloody, muddy water just as his axe finished its journey through the air and struck home below Rin's abdomen.

CHAPTER THIRTY ONE
THE BURIED TOWER

TWO STRAIGHT DAYS OF digging had been brutal. Gaelenn stuck the shovel upright into the ground and rested his forearm on it to analyze his grimy and bleeding hands. They looked just like they felt—filthy and old. He closed his eyes and tried to picture something more pleasant, but all he could see was the dirt. His fingers and palms would be happily calloused by now instead of blistering if there had been time for even an hour's rest. But there had not. For some sneaking feeling that he could not quite place, he knew that time was precious. The shadow on Sapphire Mountain he saw as they descended was eating at his mind.

"How much further must we dig?" Aydya asked him, wiping her forehead with the cleanest part of the bottom of her palm. She only managed to smudge dirt from one place to another. "In your memory, how tall was this tower?"

Gaelenn scrubbed his own face with his bare arm; he had stripped to the waist in the heat and wore what used to be a white rag on his head for relief. Once an hour he walked back to the well and rinsed and soaked it. Without fail, an hour later he would find the hard groundwater replaced entirely with brown sweat. Aydya, who refused to take off any clothes, exposed only her legs from her calves down.

She must be baking, he thought, over and over.

"You work on the shady side. We'll break for an hour at noon when the sun's strongest and eat a little and rest," Gaelenn had said to her when they started digging.

But she refused to hog the shade and suffered the heat of the sun without complaint. To the noon hour break, however, she agreed without hesitation. At night, they slept on the ground in the nearest shack that had all four walls and a roof. Each day, that sacred hour of reprieve for lunch was all they could think about as soon as their shovels hit the dry dirt.

Sometime after dawn on the third day Gaelenn dropped his shovel and massaged his aching shoulder, not yet fully healed, leaving a small imprint on his naturally tanned but still reddened, burnt skin. The sun crept up from the horizon as they dragged their tools and bodies around the ever-widening hole. Words were scarcer the deeper they went. And they went deeper and deeper.

Aydya caught Gaelenn's eye. "Is the town like this in your memory?"

"Let me think about it for a second. Maybe we should take our break early," he offered. It was not yet noon, but his body yearned for rest.

Aydya dropped her shovel, stretched her back up straight with a wince, and then nodded and climbed up, walking straight for the open hut. When she got there, she fell down on her knees.

"Why don't you lay down?" Gaelenn said, entering the hut after her. "I know that the people of your country love their naps."

She only let herself relax when she was sleeping at night, and even then it was only after she had fallen over.

"My people," she countered, "are gone. I am still a Disciple of the Eye. And *we* know the importance of discipline. Especially with oneself."

Gaelenn dismissed it with a shrug of his shoulders and smacked the dust off of a pile of decaying rags before laying down on his back. The inside of the shack was wide and dark and not entirely uncomfortable. In fact, after hours of sweaty labor, it was downright luxurious.

"Let me see," he said, followed by a long, barely audible hum. "I don't seem to 'remember' anything about the town here. The last thing I know about this place is that it was called 'Edgebound North'. Before that, it had an even older name...but I can't seem to remember that."

His eyes rolled up white and closed.

"And, well, there was a town—a different one—around it. Not with wood huts like this one. But with actual homes and huge buildings. They were stone or rock or something even sturdier. There was grass...and trees. For a time, it was used for guarding something in the north. But I...can't see what."

Gaelenn strained his closed eyes as if it would help focus his view inward. "That's right. Before that it was called Initar Dev. I think it's incredibly old."

Aydya barely blinked.

"How tall was it?" she asked for the second time.

"Very tall," Gaelenn said, repeating, "very, very tall. It was used just like you would use one of your temples to talk with your Eye. Not just that, from the top you could see great distances, this whole area north of Sapphire Mountain."

He sighed; it was not any less taxing to traverse his new knowledge than it was to dig dirt.

Aydya, who had shifted uncomfortably on her knees at his mention of the Eye, listened patiently, but her impatience for the answer to her actual question shone on her pursed lips.

"I can't explain what I remember—not exactly—but this place was significant. It was a capital, a command post. Or maybe it was used to commune with faraway places. And for...experiments. Like the kind that old man, Dean, does."

His eyes shot open. "Dean! He was here! This is where he did it!" he said.

"Did what?" Aydya asked.

Gaelenn told her of Dean's role in the Legion and the ENs.

"It's strange that I know these things, but don't *really* know them until I think about them. I can't get used to this," he reflected, then stood up, rubbed his eyes, and looked out the door at the base of the tower. The sun was waning and its rays were finally gentle enough to dig again. "I imagine that something that has stood for as long as this tower has would be hard to destroy. And I don't have any memory of this, but I can imagine what happened here. I think they—someone, somehow—buried it."

His fist rubbed into his open palm.

Aydya got up effortlessly, already refreshed, and stood next to him. "Will you continue? I will help you."

"Thank you," Gaelenn said, simply, peering deeply into her eyes from his resting place. "Yeah. Let's head out there."

The tower pulled his gaze from her and he continued his introspective, speaking lowly enough that it was as if his inner thoughts were spilling out.

"To be honest, I wasn't exactly sure why I had to come here before. It was just the answer my mind kept on coming up with. But now I think I know. In that tower hides the solution to defeating the ENs of Maynon Ohza. And the Eye. I can't make sense of it, but I can *feel* it."

"Then let us dig," Aydya said.

He gazed at her in secret as she turned to work; she did not recoil at the idea of her god being defeated. They continued.

For some days Gaelenn and Aydya followed the same pattern: dig before dawn, rest at noon, and dig some more before the freezing night pushed them back into their shack. Gaelenn's muscles ached and tightened and his body was stripped of what little fat remained on it. His face thinned.

Aydya's robe barely hung from her frame anymore, as well; it was more like a long, black scarf draped loosely around her body, further deteriorating with each scoop of her shovel. Her skin-tight bodice underneath collected enough dust to turn from black to brown, providing her with some relative relief from the heat as time went on. On the fourth afternoon since their last real conversation, Gaelenn spoke.

"Here!" he shouted. "I've seen this!"

The sun reached down into the crater, now over five yards deep all around the tower, and showed Gaelenn something he had not seen in the morning. On the tower, just at his knee, was a symbol.

"What is...?" Aydya said, coming around to Gaelenn's side. "It's a star!"

Gaelenn nodded. "It's faded, almost gone. But it's there. There is a door on this side!"

Whose star it was he kept to himself; it was Last Retreat's—and Livvy's. His heart turned. "Just another yard maybe!"

Abandoning the dig on the other side of the tower, Gaelenn and Aydya churned their shovels with renewed vigor, reaching down, down, down into the ground.

"Well, more like two yards down, but I was right," Gaelenn said to correct himself after they had exposed the door—and the solid stone floor at its feet. "It's here."

He stuck his fingers into the recessed grooves of the door, which were just wide enough for him to pry out some of the caked earth. "Now, how do we open this up?"

Aydya surveyed the door as well, pressing her hands and ears against it, pushing and tapping with the ball of her fist. It was the exact same roundness and strange material of the tower and, if not for the grooves that framed it, would not be visible at all.

"I don't seem to have any memory of how to open it, damnit. Maybe my eyes can unlock it?" Gaelenn asked, mostly directed at himself. He spread his eyelids wide and, hovering two inches from the door with his green eye awkwardly widened, inched his face around the entire thing. "Maybe this will work like the table-things do."

It did not. At knee height, he gave up and blinked.

"This must look a bit awkward, I guess," he said. "I don't think—"

SLAM

The tower shook and reverberated from bottom to top like a hollow bell. He looked up from his spidery pose after wiping the dirt that shook from the tower into his eyes.

Aydya was readying her second swing on the door with the back of the pick she had been using to clear away rocks. Gaelenn was too late to stop her or jump away. The second strike did the job, and the door swung free with a singing wail followed by a trail of metallic clinks and a cry. The darkness inside reached out to them.

She bent down and stretched her hands into the doorway. "This was not sealed with magic," she said, picking up a brittle, busted old chain link and tossing it aside.

"It held pretty well though, didn't it?" Gaelenn said. He stood up and, head first, crept inside. "Sealed from inside..."

As soon as he entered, he threw his tunic back over his shoulders. It was cool—unnaturally so.

Aydya followed, holding the small of his back with one hand and the pick just under its head in the other. It took nearly a minute for their eyes to adjust from the blinding afternoon sun to the utter blackness within the tower, but just enough light leaked in to give them an idea of what was inside: a ladder-staircase, ascending to the abyss above them; a torn and decomposed sack; and, near the back just opposite the door, the remains of a skeleton that was once, presumably, a human.

"This person must have sacrificed themselves," Aydya said, stooping to examine the crumbling bone resting in a pile of cloth on a dusty gray rug. "To ensure that nobody could come in. It is a noble death."

She bent her head down to the floor in a sort of prayer.

"Are you praying to the Eye?" Gaelenn asked her on a reflex.

She darted upright but remained on her knees. "I... Yes. I pray, but I'm... Not to the..."

Gaelenn waved his hand low, dismissing his comment.

"It's okay, you don't have to explain," he said. "Nothing else near the body?"

Aydya leaned over it, supported by her hands, and moved her hips back and forth to allow a little light from the door past so she could see. Gaelenn cleared his throat, which echoed upward, trying his best to remain focused on the dead body and not hers. Her touch as they entered had startled and confused him.

"There is nothing—wait," she said, stopping her breath as if it would help her see better. She swung the pick around and used the sharp end to lift away a part of some rotted cloth. Under it was a small glass ball the size of a fist.

"There is something here. Look." She moved to the side to allow just enough space for Gaelenn, now also on his knees, to squeeze in.

"I've seen something like this before. Not in my memory, though," he said. "With my own eyes."

He extended his hand forward, without thinking, and cupped it. Immediately blue light emanated from the creases in his fingers, and when he turned it over, it illuminated the room in that same pale blue that had been his first introduction to the hidden world he had discovered on top of Last Retreat. It felt so long ago.

Aydya shrank back at first, but reassured by Gaelenn's smile, came closer to the orb. "There *is* magic here!"

"It's not really magic," Gaelenn said, happily waving the ball around, casting a blue-black shadow show in the room. "Feel it."

She recoiled and shook her head.

"Go ahead," he insisted with a gentle push.

Aydya pressed her first two fingers against it. "It is cool. The light from fire is hot. It is magic."

"Maybe you're right," Gaelenn said, grinning in amusement. He set the ball down on the ground and its light went out. When he picked it up again, the light came back. "That's how this one works, then. Time to move on."

Aydya nodded. "Yes. Upward."

Gaelenn raised the orb and they looked up. The ladder climbed up and up, was separated by a grate, and then another ladder led up into the murky blackness. He looked at Aydya, took a deep breath, and nodded before ascending. The steps croaked in pain but held; they ascended and ascended, being as careful as they could, until after nearly twenty minutes they finally reached the top. Another door, this time in the ceiling above them.

"I've seen a door like this before—around the time we met," Gaelenn said, sucking in deep breaths of the thin, stale air. A flash of the sewer below his house shot through his mind but he set it aside. "Don't have that pick still, do you?"

"It was too heavy. I left it at the bottom."

He saw the strain in her neck, but that was the only indication that she was struggling as much as he. Her usually dark skin was a pale gray in the blue light next to her face, but it did not diminish her beauty—or her strength.

A half smile flashed across Gaelenn's face in admiration. "I know. Just a joke—somehow I don't think this one is locked from the inside. How did the door work back at your temple?"

"There is no lock. We simply guard it at all times."

"Well, then," Gaelenn said, setting the orb down at his feet and then continuing in the resulting darkness, "let's see if it moves." He raised his hands above his head and found the edges of the door. With a grunt he pushed upward with all his might, but it didn't budge. "There's no way to tell if it's just rusted shut or if it's locked, or held down by something. One more try."

This time he braced his legs, squatting halfway down first for momentum. The door cracked open a half inch.

"It moved! But it's too heavy for me," he said. "Let's do it together."

Reaching into the darkness, he found Aydya's wrists and pulled them up until her hands were also holding the door.

"On my mark, push as hard as you can."

"Okay," she said.

"One, two, push!"

They ground their teeth and groaned from the strain as they faced each other, in the darkness unaware that their faces were only an inch away and their chests even closer.

"Aaahhh!" their combined voices cried, and finally the trap door gave and bent upward on its hinge until it was stuck upright. It held there as stubbornly as it had held itself shut.

Gaelenn bent down and picked up the globe.

"You... I..." A last outward breath was enough to recover his strength and his wits. "Well done."

The blue light couldn't quite hide his blushed cheeks, though, when he realized how close they had been, painting them lavender instead of red.

"You first. I'll hold the light up," he said.

"Yes," Aydya replied, oblivious, it seemed, and using her hands as support, jumped right up through the hole in one bound.

"What's up there?"

"It is... not a normal temple, I think."

"What?" Gaelenn shouted louder than he had intended. The echo traveled up and down the spine of the tower and back up again. "Here, take the light."

Aydya grabbed it and Gaelenn pulled himself up.

"What is this...?" he said. His eyes danced around the room.

"There are twelve of them!" Aydya said. "Twelve altars. I have never seen a temple like this."

"And what are these?" Gaelenn asked to nobody as he navigated the crowded, messy floor to reach the wall.

Instead of the expected smooth barrier, the walls were blanketed with tubes and black glass, punctuated by luminescent buttons like those of a fine shirt, round and smooth, all the way around.

"Do not touch, please!" Aydya warned, freezing in her tracks.

He did not need to touch anything. The bright white lights came on automatically, blinding both of them.

A familiar voice spoke gently: "*Hello, master.*"

CHAPTER THIRTY TWO
VICTORY AND GRIEF

ASTRID'S KNEES SPLASHED MUD all over the massive axe buried halfway into the bone at Rin's hip. When she stooped over his face, her helmet stopped the rain from hitting his eyes, letting him open them and look at her.

His lips moved but the air passing through them failed to trigger his voice.

Kell crashed next to them, sobbing.

Ripping off her helmet after a second of shock, Astrid pulled at the axe gently. It did not come free. Turning to Kell, she said, in a calm but powerless whisper, "Help me."

They worked together to dislodge the curved steel and tossed it behind them into the water. Around them the remaining guards were tending to their own wounded and dead, but they all kept half an eye on their Captain. Rin groaned and coughed.

"Ah, thank the Priestess, you got it out," he said and laughed, triggering another cough.

Astrid grabbed his head from behind and held it close to her own. The rain hid her own tears as they fell on his face.

"We did it—Gaelenn got away," he whispered, smiling.

"Where did he go?" she asked.

"North of Sapphire Mountain," Kell interrupted and turned his head to Rin's. "Don't talk, you idiot."

His beard hung low from his drooping head.

"You'll never shut me up," Rin said. He tried hiding the pain from his face but his grin fell off here and there.

Kell grabbed his hammer. "The old man used this. I'm no cleric, but we should try. To stop the blood." He set it to his belt, pulling it off and pressing it again, making sure it was hot but not too hot. "Pull his clothes away."

Astrid swallowed her tears and did as Kell asked, pulling Rin's bloody tunic up and undoing his halfway-severed belt. She put her hand over the gaping wound, and then looked away as the blacksmith pressed his steaming hammer firmly against it.

It hissed and Rin howled, losing consciousness from the pain, resting his head back in Astrid's arms. She lifted it up and stroked his cheeks, wiping away the rain and mud.

Drums and cries droned in the distance to the northeast.

"We've got to get back to Last Retreat," she said, turning to Kell. They looked at each other and shared their grief in a fleeting moment before burying it away for the time being. "This was only a tiny piece of the army of Maynon Ohza. The deserter who ran will reach them soon, and then the rest will follow. We cannot stand against them as few as we are. Who was that old man?"

"Some kind of wizard. He says he knows your Priestess. I believe him," he said. "Says they're friends."

Astrid nodded and whispered, "Somehow, I know his face..."

Morning light set the air into a diffused, thick gray, and she found her shield in a deep puddle full of blood, shook out the water, and fastened it on her back.

"You must go with the others. Take your old man to the Priestess with my guard. At once," she said.

"You're not coming? What are you going to do?" Kell asked as he stood up.

"I promised the Priestess that I would bring Gaelenn and Rin back to her. Gaelenn is now beyond my reach. But I will fulfill half of my oath, at least." She stood up and called her soldiers closer to address them, instructing those who remained to assist the wounded and dying and speed Dean and Kell to Last Retreat. They gave parting prayers to the dead and dying, helped up the wounded who had a chance at survival, and set off.

Kell held back before joining them and looked at Rin once more. "Is there anything you want me to say to her...until you arrive?" he asked Astrid.

"Just tell her I will come back soon, please. And..." She eased her arms under Rin's neck and knees and lifted him up like a doll, limbs and head lifelessly swinging.

"Tell her to make ready. The war is upon us."

Kell turned and jogged to the group and they disappeared into the ruins.

"I wish you were lighter," Astrid said to Rin, and started forward in slow, plodding steps.

The rain stopped. She looked east and smiled at the clouds, surprising herself, as they gave way to a dazzling beam of morning light that kissed her cheeks and dried her still-falling tears.

CHAPTER THIRTY THREE

AI

"WHO'S THERE?" GAELENN SAID as he spun around and saw only Aydya, who had brandished her blades and was swinging at the air threateningly amongst the waist-high tables. Once their eyes acclimated to the sudden light, they found it was not quite the blinding white it had seemed at first. The room was only half-lit; most of the lights had failed to come to life.

"There are only two people in this room," the voice seemed to emanate from the walls themselves without any particular direction.

"Then who is speaking?" Aydya asked with slits for eyes.

"I am your assistant. What can I do for you?" it gushed in an overly-friendly tone.

Gaelenn and Aydya looked sidelong at each other and closed the gap between them while facing the walls.

"I've heard your voice before. What is your name?" Gaelenn asked.

"Please wait a moment... I'm sorry, I seem to have made a mistake. I don't remember meeting you. My name...?"

"I don't understand. You don't have a name? Aren't you human? Where are you?" Gaelenn pressed.

Aydya looked over her shoulder at him.

"We should not talk to it," she whispered.

"But I love to talk. No, I am not human. I am simply a helper. What can I do for you today?"

Gaelenn lifted his brow up at Aydya and shrugged his shoulders.

Couldn't hurt to talk, he mouthed to her without words.

"Okay... What are these things all over the room?" he asked the walls.

"This is a collection of various devices. There are four Keeroekoohoegee, three Sooshinsoechee, three Jeekensoechee, and two Eedensheekee."

Gaelenn pulled his brow tightly over his eyes and quipped, "I have no idea what that means."

"Would you like me to explain?"

"Yes...?" Gaelenn responded, still unsure how to properly communicate with the voice.

"Keeroekoohoegee keep records, Sooshinsoechee are communications beacons, Jeekensoechee are work tables for experiments, and Eedensheekee are used for human alteration."

"Human alteration?"

"Would you like me to explain?"

Gaelenn sighed. "Yes."

"The Eedensheekee are used in the permanent or temporary alteration of a human's physical or mental state. They were first used in the second great conflict."

Gaelenn put his hand over his green eye. "I...know that. Somehow. But let's not use the formal names, I can't remember those. Do all these things work?"

"Understood ... I'm sorry, I don't know. It's been a long time since they were used. I can check them, but it will have to be done one at a time. Shall I proceed?"

Aydya pulled Gaelenn's elbow, bringing his face close to hers. "I do not think it is wise to do this," she pleaded.

"But it's what I came here to do. All these things here...I didn't know exactly what we'd find, I just knew that something was kept here. It makes sense."

"Then, please, be careful. These altars are not much different from the alters we have used before to commune with the Great Eye. If you use the wrong one—maybe *any* one—you may summon something you regret." Her warnings came with great, exaggerated gestures, pointing at each machine in turn and mimicking those of the cult leader at the convent in Maynon Ohza.

He stopped himself from looking at her sideways. "Okay, let's see if these things work. One at a time."

"*I understand. Please wait a moment...*"

One table hummed for a moment and then ceased.

"*The first communication beacon does not work.*"

Another table came to life and then died, followed by two others.

"*Neither do the first alteration table, first work table, or first record-keeper. They seemed to have succumbed to age and are in need of substantial mainte-nance. It doesn't look very good. Do you want me to continue?*"

Gaelenn walked around the room to brush off a few of the tables. Some had yellowed with age under their thick layer of dust, and some were made of obsidian just like Livvy's and still a deep black. He used his arm to wipe one completely clean.

"This one is a...record keeper, right?" he asked, absently.

"*That's right.*"

"Okay, keep going."

More low humming, on and off, sent buzzing through the room for a few minutes.

"*The second communication beacon and some of the record-keepers are functional, but locked,*" the voice, usually so lively, suddenly had a sad tone, as if it had failed its duty.

"So does anything work?" Gaelenn shouted, slamming his palm down on the nearest table. Dust burst out from small, unseen creases all the way down to the floor. Gaelenn covered his mouth with his forearm to keep from coughing. Strange, small circles of light lit up and illuminated the ancient grime above them in red and yellow and the green.

"*That one does*," said the voice.

Aydya brushed up against Gaelenn's back and poked her head out from around his body, grasping at his arms and whispered in his ear as quietly as she could.

"That is a portal for communing—be careful!" she warned.

Gaelenn stepped closer and swept the portal clean, but held his tongue, not sure who or what it might summon. A barely visible red light, just as in the old room in the middle of the Windy Woods what felt like years ago, shot out of the table into his eyes. A crackling noise preceded a short beep.

"...Hello? Who is this? Who opened this channel?" came a small but instantly recognizable voice directly from the table.

"I don't believe it," Gaelenn said. He bent over the machine and pressed his elbows and forearms into it. His voice, without meaning, rose to a shout. "Livvy?!"

Aydya stepped backward and leered at the machine.

"Gaelenn?! What are you doing? Where are y—*Initar*?" the Priestess' voice, muffled and somehow distant, filled the room and despite its suddenly shocking volume, set Gaelenn's heart pounding.

"You know where we are?" he asked, taken aback.

"Yes. Is Rin with you? Astrid? I sent her to find you two. How did you find that place? You must have met Dean then—he's there with you? Dean, are you there?"

Gaelenn leaned over further, his face mere inches over the table, and spoke into it. "We were separated from Rin and Kell—I don't know where they are now. They went with the old man, who said he knows you. They were being chased. I have to think that if they survived, they would be heading back to you."

A long pause in the conversation set his heart racing again. "They didn't make it?"

"Just a moment, Gaelenn...it seems they're just arriving now," she replied.

Gaelenn sighed heavily, dropping until his forehead rested on the portal. "Thank the gods..."

"Kell and that 'old man' are with them—I see you've met Dean—but no sign of Rin or Astrid."

"What do you mean? They aren't there?" he asked. The skin around his eyes burned red.

"Gaelenn, are you safe? Alone? Let me talk to them to see what's happened, and then I'll come back. Don't—go—*anywhere!*"

"I'm safe," he said, dodging the 'alone' question. "I'll wait."

"Good. I'll be right back. Please wait. *Please*," Livvy said. Gaelenn could not see her face but could feel the desperation in her voice. He sat down on the floor to rest his tired legs and tied the ends of his tunic, which had been flying loosely. Aydya sat next to him, on her knees as usual.

"Who is it you are talking to?" she asked.

Gaelenn looked at her with his eyes, his head still pointing down at his feet. "That's the Priestess you've been hearing about."

Aydya examined Gaelenn's face. In her own, a sliver of compassion showed through her lips. In her voice was a thread of genuine care. "Is she not your friend?"

He took a deep breath before answering.

"I don't know. I think so. But," he said, considering how to explain with a caress of his jaw, "it's complicated."

"Who is her god?"

"I think she's a priestess without a god, honestly," he answered.

"No god? How could she be a priestess, then?" Aydya's eyebrows twisted up high on her forehead. "To whom does she pray?"

Gaelenn looked deep into her—so confused, completely earnest and innocent and yet somewhere, far beyond her eyes, she was a woman who had seen betrayal. Who had been a victim of it. She was incapable of trust. He just shook his head at her with pursed lips.

"I don't know. What about you, Aydya—what do you believe?"

Defensively, she rocked back onto her heels before settling her weight back on her knees.

"It is...also complicated," she said and smiled, faintly, showing Gaelenn a new sign of vulnerability.

He half-smiled back. "Then it seems like we've both gotten into something a little too big for ourselves."

A minute or two of total silence filled the void between them, giving them a moment to connect in their struggles without words. Gaelenn looked down at the sword he still carried at his waist.

"For such a fine weapon, it's almost a pity I haven't been able to use it yet. I haven't even really had the chance to look at it," he said and fingered it lightly.

The hilt glinted with clear jewels that cut up the light from a source above into dazzling rainbows at the slightest movement. Diamonds. He was happy for the momentary distraction.

"In all my travels, I've never seen anything like this. Swords are rare enough, let alone something so...grand," he continued. He drew a dot of blood on his thumb with a purposeful test of the edge. "And nothing this perfectly sharp, ever."

"Where did you get it?" Aydya asked, relief in her voice as well at the lightening of the conversation.

"From that lunatic—I can't seem to remember his name for some reason. Triumvir something?"

"Anwir. The Betrayer."

"That's right," Gaelenn said with an aimless look upward. "Wait."

He sat straight and faced Aydya, suddenly on edge. "I wanted to ask you. You didn't see him on the Mountain? Before we jumped down? I thought I saw a shadow. I almost thought it was him. I couldn't see *him* but...I don't know, just the way it moved."

She shook her head. "No. But the fight was so far away, I couldn't see. And the rain, and—it is possible that he was there if the beast Yajuu was. I could see the large one easily. They are usually together. All three of them."

Gaelenn rested his back on the machine behind him again, appeased but still grinding his lips. "Tell me about these ENs—Triumvir—guys. I haven't been around for a few years. Seems like I missed a lot that everybody else knows."

Aydya looked Gaelenn up and down, her eyes drawn slim with initial suspicion before she decided he was not trying to fool her.

"Everybody knows the Triumvirate. Not all know that they are the hand of the great Eye. It was they who...'liberated' the city and renamed it Maynon Ohza. Not long after I arrived," she said, her lips twitching with slow-boiled hatred.

"Wait—when you say liberated...what happened? I used to know of Sithica, I think it was, but it was peaceful. There was never any word of oppression or rebellion."

Aydya sidestepped the question but continued, "'Triumvir' is a title to denote a Councilor. One of the three rulers of the city. That much is known."

She glanced at Gaelenn. "But *we* know what it really means: one who has been chosen by the Eye. They execute the Eye's vision. And the Eye commanded that the great city should be Its Throne. And so It blessed the three with Its power and deposed the old king. The Disciples of the Eye, of course, assisted from the shadows in our own way, as we always have."

Her voice quivered with a shudder that ran through her body.

"We have never had a direct role in governing Maynon Ohza, but we are totally dedicated to the Great Eye, and in that sense, we are dedicated to the Triumvirs, who are Its hands. However, one year ago, our spies deep in the palace first noticed a change in Triumvir Anwir. He...pursues his *own* vision while deceiving the Eye. The other Triumvirs do not know it but are used by him toward that end."

"How can he keep it from your Eye? And even if all this is true, what could he hope to gain?" Gaelenn asked.

"It is obvious. He desires the city for himself. He wishes to usurp the Eye!" she exclaimed, her voice rocking the room before continuing more gently. "With his power, no man can stand against him. He is devious, and works in secret."

"—But how could he usurp the Eye? Doesn't he know what the Eye is?"

Aydya's gaze drifted to the communication beacon next to her and the usual commanding zeal of her voice evaporated.

"I cannot answer that. I am not sure even that I know what the Eye is now," she said, never more vulnerable.

"*I am sorry to interrupt your conversation,*" the room's soft voice cut in. "*It appears that the other end of your connection is attempting to reestablish contact.*"

"What?" Gaelenn asked. He and Aydya closed their mouths and focused on their ears. Sure enough, a muffled voice was calling to them.

"Gaelenn! Gaelenn! Are you still there? Gaelenn!"

He shot to his feet and jumped at the Sooshinsoechee—the communication portal—he had used to talk with Livvy before.

"I'm here!" he exclaimed.

"Good, you made it," a man's voice responded instead. Dean. "To my laboratory."

"Your laboratory? That makes sense, now that you mention it."

Gaelenn looked over the room and its scattered machines, littered with strange tools; it was just like the workshop in the mountain, but on a grander, more sophisticated scale.

"Wait—tell me what happened! How did you guys get away?"

"That's a long story. Maybe another time."

"Is everybody safe?"

"That's also a long story...I'm not sure."

Livvy interjected. "Gaelenn, we're still sorting out the details. All I can say for certain is that tensions have escalated. In the past few weeks almost every village and city in Sintarria has been wiped out. There's no time left—we have to focus now if we want to survive. I'm going to go for a little while to take care of things here. Dean will try to lead you through. If you're willing to help. *Please.*"

Gaelenn let his breath out slowly and waited for his thoughts and feelings to coalesce.

"...Okay," he said. "Now that I've seen the Eye. Now that I know."

He let a long pause sit between him here in the tower and Livvy in Last Retreat. "So lead me through what?"

"Gaelenn—thank you!" Livvy's voice shouted and then faded away.

"Listen," Dean said, taking over. "This would have been a lot easier if I were there with you. Did your friend make it, too? The woman."

"Yes, she's here. *What* would be easier?"

Dean exhaled, distorting the sound coming from the communication portal. "Everything."

CHAPTER THIRTY FOUR
Just Hang On

THE DOOR BEHIND LIVVY slammed shut, pulled by the wind her flowing dress dragged with it as she ran.

"Get him some food!" she shouted to the surprised guards waiting in the large banquet room of her building. Her thumb pointed back toward her room, where she had left Dean. Usually they got meal orders through her magic voice in the walls. And, usually, she was much more polite when she gave them. They scattered away to prepare something.

She continued running out the front double-doors. Outside, citizens were tending to injured soldiers. "So few came back...what happened?"

After a shake of her head, she decided that nobody around her was in any shape to answer. "Who's in charge?" she asked the closest group of guards. They looked at each other with wide, sad eyes before bowing.

"The Captain and Lieutenant-captain have not yet returned," one of them responded through a timid voice. "We brought all survivors here to this courtyard."

"This is all of you? Who is in charge now?"

"Yes, Madame Priestess. Ah, not all who went. All who came back I, uh..."

"Nevermind," Livvy said impatiently; until she could find Astrid, the chain of command of her army had been severed.

"I can tell you what happened," a gruff voice came from behind the center fountain.

"Kell!" she exclaimed and jogged to the other side to find him lying flat on his back, catching stray droplets of water on his forehead and in his mouth, grasping for breath.

Without sitting up, he looked at her—she was upside down to him—and asked, "Did the old man already make it to you? Where does he get the energy? He was impaled by a spear just a couple days ago."

"Yes," she said, straining to contain the semi-relieved giggle rising within her despite herself. "He has plenty of energy, just like me. He's in my room, talking with your friend, Gaelenn."

"Gaelenn's here too?" Kell gasped and raised his head a few inches, attempting to sit up.

"No," Livvy said, and Kell crashed down again with a sigh. "But we've somehow reached Gaelenn through a communication portal. We think we know where he is."

"You what? Ah, thank hell. It got a little hairy up on that mountain. We weren't sure he got away."

Livvy kneeled down near his head. "When you've caught your breath, please tell me everything. Dean has gone over the basics but I was hoping you could help with the details while he's busy."

"If I had a flank of lamb and some ale in my stomach, I'd be able to talk all day. Or...," He took another deep breath and tried to peer behind her face by adjusting his neck. "Is it night? I can't bloody tell!"

"When you're well enough, please go back to your cabin. We've kept it for you in your absence. I'll have some food and drink brought to you right away, and I'll meet you there."

She stood up and walked back around the fountain to the guards she had spoken to before and studied them as she approached: bruised, bloodied, broken, maybe—but somehow radiating pride and defiance. The peaceful blue that permeated the air from the globes all around could not soften their edge. But she passed by without speaking, nodding to acknowledge them, and they bowed again with honored, embarrassed smiles. When she was sure she could not be seen from the front on her way back to the double-doors of her house, her eyelids clamped shut and she let out her sadness in a long, painful exhale. It was happening again. The end. Again! If only she had another hundred years. Or a thousand. She pressed her hands against her burning cheeks and felt their heat in her cool palms.

Just as well that it was happening now—with the Key Line finally broken and irreparable, another thousand years would just be putting off the inevitable defeat. And this time, there was only one other of her kind left alive to share in her pain: Dean. And this time he was here with her, physically. But not, she lamented as she opened the doors, in his mind or his soul; he handled the infinite, endless sadness that surrounded them in his own, private way. Always had. He would never openly show his emotions to her. And she needed someone to share hers with after so, so long without.

ASTRID LOOKED DOWN AGAIN on Rin's face. The sun, though it had been sapping her energy for hours with its incessant stare, had brought out a welcome sweat just under the white roots of his hair.

"You're still alive," she said with a pained smile. The ground was drier now and easier to navigate, but her arms were burning under his weight.

"No time to stop now," she said to her limbs, commanding them to hold on. She shifted Rin to relieve some of the ache.

"It's funny," she kept talking, knowing that he could not hear, "usually you're the one who won't close his mouth, but now it's the only thing I can do to keep sane."

For several more hours she continued on, talking along the way, sometimes of memories between them, sometimes noting the landmarks they passed: a forest they once patrolled here; a river there. Stopping not even to drink, she marched and marched, driven by purpose.

"Is this for love? Duty?" she asked herself. When the moon came over the horizon, she finally stopped talking and found herself staring at him, almost in a trance. For the first time all day she heard a voice that wasn't hers.

"I thought you'd never shut up," Rin muttered.

"Rin!" Astrid shouted, and then dropped gently to her knees and laid him down and kissed his face.

He winced and opened one eye halfway. "Where are we?" He could only manage a whisper.

"Heading home. Can you walk?" she asked, hopeful.

"I can't...feel my legs at all." He managed to push out the words and force both eyes open to look at her.

She stifled her desire to cry by rolling up her lower lip and nodding.

"Then let's get back on track," she said, picking him up gently and marching on, again. "Does it hurt?"

"Did you not see the size of that axe?" Rin joked. "Actually, I can't really feel anything. I mean, everywhere hurts."

He looked her dead in the eye. "I don't think I'm going to make it, Astrid."

"Don't say that!" she said, swinging her tired legs faster and faster. "We will be back home within a day. You just hang on."

He smiled and closed his eyes, exhausted from the strain, and rested his head against her shoulder.

"Just hang on," she repeated.

CHAPTER THIRTY FIVE
Life Without Time

"ARE YOU *EATING*?" GAELENN asked, incredulous. Dean's responses were smattered with alternating smacks and relieved sighs.

"Yes, sorry—one of my curses," came his answer. "Anyway, let's get back to it. So that's how we got away."

He had just finished explaining their daring escape and subsequent chase and then, ultimately, their stand on the swampy plain.

"I still think we shouldn't have split up," Gaelenn protested.

"Well, we had to make a choice, so we did what we had to do to keep you safe. And it looks like it worked."

"But without you here, I can't even use any of this stuff."

"Are you sure you don't 'remember' any instructions or anything like that?" Dean asked.

"No. I have bits and pieces, but I didn't get the full picture. I found this tower, but that's about it. I didn't even know exactly what I'd find."

Dean responded with silence.

"You say the giant was killed?" Aydya joined in and changed the subject.

"That's right."

"How? It is impossible!"

"Told you, I didn't see what happened. But I believe these soldiers here. They're almost as fanatical to their cause as you are to your Eye. That giant is dead, thank God."

Dean could not see the relief pasted on Aydya's face but he heard her stiff sigh through his device.

"Did you see another Triumvir during the battle? Visha? Anwir?" she asked, glancing at Gaelenn now with worried eyes, asking on his behalf.

"Wait, wait, wait." Dean's smacking stopped. "That monster we killed wasn't the one after you?"

"No," Gaelenn said. "Well, not *the* one. Or the only one. Or...I don't think so. I'm not sure."

"There are two others, as you know," Aydya corrected. "They may all be hunting him."

"Damnit," Dean responded. "And here I thought we'd just witnessed a miracle. Now we need two more? If being alive for this long has taught me one thing, it's that nothing is ever as easy as it should be. Do you know how hard it is to kill one of those things?"

"Pretty hard," Gaelenn said, his hands rubbing the wound on his shoulder, reminding him of his last encounter with Anwir. The Disciples had done a marvelous job of fixing him, and it was healing nicely despite the constant ache. "I've had enough run-ins with the one already."

"Yes, well, it's not just 'hard'—it's nearly impossible, just like your friend there said. If it weren't for the rain and mud and the size of that big one, he'd have wiped us all out by himself. We got lucky. *Really* lucky. Shit, I should know. I helped design them."

Gaelenn stared with unfocused eyes on one of the few sections of the wall unadorned by lights or glass or iron circles, naturally drifting to a blank space so his mind could explore its new depth. "Can we get really lucky again?"

"Wouldn't count on it. Not with spears and arrows," Dean said.

"How? How do you know? They may be more than human, but are they not still human?" Aydya stated rather than asked. "Except for the woman—she is evil incarnate. I thought so even when I worshipped the Eye."

Gaelenn shot a surprised look at her, shock in his wide eyes. She had admitted it—she *had* changed her mind. Her belief had been, somehow, shaken ever since Dean's cave on the mountain. But he kept his mouth shut for the moment and focused back on the old man's voice.

"I had almost this exact same conversation with your two friends just a couple days ago; they're not just human. I know because I made them," Dean continued.

"You *made* them?" Gaelenn said, leaning closer to the portal. But it made sense. That's right. In his adopted memories he could see it. "Yes, you did, didn't you?"

"Yes, I made them."

Gaelenn ground his teeth together. "I can see them in my mind, but I can't make the connection between you and them. I...can see that they were made to fight against the Eye."

"*Against* the Eye? They are the Eye's hands!" Aydya shouted.

"You're both right," Dean explained calmly. "I'll go quick: we were desperate. We always are. Those of us who'd survived the first two wars had a vote. I had come up with a way to make a man or a woman into a kind of...super-human. I was good at that—'making potions'—you'd say."

Gaelenn nodded to himself. When he closed his eyes he saw the meeting from his long dream in his mind.

"Gaelenn," Dean said, using his proper name for the first time. "Was the tower disturbed at all when you got there?"

"No. There was a settlement around it, but the entrance was buried deep under the soil."

"Freeloaders... Well, good enough. There should be a number of those tables, like the one I had in the mountain. Do you recognize them?"

Gaelenn tilted his head and strained his memory. "No... Not really. I mean, I can tell what they are because I've seen so many of them the past few weeks, but I can't tell what each one does just by looking at it."

"Well, one of them is the very device I used for testing the first generation of ENs. With it, I could give a human unnatural strength and reflexes. I could make their skin harder, their senses keener. I could build the perfect weapon—the only weapon—that worked against the Eye."

"But how...?" Aydya breathed into the table's void.

"The whole point was to make something human into something more than human, but still one of us. Something that the Eye couldn't corrupt. Up until then, none of our weapons, no matter how powerful, could defeat it. Even when we were sure it would work, the Eye would find a way to turn it against us."

Dean's breaths deepened and his voice lowered with each successive word.

"So, you made a platoon of these things, and they turned against you anyway," Gaelenn said. "I can see it."

"Basically, yes. But it's a little more complicated than that. At first, our efforts turned the tide. We almost won. We thought we did."

"I can't tell after that...what happened?" Gaelenn asked.

Aydya sat down on the floor and closed her eyes, listening intently as she meditated.

"That bastard Eye found their weakness—"

"So they do have a weakness? Can we use it?" Gaelenn interrupted.

Dean took a deep breath. "No. It's not that kind of weakness. It's not a chink in their armor. It's deeper."

"I do not—we do not—understand," Aydya said from the floor.

"The Eye lives without time, you see? I'm old. Your Priestess is old. But we still feel time. We live every day, the same as everybody else. The Eye is an enemy without time. It could wait forever if it had to. That's one reason. It can play the long game."

Gaelenn pictured Dean raising a finger in his mind's eye and mimicked it with his own. "And two?"

"Well, we can't play the long game. Our Legion—the ENs—lived and died. They aren't like me and Livvy. They don't live forever—in fact, when you undergo the procedure, your lifespan is cut nearly in half. It's a death sentence. So, we had to keep on making them. At great cost. Great sacrifice."

"I can remember a battle. There were a lot of those things. And they were fighting each other," Gaelenn said, pinching his temples together with his thumb and forefinger as if it would help him keep the memory in focus.

"That's right. But, like it's done from the very beginning, the Eye hid its intentions. It kept its knowledge of our Legion secret until it could kill all of our forces at once. And it did, with weapons that scorched the earth. Beyond our world now, you may know, there is no place we can go. Even though it stretches on endlessly in all directions. Thank the Eye. On top of all that, before it executed the majority of mankind it stole our technology—one of these devices for creating the Legion. Which, we thought, was also destroyed in the blasts. Looks like we were wrong."

"Right," Gaelenn said. He was more confused by the minute, but somehow the words made sense.

"And that was the last war. After we thought it was over, while we rested, thinking we'd won with our great sacrifice, what I think happened is the Eye spent a thousand years becoming the god of remote villages everywhere. It didn't use a bunch of volunteers to make more ENs. It 'blessed' the children of its most devout and raised them from birth as chosen warriors. And it worked. We were this close to done with them."

Aydya, still closing her eyes, buried her face in her hands. Her village had been one such place. Triumvir Visha famously was 'chosen' from among the locals before Aydya's time. Her name was still sung, even as Visha came back and destroyed Igtao herself years later.

Dean continued after a pause. "Tell your friend there not to worry. And I'm sorry. She didn't know what she was doing for most of her life. She just saw it for the first time as she was watching some of the images being transplanted into your brain. I didn't have time to explain it to her then."

"Does it mean," Aydya sobbed, "that my whole order is a sham? That we were manipulated?"

"It's...," Dean stopped for a moment to consider how to go on, and continued in a delicate tone, "—your group is not the first. Not the only one, either. It's a small part of the Eye's strategy. To infiltrate humanity and keep us fighting ourselves. It's been more effective than you could imagine. By now the Eye doesn't even need the machines and drones it used to use against us. Now it's got real people to fight for it. Against themselves. Not to mention those ENs."

A low thump came across the communication portal as Dean smashed his fist down on the table at his end. "If we can't stop them now, there's no way we can stop the Eye. If only we could get lucky two more times, one for each of those Triumvirs. Then we'd only have the human army to contend with, and I'd feel much better about that."

"So, Dean," Gaelenn said after allowing the sound, along with the raw emotion, to dissipate, "we have your magic table here. And we have Aydya. And me. Let's fight back."

CHAPTER THIRTY SIX
EXPOSED

"LIKE I SAID," DEAN started. His fingers tapped rhythmically, as they usually did when he was thinking. "Nothing is ever as simple as you think. It's not an option. No."

He glanced sideways at the pile of food scraps and rubbed his full belly until his fingers found the almost-invisible scar on his side. It would be fully healed in just a few more days. His injuries always were.

"I'll make you a deal. You keep that machine there a secret for now. Your Priestess wouldn't be happy if she knew one still existed. That's one of the reasons I buried it—so nobody but me could ever find it again. In the meantime, try to get those archives working. They might have some information you're missing. Does my personal assistant still work?"

Gaelenn's voice crackled over the communication channel. "Yes, I think we met her."

"Good, see what she can do. She's always been a great help."

The door behind Dean swung open.

"You can take the plates, thanks. I'm done," he said without looking.

"They'll be around to do that shortly," Livvy snapped, walking around the table to sit down in her usual chair.

"Elizabeth," Dean acknowledged her with a quick smile under his thin mustache. His eyes didn't move. "Impeccable timing."

He looked down at the lights dancing within the obsidian and touched one of them. "We'll call you back, Gaelenn. Get to it."

"We'll try," came the reply, followed by silence. The call was over.

Dean looked up to find Livvy's eyes boring straight into him. "What is it?"

"I hate that name, you know that." Her clenched jaw, more than her words, told him she was ready for a quarrel. "What have you done?"

Dean shrugged his shoulders. "Nothing I had a choice about." He forced a smile, trying to disarm her. It had worked a million times before but not this time.

"We've been through a lot. Maybe never quite this bad, but we've been through a lot," he mused.

"We've done everything we can to avoid all-out war this time. To keep the enemy at bay long enough for time to take its toll. Why does it feel like time has only made the Eye stronger?" Livvy asked. She moved a few strands of hair from one side of her head to the other, using her hand to cover her face for just a second to hide her anguish.

"We did what we could. I mean, you've done what you could, at least," he replied, stretching his arms backward to grasp the top of the wide, padded seat behind him. He craned his neck backward and cracked it to ease his stress.

"If it weren't for you, Elizabeth, we'd be gone. Humanity, too. Our battle would have been lost a long time ago. A *long* time ago."

"Stop calling me that!" she exclaimed, her hands now at her sides in fists.

"Be serious for a minute," he chided. "I've been next to useless. And now, because of me, our only weapons against that Eye are in its possession. Our line of keys is broken, and the only Key Master left alive—the last in a line almost nine hundred generations long—is stranded up at the northern reaches. Oh, and his key only half-works. All because of me."

She looked at him and broke, pity pouring from her shimmering but not-quite-crying eyes, moved by the weight of responsibility he bore.

"But without you, I wouldn't be here, either. We would have all died before the second era."

He smiled again. "It feels like we've had this conversation before."

"We've had *every* conversation before, Dean," she corrected.

"Then I guess," he said, "we both know that ruminating on the past will get us nowhere. It's all about what we do from now."

"Fine," Livvy surrendered. She was not quite angry anymore, but having spent so much time with Dean she knew the lengths he would go to prove his point. Her half-closed, suspicious eyes let him know she was onto him.

"What do you think we can do?" she asked.

"Well, we have two options that I can see. Both are risky. One, we see what kind of information your Key Master can still extract. Plug him in, see if his key still works, look for any information we can use in those databases. Who knows, maybe he can do what his father Ricar couldn't—fix our key machine. Like I've been trying to do since he was born."

"We should start that right away," Livvy said.

"I've already got him trying. We'll see how it turns out. There's only about 20 millennia riding on it. That's risky enough; only a matter of time before the Eye detects his probing. It happened already on the mountain."

Livvy sat silently, wearing no particular expression, waiting for Dean to continue.

He swallowed his sarcasm in a big, profound gulp. "You're not going to like option two."

She sat forward and put her hands in a ball on her lap, her unblinking focus on Dean. "Try me."

"So we can assume that we're going to have a fight on our hands now that we've come out into the open, more or less," he said. "Your Captain saw to that on the battlefield. I'm sure the Eye knows we're up here now. Or will figure it out soon enough."

"So we should also assume that it will attempt to lure us down," Livvy said. "Or cut us off up here."

"Yes, we should. How many guards and troops do you have?"

"A few thousand."

"From what I've been seeing, there are a lot more than that running around that damn city. They've enslaved whatever they haven't been able to recruit. We'll be outnumbered. By a lot," he continued, "Listen—our little fortress up here has held up remarkably well for this long. But it's our last stand. With their numbers, they'll probably even make it up here sooner or later, if they can't force us down."

Livvy let out a measured, calm breath and examined the walls inch by inch, as if appreciating the safety they gave her for the first time.

"It's funny, isn't it, Dean? 'Last Retreat.' It used to be a vacationer's resort, didn't it? I think my parents came here once."

"Built from the ground up, the whole structure, to 'get away from it all.' I can still remember the commercials."

"And now it's actually going to live up to its name."

She rolled her shoulders and stretched her fingers between her knees. "So, I didn't catch it—what was option two?"

"Well," he said and leaned forward, uncrossing his legs, "we know they'll be coming here. They know that we know they're coming. Option 2 isn't really an option, per se. It's a certainty. Because any which way, we're going to have to fight."

CHAPTER THIRTY SEVEN
DANGER IN THE DESERT

"ARE YOU THERE? HELLO?" Dean's voice broke the silence in the room.

Gaelenn's knees creaked as he stood up.

"Does the air in here move?" he asked, but only to himself.

"There should be adequate airflow," the room's strange voice replied.

"Um, thanks," Gaelenn said. "Yes, I'm here."

"Good. Let's get started," Dean said.

Gaelenn caught Aydya staring at him as he turned toward the device that Dean's voice originated from, and they nodded to each other. He tried to hide his confused brow from her, unsure why she would be looking.

"You need not concern yourself with me right now," she said. "There is much to be done, I think."

He smiled, thankful for her presence. "So, before we start, Dean, tell me, what's going on there?"

Dean's muffled breath came through the machine for a long, drawn-out moment of thought. "Right now, nothing. But soon we'll see this whole thing come to a head."

"Come to a head...?"

"For now, we're going to see what kind of progress you make. We'll decide what to do from there. But there's a fight coming, no doubt. So all we can do now is wait. Wait and prepare for the worst."

Gaelenn hesitated.

"I know what you're trying to do here. You want to use me to see if there's a safe place we can go to fix my eyes, right? Or a hidden machine somewhere? Or raw materials? I didn't find anything in the place at Sapphire Mountain. Or are you asking me to go look for a weakness in the Eye again?"

"Yep, that's the gist of it. Big 'yes' to all the above. The place you're at is safe but you'll still need to hurry. Gosh, in a lot of ways we're lucky that the northern tower is the place you decided to go. It's less used. Further away. You should have a lot more time to search. But your real limit will be us here. We need to you to get that information to us before we're overrun by Maynon Ohza. This old signal might not cut it."

"Right...so, what does it matter anyway if I can somehow acquire all this...wisdom? Or if you can fix me?" Gaelenn asked.

"Well, it brings us back to even footing. It means that all the work we've done for two-hundred centuries wasn't for nothing. But it's not all about you, I won't lie—it keeps our plans alive. We can fix the line that is going to break with you. You have no idea how long and how hard we've fought to outlast our enemy. You don't know what your 'Priestess' here has sacrificed," Dean said, cutting off suddenly at the last word, and all was quiet for a long minute.

Gaelenn nudged, hesitant, "Dean? Are you still there?"

"I'm here," the old man answered and continued where he had left off, "so, we find some information by continuing your procedure on Sapphire Mountain, our old plan survives, and we live to fight another day and save our strength up here at Last Retreat while simultaneously looking another place to hide. With our enemy, you can't just take the fight to him, you know? Now, any more questions? Or can we start?"

Swallowing hard, Gaelenn looked at Aydya, still staring at him, and offered her a chance to interject. She gave him only a single, approving blink and nod in return.

"We're ready."

"Okay," Dean said, his voice coated suddenly with an excited twang. "We used to have this saying when I was younger: 'this may sting a bit.' My doctor used to say that before shooting my arm with medicine. I gotta tell you, it's a lot more fun to be on the stinging side."

Gaelenn scoffed. "You didn't say this was going to hurt."

"Take off your shirt and lie on the table. The assistant should highlight it for you."

The room's light shifted slightly at his words, dimming everywhere except for one strong, bright beam focused on a table a yard away.

"*This is the one. Please be careful when using this device,*" the room's airy voice said cheerfully.

Gaelenn stepped over with Aydya, pulled off his shirt, and laid down on the cold, stony-glass surface, sending a wave of goosebumps across his body. There was, just like the one he had used in Dean's cave at Sapphire Mountain, a slightly softer area for his head rising a few inches above the rest.

"I didn't have to take off my shirt last time," he noted.

"This device is a bit more old-fashioned," Dean replied.

"Old-fashioned?"

"Never mind. Just know that it's going to take a lot longer to start up if it still works. You'll have to be knocked unconscious. Aydya, was it? I'm going to need your help."

"Yes, anything," she said without even a moment's pause, her eagerness painting her voice with fresh zeal.

Gaelenn's gaze shifted over to her and he smiled. "Nothing about you is halfway, is it?"

Aydya blushed.

"My assistant—her name's Ai—will guide the way, but you'll have to do most of the physical work," Dean said. "Is that *Keeroekoohoegee* still loaded?"

"I...?" Aydya started to say, confused.

"*The working portals are partially supplied, however most of the fluids are past expiry,*" Ai answered Dean's question.

"Oh, I designed them to last pretty much forever—they'll be fine. Activate the intravenous, please."

A compartment opened on the side of the solid table, just under Gaelenn's right arm, and a skinny hose with a long, impossibly thin spike eased out a few inches.

"Better hold him down. Palms up, my boy," Dean said.

"Wait, won't the Eye find us out as soon as this starts?" Gaelenn asked as Aydya leaned over and pressed down on his wrists, and Dean went on.

"Nope, at least not for a good while. Ai does a bang-up job of keeping those channels separate. She has full control up there. And there's no way she'll let the Eye in. You'll be safe. Trust her."

Ai gave no response, but a high, almost cheerful hum reverberated through the room as Dean spoke.

Gaelenn took a huge gulp of air and then held the tops of his hands against the table just as four holes opened up under them. Two flat ropes rose out and wrapped around his forearms above Aydya's hands, finding their homes on the other sides like snakes coming out of one hole in the ground and going back into another. The right side pulled down harder, popping the veins out at his elbow. As if lit up from the inside, one of his veins began to glow, highlighted in bright green.

"Ai can do this, but it's better if you do, Aydya. She's been out of practice for...a good while and her guiding sensors might be out of calibration. Insert the needle there into the green area at a shallow angle, just under the skin."

Gaelenn raised an eyebrow, but beckoned Aydya. "Well, I'm sort of used to pain by now anyway. Go for it."

She picked up the hose, which seemed to magically be only as long as it needed to be, and pressed the needle against his skin.

"Are you ready?" she asked as a short hiss came from the top of the spike, wetting the precise area it was about to pierce.

"Ready," he said, but before the breath came out of his mouth, she had forced the steel into his arm.

He let out a quick yelp. The needle was thicker than he thought.

"*Please pull the needle slightly back,*" the voice instructed. Aydya pulled it back a quarter of an inch, and another snake-rope slid silently around the needle's tube and back into the table, securing it in place.

Aydya took a step back as Gaelenn's head sunk into the thin pillow underneath. A light glowed briefly over his eyes and disappeared, then two tendrils crawled out of hidden holes at his neck and attached themselves to the sides of his head. His eyes rolled white, back into his head, and then his eyelids closed.

"That should do it. I'll call you two again later. I can watch some of the progress from here. Please watch over him, Aydya. Good luck," Dean said, and was gone with a crackle.

Tears began falling down her cheeks before Aydya took another breath. Her dam—the wall she had been holding up with so much of her being for so many days now—broke and unleashed the torrent that was welling up behind her eyes. Her life as she knew it was shattered and it had taken all her strength not to succumb. And now, here in front of her lay another who did not know her, did not know her struggles, and had no idea just how much he meant to her. She cried and cried and gave thanks to no god—just to the infinite, to the void, for giving her someone she could call a friend.

"Don't go for long," she said, touching his fingers gently.

"I'm still here," he said and smiled. His fingers wrapped around hers and squeezed. "I'm still here..."

Aydya sniffed her tears away. "I cannot see what you're seeing this time. Last time I saw but a little, and it changed everything."

"What did you see? What changed you?"

"I saw that the one thing I believed most in this world was a lie. I saw the Eye destroy the world, not save it." Her jaw set. "So, whatever you learn this time—keep it to yourself."

Gaelenn laughed and said, "I wouldn't know where to begin, even if I could tell you." He then trailed off, his head reaching further and further back until his neck looked like it was about to snap.

He truly did not know. Explaining the faces and letters and colors that he had never seen before was impossible. Somehow, these machines plumbed the nether reaches of the endless chasms in his mind, drowning them in a sea of knowledge that flooded each and every space within. A strained groan crawled from Gaelenn's lips and his mouth drew thin.

"You do not push yourself too far. Do not push yourself too far," Aydya said, correcting herself. For five minutes she watched him writhe gently on the table until he was finally under. Then, slumping to her knees, she fell into a trance and lost herself to her thoughts. It was not apparent how much time had passed when she was next awoken.

"*Excuse me*," the room—Ai—spoke in its usual gentle tone, breaking the not-quite-silent whir of the machine under Gaelenn.

"*But there are three individuals approaching from the South.*"

Aydya spun around as if to meet someone face to face, her eyes round and her hands at the hilts of her daggers. "What?"

"*Would you like to see?*"

She paused and took several breaths, trying to ease her heartbeat back to normal. But it would not budge.

"How can you show me?"

A light to her right blipped into existence and she waded through the machines to it. An image of the desert around the tower faded in from a canvas of pure blue and grew around a group of three people walking side-by-side, straight toward the tower. She took a long step backward.

"What is this?" she exclaimed, grabbing either side of the image in vain after determining she could not be heard or seen. Her hands, blindly searching for something to hold on to, found nothing but complete smoothness, and she resorted to slapping them against it.

"It is a view of outside this tower. The individuals are approaching from the south."

"Is it...happening now?"

"Yes."

The figures slowly grew larger and larger until they transformed from mere dots into blobs and finally into humans.

Aydya pulled her face within inches of the wall and gasped. The bright blue of the horizon and the blazing yellow of the sand outside cleaved the specter of her eyes, and in the middle of the image were three figures completely robed in black.

"How did they find us...?" She whispered under her heaving breath.

Two minutes passed before she blinked and snapped back to the present, her mind's wandering complete. She looked at Gaelenn lying motionless on the table across the room.

"Gaelenn, can you hear me?" she asked and followed it with a louder call of his name: "Gaelenn!"

There was no response.

She gave a blank stare down at the daggers poking out of her sleeves and rubbed the ends of them with an empty touch. Her hands went to the veil hanging at her neck, but just as they lifted it up around her head, she stopped them, and the wispy cloth fell back loosely to her shoulders. Without a word she walked to the porthole center of the room, lifted the heavy iron door, and jumped down.

She spoke up into the room, "Keep him safe. Danger has come."

"I will do what I can," Ai answered dutifully. *"Though I have limited means. Unfortunately, I'm not able to give an estimate on completion time, but the information upload is still in the early stages."*

"Then I will buy him some time," Aydya said, her voice suddenly sharp, set, and cold. "You will do what you can, as well."

She pulled the handle to shut the door and jammed one of her daggers into the crease just before it sealed completely. Finding her way with her memory and her hands, she raced down the staircase and ladders, leaving a trail of soft footsteps and creaking iron in her wake.

The room went silent and darkened a few shades. Gaelenn sat motionless, little more than dead, with only the occasional rising of his chest marking that he was not. All the while, the moving painting on the wall cast its yellow-blue light on the tables of the room. The three figures grew and grew, and when they were large enough, the glint of steel at their sides shot brief sparks of light.

Not a second after, the room moved. The syringes in Gaelenn's arms made no noise as they slid out of his veins and back into their table. Two others replaced them moments after from the table next to him.

Ai had no body, no hands, not even a presence in the air. But she had a mind, and a keen one at that. If anyone was there, they might have seen her use it.

CHAPTER THIRTY EIGHT
A Last Homecoming

Astrid pulled the last part of the rope, securing the knot around Rin like a spider's web around a fly.

"This will have to do, Rin," she said to him, and raised her hand and waved.

Almost immediately his limp body began ascended. She wrapped a separate rope around her forearm and foot and waved again, following him up. She looked around but the sun setting over the country below could not calm her nerves like it usually did on these long climbs up to Last Retreat. The fires she had seen on her way down to find Rin and Gaelenn had gone out, and even the smoke that she expected to see smoldering up to the heavens had ceased. It was as calm and peaceful as she had ever seen it and all the more terrible and frightening for it; she knew that the last fight was coming.

"I risked it all for you," she said up to Rin above her, swaying back and forth gently as they rose together. "But I think the fight was coming eventually either way."

At the top she exchanged quick, customary greetings with the guard and commanded her to summon whoever she could find immediately. Four guards arrived and eased Rin onto a canvas stretcher, and guided him through the darkness. After that Astrid made the longest trek through that familiar forest she had ever been on.

"How bad is it?" The Priestess greeted Astrid with a barrage of questions as soon as she had cleared the trees. "How long ago? Was the wound cleaned?"

Genuine concern drew lines in her normally blemish-less skin, though it did not age her. Astrid fought to stop her feet from moving alongside Rin just long enough to bow to Livvy, but then caught back up with him as she answered.

"I did my best to clean it, but I only had drinking water and cloth. I haven't looked at it for about a day, my Lady. I couldn't."

The Priestess caught up with a few quick, light steps and walked side-by-side with her Captain. Onlookers stopped their daily rituals to recognize with knowing looks the deep respect the Priestess showed the Captain of the Guard. Astrid was expected to walk a step behind.

"Something's happened," she heard one of them say, and her cheeks flushed when she realized what she was doing. She tried to take a few slower steps to meet the proper protocol, but the Priestess matched her gait, step-for-step.

"I—" she started to say, but Livvy smiled warmly and cut her off.

"I'm sorry about what's happened. I know it must be hard on you, but we must leave it to our healers for now," she said. Her hand caressed Astrid's forearm just above the gauntlet on her forearm, caked with dried mud and blood, and pulled her to a stop.

"You must let go for now," Livvy explained gently. "I've instructed them to keep us up-to-date on his condition." She stood nearly a foot shorter than the Captain but gazed up into her teary eyes with a mother's pity. Astrid's head fell, but she caught it just in time to turn it into a deferential bow.

"Good," Livvy said. "We'll visit them after they have had time to help him. I know this will be hard, but there are more pressing things we need to focus on. You've been through much in the past few days, but things are about to get more serious. And I'm sure, more than anyone, you can understand this."

The surrounding faces had multiplied immensely; a crowd had gathered, and though it kept its distance out of awe and respect, the most eager among them hovered within earshot. Livvy felt the eyes upon them and, rather than grabbing hold of Astrid's arm, gestured politely for her to follow and led her to the main fountain. There they sat down—the Priestess first, according to custom—but together. The guards fanned out and carved a large circle to ensure that the conversation between them was drowned out by the water splashing out of the elaborate, cherub-shaped jets.

"I know what we've done," Astrid said immediately. "I am sorry, Priestess."

"You did nothing I didn't ask you to do, which was to bring Gaelenn and Rin back. We found Gaelenn ourselves, though."

"You did?" Astrid exclaimed. "Where is he?"

The priestess calmed the captain with a gentle grin. "Safe, for now, far to the north. But I'm afraid we've finally been exposed, haven't we? What did you see when you were out there searching for them?"

"Nothing but destruction, just as we saw on your map."

"Any survivors or stragglers? Anything intact?"

"Not a thing. Not even old ruins were left standing."

"Exactly. The Eye has finished its preparations. It has destroyed every sliver of humanity on this continent. And years it culled all the other ones long ago. And now, I think this is the last stand. We are exposed."

"I'm so sorry," Astrid apologized again.

Livvy shook her head. "No! Don't be. It was only a matter of time. The Eye is always a step ahead of us."

A deep breath gave the Priestess a chance to catch her thoughts. She watched the fat little angels of the fountain shooting water over each other.

Then she turned to study the faces of her people. They were all new to her. But they had lived in this small paradise for all their lives along with their parents and their parents before them, and on and on for thousands of years. They had just as much a stake in what was happening as Livvy herself. More.

"Lady?" Astrid asked, interrupting Livvy's trance. "What can we do now?"

"You know what we must do," she replied, setting her all-knowing gaze directly on Astrid. "We must get ready. This might just be humanity's last stand."

The captain stood and bowed deeply. "I will start right away!"

"No—get a few hours' rest, first! I've already told your forces to start. *You* need it."

"There you are!" A man's voice drifted over the slapping of the water. Astrid froze in place just as she was about to leave, and Livvy rose to her feet.

"Hello there," Dean said, greeting Astrid as he shuffled around the fountain holding his side. "Elizabeth, it doesn't look good. Your Lieutenant Captain... I'm afraid there's not much we can do."

"Can you save him?" the Priestess asked.

Dean glanced sidelong at Astrid, who was standing purple-faced and breathless, gripping the helmet at her side with white knuckles.

"Well...there's a chance, but not much of one," he said, carefully choosing his words but racing at the same time. "Even if he does survive, it's a matter of how much of him does. Where is that blacksmith from Gaelenn's village? I need him. Now."

"In the cottage right next to mine," Livvy responded.

Without a word, Astrid grabbed Dean by the wrist and dragged him with her, cutting a line in the crowd directly toward the center of Last Retreat.

CHAPTER THIRTY NINE
NOW OR NEVER

THE LIGHT REFLECTING OFF the sand was so bright that Aydya held her hand under her nose instead above her eyes. The wind blew her tattered robe against her thinned frame as she closed the distance between her and the approaching figures. By now, she knew exactly who they were: Disciples of the Eye.

"Sister! Where have you been?" the middle one, a woman, shouted as soon as they had come within speaking distance.

"Where is your veil?" another asked, a man.

The third, also a man and slightly taller than the others, remained silent, with hateful slivers of eyes boring through the slit in his hood. His robe was immaculate, unlike those of his salt-stain-ridden partners. An Enforcer, no doubt, Aydya thought. He looked to be used to the heat, and he seemed to absorb the light like a hole of pure blackness.

"First, tell me why you have come," Aydya responded, avoiding the questions. "Surely my charge has not been replaced at this young hour?"

"The hour is not as young as you think, Sister," the woman said dryly. "Already the city overflows with vermin, and the Great Eye sets his focus abroad. Have you accomplished your mission? Has the prisoner acquiesced?"

Aydya looked at their eyes, one-by-one, while carefully constructing her response. "He has. But our quest has not been without hardship. We have come this great distance to finish it."

She looked downward in feigned deference and continued with a suspicious, sidelong glance at the tallest Disciple, "You have done well to find us. I would expect nothing less from an Enforcer."

"Where *is* the prisoner?" the Enforcer finally spoke, and his cold, serpentine voice sent a shiver down Aydya's spine.

Enforcers. A bitter taste rose in the back of her mouth. The worst of the Disciples. Useful tools, but little more. They were the instruments of punishment—and that was usually death.

"I have restrained him in a building in this old settlement. He had threatened not to fulfill his end of our contract, so now I am...convincing him."

The shorter man's eyes creased at their corners, poorly hiding the smile beneath the black cloth over his face. An Inquisitor.

"You were able to restrain him yourself?" the lead Disciple asked, her doubtful eyes not as easily convinced. She was older than Aydya, perhaps by ten or twenty years, and that much more zealous.

"Do you think I would allow myself to be overpowered by a common vagabond?" Aydya asked, throwing in an extra dash of incredulity with an angry brow. "He will fulfill his promise, or I will perform the ritual myself with his head."

"Hah!" the Inquisitor laughed and snorted.

"Take us to him," the leader asked. She was just a 'Sister,' like Aydya, which meant that she had proven herself dedicated enough to not be pigeon-holed into one role and therefore was destined to scale the hidden hierarchy of their order.

Aydya studied the cruel eyebrows through the thin slit in the Sister's veil to glean a hint of the true reason they had come, but there was nothing deeper behind the hollow eyes within.

"Of course," she replied at length. "Follow me."

She turned around and marched with feigned conviction, but bit at her lips as soon as her face was away; there were only a few hundred yards between them and the settlement. Her feet moved just slowly enough to buy time while not raising too much suspicion. But the lines digging their way across her strained forehead as she scoured her mind for some way out would have been damning if they had seen them.

The shack! Her eyes searched among the tattered wooden buildings to find it. Right next to the well and by some stroke of fortune—not the grace of the Eye, she now knew—on the opposite side of the tower from where they had dug up the door.

The shack had a door.

They walked in single file now, following Aydya through the stifling heat. The biting sand penetrated their robes and lodged itself in every crease it could find. She breathed a sweet sigh the wind swept away quickly, full of thanks for the heat. The sun was the perfect excuse to stall for more time while the group drank and rested.

"You will be tired, having traveled so far in the desert," she said in a genuine tone as they approached the first line of ramshackle huts and garbage. "Have you depleted your supplies?"

"We brought nothing but our faith, Sister," came a zealous reply.

"Then let us first visit the well so you can sate your thirst."

With the hope of the plan forming in her mind, Aydya suddenly grew more conscious of creating a convincing impression and pulled her veil over her hair. She stopped just short of covering her face, though, thinking it might be too much too quickly and raise suspicion, which she was sure she was already under enough of. Her guests' stinging looks were all the evidence she needed. She took a winding path through the buildings and rubble, pretending to have lost her way, always looking to balance on that razor edge of too much or too little; she had never had to act so much in her life.

And then she remembered, for a split second, the first few months following her recruitment by the Disciples of the Eye. How, before she had truly believed, she had had to fake her zeal to become a part of the order. At what point she stopped faking she could no longer recall; until now, she had forgotten that she had even once had to fake it at all.

Grabbing the bucket wildly in her distracted state, she dropped it into the well and smacked it against the walls before snapping back to the present. Despite its age it somehow held its shape and refused to crack. Thank the Eye. No—thank something else, she thought. Anything else. She calmed herself with a controlled breath and eased the bucket down the rest of the way.

Behind her she found the Disciples scrutinizing her every movement. The Sister was resting on her knees, careful not to show weakness. The Enforcer was standing perfectly still, hands wrapped around his torso and feeding back into the loose sleeves of his robe. The Inquisitor, plumper and slovenly—which is probably why he was given such a lamentable duty in the first place—had parked himself on the ground and pulled the mask from his face, swallowing great gasps of air.

"Where is the prisoner?" he asked before nearly drowning in a deep swig of the cool well water. He coughed up what had slipped down his lungs and continued to stare at Aydya expectantly.

The others partook in measured draughts, stretching their masks to just below their lower lips, never once taking their eyes off of her, taking copious mental notes of her every breath.

"I have restrained him in a nearby shelter, where he is contemplating our contract as he recovers. He collapsed from the heat a day ago," Aydya said, lying convincingly with an emotionless gaze.

The Enforcer put his hands down. "We wish to see him. But before that, we have questions."

Aydya felt the same uneasiness every time he spoke. She could not help but squint and cringe at his every word.

"You must tell us, Sister, what has happened. Mother demands exact details," said the leader of the group.

Mother—who knew who she was? Behind a mask since before most disciples had even been born, nobody had seen her face. Nobody really even knew if it was the same person or just a series of old women plucked from the strictly ordered line of Sisters.

"You may tell Mother that although we encountered difficulty, we have continued the pursuit of our goal, and have stopped at this abandoned camp in our travels north, where the prisoner believes a working portal can be found," Aydya lied again. The acting came a little more naturally now. "How did you track us here?"

"Our Enforcer is an expert tracker," the sister said. "Among other talents."

She glanced at him, her lips curled up in a grin of satisfaction, continuing, "And the Disciples have known of a portal in this area from time immemorial."

He looked back at her but instead of returning the lustful gaze, his eyes betrayed only scorn. Sexual maneuvering was not the only way to move up, but it was the quickest ticket. This man had paid for his.

Aydya shivered under her robe, which had dwindled to so little that she could not hide the movements. But her visitors were more interested in the water at this moment than in analyzing her.

When they had sated their thirst, Aydya took a long, last drink from the bucket herself. She needed to buy a few more seconds and hoped that its cool water would give her a bolt of courage. It did not. She tried but could not imagine what was about to happen. She only knew that one wrong move would result in her death and most likely Gaelenn's as well.

Her throat rose up and down in a hard swallow. Still dry.

"We are waiting," the sister said and stood up. "And we are eager."

Aydya turned around, finally deciding the time was right to pull up her veil. It covered up her clenched jaw perfectly and she was glad for the respite—she could act a little less.

"Of course," she said. "Know that he is in a vulnerable state from the heat. His faith and constitution are not like ours."

The Disciples followed her through the dirt roads after a grudging nod from the Inquisitor. Aydya was careful to keep a line of shacks between them and the tower to obscure their view; the trench must remain hidden for as long as possible. She eagerly scanned through holes and gaps in the old wood and stone—if she or Gaelenn had left a shovel or pick haphazardly on the side, things could go awry in an instant. This Enforcer was too observant.

Only a few hundred paces now separated the well from the shack. Aydya waited to announce it until they were almost upon it so she could examine it with a critical eye—she needed to make sure it would be fit for her plan.

The walls were sturdy wood, but there were spaces between the boards where any mud had long eroded away. The door wavered in the wind and creaked back and forth but held on, somehow, to its foundations. And an iron latch, thankfully, clung from its edge. Aydya smiled underneath her veil at her good fortune. It was her first smile in ages; it would be her last for ages more.

"In here," she said, walking around the hovel to the entrance and offering her palm to guide them in.

She looked inside at the shadowy shapes: a few old canvas sacks, straw, bags of dirt stacked up randomly—the makeshift beds upon which she and Gaelenn had slept the days previous.

"He is sleeping. In the far back of the room."

The Inquisitor walked in first, squinting his eyes hard as he entered to adjust to the relative blackness. The Sister did the same.

The Enforcer stood for a moment at the door, looked in, and then glanced back for a terrifying moment at the tower.

Aydya's eyes swelled up with blood, horrified that she had been found out. She swallowed hard, and her act came one wrong breath away from faltering only seconds before it was to finish.

But the moment passed. The Enforcer turned back to the hut and ran his hand across its frame with his hand. His thumb was gone above the knuckle—a recent wound—and he held on to the edge with the red stump before stepping into the darkness.

Aydya blinked hard at the entrance and took a deep breath.

Now, or never.

CHAPTER FORTY
THE MOUNTAIN SHAKES

"THAT'S ALL WE CAN do," Dean said, patting Kell on the shoulder. "Good work."

"Thanks. Now can you tell me what we just did?" Kell asked, panting. Sweat on his forehead mixed with black soot and grime and dripped onto the work bench below them, sizzling away.

"You just saved your friend's life, that's what."

Dean wrapped up the chunks of rendered steel in a blanket and tied the end to make a large satchel.

"Damn, that's heavy," he said as he hoisted it over his shoulder.

"And how did I do that? Give me that sack," Kell said, pulling it from the old man's hands and put it on his own back. He nodded toward the door and huffed. "Lead the way."

They shuffled out of the workshop and wheezed, thankful to be liberated from the stiflingly hot air. It was lined with open windows all around, but the roof trapped all the heat and smoke right in the center.

"Not originally designed to do that kind of metalwork, that hut," Dean said, pointing a thumb back toward it. "But good thing they've got it here."

Its regular patrons, who had been waiting outside, hurried back in and started up again on their busywork, getting back to their swords and arrowheads and armor. There was a fight coming they had to prepare for.

"Thanks, guys!" Dean waved back to them, but received no response. He shrugged his shoulders and walked on with Kell and the bag of iron in tow. A minute later they reached a completely closed cabin, two stories tall and painted white, contrasting with the natural yellow of every other building in Last Retreat.

"What's this place?" Kell asked.

"Thank you again," Dean said. "You can leave the bag there. You're not going to want to see what happens in here. Rin's inside—you'd better go back to your place and wait. This'll take a while."

"I can—"

"There's nothing left for you to do. You've done enough."

Dean cut him off, held his hand out, and Kell, recognizing the gesture from his brief time at Last Retreat, grabbed and shook it in silence.

"Your work's perfect," Dean said. "I would have had to try myself if you weren't here. But I'm not very good at shaping steel. I'd need at least a couple thousand years' more practice to do what you do."

Kell pursed his lips, concentrating his red beard hair into a dark bunch in the middle of his face. It was a compliment, but he was not sure what it was for.

"Well then, you know where I'll be if you need me," he said, and walked away.

After a wave, Dean grabbed the sack and dragged it out of sight through the door of the building.

"What was that all about?" Kell muttered to himself, looking back to see the door slam. His dirty hands dripped sweat, so he pulled a rag out of his back pocket to wipe them. He had spent the better part of a day making odd shapes of steel for Dean.

But whenever he asked what it was for, all Dean would say was, "It's for Rin. Too hard to explain now."

He sighed and stopped in front of a cluster of glowing blue globes at his feet, still a few minutes from his own house. The past few weeks and all that had happened hit him all at once. His life had changed in a whirlwind of tragedy and bittersweet reunions: his parents and friends, dead; any hope of a good marriage, dead; Gaelenn had come back from the dead. And all the adventures since.

A small tear ran down his nose and buried itself deep in his beard. It was the most emotion he had shown since he was a small boy. In all his life he had not experienced more than he had in the past thirty days.

"Kell," Astrid said from behind, startling him.

He wiped his eyes haphazardly with his rag, leaving a ring of black around them, and turned around to face her. A nod of acknowledgment was all he could offer, sure his voice would crack if he used it.

"Thank you for helping Rin," she continued. "Dean said there's a chance he may survive."

She spoke with her usual stern, stable expression, but her voice was woven with a new vulnerability—a softness Kell had never heard from her when she, Rin, and her guard had rescued the survivors of his village. Nor as she barked orders and directed the soldiers in their jobs around the compound.

"Tell the truth, I don't even know what I did for him. But if it helps, I'm happy," he said as he rubbed the grease around his knuckles. "I owe you all here a lot more than that."

Astrid stared at him, offering neither a reply nor a gesture of acknowledgment, contemplating something behind her stony eyes.

"You owe us nothing," she said at length. "Yet...there is more I must ask of you."

Her hesitations bore more weight than her expressionless face. "You fought with us in our battle with the giant and the Maynon Ohzan army. I know you are a fierce warrior. Can I convince you to join us again? That battle was not the end of our fight. It was the beginning."

Kell's eyebrows bunched up between his eyes. "Now, just so we're clear, that was the second time you saved me. I owe *you*."

He fit his thumbs behind his belt buckle to rest his arms and stretched his stomach forward, providing a distraction away from his ruddy cheeks. "And it's not like I'd say no. I've got nothing else to do, anyway. Where do you need me?"

Astrid almost smiled.

"Thank you. We are far from ready. If you're not too tired, I know you have skill with that hammer," she said, eyeing the tool hanging at his side. "If you would lend a hand at our forge, we would be grateful."

"Well, I was just there—I know the way back," Kell sighed. "And I've rested enough."

"Thank you. I fear we don't have much time. Thank you."

Kell bowed his head and raised a hand in farewell as he walked back to the forge and out of sight.

"What else…," Astrid said aloud to herself and grabbed her pounding forehead, swollen with an endless list of to-dos. She shook it off; there was no time for pain. "Right."

She pulled her shoulders back and straightened her spine. The next item on her list. In the days since her return she had prepared so much, it was all a blur in her mind. She began a brisk walk toward the center of Last Retreat.

BOOM

The earth beneath her quaked so hard that she fell to her knees. "What was th—?"

BOOM

Another fierce, deafening shock sent blue globes flying and left them jumbling around on the ground while the trees rocked hard back and forth, shaken to their roots. Houses cracked at their foundations and door frames, clouding the air around them with what was once solid plaster and cement.

"Guards, to me!" Astrid yelled to two nearby soldiers. They sprinted to her, losing their own balance a few times before they reached her, and bowed down to her level to receive her instructions.

"Get to the barracks and form teams—send pairs to the infirmary, forge, schools, and send a goddamn legion to the Priestess' quarters. Go!"

They bumbled up to their feet with wide eyes and took off. Astrid struggled to stand herself and as soon as she had turned toward Livvy's house, a pair of guards popped around a corner of vibrating blue lights.

"Captain!" one of them yelled.

"Lieutenant!" Astrid shouted in reply, using her forearm to swish away some approaching dust. "Why aren't you at your post? The Priestess...!"

"We have just come from there! She demanded you come immediately!"

Astrid used his shoulder to catch her footing. "Stay near me," she commanded with steel in her voice. Her headache was gone and she was off.

"GET HIM UP ON this sling!" Dean yelled at the two doctors flanking him over the din of the quake. He was pointing at a thin, wide cloth hanging up from a wooden frame on the other end of the large room. "This shaking's going to kill him! God damnit, what is going on?"

The two medics looked at each other and then reached under Rin's torso and pulled him up. He was still unconscious.

"Grab the legs, too! Never mind, I'll do it."

"Is it safe to hold those?" one doctor asked.

"Well, if they don't hang on when I lift them up, then this shaking's gonna pull 'em off soon enough anyway!" he snapped back, then stepped between Rin's legs and held on at the knees, letting the calves and feet fall limp. The steel was still warm to the touch.

The three of them shuffled over to the sling in a mighty struggle to hang onto the lifeless body.

"He's too heavy!" the other doctor complained. "I can't hold on!"

Dean used his foot to spread the sling apart and eased Rin's new iron legs into it. "Don't drop him! There you go, there you go... gentle with his hips!"

Once the metal from the lower half of Rin's body had enough support, the doctors delicately secured his torso and head. A groan crawled out from between his lips and they tried to adjust his position until he looked a little more comfortable. The shaking would not stop.

"This building had better hold together. You guys had other earthquakes up here lately?" Dean asked sarcastically, his eyes tracing the growing cracks in the house's ceiling.

Both of the doctors shook their heads.

"Shit," Dean deadpanned. He grabbed a box full of random, exotic-looking tools and colored wires and ran his hands through the junk until he found a few trinkets he was satisfied with, then pulled them out and stumbled toward Rin.

The doctors, as they had during the entire procedure, watched with slack jaws as Dean did things they had never seen before—perverse, unfathomable things, fusing flesh and iron together into one—even as they scrambled to catch falling vases and receptacles full of all sorts of powders and liquids, they kept one eye glued on the grotesque operation.

"Dean! Dean! Are you there? I need you here!"

A voice drifted from the walls, barely audible; the crashing glass and the constant, deafening rumble of the earth rendered any communication through voice almost impotent.

Dean craned his neck and his blank eyes traced the faded fresco above. "Elizabeth! What's going on?"

"...I need you at my house *now*!" she responded after a great crash interrupted her first words.

"I can't be two places at once!" He wiped his forehead with his arm, leaving a smear of red blood. Another massive series of quakes crippled his balance and he fell as if someone had kicked him behind the knees.

He grabbed the edge of the table and used it as a crutch to stand high enough to hear Livvy, who was still calling, "Dean! Dean!"

"I'll be there in three minutes!" he responded, not knowing if he had been heard or not, and bent down over Rin. "Sorry, young pup, this is going to have to do for now."

He spent one precious minute finishing his work and then spun around toward the doctors who had come been shadowing him. Then, pulling a glass vial of liquid attached to a long, thin needle from a sack at his waist, he handed it to one of them. "If he doesn't wake up when shit starts going down, shoot this into his chest."

"And if you see any part of him come open, sew it up!" he cried as he raced out the door.

CHAPTER FORTY ONE
PROTOCOL 51

"I'm sorry to wake you, but I thought it was important."

The calm voice of the room stirred Gaelenn: Ai's.

"I believe your companion may be in trouble."

His eyes drew open, needing no time, strangely, to get used to the lights.

"What is it?" he asked. For the few seconds he lay dormant, catching his thoughts. His face was peaceful, but, pulling himself up to sit, he grabbed the top of his head as pain and nausea came flooding into his brain.

"Oh god—what's happened to me?" He winced deeply and bent over his knees, descending from the table.

"Perhaps you understand what happened," she said.

Still wincing, Gaelenn nodded. He had few, if any, new memories compared to the last time he underwent this procedure. There was only one other possibility.

"Why did we do it, then? Is it finished?" he asked, expressionless and emotionless.

"No, it is not—and usually it's not advisable to interrupt the process. But if you'll come closer to the portal on this wall, I can show you the situation."

A light began blinking on a single wall panel of the room, showing him the way.

He drew a breath and replied, "Give me a second."

By now he was kneeling, supporting himself with one arm on the ground and spitting out whatever saliva he could muster onto the smooth floor. It came out in dry heaves.

"Okay, I think I can stand now," he said and stretched his legs, which gave out before he reached full height. Another heave and a groan followed; his body was tearing itself apart. He wobbled over to the wall where Aydya had watched, in disbelief, the Disciples approach. Even though it had not yet begun to glow; he knew—thanks to his borrowed memories—exactly where it would.

"I'm ready. Please show me," he said, resting his frame on his forearm against the wall.

A whir, only audible in the utter quietness of the sealed room, preceded a sudden painting showing the outside world. It was from high above—somewhere on the tower he was in—and faced almost straight down.

Gaelenn snapped upright. "Who are they? When did they get here?" he demanded.

He recognized them in an instant; the sight of the Disciples awoke his still sluggish mind, which had been swimming and nearly drowning and unconscious for hours, back to the present.

"Your companion seemed to recognize them even though they are wearing masks."

Gaelenn pushed his face almost until it was right up against the image, searching for details.

"At least Aydya looks safe," he said, followed by a sigh. "Wait."

She and the three hooded figures stood in front of the shack that had been their shelter for many days as they dug their way into the tower. One by one, Aydya waved them inside.

"This is...now, right?" Gaelenn asked the voice.

"Yes, this is happening currently," Ai replied, as calm as ever.

"She must be trying to—" His mouth gaped open, but no sound came out. As the last Disciple entered, he set his hand on the door, revealing a thumb-less hand.

"No!" Gaelenn cried out in disbelief. "Is there a way to talk to her? Can you do it?" His voice raced so fast it came out as one long word.

"*I'm afraid I can't. I'm sorry.*"

"But that is an EN! The Legion! Anwir!"

"*Yes, I assumed so by the characteristic gait. And the man was concealing a weapon. But I am limited to communications in this room alone.*"

Gaelenn watched helplessly, fresh sweat pouring down his torso, as the door closed and Aydya locked it from outside and stepped backwards.

"Attagirl—smart. Lock them away and get up here!" Gaelenn shouted with a pound on the wall. The tower shook, but he took no notice.

Before she turned around to run, or whatever her plan was, a long sword draped in blood eased out from a crease between two boards in the door. There was no sound from the image, but after a short delay, a dull, painful scream climbed up the tower and through the door in the floor. It was not Aydya's voice.

Gaelenn cast his gaze at the latch in the room's center and a glinting light caught his eye. *Aydya's dagger!* He dashed to the center of the room and grabbed its immovable handle.

"What if she comes back up here?" he thought aloud, and looked back at the image on the wall—the sword had disappeared from the shack's door, leaving a line of blood oozing to the ground.

Aydya, in the image, turned around and looked up, pointing directly at Gaelenn, it seemed, and then raised her palm.

"Stop, stay," Gaelenn translated.

Using her other hand, she pointed to herself and then toward some place out of view. *I will run,* she seemed to say. It was her plan.

"Okay," Gaelenn mouthed, as if she could see him, too, then wrenched the dagger free. The portal slammed shut and his eyes darted around the room, analyzing it.

"I can't stay up here forever," he said. "How much of that procedure is left?"

"*One more hour. However, the recovery period is not immediate. And the side effects are severe.*"

He knew it. His eyes closed and in his borrowed memories he recalled the first generation of ENs and the very first trials. Dean appeared, smiling with apprehension and pity as the original pioneers strapped in. But it was an incomplete memory and ended there.

"I can't see what happens after the procedure," Gaelenn said. "Will I still be...me?"

Ai hesitated. "*I'm afraid I don't understand your question exactly.*"

"I know that my body will change. But will my mind?"

"*It is possible, but I can't say for sure.*"

"If there's a risk, then why did you start it?" Gaelenn's fingers balled up into a fist, held for a second, and then softened again. He looked at the image on the screen. Aydya had vanished and the door to the shack was being ripped to pieces. Triumvir Anwir would be free before long. Gaelenn understood.

"Nevermind. I know why," he said, continuing, "You know, you're a sharp girl, Ai. Thank you."

"*I also regret to inform you that your life span will be significantly reduced.*"

"Hah! One way or the other, right? Depending on how long he takes to find me here. Well, too late for regrets now—we'd better finish what you started. Otherwise, I'm not making it out of here with *any* life span."

Instantly, dull white lights emanated from the table next to the one he had just rested on and he limped toward it.

"Do it quick. Who knows if we have an hour. Don't bother putting me out."

He crawled on top and drew a deep, slow breath. "Ready."

"Of course."

He glanced at the screen once more as the hoses and needles snaked around his body and straps pulled him down tight; he had already missed the part where the door had burst open below. Now, there was only an infinite, hollow black shadow where the door had been and a robed body lying flat amid a growing pool of blood. Triumvir Anwir stepped out, disrobed, and stared directly up at the tower.

Gaelenn swallowed hard. "Better get moving—fast," he said, his mouth set.

"Understood. General preparations are complete, but this will work faster if we use gravity to push your blood around," Ai replied. After a series of rapid clicks, the table itself rotated until it was perpendicular to the floor.

"Whoa, whoa, what are you doing?" Gaelenn asked, surprised.

"No time to explain, sorry."

Fluid hit his veins and set them on fire, but Gaelenn kept his focus on the picture. A bucket—the one from the well, severed from its chain—careened from out of frame and smashed into the side of Anwir's head. Its force would have toppled a lesser man, but the twisted warrior simply staggered half a step, looked at his assaulter, smiled, and took off.

"Push it! As fast as it can go!" Gaelenn cried to Ai. The hoses pulsed under the added stress.

"Thank you," Gaelenn said through the pain. "For all your help. From Dean, too. I hope I'm not so mad after this thing that I can't thank you then, too. You made the right choice, Ai."

The room lights dimmed and flickered.

"From Dean, too..." Ai repeated.

CHAPTER FORTY TWO
MOUNTAIN SIEGE

DEAN BURST INTO LIVVY'S room, utterly out of breath. "What the hell's going on?" he screamed.

Astrid and the Priestess turned around from the glowing altar and waved him over.

"Come here!" Livvy beckoned. She and Astrid pointed at a still image she had enlarged.

"So that's what the hell's going on," Dean said, his mustache flat above pursed lips. A battalion of gigantic boulders held from strings were in mid-swing and crashing into the bottom of the wall from the north. "How many of them are there? How did they build them?"

"We don't know, but this is happening all around Last Retreat," Livvy responded. She used her hand to swipe and summon several other images, all showing the same destruction but with all sorts of different mechanisms—battering rams, huge drills, massive, twisted iron contraptions with arms that smacked the wall and shattered it.

"Do you think they're doing this to scale the mountain?" Livvy asked.

Astrid nodded and kept her head down. "It must be so."

"I don't see what else they could be doing," Dean said and looked at the Captain. "Your army ready?"

"No," said Astrid, stone-faced. "But we couldn't be much more ready than we are. We will fight to the last person."

Livvy touched Astrid's arm and nodded. The bond of complete reliance on each other that had grown between them shone bright. "Thank you. We are out of time. Dean, do you have any tricks up your sleeve?"

Another great rumble shook the house and shifted the table a foot-length to the side. They all held onto its sturdy edges to keep from falling over.

"I'm fresh out. Maybe I can scrounge something together, but—"

Further shakes, increasing in frequency, powdered the air with dust and soot.

"Right, right—I'll go right now!" Dean shouted and turned to go, but he paused mid-step and craned his head around in sudden realization.

"Anybody heard from Gaelenn?" he asked.

"Wouldn't he still be under?" Livvy asked, her hand hovering over a circular depression on the table.

"With any luck. But when's the last time we had any of that? Ai will tell us, either way. Push it," he said, his wide eyes on the button.

She did so, with Astrid biting her tongue in an attempt not to interfere; this—*man*—had just told the *Priestess* what to do!

"Gaelenn, are you there?" Livvy spoke through the table, pushing her voice a thousand miles away in an instant.

"*Hello—I'm sorry, he is unavailable to speak right now. He is currently under procedure,*" returned Ai's soft voice.

Dean's and Livvy's shoulders dropped, simultaneously, in relief.

"Oh, thank god," they muttered.

"Ai, this is Dean...hello, honey."

"*I know. Hello, Dean.*"

Dean closed his eyes. "How much longer before the transfer is complete? We've got a bad situation here."

"*...the transfer was abandoned.*"

"Long story, but we've had more important things to do—wait, what do you mean, abandoned? But he's still under?" he retorted, his rising voice accompanied by a host of sinewy veins in his neck and temples.

"Can you explain now? How about Gaelenn's companion?" Livvy added in a slightly calmer tone.

"*Of course. His companion descended the tower to meet with our visitors—*"

"Visitors? There?" Dean interrupted. His grip on the table was so tight that it spread his dark skin completely colorless on his knuckles.

"*Yes, and she appeared to recognize them. Gaelenn, too. I'm sorry, but I...took the liberty of switching his procedure. It was the best way to maximize his chance of survival.*"

Dean, now in full shock, released his vice-grip on the table and sunk to one knee. He swallowed, gained control of himself, and drew a single, steady breath.

The priestess, having seen this before, showed a warning hand to Astrid, who had nearly stooped to help him up. Stay away, it meant.

"Ai...which procedure?" he said without standing up.

"*Protocol 51.*"

"51?! Why would you let him do that? You know what that does to a human."

"*I am under no orders,*" Ai refuted.

Somehow, her voice was cold. It was like a spat between lovers. Neither was truly angry, but then again, outside observers could not fathom the true depth of the argument.

"But you know as well as I do that after that procedure, he'll flame out in a matter of years, if not months—no one can accurately predict the results."

"*I believe there was no choice. His companion was assaulted and may not be alive. I am no longer able to track her. I believe Gaelenn knew the risks—*"

"Excuse me, Ai," Livvy broke in with an even colder voice, wresting control. She glanced at Dean with jaw clenched before speaking again.

"Right now we don't have time for whys and hows. We are under attack at Last Retreat. When Gaelenn wakes up, make sure he stays as far away from here for as long as he can. Tell him that the entire the Maynon Ohzan army has come and probably the ENs and until they're destroyed, our enemy will *never* stop hunting him. He *must* stay away."

"*Yes, I will tell him,*" Ai responded, more apologetic than cold this time. "*But—*"

"And Ai, if there's anything you can do to help him—anything at all—please do it. We can't lose him. I trust you," Dean interjected. He finally had the strength to rise to his feet.

"*...I will, Dean. But—*"

Livvy touched the table once more and the connection cut out. Torn in two—unable to help Gaelenn but needing him desperately and singly responsible for all the lives here—she mustered her steely nerve and wrested control of herself from the pit of despair.

"We had better get going. Astrid, Dean, I'm counting on you."

Ai DID NOT NEED to speak aloud. Nobody could hear her. But she still felt that she needed to, even if the communication portal was closed. If only to keep from guilt. What a human feeling.

"*But there is an EN here, too.*" Her solemn voice echoed throughout the chamber, almost in harmony with Gaelenn's groans and cries.

AT THE WESTERN END of Last Retreat, Kell looked over the edge.

"This is where they brought me the first time I came up here," he remarked to the nearby soldiers, who were lined up, emanating discipline and hardness but also fear and uncertainty. They braced themselves from the quaking earth with their long spears. Nobody had ever attacked Last Retreat.

More guards appeared from the forest onto the clearing on the ledge.

"It doesn't look like the structure will hold much longer, but we're not sure where it will fail first," one of them said through labored breaths. "Be on guard."

Other soldiers carried the message around so that all were aware.

"So you've never fought before?" Kell asked them. He shimmied a bit to the edge and bent his upper body down to see over it.

"Sir, please back up!" one guard chided.

"Most of us have fought, but not to defend our home," another said.

"Ain't gonna be pretty," said Kell, a veteran of exactly two battles, both within the last month. "But stay together. That's our best chance."

A hundred yards south, along the edge, originating from the base of the artificial mountain, a massive shockwave burst forth. With it came a ghastly, snapping blast wave that knocked all of them off their feet. Terrible, utter silence followed.

A faraway rumble snowballed over an excruciating minute of dread and confusion into a furious roar, and just as the evil sound stopped, the top of the wall where the shockwave had originated simply disappeared. The soldiers looked at one another, wide-eyed and paralyzed, horror on their soundless lips. A few excruciating moments later, the sound of the resulting crash below reached its way up top.

Next to the now-missing edge, another twenty-yard section snapped, and again another section next to that. In the end, 100 yards of wall vanished. The last moment of dread to precede the inevitable was the twenty seconds when every soldier on the mountain who had seen the impossible just become reality prayed to their Priestess to deliver them from this unfathomable evil.

Then, the dam of ancient earth and iron broke with a deafening growl.

A hundred troops, caught in the catastrophe, plunged into the abyss along with the failed structure as it burst out and down. Giant swaths of earth and dust shot up high into the air, clouding the entire western side of the man-made mountain in a brownish-red haze.

When it settled, the once completely vertical side had collapsed into a gradual slope, taking a fifth of the dense trees atop Last Retreat with it, extending for almost a half-mile into and over the forest below.

Both sides lost whole battalions of warriors in an instant, buried under the dirt, but the advantage was clear: the army from Maynon Ohza—and whatever it brought with it—had forced opened the gates.

Kell choked on mouthfuls of thick dust and spat out rough grains of sand that had lodged themselves between his teeth. When his vision cleared, he inched toward the new hill and gasped at the scene below: an ancient latticework of iron roots had been partially exposed, but otherwise a great, smooth pathway led all the way to the ground below. At its base, sparkling steel glinted, moving up toward Last Retreat.

"They're coming!" he bellowed, and the soldiers echoed his warning.

"Form up!" a guard ordered the nearby guards. It was relayed around, repeated, and the soldiers formed rank.

Their shock could not completely be forgotten, but pasted on the soldier's faces, beneath the layers of caked, cracking sweat and soot was sharp determination; they knew that not only was this the battle of their lives, but the battle of the lives of their ancestors.

At the center of the top of the newly-wrought slope, the formation of guards stepped aside. Horns blew on either side, and the clamor of voices and chaos ceased.

"Soldiers! Men and women of the Last Retreat!" Astrid appeared at the front and her voice boomed and echoed throughout the freshly-carved canyon.

"This is it! Hold fast! Do not let one enemy through!"

She raised her spear at its very end and held it up as high as it would go, creating a statue of a being that was no longer just human but a titan—a symbol of righteousness and fury that stirred the heart of every defender. They screamed in unison, creating an aegis of fury.

"For the Priestess!" Astrid called, and the archers hidden high in the trees let loose their arrows and the footmen launched their throwing spears.

The fight had come.

Livvy's brow knotted tightly above her eyes as she leaned over the shaking table.

"It's going to take a minute to get a visual of what's happened," she told Dean, motioning him to wait.

He said nothing, but pursed his lips and nodded.

The image of the perfectly circular compound from miles above flashed onto the surface. With a few rapid strokes of her fingers, Livvy brought into focus two pictures that were almost identical.

"A half hour ago," she said, pointing to the left one, then pointed at the other and continued, "...and this one, taken now."

"God damn. Did I mention our shitty luck?" Dean said.

Livvy rubbed her pendant between her fingers nervously, and muttered, "This has nothing to do with luck."

On the right image, a section of the southwest wall was simply missing, along with a large part of the forest. A light brown line cut across where it should have been all the way into the Windy Woods.

"That's that, then—the fight is on. If we can't hold out here, then Gaelenn is our last hope," she said.

Tears welled up in the bottom of Livvy's eyes where thousands of years of pain gathered, threatening to burst forth.

"Can it all have really come down to this?" she whispered through choked lips.

Dean did not console her; the wheels of his mind were churning behind his squinting eyes. His finger and thumb traced his mustache over and over again. "If we could cut off the head, as they used to say."

"We've tried it a dozen times, Dean!" Livvy wiped the tears from her eyes. "The Eye can't be killed. It has no head, no weakness!"

"No, no, no—I don't mean kill the Eye, I know we can't do that. But we can get out of here alive. We can keep this thing going. That's all we can hope for right now."

"And then what? Where will we go?"

"First, we worry about living to fight another day. Then we worry about the rest. Damnit, Elizabeth, listen to yourself!" He shouted, half angry and half pleading. "At this point four thousand years ago you were telling me the same goddamn thing!"

Livvy paused and crossed her arms, instantly sober. "So where's the monster's head?"

"The Legion. That's the Eye's trump card. There's still two left. Just two, thank God—and you can bet that it doesn't have the right resources to make more or it would've done it!"

He yelled louder with each statement, and then added coldly, "And I'm sure as hell they'll be here for this party."

"But we're talking about your super soldiers. I instructed Astrid to tell her troops to stay as far away from them as they can. I will not have them throw away their lives in needless sacrifice."

"Yeah but somehow, some way, we killed one last time. *Killed* one. Can you believe that? There's hope!" Dean shouted, grabbing her shoulder.

Livvy nodded.

The ground rumbled low again, though this time in a steady, growing drum. The old man and Livvy ignored it for the moment.

Dean pressed his point: "Look, the Legion—those ENs—are the Eye's only real power right now, but also his weakness. He can't just turn every follower he wants into one of those freaks. They're too unstable, too short-lived. And too damned expensive to make! I don't know how in the hell that machine found out my formula in the first place, but it's not like it has the arms to mine the materials itself. It needs lackeys to do its dirty work for it. It would take time."

Livvy kept her eyes on him. "I know all this, Dean."

"Point is, the Eye made the mistake of making those ENs its right-hand men, so to speak. Without them, its army is lame, limp—and it is too! It can't just replace them. We take them out, we take out its whole goddamn army. Now *that* will buy us some time. Look, let's do what we can. It's either that or sit here and die—I don't see anywhere to run anyway, do you?"

The Priestess only stared blankly and blinked.

"That's right," Dean said, his voice gentler, closer, like a father to a loved daughter. "Listen, Elizabeth. I know that every time we've done this it's taken a piece of you with it. Well, me too."

She looked up at him, eyes, nose and cheeks as red as fire. "I just can't do it again."

"Elizabeth, without you we wouldn't have survived even a hundred years. Humans would've been wiped clean off the planet. But look at us—we've made it twenty-some-thousand. Someday, if you just hold on, we're going to take the world back. And then you and I can get rid of these fucking machines in our blood and finally grow old and die."

She chuckled, despite herself, at his foul language and let a final tear drop, adding, "As long as we do what we set out to do in the beginning—make sure that nothing like this never happens again. That's what this is all about, Dean. Not just about survival."

"There you go," Dean said, holding her arm with a warm hand and smiling. "But we still have to go out and earn it. The hardest anybody's ever had to work for anything. Ever."

He looked at the table and used his dirty fingers to change around the glowing tapestry. "Let's see..."

A few moments later, a new image appeared; the light-brown strike through the southwest part of Last Retreat had turned gray. The Maynon Ohzan army was almost at the top.

"It's starting," Dean said. "First of all, you stay here. I'll make sure a garrison stays around the house in case they make it this far."

"I'll take care of myself," Livvy said with a sharp look.

"I know you can, hun!" Dean smiled back and followed it directly with an ice-cold stare. "But if those two Triumvir got in here...I can't be worrying about that. Now, after that I'm going to need two people in particular. And then we're going to go on the hunt for those EN bastards."

CHAPTER FORTY THREE
TOWER OF TERROR

THE LOW LIGHTS WENT bright again the exact moment Gaelenn's head jerked up. Within 30 seconds, the straps fell loose, and Gaelenn spilled out onto the floor in a sweaty mass of man. His lips bent to one side of his head, struggling for air since he could not move his neck to rest his skull sideways on the floor instead of kissing it. His pants were drenched with sweat and the ribs along his back writhed and pulsated with labored breath.

Steam spilled from the holes in the table and its hoses as it silently returned to its previous form. But even after that, Gaelenn still could not stand. Along his arms and spine he wore thin red dots where small pieces of skin had been removed or grated away.

"What happened?" he asked himself.

"*Hello Gaelenn,*" Ai responded. "*I'm afraid the accelerated procedure is...a little jarring.*"

"Yeah, a bit, I'd say."

"*I'm also afraid that it was not totally complete once again.*"

"Not totally complete? Why?" Gaelenn looked up to the ceiling, his head spinning.

"*Because a few minutes ago the man who chased your companion entered this tower and is, I assume, currently ascending it,*" Ai continued. "*I terminated the process as soon as he entered. It was mostly completed, though, except for the rest phase. Since you didn't have it, you may experience some side effects.*"

"What side effects?" Gaelenn yelled. He curled his fingertips around the edge of the table he had just fallen from and with a curdled, stifled half-scream pulled himself up with only his arms and his will. "I...can't..."

"*What can't you do?*" Ai asked to elicit the rest of the statement as Gaelenn nearly fainted on top of the table.

His breath slowly came back to him. "The man...who is coming for me...was enhanced by one of these very machines, wasn't he?"

"*Yes, not these specifically, however. Oh—I have a message from Dean and Elizabeth.*"

"Eliza...? What is it?"

"*Their home is under attack by the Legion and the Maynon Ohzan forces. They have instructed you to stay as far away as you can and hide until the battle is over.*"

"What? So ENs are here *and* there? ...Are they okay?"

"*I am unsure. I haven't been able to regain contact with them since we last spoke, some time ago.*"

"Oh, god...I don't think I'm going to make it out of this tower," he said with a dry cough.

After what he had seen in the images of ages past, sticking in his mind like thorns, he knew, more than he had even after his two previous confrontations with his stalker, that resistance was pointless. If, indeed, Triumvir Anwir was on his way up the tower, he had only minutes to live—or less.

And at that very moment, the portal door in the middle of the floor whined with a slow squeak, pushed from below.

"*I have tried to engage a backup locking system,*" Ai whispered. Her voice came from the wall closest to Gaelenn. "*But I'm not sure there's anything else I can do. Please try to hide—maybe I can distract him somehow, and you can escape.*"

Gaelenn crawled as far away as he could and sat back against a solid table near the edge of the cloister. The cool, sleek surface dried the sweat on his back, offering a small comfort before his judgment.

He spoke aloud, either to Ai or to himself. "There's no running this time. I wouldn't even make it down the stairs."

Deafening clicks, the sound of a bare metal brake failing its purpose, began firing from the porthole as backup locks attempted to catch. But the door was already an inch or two past its resting position and most of them only caught on air. Two or three of the lock's fingers found a home in the grimy lower lip of the door, stopping its upward progress temporarily. After a brief moment, rabid, incessant hammering sent forth a jarring clamor.

Hands on his knees, Gaelenn spent a half minute to reorient himself.

Where did I leave my sword? He thought, cursing himself. At his feet, the cold sheen of iron looked back at him. But it wasn't the right length. *All I have to defend myself with is Aydya's dagger.*

He stared at the weapon under his palm, analyzing the curved blade and tarnished bronze hilt. It was wrapped in tacky skin and sharp—a deadly weapon at close range, but more than likely useless to him now, given the enemy he faced. He blew out a measured, helpless sigh as a series of loud bangs shot through the room. It was starting. The end.

The banging became louder and louder until it the last lock snapped, the door slammed open, and rusted metal fingers shot around the room. The room's lights dimmed at once, as if in warning, creating a heavy, orange atmosphere. Then, all sound stopped, save the clanking of a heavy metal rod falling down the center of the tower, striking ladders, stairs, and walls until it hit the stone foundation far below.

Gaelenn wound his neck around the corner of the table and found a sliver of a view between the mess of machines. A lithe, black figure ascended into the room without a sound. Gaelenn sat back against the table and closed his eyes. His sweat had evaporated, and now his throat was so dry he could not swallow his fear.

Recalling his time in the sewers below Key Rock, he abandoned his eyes and used his ears and his memory to scan the room. It was a dark maze of machines, order-less, surrounding the porthole randomly all around but leaving a nearly perfect circle of space around the door where his doom now stood. Nothing moved and nothing spoke except for the gentle whir of the room's machines and the oddly horrifying sound of fabric falling to the floor, as Triumvir Anwir removed his black costume.

"I can smell you," came his voice, like a snake's, slithering into Gaelenn's ears and poisoning his courage. "You might as well just stand up and come to me now. There's no sense in us painfully reenacting of our last meeting—there's nobody to save you *here*. Ah! My sword. Thank you very much. A gift from my master, I've quite missed."

Gaelenn cursed under his breath—he had left it right in the middle of the room. Anwir took a few heavy steps in the opposite direction.

"I hate games, you know," he said in a calm breath before violently flinging one of the tables onto its side. It crumbled under the ensuing rain of enraged kicks that followed. When the terrible clamor died down, he walked to another random table to do the same.

"Just come out! I'll level this whole place if I have to!"

Gaelenn gripped the dagger. It was small in his hands, he noted with regret, made more for concealment and surprises than for open fights. He opened his eyes and, as quietly as he could, brought his feet under him, testing them. They moved like granite.

This will be the shortest last stand ever, he thought with a sardonic smile.

A low, escalating hum erupted from a table between him and Anwir—it was coming to life.

"Ai? What are you doing?" he whispered toward the wall.

Another started up, and then another. Strange, unnatural sounds filled the stuffy air, the mechanized tables talking in long-lost tongues. Then they moved.

Ai's voice projected itself toward Gaelenn where only he could hear and pleaded, "*Close your eyes!*"

Just as he did, all lights in the room flooded, drowning out every single shadow, bathing everything in pure bright white.

"Devious!" screamed Anwir. He covered his eyes with his arm as quickly as he could but was still momentarily blinded. "Foul, wretched magic!"

The lights continued their course, becoming brighter and brighter, and then burst out into sparks and died, leaving pocks of sizzling red on Gaelenn's back and smoldering holes on Anwir's green shirt. After a moment of darkness, several dim, orange globes flickered on around the domed ceiling, but neither of the men in the room could see yet. Gaelenn rubbed his eyes, blinded even through his eyelids and hands, and Anwir cowered in a heap, covering his head.

He did not see the tendrils and metal arms creep out of the tables around him and surround his turtled form. As soon as he dared to look up, they struck. The room was alive, and all the functional machines united in a frantic, mechanized attack aimed at the intruder.

"Ah!" he yelled, stung in the back with a long needle. His reflexes were sharp and even though his vision was still clouded, he struck and snapped it off before it even left his skin. Soft tubes tried to wrap around his wrists and legs and he writhed in a furious dance.

Gaelenn's eyes returned to him and he looked between the tables to witness the wild, surreal battle of man versus machine.

Man? Not a man—a monster. Much like himself, now. Sudden strength came to the Gaelenn's hands in spasms. He was still weakened. But he was changing.

Steel and stone and cloth flew about the room as Anwir went from defense to offense and began attacking the machines. With his unreal strength he lifted a nearby table, solid obsidian and steel, over his head and heaved it effortlessly with enough force to take out two other machines.

The resulting amalgamation of twisted obsidian slammed into the wall, unleashing a gush of sparks. Then another round of attacks came at him.

"*Go! Gaelenn, run!*" Ai yelled into the room—she saw no use for stealth any longer. "*Now is the only chance. Please.*"

But he knew it was useless.

"I can't do anything now. I know that if I don't stop him now, he'll catch up with me eventually. Tell Dean and Livvy thanks. And I'm sorry," he said straight to the wall and stood up.

Before he turned around, he squeezed his fists and marveled at them. Something was different. They were stronger. Iron made flesh. His legs flexed involuntarily, unbalancing him for half a second before adjusting. Instantly he could feel control returning to them, and more: power. He did not spend a single second more to ponder whether it was the call of battle or the strengthening magic taking effect—he sprung.

Anwir had been too busy to notice Gaelenn's approach, but his animal senses felt the wind from the dagger's swing just before it landed and he deflected the arm of the incoming attack with a slap. In a single motion he lifted his sword and swiveled to face the attack, swinging wildly at both Gaelenn and the machines' devices.

Gaelenn lunged backward to dodge the blows. His strength was returning, enhanced, little by little, and with each pulse of energy he initiated a fresh counterattack. Most of the blows from the two men fell devastatingly onto and into the machines around them and they chased one another around the room in a frenzied war dance.

The Triumvir, though, was slowly winning. His sword, when not occupied cutting ropes and staving off knifes and needles, gashed his opponent's bare skin.

"You bastard!" Gaelenn yelled, flinging bloody saliva into the air. His swings were ever more powerful but every time their speed increased, so did the blows of Anwir—the help from Ai was faltering.

"Run! Gaelenn!" she blared through the room loud enough for her echo to bounce back from the tower floor below.

Another wave of machine attacks—the last, perhaps—wrapped all around Triumvir Anwir's arms and legs and finally seemed to restrain him. But just as he was driven back, his left hand came loose and he struck Gaelenn's fingers, flinging the dagger to the floor. Gaelenn drew back several paces.

"What do you want with me?" He asked the bloodied face of the bloodthirsty man in green. "Why? Why do you pursue me?"

Anwir sneered. "You don't need to know. You only need to submit to me or die." He moved his leg and dragged the impossibly heavy mess of tables, three or four at once, with him.

"What are you going to do with me?" Gaelenn pressed again.

"Before I do anything I am going to rip your eyes out of your head," he continued, blind with rage, inching forward. "And I'm not in the business of chatting while fighting!"

Gaelenn stopped. His green eye caught the orange light and sparkled. His gray, mist-colored eye, did, too, from beneath his bent brow.

That's it. Anwir's secret. The only chance. A longshot, but...I trust Aydya. He shot a taunting grin at Anwir.

"Ai, can you activate the last Sooshinsoechee for me?" The term came easily to him now, his mind clearing.

"Do you mean 'that' one?"

"Yes." Gaelenn said.

"*But—*"

"Is it possible?"

"*Yes. As you wish,*" she replied after a short hesitation. The room vibrated with her thoughts and the profundity of the emerging concept. "*I understand what you mean now.*"

In that half-second delay, not a lifetime but a timeless, infinite eon for a machine that a human could never comprehend, she felt anger. And bitterness, and coldness. And warmth. Envy, sadness, and longing. And finally, hope. In that quantum of silence she felt all that she would ever feel. And in the end, it was love that won. A machine's love. But love nonetheless.

"*Thank you, Gaelenn. I wish you the best of luck,*" she finally said, and went silent.

The last machine in the room—the one that was fated to rest forever—woke up.

The dull orange lights in the room flashed red.

Triumvir ignored the strange exchange he had just witnessed, creeping closer and closer in his bondage. The hoses and straps could not hold him much longer.

The lights flashed red again, this time for two seconds, and then again for three. The struggle for dominance between Ai and the Eye raged on an unseen, unfathomable battlefield in this very room, dwarfing the struggle between the men.

The flickering red and orange lights, punctuated by yellow and blue sparks still spewing from the walls, ceiling, and tables, played a strobe-like song with the shadows on the faces of Gaelenn and Anwir as they drew closer and closer to one another, readying for the final duel.

Finally, when the Triumvir was an arm's length away, the orange light died, along with Ai, and the room was as red as blood. He gave one last push against the suddenly lifeless rope and came free, then stuck his sword a fingertip's length into the sinewy muscle on Gaelenn's naked breast. It pierced the muscle and rested neatly on the bone.

Gaelenn refused to react to the pain—he did not even feel it—and stuck out his chin and asked with a wry smile, taunting, "And now who gets me, you or *your master*?"

A shocked flash of white eyes preceded a sneer and the crazed stalker finally gave an answer. "With you, I will *own* my master. With your key in my hand, *he* will bow to *me*."

The trap worked.

BRRRRRAAAAAAAAAAAAHHH

The room screamed, deafening both of them, and as they winced and covered their ears in pain, the remaining machines moved on their own and crashed down on Triumvir Anwir with the fury of demons, smashing all their weight into him from all sides, their wild tentacles flailing with rage and stabbing every skin and orifice. A bloody minute later, they stopped.

Broken and twisted, Anwir slid into a heap on the floor; the Eye had meted out its punishment for treason.

When Gaelenn opened his eyes, he saw the pile of man and blood before him with pitiless, cold eyes. Anwir stared back, his broken face full of hate and shock, bloody foam leaking from the sides of his mouth. Gaelenn picked up the fallen sword nearby and drove it slowly into the Triumvir's heart until at last it stopped beating.

"For my mother," he said.

He could not hear yet, but ears were not necessary to understand his new plight—the machines turned and began to swoop in his direction.

"Guess that means I'm next!" he yelled as he somersaulted, narrowly evading a swinging blade and the end of a mechanical noose.

The gust from an impact where he had just been standing—a table smashing into the floor—pushed him just into reach of the rusted steel door that had been blown off minutes earlier.

He picked it up with a grunt, anticipating having to struggle with its immense weight, but instead it came off the ground like a feather. Surprised, he used it as a shield to fend of the onslaught that had, until now, been protecting him from the Triumvir.

What am I doing? he thought, observing himself from outside his own body as he darted weightlessly from point to point. Then, he stammered aloud, almost panicked, "Am I really doing this? Give...me...control!"

He yelled at his own limbs, but they failed to respond to his consciousness. When he was just on top of the room's porthole-door, he stopped. His voice, at least, was still his.

So, this is what it feels like to be an EN, he thought, and willed his feet to set themselves.

"You bastard. When we destroy your army, you're dead too. You'll pay for what you've done. To the world. To the people. To Key Rock," he screamed, adding a deathly sneer, "and to my family!"

He flung the door-shield in his hands. It sliced the air like a rotary blade and cleaved the communication portal from which the Eye had been summoned clean in two.

All light in the room died as he dove into the hole and to freedom. He had not a second to spare.

CHAPTER FORTY FOUR
Bring it Down

Growing up, Kell had always been known as quiet—a gentle and weak-willed child who kept out of trouble, kept his head down, respected his elders, and, above all, never started a fight.

Any trouble he had ever been in was directly attributable to Gaelenn, his inseparable polar opposite of a best friend. In fact, Kell had long ago lost count of the number of times he had kept Gaelenn from doing something spontaneously disastrous. He did not need to count how many times Gaelenn had done the same for him. Zero. He never needed to. No one from their old town, if they had been alive to see it, would ever have believed that at this moment, Gaelenn was using his wits to escape from danger while Kell was forgetting any wits he ever had to seek it.

Another swing of his fiery hammer smashed into the bare skull of a Maynon Ohzan berserker, sending the lifeless body of its owner cartwheeling into the ground sideways and triggering a wild battle cry from Kell's throat; he was alive like he had never been before.

"Kell, behind you!" Astrid shouted from several yards away as she dispatched a pair of attackers with a sweep of her long spear.

He swung around, writing a line of black smoke in the air just in time to catch an axe and stop it from splitting his shoulder. It shattered and its wooden shaft smacked onto the red-hot anvil in Kell's hands, instantly charred and smoking. He bared his teeth and shoved the hammer right into the shocked face opposite him. The smell of melting flesh would have affected him any other day. But today it only fed his rage.

"Thanks!" he shouted back. "I'm coming over!"

He jumped over piles of bodies and limbs until he was at Astrid's side and the two fought together.

"There's no end to them," he said.

"We need a miracle. We need the Priestess!"

"What's she going to do? She's half your size!"

"You wouldn't have faith, of course!" She stabbed another attacker through the abdomen before continuing. "Haven't you come to believe in her power since you've been here? Look at your own mace!"

"She didn't make this! The old man did."

Astrid spit blood onto the ground. "They're cut from the same cloth!"

Both the fighters were exhausted and aching for a break to the fighting, but there was no end in sight.

"Captain!" came a guard's voice from a line of trees nearby.

Astrid looked behind, just now noticing how close they had been driven toward the trees before finding the guard. "What is it?" she replied, screaming over the battle.

"The Priestess demands an update from you personally."

She gritted her teeth, unable to hide her initial wave of contempt. She quickly recovered, though, and responded with a simple answer: "...Understood. Back to the battle, soldier—we must protect her!"

Turning to Kell, she began a confession, "I can't leave—even under *her* orders. I must be here with my army. For her sake and theirs."

They continued fighting, speaking just loud enough to hear each other but safely out of earshot of any others.

"What are you going to do?" he asked.

"Ask you to go in my stead."

"Me?" His beard bunched together with his lips. "I don't think that's going to help anything."

"Please—without direction I am afraid that we will fall in minutes." Astrid looked at him, shock plastered over her face with what she had just said. "—Don't tell her that, of course! But do tell her that we are in dire straits."

"But I haven't agreed to go!"

"Please...please!"

Kell smacked a lazy arrow out of the sky. "Fine. Anything else I should say?"

"I know you have no faith. But I am sure that the Priestess has some power to help us. We have lived for countless generations believing so."

"So ask her to use her magic, is that it?"

Astrid relaxed her battle stance for a short moment, her blank stare at once innocent and desperate. "If that's what it is—yes. I know there is something she can do. And she needs to know we cannot hold forever. Go!"

Kell nodded and ran off toward the trees.

"I WANT YOU TO know that I used the last of my power to help Gaelenn. I cannot tell you if he will survive, but I tried. And I must warn you, as soon as I sever this connection, I will turn on the unencrypted Sooshinsoechee. At his request, but also at mine. This is my choice. And you know what that means—you can never come here again. I love you, Dean. Good bye."

The signal went dead, the recorded message complete, and the old man pressed his fists against the table, bent over as if in prayer. The tears had nothing to do with any gods.

"Me too, old girl. Me too," Dean muttered, broken.

Elizabeth put her hand on his shoulder. "I'm sorry, Dean. I know what she meant to you."

He bit his lower lip, stretching out his mustache across his face, and nodded. "I left her a long time ago, already. But you know, if anybody could help Gaelenn out it would be her. She is—was—is—something else."

Swimming in his head were the thoughts and feelings he could not express: the father-like instinct he felt for an ethereal being, having rescued her from a long-forgotten corner of the world and recreating her in a perfect, pure image. And the bond that grew between them in the thousands of years he toiled away with nobody at his side but her. And the sacrifice and suffering she must have felt when she gave herself up to her deranged alter-image. In her own lifetime—an infinite, immeasurable age—she had suffered just as much as any human.

"But why would she do that? Let the Eye in?" Livvy abandoned her empathy and began a battery of questions. "Do you have any idea?"

"Not at all," he said, burying his thoughts with a shake of his head. "Unless..."

She crossed her arms and made a half-step toward him to hear better over the steady drum of battle, which was growing ever louder.

"Unless," he continued, "unless, well—there was some reason Gaelenn would have asked her to do that. I'm pretty sure it wasn't suicide."

"Well, we've lost the North Tower as a possible refuge or for supplies and parts, we know that much," Livvy said.

"That's right. We'd better get back to checking those old blueprints of this place." Dean smudged the wetness from his eyes with the thumb and index finger of one hand. "Bring it up."

Livvy summoned a strange image of thousands of striking white lines buried in a blue cloud. It was an abstraction, nearly impossible to fathom by sight.

"So if we're lucky and time hasn't taken the lower passageways, what do we hope to gain?" she asked.

Dean's mind absorbed itself in the image before him; his gaze would not be diverted, but he spared enough cognitive function to offer simple answers. "A safe way out. We're outnumbered and I'm out of tricks. Damnit, I'd need a month to analyze this properly."

"But we have Astrid and her guard and all the people of Last Retreat. I have trusted them with my life for thousands of years. They'll hold, and then we can escape. Everyone."

"The walls had never been breached before today too, right? They were built to last a hundred thousand years. The Eye broke them down anyway in a matter of minutes once it figured out it wanted to. And the ENs are after us. We can't stand against them. Not even you can."

Livvy crossed her arms in a huff. "I can hold my own."

"I know you can, but not against this. We need to prepare for the worst. How's the fight looking?"

"Not good," she said. On another part of the table she conjured a bird's-eye view of the battle. The new hill, which had been covered in a mass of humanity, was now mostly bare—the battle had moved into the trees. "Very bad, actually. We've been driven into the forest."

Dean cupped his hand under his chin. "That'll work to our advantage—for a while. It's as black as night in there."

"Dean, please tell me you were joking about being out of tricks. We need something, and quickly."

He reached backward and found the worn armrest on a once-well-polished luxury chair and collapsed into it, the pressure to yet again be the savior pulling him down like an anchor.

"I truly don't, Elizabeth. All we have now is hope. Faith, your acolytes here would say," he said through a deep, exhausted exhale.

"What's this?" Livvy jumped almost onto the table, pointing emphatically.

"What's what?"

"Here!"

Dean pried himself out of the chair and scanned the area her finger was tapping, a tiny portion of the massive blueprint, and watched her slender finger trace a series of lines to the edge of the table.

"That's it!" he shouted. "It's an old maintenance tunnel. Sealed, but only at the very end. I should have at least enough magic left in me to open that door."

He fingered the black brick in his bag. "Let me transfer this data over." He said, pulling the old black stone from the pouch at his side. After a few taps on its surface, he fastened it back safely.

"How far away was the entrance inside the structure? I've never been down there," Livvy asked.

"Not far, a minute if we run. And if we have to go in there, I'm sure we'll be running. It's a long way down to this maintenance exit, though, by the looks of it—all the way down. That's if we can navigate this maze."

Livvy looked up, an epiphany hitting her between the eyes. "Running...running...where is Astrid? She should have checked in by now! Without her we don't know what's going on out there."

The door opened and blew a gust of wind at Livvy and Dean. In the doorway stood Kell with his great chest puffing in and out rapidly. "Astrid sent me. Things aren't going well. There are too...too many of them."

The Priestess ran to him and handed him a large cup of water. He drank it down, stopping every few seconds to gasp for breath, and slammed it down onto the table.

"Astrid told me to tell you that they're still fighting. But things are grim. She won't leave her guard, and her guard won't leave the people."

"I know. She wouldn't. I was hoping. But she never would. That says more than any words. Dean—we might want to think about evacuating everybody," Livvy said.

"Wait—everybody? There are thousands of people here! Tens of thousands!"

"Everybody. I won't go without them."

"You've never made anything easy, have you?" Dean said, but not without a faint smile. "It's going to take some time."

She nodded. "Good. Let's organize the people around—"

Another great earthquake shook all three of them to their knees. It lasted for a full minute, threatening to bring down the entire house. It succeeded in leveling several buildings nearby in a steady series of aftershocks.

"Now what?" Dean asked, following his question with a sickened grumble, his head spinning.

Livvy shot up to her feet and stepped toward the table. Her focus was imperturbable and with an utterly steady hand she brought up another view of her fortress from the heavens. "We had better start that evacuation now."

Kell shook the dust out of his beard. "What happened?"

Dean shuffled to the table and answered the instant he saw it: "They brought down the wall on the other side, too. There goes our hope."

THE SUN BEAT ON his back and the wind shot sand in his eyes, daring Gaelenn to stop and rest. His mind had long since given up. But his body pulled him along, possessed with power and undying energy.

He had left the tower a day earlier and run through the night after filling his belly with two whole buckets full of well water and a few strips of dry flatbread he found among the packs of the mutilated bodies and his and

Aydya's own dwindled supplies. In vain he had searched for her but found only her footsteps in the sand leading away from the tower and those of Anwir after her.

They led away too far to follow; only his footsteps came back.

"I've got...to get...back to Last Retreat," he said against the current of air.

There was no one to talk to but speaking out loud made his mind and thoughts feel more real. Inside himself, he no longer trusted his inner voice. He ran and ran, throughout the day and night and all the next day, pausing for a quarter hour here or there to recover, but he found that much to his own surprise he needed none of the rest and that it was more out of habit than anything else to stop.

"I have to save them. I have to get back to them," he repeated over and over again.

Finally, a line of low mountains appeared on the horizon south, and soon the great Sapphire Mountain also showed its monstrous girth, though the brilliant glass that gave it its name still hid from view in the northeast. Gaelenn's legs carried him even faster now, and the relentless sun was powerless to stop him.

At the edge of a decrepit, abandoned village just over the mountain line, he spotted a rogue band of vagrants watering their horses at a small stream. Tossing Anwir's sword at their feet, gathered at the last moment of his escape from the tower, he grabbed the reins of one of the animals and nodded in affirmation of the transaction. He needed the speed of the animal but not its strength. His will led it south.

His only enemy, aside from the Legion, the Maynon Ohzan army, and its master, was time.

CHAPTER FORTY FIVE
THE BATTLE OF LAST RETREAT

"GUARD! SECOND BRIGADE TO the north!" Astrid yelled into the trees behind her. There had been no news since the quake, but her senses were sharp. She faced the lieutenant beside her.

"There must have been another breach of the wall somewhere. Take as many soldiers as you can!"

The black of the forest gave her and her remaining warriors the advantage, but torches had made their way to the enemies on the front lines and after endless hours of fending them off successfully, she felt another push coming.

If only Rin were here, she thought. She needed him to be her light in this dark hour. But she had no time to cry. An axe swooshed through the air and brushed her arm, leaving a deep cut in her skin. Her grimace would have remained invisible if not for the burning torch thrust into the dark in front of her face. She resumed her fight, expertly weaving backwards up and over and under the knotted trees as her assailants tripped and plodded forward in vain to catch her. Her personal Guard tried to form a barrier to protect her, but every time they did she split their formation asunder with a fresh, raging attack.

"Don't worry about me!" she scolded. But their love for their Captain was too much to overcome. When the first of the blue globes marking the boundary of her city caught her gaze, she panicked. "Soldiers! Hold! This is your moment!"

She wheeled back toward the lights and let them illuminate her from below; she was a beacon in the dark.

"We must make our stand here! This is the moment of our lives! Fight!"

Arrows smashed into trees haphazardly around her—opposing archers could not get a clear shot. She leapt out of the light and circled around to other points, repeating her plea to the soldiers all around the battlefront, stirring them into a frenzy, refreshing their dwindling spirits.

They fought with renewed zeal and beat back the attack, leaving a fresh trail of bodies, not losing a single defender.

"Yes!" Astrid screamed. "Send them back! They will never take our home!"

Within an hour, the attack had dwindled to nothing. The sound of clanging metal had faded, leaving the forest black and silent, as it always was. Only the smell of the wounded and dead lingered.

"We did it!" a soldier shouted, and several of his comrades followed him with a cheer. Others all around the southern front did the same until the silence was drowned out in celebration.

Astrid kneeled next to a blue globe and set her hand on it gently. The coolness comforted her, lending her a moment of peace. They did it. She did it. It took several minutes for the cheering and singing to die down. As the last voice laughed and went silent, Astrid jerked herself to her feet.

She sniffed the air. Smoke.

Clamping her eyes shut, she turned her head and probed ahead using only her ears. The sound was low, almost imperceptible, but unmistakable: the popping of wood. "Soldiers! Fall back! FIRE!"

ARROWS THUDDED INTO THE back of the great house. From inside, it was a chilling hum, sending the spines of the holdovers shivering.

"They're here. Shit! Let's get going!"

Dean waved his arms wildly at Kell and Livvy and at the few guards still stationed around the mansion.

"That was too fast," Livvy said, a sudden gloom forming over her like a cloud.

Outside, screaming and shouting littered the air as panic took hold in Last Retreat.

"We did what we could—let's get moving!" Dean replied.

He grabbed her hand and yanked her out the front of the house. Kell followed, eyes on the trees and houses behind them.

They had spent the better part of the past day making preparations and organizing the citizens into escape groups. Guards were assigned to each one, though they were woefully outnumbered. As many as a hundred people to one soldier. It was the best they could do, but it still was not enough.

Dean led them straight to the center of the ancient resort, where thousands of villagers had gathered, scarcely ready for a mass exodus, strapped with packs and satchels full of whatever goods and food they could carry. Fear lined their faces, young and old; elders, parents carrying their newborns, young children, all those who could not fight had gathered here. His hands rose over his head, palms outward.

"Listen! It is time to leave your homes. You have been told to bring only what you need to survive. I will open the way out now. Enter only when you are called!"

He approached the fountain in the center of the courtyard and stepped into the clear water. Its icy embrace sent goosebumps around his body, and he walked to the center statue and looked up. In its time, this place had been the pinnacle of human expression—or maybe at least the acceptable facsimile of an original. But now, after millennia of restoration and painstaking care, it did not matter whether it was made 20,000 or 2,000 or 200 years ago; it was the last of its kind on earth.

"At least we still have pictures," he said to himself and bent down, sticking a rough black box onto a slight, round depression on the ground under the water.

"Just a moment," Livvy interrupted as she climbed into the fountain herself. It was the only way she could see into the eyes of her people.

"My people of Last Retreat," she said, "Thank you for gathering."

The crowd was completely silent. The Star Priestess had never in their lifetimes—nor those of their parents—addressed the people directly.

"There's only one way out for us now. But before we leave our home, I wanted to talk to you all. And see you. I feel that you are all my children. I have seen you all grow up. Born. And your parents and their parents."

Livvy sobbed and continued, "But I am not your mother. I don't deserve to be. And I refuse to pretend."

Then, her voice grew as she found her strength, searching her long-dormant heart and finding her thread of humanity still beating. She was kept alive—kept perfect—by the machines inside her. But even though they made it hard to appreciate her emotions—even to feel them—they did not kill them. She was still, after all, human.

"I love you all, though, as if I were your mother! But also as your sister. And in some ways, as your child. When we leave here, no matter what happens—you must spread what you have learned all your life. We are equal. All of us. Me, the Captain, you—"

She stifled a tear. "Every one of you. I love you," she said at last, and stepped down from the fountain. Holding up the soaking bottom of her dress, she walked toward a gaggle of guards, who shielded her.

"Everyone, look away until I say!" Dean shouted.

He shuffled out of the water himself and kneeled down a few yards away.

"Close your eyes!"

A smoky explosion blasted a hole in the fountain and sprayed water on everything within twenty yards. The statue groaned and fell on its side and Dean got up and jogged back to the fountain. Water jetted randomly from pipes, but drained quickly into the large, black hole exactly where the depression had been.

"Let's go!" Dean yelled. "Single file! Group one, please!"

The guards led their groups to the fountain as agreed to beforehand, but just as the first of the villagers reached it, Maynon Ohzan soldiers burst through the tree line and fired a volley of arrows into the crowds. Some soldiers fell, but most of the arrows found targets in the general populace, causing an eruption of screams and panic.

"Run, run! Fall back! Everybody!" Dean shouted again, but the chaos muted his voice completely.

Enemy soldiers ran amok and the guards abandoned their posts to fend off the attack. Old men and women fled with their grandchildren through the trees and between houses and rubble, out of sight. Attackers ran them down, stalking the easy prey with satisfied grins.

"We've got to go, too, Elizabeth." Dean said, grabbing her wrist. "Alone, if we have to."

"But...!" she protested. In a last gasp, she screamed at the soldiers nearby, "Gather the people and get them off this mountain!"

Then he jerked her arm so quickly that she had no time to set her feet, shoving her down the hole in the fountain. She found herself descending a sloping path of steep stairs built into a tunnel.

Kell followed after, careful not to alert the mob of Maynon Ohzans. Before his head entered the darkness, he looked out to see the carnage. Many of the people had somehow escaped, and the guards had created a perimeter around the stragglers. Another fierce battle raged right in the middle of Last Retreat, but luckily, it seemed that the commotion had been enough cover for the three of them to escape.

Kell made one last check—he was only a month removed from his own town's destruction and his own people experiencing the same horror—and his heart bled not to help the citizens of his newly adopted home. His face flushed with grief, and he gave one last look over just in time to see, between the moving sea of legs and feet, a woman clad in green emerge from the trees directly opposite. She wore a purple arm band.

His eyes strained, hoping to see her more clearly over the distance. And his mouth dropped open when his eyes caught the glint of her wretched steel armor and the heavy chain at her side.

She was the EN. The last Triumvir. And she was grinning straight at him.

Into the hole he shot, tumbling down the bruising steps onto his back. He ground his teeth in pain but swallowed it and dashed on, Dean and Livvy having already gone out of sight. There was no light in the tunnel, so he ran with his arms outstretched, using them to feel the walls of the corridor.

"Hey! Hey!" he projected a whisper that came out more like a shout.

A small white light appeared a few yards in front of him. "Come on!" Dean said.

Kell rushed to catch up. "We've got to hurry! There's a...there's one of those things! And she saw us."

"Are you sure?" Livvy asked. "Things meaning an EN? Legion?"

"Yes. Whatever you call them. It was the she-one."

"Damnit. Let's go!" Dean whispered harshly.

The smooth stone in his hand became a lantern—from a tiny pinpoint on its surface it lit the path two or three yards in front of them. On the other side of it, Dean studied the blue-lined image that Livvy had conjured up on her table and used it to direct their path.

The tunnels wound in unfathomable patterns, and for every path they took there were three that had collapsed and were no longer passable. Dean led them on, his miracle device leading the way.

"These were access tunnels way back when…they used them during construction and then for maintenance and storage after the place went operational," Dean explained. "I think people even lived in them, the staff."

His mouth, at times, moved independently of his brain, which was currently totally focused on their journey. "Did you know this entire mountain is man-made? A vacation resort for the super-rich to escape the trivialities of the world below—"

"Dean, he does not need a history lesson right now!" Livvy said.

Kell gave no response, too confused by some of the words. *Vacation?* His bare elbow caught on the jagged edge of some old metal, rusted so badly that it was basically rock. He stopped for a second to rub it and turned his head to the side.

In the distance behind them, the thumping of footsteps followed.

"*Shh!*" Livvy said in a forceful whisper. Dean's little black box shone on her—her pupils, despite the light, had devoured her irises. She stared behind them with wide eyes. "She's coming. We have to hurry!"

They doubled their pace, and now little scrapes, five times as frequent as before, went ignored as they descended further and further down the old tower-mountain.

"Go! Go!" each of them said at intervals, prodding each other at a dangerous, necessary pace. Deeper and deeper into the mountain they descended, fighting against the earth and time. The reek of rust and rock and stale air and *age* began to overpower their senses.

"The ventilation systems are probably just going to get worse," Dean said, covering his nose with a loose bit of cloth from his sleeve. "Keep going."

The walls disappeared as they passed into the largest room they had yet found, empty except for a few ancient tools scattered about for them to trip over. Any wood had long rotted away but some of their fittings were still intact.

Kell picked up a small stake-looking object and used his hands to explore it. "This stuff feels like the walls in that room in the forest."

"It'll last longer than I will, even," Dean said. "Drop it. Let's keep moving."

As soon as they found the exit on the other side of the room, a blue light in front of them and around a corner stopped them in their tracks.

Livvy spread her arms and physically barred the two men from advancing, then put her finger up to her lips. *Quiet.*

After half a minute, she dropped her arms, whispering, "It's safe."

"Are you sure?" Dean asked.

"Yes."

She led them into the room. The walls were several yards high and piled to the top with the same blue globes that had lit—and still lit at this moment, she chose to believe—the forest and city above for thousands of years. The room was alight with their steady blue glow.

"What are these things anyway?" Kell asked, stepping over one carefully.

"Just lights," Dean said. "That never die. Like Elizabeth. This way!"

The footsteps behind them grew yet closer. The faster the three escapees walked, the nearer they came. Sweat broke out on Kell's forehead and stung his eyes even though the air was cold and dry.

I need to get out of here, he thought, grinding his beard between his teeth, as the walls grew narrower and narrower until they were forced to progress single-file.

They continued to descend the heart of Last Retreat through rooms and tunnels and down ladders and stairs, navigating the decrepit halls that at any moment could become their tomb.

Occasionally they found long, vertical columns. "Elevator shafts," Dean called them, and they used them to descend large distances all at once. But each time it required a minute of setup for the rope, and their hands ached from the strain.

After hours of descending the labyrinth, they dropped through a final shaft. And at the bottom, the hollow feeling of the floors disappeared. They were on ground. Solid rock.

They moved on. Room after room after room.

"We are almost at the final corridor. After that's the home stretch and we're free," Dean said. His eyes bulged out toward his hand-held machine and his gaze never left it.

Just as they reached the ends of their limits and the mountain began to destroy their wills, the walls spread apart in mercy and the scent of fresh air rescued them from the gloom.

"We're there! Do you smell that?" Dean shouted. "Look for a door!"

Look? Kell had not noticed the pale light at all—and it was not the blue of the globes of Last Retreat, it was the white light of the sun, so faint that it was nearly imperceptible. But it was there in the room. "Where's the light coming from?"

Dean pointed up. "Ventilation shaft."

"What?"

"Like a chimney in a forge, young man, cutting through the entire hill," Dean said. "Now find that door!"

The edges of the room were still vague and too black to see, so Kell and Dean used their fingers, which still throbbed with the pain of countless cuts, to search for the edges of the door.

"I've got one last charge I can use to blast it, so let's make sure it counts."

Livvy snapped her fingers lightly. "Over here!" she said, and Kell and Dean dashed over to see her standing on the tips of her toes. Her hands were halfway deep in a thin crevice. There was an old, sealed gate under her fingers.

Dean tapped on it with his wrist. "This is solid...we only get one chance. If you have a god, it's time to pray."

"It was time to pray a week ago!" Livvy said. "Do it, please."

Reaching into his pack, he replaced his black stone with another round explosive—his very last.

"You two, go into the corner over there," he said, pointing into the darkness where they had come from. "And cover your heads. You're going to catch some spray."

They scurried back into the darkness where they felt for the edge of the room and together huddled down toward the floor. Kell made sure he was closer to the room entrance, just in case.

"Here goes!" Dean's voice carried throughout the room and his footsteps followed it to the opposite corner.

The explosion was muffled but still loud enough to force a quick scream from Livvy. Their ears rung in pain even though they had all used their palms to cover them. Stony shrapnel bruised their backs—the room must have been 5 yards long or more but sharp flak shot like darts all across it. Kell, who had been covering Livvy from a direct line from the blast, bit his lips in pain.

When there was enough air to breathe, they stood up and walked over the fresh grime and rubble to the gate. Dean shone his light and Kell and Livvy flanked him, gazing hopefully into the blast hole, desperation painted on their dirty faces.

"Damnit," Dean said.

Just beyond the new hole, completely intact, the latticework of a beautifully ornate, locked iron gate stood strong.

Now, they were surely trapped.

CHAPTER FORTY SIX
SALVATION LIES BELOW

ASTRID SPRINTED FROM HOUSE to house. Only half or fewer still stood. The blazing, merciless fire had taken what the earthquakes had spared. Around her the battle continued to rage and her soldiers fought valiant last-stands, but one by one they submitted to the onslaught. The end, she knew, was only hours—or mere minutes—away.

"Priestess! Rin!" she screamed in vain.

Her home, the place she and her parents and their parents for thousands of years had protected and maintained, was up in smoke. Grief threatened to overtake her with every breath, and her tears now flowed as freely as her rage. But there was still work to be done.

"Soldiers! To me!" she commanded, and three soldiers broke off their engagements and ran to her.

"Captain!" they reported in unison.

She pointed west. "The citizens have mostly fled into the woods, but if we don't get them out the fire will consume them. Get a search party and find every last one of them!"

"But Ma'am," one of them, her spear bloodied and bent, protested, "if we bring them out here they'll be slaughtered like sheep."

Astrid pursed her lips. "Then group them up and take them as far north of here as you safely can, toward the breach there. But stay in the woods and out of sight. I'll draw the rest of the Maynon Ohzans there now into the forest away—as far distant as I can manage—and when the path is clear, you take our people down the hill as fast as you can and flee. Carry them if you have to."

"Flee? To where? And where will you go?"

"I will go nowhere. But our people will live on. Take them wherever is safe. Across the seas if you need to."

A thought set fire to her eyes.

"Take them to Maynon Ohza. There's no army there now. We'll take the city...by peace," she said, smiling to herself, before continuing, "and show them a thing or two about civilization."

"Captain! Let me stay with you!" another soldier said. His love and respect for her colored his cheeks and left the corners of his eyes wet.

"No, Sab—you must lead our people to safety. I will join you all later," she said with a warm, calming smile. "I swear."

The trio left reassured, though not without aching hearts. Astrid had led the Priestess' guard since she was 18—the youngest Captain in generations—because for her whole life she had been honest, true, and brave. Her Guard's trust in her was unbreakable.

And because of that, the lie she just made was that much more painful to tell. She knew she would stay until the end. A true last stand.

She wiped her eyes dry and watched her soldiers escape. The fire behind her had grown into an inferno and she felt the heat melting the iron on her back. Black smoke plumes shot high into the air and for the first time in many years—maybe ever—the sun found a path in the canopy above and touched the ground at Last Retreat. The fight had already moved onto cooler places to continue, but she stayed to take one last look at her home before it was lost forever. At least she could save her people. She tightened the strap of her Captain's helmet and walked slowly, purposefully, to the giant hole in the tower's wall. When she arrived at the edge of Last Retreat she looked first to the horizon and the breathtaking view refreshed her, empowering her with new strength.

To the northwest, Sapphire Mountain sparkled brilliantly and the setting sun painted the sky in pink and violet streaks. Its beauty distracted her at first from the view under her feet: a brown hill, leading all the way to the ground below, and not 50 yards away from her, the remainder of the filthy Maynon Ohzan army waiting to catch any runners.

The closest of them, surprised and curious, stood up to inspect her. There were nearly a hundred soldiers in all, idle, bored, and playing games and telling stories, angry at being relegated to the reserves for this, the monumental, final battle of the final campaign of the final war—or so it was said. They were simply waiting for the call: *The battle is won! Come reap the spoils! The loot! The women!*

And here was one right in front of them. A beautiful and fiery and proud woman, coming to them willingly. She would be so sweet, an appetizer to the main course to come. Soon, they were all standing and watching.

Astrid marched forward, indeed proud. A streak of smoky earth ran diagonally across her face, dotted by her piercing, almost-colorless eyes. She dropped her spear onto the dirt, kicking up a cloud of dust, and unbuckled her helmet and threw it to the side to reveal her hair, slicked back in sweat, dyed jet-black fresh for her last battle.

She loosened her breastplate and let it fall to the ground, exposing the loose, thin tunic underneath. For protection she wore nothing but the shield strapped on her back; she was going to give these men what they wanted. Or rather, she was going to give them a taste of what she was really worth.

One of the men whistled. "Look, the captain's given up! Come to surrender like a good lass, have you?"

Astrid recognized him at the same time he recognized her—he was the Maynon Ohzan who had run from the fight in the field many nights ago. The night Rin fell. The fire in her heart blazed, but her face remained as plain as fresh snow. The man simply leered.

"Attagirl, better to spare yourself the pain of resisting! Smart one, she is!" another soldier said.

The others shouted lines of agreement and other far worse declarations, but Astrid closed her ears to them. Some of them, conscripted from conquered cities and lands, shook their heads in shame and embarrassment. She held no scorn for them. In fact, she held pity. Maybe some of them would make it out of this without meeting the end of her spear. She held her temper in check, blocking out everything, focusing on each step as it came. But she did notice that her plan was working; the men—more like 80 of them now that she was up close—did not even bother to put up their guard.

Why would they? She was just a woman, and unarmed at that. And Captain of the Guard! Not fit to fight, let alone lead.

Bigots. Crude. Cavemen.

Stop, she thought, refocused. *They don't know what they're doing. Just save your people.*

A man in the center, the ranking officer, maybe, took a few steps away from the group toward her. He still held the brass spoon he had been using to scoop rancid stew into his wide, slack mouth. He grinned with his mouth still lined with the brown broth, exposing a single front tooth.

"Captain," he said and mocked a bow. "Well fought. A lass like you oughtta be treated right. I'll 'ave a tent made for you tonight."

His smile stretched his whole disgusting, ragged face. That was it.

Astrid's fist broke his jaw in two and sent his only front tooth flying into the crowd. In one deft move, she grabbed the spoon out of his hand and jammed it straight into his throat, splitting his jugular and sentencing him to an excruciating death. Before he reached the ground, she reached under her tunic, pulled out two small knives and launched them with one hand into the bellies of the two closest men, then she kicked the commander's nose into his skull and his body rolled into the bulk of the men, knocking over three of them.

"If you want me, come and get me!" she roared. Her taunt was half challenge and half satisfaction.

It was five or more seconds before the stupefied Maynon Ohzans reacted, and by then Astrid had taken off, the large shield on her back deflecting the poorly-thrown spears and rocks. They could not see her almost-gleeful smile as she ran into the woods to their right, but even if they had, it could not have made them run any faster. All of them except for the three fresh corpses stormed after her into the forest, leaving the path down completely open.

DEAN, LIVVY, AND KELL held their breath. The footsteps had arrived. They hid in the far corners of the room, now pitch black—the sun had set hours ago. Soon their own lives would flame out, as well.

Pale light accompanied the footsteps around the corner and the first thing to enter the room was one of the blue light globes, tied at the end of a chain whip, swinging quietly back-and-forth just above the floor. Its light was only strong enough to illuminate the legs of its owner, but it succeeded in projecting a terrifying apparition.

The light stopped in the middle of the room, where the ghostly feet stopped and the globe dangled silently, threateningly. After a minute, it moved again. Dean watched it grow closer to the edge of the room. Where were Elizabeth and Kell? He could only hope they would run back out the door.

The ball stopped just as its light reached the far wall; it found more than stone and rose slowly, tracing two pairs of legs and then the torsos of two women. At its apex, it stopped and dangled between two faces: The last of the ENs—Triumvir Visha—with a devilish grin, and Elizabeth's, frightened but defiant. Both were painted in a haunting, pale blue.

"Well, now. Looks like my bet was right on the money, after all," Visha said, smiling wide. "I'm not sure if my master would prefer you alive or dead. But I'm sure he won't mind if you're a little...damaged."

She looked Livvy up and down and licked her lips.

The Priestess sneered and slapped her with surprising quickness; even the reflexes of a Triumvir were not fast enough to dodge.

"You wish."

The hand mark on her face was gray in the blue light. She smiled harder, twisting the ends of her lips in perverse pleasure, and grabbed Livvy by the neck with a hard, choking squeeze that was just strong enough to paralyze her but not enough to kill. The Priestess' head rolled around helplessly in the stone hands of Visha, who examined her trophy from all angles.

"You other idiots in this room would do well not to interfere," she threatened, aware of Dean and Kell. "Stay where you are and keep breathing heavy. That makes it easier for me. This one and I are going to leave, and if you try anything, I will not only bash your skulls in, I'll do even worse things than I have currently planned for this woman here while I make you watch."

Dean wracked his brain for something he might do, but he knew it was pointless. All he could think of was how his sins had finally all come home to roost in one final, ironic moment. He cursed himself one last time. And then he noticed a tiny spark, waist high, somewhere beyond the Triumvir and Livvy. Immediately he started grinding his feet on the ground to create a distraction.

Visha turned her head toward the noise, and a split second later the air exploded into fire—Kell's heated hammer knocked the light globe out of the chain and followed it into the ground, smashing it into a million pieces and spreading a bright blue, luminescent stain over the floor all the way to the walls of the room.

Glass embedded itself into boots and shins, and suddenly it looked as though the floor of the room was a shimmering, iridescent pool and everyone was floating on it.

Visha recovered from a sliver of surprise and snapped to rage. Before Kell had time to raise his hammer off the ground, she slammed Livvy against the wall, spun around and whipped Kell's shoulder with such force that he flew two yards before falling over and tumbling head-over-feet.

Dean's mind recovered and pulled his body to attention. He grabbed his black stone and leapt forth, shoving it into the Triumvir's face with an intense white beam of light to blind her.

It worked for a few seconds and she drew up her hands to her eyes, leaving her momentarily defenseless, but Kell could not get up in time to take advantage and Livvy had shrunk to the floor in pain. A quick backhand struck the device from Dean's hands and shattered it against the adjacent wall.

"No!" Dean called out, but the answer was a kick in his gut, exactly where the spear had traversed his body days before. He grunted and fell back onto the floor with a defeated grimace.

Kell stood up and, picking up his hammer, swung it once again with his left hand—the blow to his right shoulder had rendered that arm a useless stump—but Visha swung her chain and caught it in mid-air, jerking it out of his hands. It sunk to the floor with a silencing thud and hissed as it boiled the liquid it landed in.

Resistance *was* pointless, just as Dean had intended when he had designed the ENs millennia ago.

Astrid cursed. She had saved her people and, in the meantime, put 80 enemy soldiers on her tail. Just according to her plan, but the blaze still surprised her—she had almost forgotten about the inferno. A quick death, a warrior's death, was one thing. Burning alive was quite another.

"These savages would love nothing else but to keep me from the pleasure of a quick death," she said to herself as she looked up at the towering wall of fire growing closer every minute. The heat pouring out penetrated all the way to her bones and made each step a painful exercise.

And on the other side of the wall of fire, the Maynon Ohzans that were not hot on her trail gave chase to the vanished villagers, hoping to clean up the scraps of resistance and put the finishing touches on the last conquest on the continent. The world would be theirs.

More accurately, it would belong to their masters, and therefore the Priestess' enemy, the Eye.

The Priestess. Astrid stole a moment of thought from her chase. She herself might not make it off the mountain alive, but at least her people might. Maybe—with luck and faith—the Priestess with them. Maybe she was running down the slope with them right now!

An arrow split the air next to her head, waking her from her daydream.

"Alright you idiot bastards, let's see how long I can keep you busy up here before we all die in this fire," she said and bounded off further into the woods toward the city.

"THERE, THAT SHOULD GIVE you a good view—I warned you fools to stay put, and I am always good on my word," sneered Visha. "So let's start, shall we? I don't know whether I'm more excited to punish your Lady here or to smash your heads in."

Her eyes almost rolled back in pleasure.

Kell and Dean were sitting against the wall of the glittering blue room with the Triumvir's thick chain binding their torsos and arms in tight, painful knots. Small spikes dotted each link and dug into their skin.

"It's too bad I couldn't fit my spear down here. Now *that* would have been fun to play with," Visha taunted again.

Livvy was kneeling, sitting on her heels in the center of the room as if it were a stage. Her shins bled from the glass of the light globe and although she must have been in pain, she did nothing but stare, emotionless, at Kell and Dean.

Triumvir Visha, unaware that she was the last and therefore highest ranking of her order, wore the smug grin of a person used to abusing her power. She drew a long dagger from a strap on her thigh, savoring the sound, and wet both sides of its blade with her tongue before slicing the sleeves from Livvy's dress, digging into the flesh all the while with purpose.

The Priestess shook her head at the unwilling audience. *Don't react.*

Kell could not help himself; he growled like a bear.

Dean closed his eyes and looked away as the ceremony continued and the white dress fell apart slowly, in pieces. Here, at the end, he faced not only his death—which was inconsequential, and, truth be told, a long time in coming—but the torture of the girl he had been almost a father to for more time than he could even remember was more than he could bear. He had not drunk so much as a drop of water for nearly a day, either, and his throat ached. But, somehow, he still found enough moisture for an anguished tear. It was too much.

But somewhere in the void of grief and pain and the humiliation that he had somehow been the unwitting architect of humanity's last true breath, came clarity. When he accepted the end, he found light, and his tears stopped.

Visha, working in a deliberately plodding show of horrible artistry, bared Livvy's arms and her legs from thighs down. Then she etched artful, bloody lines into her victim's skin with her dagger.

She leered at Kell and Dean to make sure they were watching and screamed, "Keep your eyes on her or I'll gouge them out! I keep my fucking promises!"

Dean obeyed but snuck a quick glance toward his obsidian stone on the floor a few feet away. The glass on its surface reflected a web of cracks, but it was still whole.

Maybe...just maybe, he thought. If it still worked and still held the blueprints to Last Retreat, then it would hold the answer. He elbowed Kell, triggering a quick confirming glance.

In the lowest whisper he could possibly breathe, he mouthed: "Belt. Chain."

Visha shot another evil look back at them but not fast enough to catch them talking, and turned back to her perverted ritual of torture.

Kell made a hair of a nod and maneuvered his thumbs, which were hidden from view by his knees, having been set down cross-legged, onto the chain the Triumvir had fixed around his belly. His right hand burned with pain and caused a bead of sweat to run down his forehead and his eye to twitch. Slowly, silently, he brought the chain down, down, down to the buckle of his belt, where he held it for five seconds. The iron melted clean away, burning his thumbs and dripping embers of molten metal through his trousers, branding his thigh. Never had he shown the restraint he did then; never had he been required to.

By now, Visha was consumed with her bizarre ritual, smiling with her twisted teeth and belting out disturbing laughs each time she sparked a response from Livvy. But the Priestess never yielded more than a wince, keeping her eyes on Dean and Kell. She was so convincing that the Triumvir did not notice Dean slip out of the chain, nab his broken stone, and flee out of the room until he had already gone.

When the chain whipped around the base of her neck, slicing open her skin, she knew.

Kell stood against the wall, holding her neck with the whip that had just been binding him and Dean.

Visha rotated around, wearing the most horrific mask of anger and happiness he had ever seen. "I was wondering when you were going to take part. Now, let's have fun."

DEAN SCRAMBLED THROUGH THE halls, his breaths short and nervous. He knew that there was another room somewhere back with a vent to the surface that just might send his wish up to the controls there—if they were still there. From this far down, no signal could penetrate the iron and earth, but a clear path of air might do the trick.

He looked at his stone and caressed it, scratching his fingertips on the jagged glass.

"C'mon, c'mon, work!"

It responded with a breath of life and lit up his face. A sigh of relief was all the reaction he had time for.

He summoned the map once more and squeezed his eyelids together to decipher which lines were glass and which were part of the blueprint. The ancient technology in his hand was built to last as long as this mountain. The frown he wore suddenly became a smile—the vent was right next door. He plodded to the next room, his head still buried in his miniature obelisk, to double- and triple-check that he was right. But all he needed to do was to stop in the middle of the four corners to feel the slight current of air from above. Here it was, and now, his very last trick in a long, long line of tricks was ready to commence. He had to wipe his damp and sweat-sticky fingers off on his robe as he tapped and slid his fingers over the stone. It took a minute or two, requiring intermittent shakes of his head to rid his thoughts of what might be happening in the room with Elizabeth, Kell, and that *thing*. But he needed faith right now. Faith that the evil spawn of his own mind two rooms away would stay occupied for long enough.

It was better this way. To die down in this mountain.

My comeuppance, he reasoned. At least they could cut off one of the hands of the Eye before they bit the dust. And who knew, maybe Gaelenn with his newfound strength could find a way to deal with the last of the Legion. With the Eye, even.

If he doesn't go crazy first. Wouldn't that be a stroke of bad luck?

Dean shot out a long jet of air through his whistling lips as he summoned and then stared at a large, red circle on his device.

"Here we go."

He pushed it. Up on top of the mountain, on top of Elizabeth's old house, surrounded by the flames of death and crumbling, behind the ornate door at the top of her stairs, a single, polished steel pole still stood in the center. It lit up yellow. Then it blinked orange. Finally, it went red, and stopped.

The mountain beneath screamed. Self-destruct.

CHAPTER FORTY SEVEN
TURN OF THE TIDE

ONLY 70 OF THEM left, Astrid thought to herself. Not without a little pride.

She had been picking off her pursuers one by one, whenever one or two had split off from the main group, all the while dodging hellfire and trees. She was an animal now, meting punishment with her bare hands. The fire raged stronger than ever before, eating the forest around the city at a shockingly fast pace—it had already almost reached the opposite end of Last Retreat, where her people had, with luck, escaped an hour earlier through her diversion. The sparser trees in the city and the solid stone statues and buildings had slowed its progress there, along with the thinning air.

"Shit," she said.

A great tree before her lurched forward and snapped, crashing into an already-crumbling cabin, sending a cloud of dust, fire, and smoke directly at her. Astrid hid behind a large rock, which might have been a statue of a man a day earlier, and covered her face with her hands. Her ears stayed open, and sure enough, she could just hear the shouts and voices of the Maynon Ohzans.

Despite the intense heat, her heart froze—the voices were coming from both sides of the fire. By the time she stood up, she was within ten yards of a dozen enraged soldiers shouting curses at her. They had gone from titillated to irked to incensed. Now they only wanted to finish her off and get off of this rock. Besides, there were no survivors and no spoils left untouched by the inferno.

Not that Astrid was about to go without a fight.

"Let's finish it," she taunted, and settled into a bare-handed battle stance, her fists spread wide and wild in front of her body.

Another tree tipped over and fell on top of five of the assailants. But it was not from fire that its trunk had broken—the ground was shaking again, this time more violently than it had before. But the Maynon Ohzan army was already here. It had already won. This was no attack.

Her blazing heart jumped up in her breast. She looked around. Nothing had changed aside from the violent shaking. The remaining seven soldiers were still charging at her, and a dozen more shot out of the trees behind them.

"Come on!" she yelled, ignoring the strange, revolting sensation under her feet. But then it happened again—her feet did not leave the ground and yet she crashed to her knees as if she had jumped from a house. The mountain was falling, she realized with a horrified gasp. An arm wrapped around her waist from behind and pulled her up. Before her elbow could find its owner's face, it spoke.

"Come on, Dear, we'd better get out of here."

The voice was gravelly and weak, but warm. And loving. And familiar.

Astrid spun around, grabbed the face at the neck, and kissed Rin's lips so hard that she sucked the air right out of his lungs. Her heart melted. She could not speak, but in her passion she stared wide into his face, jumping from eye to eye, studying the lines and curves to make sure, in her delirium, that he was real.

"Stop staring! This is no time for a public display. Let's get out of here!" he said, a weak but decidedly Rin-like smile passing to and from his pale lips.

They stumbled in the opposite direction of the wall of fire and the Maynon Ohzans, racing against them and against time and against the mountain itself, which continued to collapse into ruin. Astrid held Rin's hand, pulling him over fallen ashes of tree trunks and rocks and rubble. Her eyebrows shot up in realization.

"You shouldn't be able to walk!" she said.

"And yet—" he said as he dodged a sinkhole, "here I am!"

"Keep moving!" Astrid said. He was moving, if a little slower—and heavier—than usual. "Almost there!"

They broke the line of trees, the last twenty yards or so that had not yet been consumed by the flames, and where the steep wall around the edge had once stood lay nothing but air. She had been right: the mountain was falling, and now, so were they. The ground fell beneath their feet.

As she and Rin tumbled through the air, she finally got a good look at his naked legs—or what were in their place. The dawn light at this height reflected coldly off their smooth, unnatural contours. They were not his flesh legs anymore. They were steel.

A chunk of earth falling slightly slower than they were broke their fall temporarily and stabilized their descent. The rest of the ground, still tumbling, was coming into focus below quickly.

Rin grimaced in pain but also in thought. Astrid knew he was trying to find a way out of a hard spot, as he always did.

"Hold on!" he shouted, and he reached for her in the air. He held onto her body like a vice, his love fueling his muscles where his body's strength failed. Rin's new legs obeyed his mind's commands and stretched out and braced against the rapidly approaching ground.

When they hit the still-settling earth below, a fresh cloud of dust shot up and covered the two for over a minute. As it settled, Astrid kissed Rin again, gently this time; alive.

GAELENN TRIED TO REACH into his own consciousness. He had no control over his body. Or, at most, a distant, minor vote.

The wind broke in front of him and snapped the tunic at his back so forcefully that it shot painful little shockwaves into his skin, propelling him even faster. He had abandoned his exhausted horse a mile back, its strength and spirit spent. Last Retreat was a huge, black shadow against the morning light. And it was crumbling in on itself.

I'm not going to make it to the top in time.

He searched his memory of the place—his artificial memory—closing his eyes even while running in full stride. They blinked open with new purpose and he set his course to a certain part of the base. He would have to risk going *through* the mountain to get up. It was the only way.

The speed with which he reached his destination surprised even him, and the legs that were his but not his and that had carried him without rest from the farthest reaches north all the way to where his quest had started were not the least bit tired.

He arrived at the base of Last Resort and without hesitation, knowing directly where he was, he stuck his fingers in a barely-visible crack in the otherwise flawless wall of the artificial mountain. It was long corroded and fused solid, but the butt of his fist shattered a hole in the inch-thick granite and revealed a recess. He stuck his hand in and fiddled with something inside, completely invisible in the dark. A door opened in the mountain, the light of dawn flared up and stirred his hope, and he went in.

At the end of a long, perfectly straight tunnel there was another door, but this time there was no lock. It was glued to the ground by its own massive weight, a wrought iron, intricately carved barrier.

But Gaelenn had strength. More strength than he would ever have imagined. And he could feel it coursing through his bones and muscles, and, part of him lamented, his mind. He let his hands form a bond with it, pushed them right into the metal and upward just enough for it to crawl an inch above the ground. His fingers reached under the edges and gained hold.

With all of his new strength—his legs driving into the floor, his back buckled, arms pulsing and stretched to their physical limit, he willed the door up. And, overcoming the inertia of thousands of years, slammed it upward with enough force to keep it there, stuck forever.

Of all that he had experienced in the last weeks, all the changes and shocks and violence and epiphanies, nothing in his wildest imagination could have predicted the scene before him. On a shimmering, glowing blue floor, Elizabeth huddled, her dress torn to pieces and her naked arms and legs bloodied and scarred. His best friend, Kell, fought for breath on his knees, tearing at the chain at his neck that was strangling the life out of him.

And at the end of the chain stood the last of the Legion, the final servant of the Eye. She looked at Gaelenn with the eyes of a hungry lioness, starving—lusting—over her doomed prey. The mountain above shook and rumbled. Dust snowed over all of them.

Gaelenn gritted and bared his teeth. He was a tiger, come to protect his brood. No words needed to be exchanged; they both knew it would be a fight to the death.

Visha loosened her chain whip and kicked Kell in the center of his chest, launching him against the far wall, where he fell and wrestled for breath. The chain swung around like lightning and snapped at Gaelenn's head. He stuck up his forearm and let it wrap around, slashing open the skin. He grinned, pulled his arm down, grabbed the chain with other hand and yanked.

The Triumvir shot toward him like an arrow, shock in her face at Gaelenn's strength. His fist connected with her chin before she could recover, and she sailed backward, staring back at him with boiling rage—and fascination.

The walls suddenly buckled and a series of muffled thuds echoed in the chamber and upward through the mountain in perfect sequence. Both fighters ignored it and launched at each other, tearing at each other's throats, tumbling to the ground in a frantic, animalistic battle, even as the mountain itself died.

Gaelenn tried to get a clean shot with his fists but each blow was refuted with deft slaps and opportune scratches and bites. His opponent even growled like a great cat.

He tried to shout, "Run!" but in between swings and blocks, he could see that neither Kell nor Livvy would be capable of running alone; both of them were struggling just for life.

As strong as Gaelenn had become in the time since the tower, he was still caught off guard by the ferocity of this last EN—she fought with a tenacity he could not match, and soon, he found himself on the ground, straddled in a vice-like death grip at his waist.

The Triumvir's slashing nails and fists and teeth cut him up, a perverse mix of pleasure and anger cast over her grotesque features, painted in bright blue, directing her every move. At length, she wore Gaelenn down enough; grabbing his wrists, she pinned them to the ground. Her strength was beyond any capacity he had to resist. She was simply not human.

"You have my thanks for making things interesting," she said, livid. "And for opening the door."

She ran her tongue over her bloodied teeth and savored the taste. "This has definitely been fun."

Her knee took the place of one of the hands pinning Gaelenn down. Then she pulled a small, slim blade from the middle crease in her now-mangled breastplate. With the same perverseness but with less patience than before, she brought it before his throat.

"Pity," she mused, "we could have been great friends."

Those were her last words. Kell's hammer, unlit but still whole, smashed into the back of her skull, crushing it. Her body and the knife at Gaelenn's throat went limp and she fell over, dead.

Livvy dropped the hammer and stood in front of Gaelenn, her hand outstretched.

"Too little, too late, you bitch," she said with a smile and then fainted onto him.

The mountain groaned its final protest, and fell.

Looking back, Gaelenn could not remember what happened. He could only remember that after he carried Kell and Dean, who he found limping further in the catacombs, clear of the collapsing mountain, the second thing he did was tell the old man: "You wouldn't believe it if you were there."

The first thing he did was cradle Livvy in his arms and press his scruffy cheek to her forehead.

"This, Priestess," he said, "was all for you." And he was in full control of himself when he said it.

When she came to, she smiled. Somewhere in her ancient, closed heart, the key to a lock that she had long forgotten had ever existed turned and opened.

AYDYA STOOD AT THE side of Sapphire Mountain, watching the giant plume of smoke from afar as Last Retreat crumbled to dust. Somehow, she had faith that Gaelenn was there, and that he had done something extraordinary.

And in her own way she took lonesome comfort that she had aided him in his quest.

He was not a god. He was a man, a person, and that was enough.

She would be at his side again, she was sure—not as a captor, nor as a servant. Just as his *friend*, something she had never had. She smiled.

LAST RETREAT, CONSTRUCTED BY humankind to demonstrate its permanence and glory was now a broken monument to its temperance and fragility. It came to rest in a smoldering pile of rock and earth and flesh, having swallowed up the armies of Maynon Ohza and the body of Triumvir Visha, last of the Legion, the world's last EN. Except for Gaelenn.

ASTRID AND RIN AND his metal legs descended the ruins in the morning light, hand-in-hand, linked now not only by love but in their struggles. They joined their people who had fled to the safety of the forest below as they looked toward the city at Maynon Ohza, and several days later, the two lovers led their masses peacefully through the gates and the people on either side marveled at each other and accepted each other with neither a welcome embrace nor resent. All of them, whether they had come a month ago or a year ago or a century ago, refugees. Each of them, down to the last newborn child, human. Equal.

"WHERE DO WE GO from here?" Gaelenn asked. He rested his hand on Kell's good shoulder, who responded with an agreeing nod. They had spent the last hour catching up. The Legion was gone. The Eye, defeated. For now.

"What we've always done at this point," Dean said. "Find a new home. Regroup. Get ready for the next wave, whenever that may be. But I've got a good feeling that this time we've turned the tide."

"And take a break, I hope," Kell said, pulling a grin from Gaelenn.

Dean laughed. "*Definitely* take a break."

They all looked one last time at Last Resort before turning to walk away. Elizabeth lingered a moment longer than the others.

"I feel it, too. Something I haven't felt in a long time." She glanced at Gaelenn, the flicker of a smile at the ends of her mouth. He blushed.

"The tide. This is our world. Let's take it back."

THE END

ACKNOWLEDGEMENTS

Though this has largely been a solo project, the real heavy lifting was done by those who have hoisted me up.

Deniz, my cover artist. A true artist in every sense of the word, and a beautiful soul. You added something to this book that I couldn't write. Find her on X: @PersephoneLines

Kyle, in whose basement I first conceived of the idea. You didn't know, but I was writing scenes while we played games. Two fighters, or one fighter and one thief? It's the universe's ultimate mystery. (This is also for your parents, who did more for me than they'll ever know. YES I will have a bagel and cream cheese for the fifth time this week, thank you very much!)

Sarah, for always believing in me. There isn't a thing on Earth I could ask you for and not receive immediately. I could not have done this without you.

My dogs, who kept my feet warm (and wet, you lickers) while I wrote.

Molly, my emotional anchor. I'm as steady as she goes, but when I'm not, one chat with you and I'm straight as an arrow—thanks for attracting all the crazy in the world so it doesn't somehow latch itself onto me. Live pecans!

Rich, Bob, and Jake. I wouldn't be who I am without you. And I'm sorry my PC is better than yours.

Andrew, for educating me on the finer points of nerddom and sacrificing your time to hang out with boring ol' me. There isn't anybody I'd trust more in the ways of Nintendo or board games. Make sure to watch for book 2 (hint hint). Expert!

Mom, for knowing me more than anybody. Miss you. I hope you enjoyed this story, because it's for you and Dad.

My Nova friends—you know who you are—for wild times and laughs. We're getting older but we must not forget to raise a little hell every once in a while. Osaka will never see the likes of us again.

Rinoa, Julia, and Lydia. You don't know it yet, but you've been my inspiration. Ask me about it sometime.

Shoko, for tolerating me, my quirks, my antics, my lectures, my hobbies, and my horrible jokes. I can't help being interested in everything on God's Green Earth, but what I'm most interested in is you.

About the author
Guy W Nettleton

Guy W Nettleton was born and raised in the deep midwest, U.S.A., but has spent half his life in the furthest place from it: Osaka, Japan. That's not a statement on his feelings about corn and soybeans, but rather an endorsement of his favorite big city in the world. No place else has that just-right mix of earth, water, wind, and fire. Oh—and heart.

As a writer, he focuses on Fantasy and Sci-Fi, but dabbles in thrillers and suspense when the mood strikes. Inspired by his many experiences travelling both in the U.S. and abroad, his stories also tend to challenge borders and examine the truths (and falsehoods) that affect us all, no matter where one might call home.

www.guywnettleton.com

To be Continued...

Gaelenn and Livvy will return to save history in 2026.

The Last Eye of Time series BOOK 2 (of 3) is currently being forged. New adventures, new characters, and new complications await.

To you, dear reader: thank you for reading my story and for giving it a reason to exist. If you enjoyed it, please consider reviewing on Amazon, Goodreads, or the storefront you prefer. Your support means the world to me and will continue to help other readers discover the world within these pages.

Visit me and join my newsletter at:
www.guywnettleton.com
or on X: @gw_nettleton

There is more to the story than in these pages and you will find it there, whatever it is—side stories, history, excerpts, and exclusive short stories.